John Kemp

Wild Dayrell: a Biography of a Gentlemen Exile

John Kemp

Wild Dayrell: a Biography of a Gentlemen Exile

ISBN/EAN: 9783743338838

Manufactured in Europe, USA, Canada, Australia, Japa

Cover: Foto ©Raphael Reischuk / pixelio.de

Manufactured and distributed by brebook publishing software
(www.brebook.com)

John Kemp

Wild Dayrell: a Biography of a Gentlemen Exile

A PIC NIC IN THE PYRENEES.

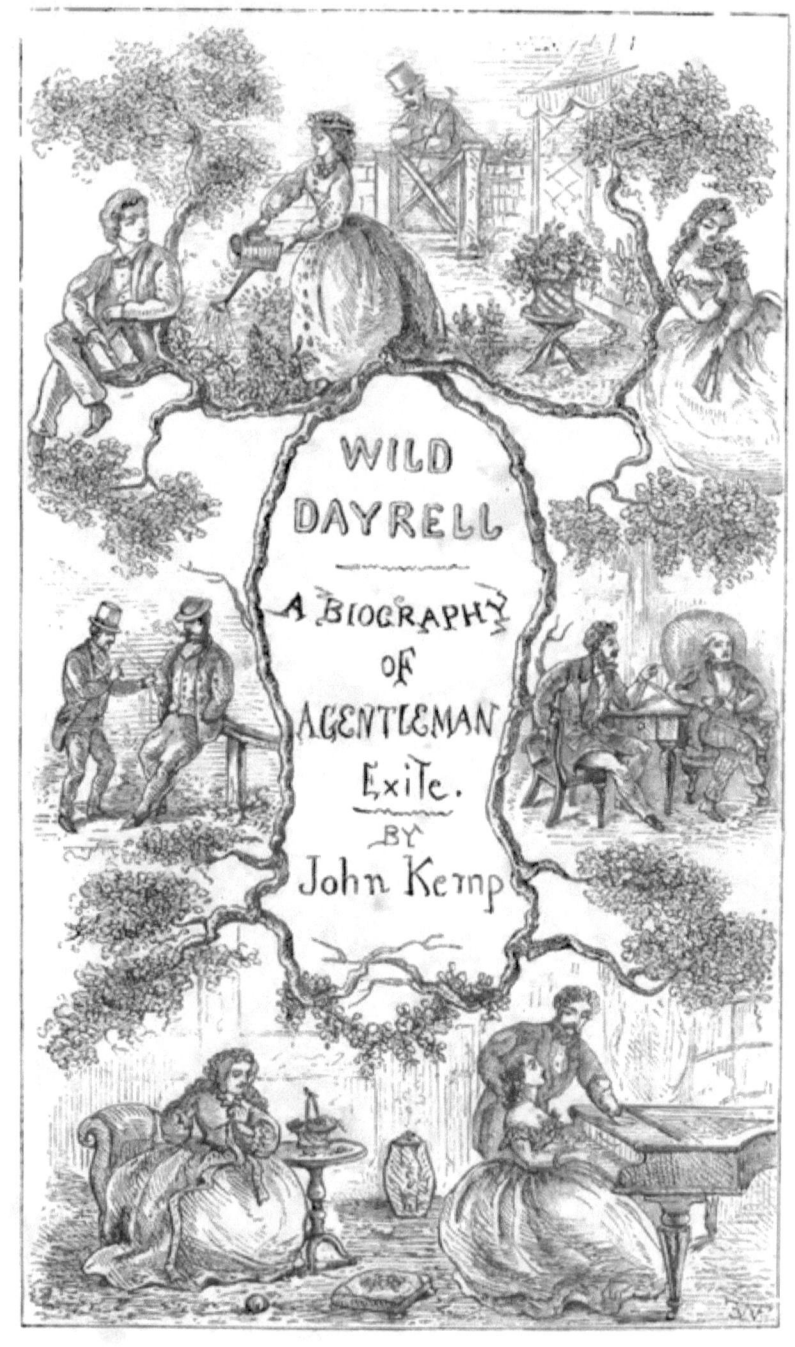

WILD
DAYRELL

A BIOGRAPHY
OF
A GENTLEMAN
Exile.
BY
John Kemp

LONDON:

LONGMAN, GREEN, LONGMAN, & ROBERTS.

WILD DAYRELL;

A

BIOGRAPHY OF A GENTLEMAN EXILE.

BY

JOHN KEMP,

AUTHOR OF

"SHOOTING AND FISHING IN LOWER BRITTANY," "SKETCHES FROM THE SOUTH OF FRANCE," &c.

SECOND EDITION.

LONDON:

LONGMAN, GREEN, LONGMAN, AND ROBERTS.

1862.

LONDON:

Printed by Truscott, Son, & Simmons
Suffolk Lane, City.

PREFACE.

WHAT has become of them? What has become
of some of our contemporaries, who, as boys,
started in the great race of Life on equal terms
with ourselves, but in whose career at the
University, London, and elsewhere, we saw only
"the beginning of the end?" They have failed,
been removed from the scene, and are now forgotten, save when old comrades call over the roll
of men of their day. This true Biography of
Wild Dayrell, the author hopes, may supply a
missing link in the record of our lives, and clear
up any mystery enveloping the fortunes of—to
Anglicise a French phrase—the Forgottens.

LONDON,
  July, 1861.

WILD DAYRELL.

CHAPTER I.

" Is the favourite to win?" asked a young lieutenant in one of her Majesty's crack regiments, of Dayrell, who sat opposite him eating his breakfast. " Did you pick up any news when you went to see the thoroughbreds air themselves on Doncaster moor?"

"You know quite as much as I do," answered the latter: "that is, what a good horse Sellington is; how he won the Derby easily, and at York last month beat most of the horses that have to meet him in the race to-morrow. His only dark rivals are Boanerges and Nutmeg, and they, I should think, cannot be of much account, to judge from the disgraceful way their stable companions were beaten when they tried to get the favourite's measure. I consider it a moral certainty, and, turning a deaf ear

B

to the shaves of the race-course, shall stand or fall
by the fortunes of Sellington."

"I shall follow your example," said the young
lieutenant, "and, if the favourite wins, I have yet
six months' leave, and, after the settling, shall carry
on the war for that time; if, on the contrary, he is
beaten, I shall join my regiment in India. To tell
the truth, I am tired of the depôt at Maidstone, and
would just as soon be roughing it on the banks of
the Sutlej as stay here without plenty of money to
enjoy my leave and hunting in Northamptonshire."

Thus, over their coffee and muffins, chatted two
average specimens of our rising generation in a small
lodging at Doncaster, on the morning preceding that
which was to witness the great race of the North.

Our hero, Dayrell, was now about twenty-five
years of age, of good family, prepossessing manners,
and, as the ladies would say, decidedly good-looking.
At an early age he had been sent to a public school,
where he had shone as a leader at foot-ball, cricket,
and other games—a fact that tended to exalt him
much in the good opinion of the boys, but considerably disgusted the head-master, who only tolerated, but
by no means loved, such unacademical amusements.
His talents were above the average—another fact
that rendered other backslidings doubly disturbing to
his worthy pedagogue; and when he did occasionally

put his shoulder to the wheel of learning, and send up a copy of verses or Latin prose worthy even of the notice of the Hertford examiners, his plodding companions had good reason for thinking that he would have been a dangerous rival in the race for honours. His tutor thus graphically summed up his character: "He was a good fellow, with plenty of talent, but ruined by his love of field sports." So on making his bow to the public school, his prizes were not the gift of his master, but of his companions, who testified by a shower of leaving books how deeply they regretted the loss of their cricket captain.

Alma Mater, to whose nursing he was soon afterwards confided, was (and, perhaps, is still) a dangerous mother for such a character as Dayrell. Untrammelled by the wholesome fear of a father, who died when Dayrell was yet a boy, and supplied with more money than most other men of his college, he did not find his own level, but took a position above his less fortunate compeers. Hence he was quite an oracle to the men of his year, and an object of "attention" to those townsmen of the university, who quietly prey upon open-handed youth at the same time that they pander to their tastes. No wonder that Dayrell soon saw more of the interior economy of the old Berkshire kennels than the

inside of the musty lecture-room, and thought the
chances of the favourite for the ensuing Derby more
worthy his attention than an Aristotleian theory or a
problem in Euclid.   In fact, his idle habits grew upon
him to such an extent, that it is difficult to imagine
how he scrambled through his Little-go.   Some
people did affirm, that when he wanted the figure
for an Euclidian definition, so kindly set before him
by the examiners, he solved the difficulty by tossing :
—heads, a parallelogram—tails, a triangle ; and that,
acting on the result obtained by that original pro-
cess, he selected the right framework for his proposition.   That he escaped rustication was partly
owing to his sedulous attendance at chapel—the
performance of which duty covers a multitude of
sins in the opinion of the authorities—and partly
to vague hopes of the Master, that his clever scapegrace might yet do something for the honour of
his college.   Dayrell did not fulfil any such anti-
cipations.   He certainly never was plucked, though
how he obtained his degree was a greater mystery
than his passage of the *pons asinorum.* The " three-
fold " torture now in vogue was, luckily for Dayrell,
not invented in his day.

   At the age of twenty-one our hero left the University, and took up his quarters in London, where
a larger field was open to his talent for readily

calculating the odds, and obtaining a practical acquaintance with the doctrine of chances—a more necessary accomplishment on the Turf than any knowledge of the condition or capabilities of the horses themselves. Here also he earned his soubriquet of "Wild," not because he was guilty of excesses, such as the epithet might seem to imply; on the contrary, he was rather a quiet man, and bet more for the *éclat* of the thing than from love of money; but simply from the lucky hit he made when the animal of that name won the principal race of the year. His success for three seasons was unparalleled. "Lucky Dayrell" was in everybody's mouth as the rising guide to fortune. Whatever "Lucky Dayrell" did, should, they said, be implicitly followed. If the gentlemen lost by the defeat of the favourite, it was soon bruited about that Dayrell had laid against him, and had reserved the actual winner to carry him through triumphant. If backers of horses, suspicious and afraid of the intentions of an owner, held aloof from investing on some good public performer, Dayrell appeared in the market, took the odds heavily from some of the ring, and, when the event was over, simply remarked to his chagrined friends, "I told you how it would be." Altogether our hero, in spite of what sagacious old stagers said, was considered to be the

man who had at last cut the Gordian knot, and discovered the short and certain road to wealth.

The tide, however, turned at last; Fortune, weary
of her favourite, had been very unkind during the
last six months. The results of every great race
had been disastrous, and even in those of smaller
consequence, where his luck had hitherto been
proverbial, his calculations were completely upset.
The present St. Leger was to make or mar him.
In the former case he had determined to quit the
Turf, and take to some less perilous pursuit; for
the latter emergency he was not equally prepared,
although he clung to the delusive hope that he could
still enter upon some plodding path of life, which
might offer him a competence, if not steadily lead
him on to fortune. Many like him have been led
away by the same will-o'-the-wisp, in fancying that,
without years of probation and a formed character,
they could be received into those professions for
which other men qualify by a long course of preparation and study.

Dayrell, although he attended the first day's
racing at Doncaster, took but little interest in the
proceedings, albeit a goodly show of jockeys answered to the starter's summons, and the decisions
of the judge were received with the customary
enthusiasm by winners, and ill-concealed regret by

the losers. He regarded it, as we should the tuning of the instruments that preface the grand efforts of the band at an opera—a kind of prelude and foil to the all-absorbing event of the following day. When he felt the morrow would see him "*aut Cæsar aut nullus*," he had no inclination for winning or losing a few pounds, which could make but little difference in the balance that was to be in his favour or the reverse. So he spent his time in loitering near the ring, where stentorian voices proclaimed their willingness to lay against anything, from the favourite to the most hopeless outsider, and persuaded himself, from many investments made, that his horse still basked in the sunshine of popular favour.

That night there was a mighty gathering in "the rooms," devoted for the nonce to speculators in racing, and devotees of Mammon in yet more exciting games of chance. Thither had flocked the *habitués* of the Turf, the gentlemen just returned from the moors, the representatives of the army, and all the mixed assemblage that nobody knows anything about, but who are sure to be present on the evening before the St. Leger. There were the betting men in full evening costume, as though they had just left the most *recherché* dinners instead of their quiet "chop or steak feed" at the Salutation,

gliding about the room, book in hand, and plying
their trade with untiring energy. Knots of men
would suddenly congregate round some well-known
speculator, listen eagerly to his offers, as if they
could thus fathom his secrets, and would as quickly
disperse to form again elsewhere. At intervals
might be seen a well-known character, dressed like
the most dapper of linen-draper's assistants, who
moved from one circle to another, and invested
largely against Sellington, wherever a chance backer
could be found. Dayrell recognised him as the
agent of a magnate of the ring, and knew the
commission looked ominous, when he offered 6,000
to 4,000 against the favourite, and met with no
response.

> " Quem Deus vult perdere, prius dementat."

No other explanation could be given for Dayrell
being so obstinate as not to take a hint like this.
Even Andrews, whose business it is to take subscrip-
tions, and see that improper persons do not enter the
subscription-room, said to him, winking at the same
time, " A deaf man could understand that. Poor
Sellington, he is dead to-night; I suppose we shall
have his funeral to-morrow."

Like a troubled spirit, Dayrell left the large room,
and went to one of the smaller, where were roulette

tables covered with sovereigns, which moustachioed gentlemen picked up and relinquished with a non-chalance which savoured strongly of co-operation with the proprietor. But this game was unpopular, so he went up-stairs to the two tables, where the oft-repeated " Make your sets," and " The main will be," had collected a double row of players. But he did not join them. His mind was pre-occupied. He was not even enticed by the plethoric, gouty-toed Norris, who, with his hands in his pockets, and shaking his head, repeated his old, old story: " The bank, sir, has been nearly ruined to-night by the good luck of the gentlemen; only five minutes ago Mr. Digwell threw eleven mains."

Restless and disgusted with the scene, Dayrell left the rooms and passed through the mob that thronged the entrance, and the knots of idlers who, regardless of the drizzling rain, conversed on the pavement, or the middle of the street, or wherever they could find standing-room, in their anxiety to pick up informa-tion that might be turned into gold on the morrow. He returned to his room, whither the hum of voices from the centre of operations still followed him, and whose interior was rendered more gloomy by the sickly light that came from the gas-lights in the street below. Let us pass over the wearisome night. We have none of us reason to envy the state of the speculator's mind when awake, or the tossings and unquiet rest, when fitful slumbers at length fall to his share.

At the first break of day, Dayrell was aroused by the roll of vehicles and the clamp of feet, betokening the arrival of fresh patrons of the great northern carnival. It was a foggy morning, and from his window he contemplated the living stream that passed below. Here a party of stout graziers, with greasy Macintosh coats on their arms, and their pockets bulging with substantial luncheons, making the best of their way to their customary halting-places. On their heels followed jolly-looking farmers, breeders of short horns, tradesmen, and Yorkshiremen of every grade; some speculating, in their broad dialect, on the result of the race, others laughing and joking, as true holiday-makers should. In the square opposite Dayrell saw the stall of the old game-vendor, sole occupant of that area, who, sticking his hands cabman-fashion against his sides to promote circulation of the blood, looked out for customers among the better-dressed, or cracked jokes with his poorer brethren. Looming through the mist, and suspended by the lower mandible, hung the spectral corpses of four grouse, changed, indeed, in appearance since they saluted the rising sun with the proud gestures and shrill crow of their species. Tell us, Mr. Gamedealer, what superstition inclines you to the mystic number four? Why have we never seen more or less in your stall on any of our visits to Doncaster? Tell us, are they dummies, or are they the ghosts of their unfortunate predecessors?

Dayrell hastily dressed himself, and, as his custom was, started for the course on foot to see the sheeted strings take their morning canters. Bent on the same errand, a sprinkling of gentlemen, snugly wrapped in coats and comforters, had already made their appearance; as well as a legion of touts, who occasionally made frantic rushes towards the rails when the horses cantered by, in the hope of gathering information for their credulous employers. Gentlemen sportsmen, as the card-sellers call you, you are not likely to realize much benefit from your early attendance. Any conclusions that you amateurs may form from what you see of the horses at exercise will probably result in delusion and loss. Few of you know one horse from another, swathed as they are from head to knee in their thick clothing. Like an opera-girl reft of her spangles and paint, and removed from the foot-lights, the animal, that you attempt to recognise this morning, is very different to the gleaming satin-coated thorough-bred that you remember to have seen stretched in a preliminary canter on some other race-course. Granted that you

know the horses apart, and that you are good judges
of action and style of " going ;" whatever new ideas
might be grafted on your germinating mind will bear
no fruit; for, alas, your opinions have been already
formed, and certain figures are even now entered in
your " little book," which will inevitably warp your
better judgment.   If you only congregate here this
morning *pour passer le temps*, well and good : the
fresh air of Doncaster Moor is as healthful and in-
vigorating as that of the mountains you have so
lately quitted.

" Good morning, Captain."   Each new comer was
a captain with the individual who now addressed
Dayrell, as he leaned on the rails of the course.   The
intruder on his meditations was one of those Bedouins
of the Turf, who are always on the watch to earn
half-a-crown, honestly if possible, but at all events to
make it somehow.

" Si possint recté, si non ——"

He was known to the world by the soubriquet of
" Scrapings," and report said that he " lived by his
wits ;" but as he had by no means a superabundance
of that commodity, it would have been nearer the
truth to say that he throve on his consummate impudence.   His character may be easily guessed, from
the answer of a wag who, when asked where Scrap-

ings was likely to be found, replied, " If he is not borrowing a shilling, picking a pocket, or fighting, you may be certain to find him in the nearest horse-pond, being ducked for some piece of rascality." Scrapings, however, had lately had a turn of luck; and, presuming on a new coat, and the possession of a little ready money, had approached Dayrell, and accosted him.

" Good morning, Captain," said he; " I beg pardon, but they do say that you are backing the favourite for this race. Now, I tell you he can't win—no how."

" Why, what on earth," exclaimed Dayrell, " can you know about it, you who never told me anything by which I could make a sixpence?"

" Don't be too hard upon us, Captain; you've given me many half-crowns when I've been out at elbows, and I'll just tell you how it is: I've been talking to the lad who exercises Sellington every day, and has ridden him this last eighteen months, and he says as how he does not go free-like in his gallops, and how he seems quite a different horse to what he was before he won the Derby. Just take my advice this once; it is all true that I am telling you. Thank'ee, Captain," continued Scrapings, pocketing the douceur tendered him by Dayrell; and holding up his finger, as if in warning, " Don't forget; the favourite will not win."

The sun had cleared away the morning mist, and now shone brightly on the thousands thronging every part of the Doncaster race-course. Ding-dong, ding-dong, from the top of the stand rang the great bell, that never seemed to cease uttering its warning notes, save when the horses were actually engaged in the strife for victory. Ding-dong, ding-dong; clear and loud it pealed above the hubbub of the betting-ring, the jargon of would-be judges of horse-flesh, the persuasive vociferation of those who proffered the odds, as well as of the thousands of less agitated spectators congregated in the wide area near the Grand Stand. Ding-dong, ding-dong; it was heard above the stentorian voices and trumpets of booth-proprietors, the shouts of vendors of correct cards, the drums of the juggler-troops, the bones and banjoes of *soi-disant* Ethiopian melodists, and all the motley herd that strove so incessantly to relieve the visitors of their superfluous cash. Ding-dong, ding-dong; it drowned the hum of voices proceeding from the crowds of admirers that followed the sheeted quadrupeds, as they were led up the course to be saddled for the part they were to play in the coming struggle.

The various scenes in the Turf drama that precede every great race were duly enacted. Formed under their inspector's eye, a solid phalanx of policemen advanced, to clear gently, but effectively, the long

green lane of the gaping multitude. The elastic
thoroughbreds were divested of their clothing; the
jockey boys, those precocious nondescripts, were
hoisted into their tiny saddles. In twos and threes
they cantered up the course, ere long returning
past the stand at a pace equalling in severity that
for the actual race itself. Individuals, who had been
separated from their friends, made a rush for the
opposite side, pursued by an indignant policeman,
fiercely wielding his truncheon, but whose efforts to
catch the offender were generally ineffectual, and
provoked a burst of laughter from the good-humoured
lookers-on. That time-honoured institution, the
inevitable dog, was turned out, and, hooted by a
thousand voices, rushed hither and thither in frantic
haste, to disappear no one knew where, though
"Surtees" has attempted to follow his vagaries.
The last loiterer—I think the great Mr. Toole, of
trowser-making celebrity—has been let into the
Stand; the gates are closed, the course is cleared,
and even the monotonous bell has stilled its warning notes.

All the horses have taken their preliminary canters,
the last to pass the Stand being the favourite; he
was, of course, the cynosure of a thousand eyes.
Good judges saw with suspicion symptoms of lather-
ing and hurried training; more than one sage old

lover of horse-flesh shook his head ominously, and
pronounced an adverse verdict. The occupants of
the ring became quiet, and adjusted their glasses, or
listened to the prattle of adventurous souls, who, by
their comrades' help, had mounted the rails of the
betting circle, and thus commanded a more extensive
view. Dayrell nervously watched the line formed by
the sixteen competitors, as they were led up to the
post by the skilful, but nonchalant, Hibburd, and
his heart beat high, when the flag dropped, and a
somewhat straggling start was effected. No reason,
however, had he for complaint. Sellington was one
of the lucky horses, and in the front rank—a position
that his jockey maintained, but did not injure by
attempting to force the pace. Round the hill they
sailed, and, as the pace improved, the tail of beaten
horses became longer, and the shouts of the backers
of the different favourites were redoubled. Down
the incline they rattled, a cloud of dust forming as
background for the display of the advancing wall of
parti-coloured jackets. The shouts soon merged into
a roar, till, at the distance post, Sellington was
evidently in trouble; his jockey's arms and legs
were at work; and "The favourite's beat," was re-
echoed by a hundred throats. Past the Stand they
rushed like a whirlwind; the three leading horses
cleared the winning post, and the hubbub ceased;

for no one, but the judge, could tell who had won. This breathless suspense, however, was but for a second; the number of the winner upon the tele-graph was the signal for half a dozen hats to fly into the air, and for a general rush to the exit from the stand, when all was over, save the exuberant joy of the Yorkshire lads, who thronging round their pet, as he returned to scale, shouted at the top of their voices, " Now, boys, one cheer more. Malton, Malton, for ever."

With an almost insupportable load at his heart, Dayrell threaded his way through the ground sacred to stick-throwers, proprietors of gorgeous aunt Sallys, exhibiters of the noble game of prick the garter, and, heedless of all invitations to try his luck, made his way to a carriage drawn up on the opposite side of the course. Here he found his friends, elated, or depressed, as they happened to have won or lost, and listened apathetically to the stories, already passed from one to another, accounting for the defeat of the favourite, many of them as incredible as they were false. That cunning reader of physiognomies, the tall, sun-burnt, gipsey Ellen, guessed what had happened from simply seeing Dayrell's dejected air, and wisely forbore to ask for her accustomed present. That quiet, respectably-dressed individual yonder, whom the London club waiters designated " Mr.

Dayrell's agent" (meaning touter), prudently stood aloof and waited for a more convenient moment to offer consolation and to borrow a fiver. Even that short man with the red face and black whiskers, Mr. Wiley's assistant, took the hint, and did not present his card of invitation for an afternoon visit to what he called "his place for a little amusement."

Dayrell must indeed have been hopelessly out of sorts, otherwise he would have been amused with the new manœuvre for raising money that Scrapings was practising upon the occupant of a neighbouring carriage. This worthy, in making his rounds, had spied a pale-faced, mild-looking young man of five and twenty, who held the responsible situation of trusty clerk to the famous house of Silvercorn and Co. He sat on the box of the family four-wheel, and detailed to his mother and sisters some particulars respecting the horses and their riders. The scoundrel marked him as a victim, and sideling up with a wink and a leer, exclaimed,

"Ah, Captain, here we are again. You don't forget your old pal, I see. You'll give him something for the sake of old times."

"Go away, man," said Paleface; "I don't know you."

"How can you say that, Captain?" said Scrapings, in a louder key; "have you forgotten our good luck at Hampton and Chesterfield, and how you gave me a sovereign and said, 'Scrapings, if ever you want a trifle, come to me?'"

"Go away, man," reiterated Paleface, his complexion changing rapidly from white to red, for he had been to Hampton races unknown to his family, who thought at the time that he was paying a visit to an old schoolfellow in the country.

"What! have forgotten, Captain," continued Scrapings, "the fifty half-crowns we won at roulette, and how, after the races, you and I, and the la—"

Down dropped poor Paleface from his perch, and rushed across the course to speak to a friend (as he said afterwards), in a state of hopeless horror at the advent of so terrible a dream; and before he hid his head again in the family carriage, he had made a three-mile circuit round the course.

In the good old days when noblemen and gentlemen attended races in greater numbers than at present, the wholesome practice of settling debts of honour on the morning after they were incurred was rigidly adhered to. Then, if Major McSwindle or Captain O'Tryon did not put in an appearance and liquidate their heavy liabilities, the usual penalties were inflicted on them as defaulters, viz.—they were prevented from entering the Grand

Stand, and perhaps compelled to leave the town
by the importunate demands of their creditors.
Hence the beautiful allegory, oft quoted by the
veterans of the ring, that describes an insolvent
gentleman, the morning after the race, as having
been seen crossing London Bridge—his only luggage
a carpet-bag, his face set towards the Continent.
Mais nous avons changé tout cela, much to the
disgust of the legitimate speculator. By tacit
agreement the settling hour is postponed, and bills
do not fall due till the next gathering at Tattersalls.
A few sanguine individuals, however, still cling to
the old system, attend early in the subscription-
room, produce their books, and by make-believe
settling try to induce a tyro at least to part with
his cash; but their efforts are unavailing. They
may look hungry, and expect, but their debtors
know better than to come and be bled. The
pleasure and grief connected with paying and
receiving must stand adjourned till the following
Monday. Of this new system unprincipled adventurers, who have lost quite as much as they can
pay, if not more, take unfair advantage; they know
they cannot be in a worse position than they are
at present, and so make fresh bets, with a view of
recovering the whole of their previous losses.

But Dayrell, now that the great event had come

off against him, laid down his book and pencil, and thought only how best he might satisfy his numerous creditors. This was not an easy matter, seeing that a ring-man loves deeds better than words. He owed some small sums. Such creditors are inclined to be troublesome and clamorous, so they were paid at once. Luckily he found those to whom he owed most in a good humour, being large winners on the race. They did not object to a piece of stamped paper, a promise to pay at some not-far-removed future. As to interest—"A trifle like that, Mr. Dayrell would not refuse," they said; and the trifle, which turned out to be sixty-five per cent., was accordingly added to the amount. "Well," thought Dayrell, as he handed the last bill to the plethoric Norris, "there's the end of my folly; it did not require a prophet to tell the result of my betting. What is the use of blaming myself for not backing Scott's horse, or the Field, when the real question I have to ask myself is, Why did I bet at all? Does not common sense tell me that every gentleman in the long run must lose? Has cleverness, age, or brains ever been able to cope with chicanery and unfair odds? How is it possible to win without associating with people below one's station, without departing from the honourable principles that govern gentlemen; without

sacrificing health, heart, and every moment of one's
time to that abomination—the betting-book?"

"No, thank you, Pavis," said Dayrell to the
leviathan speculator, of the eagle eye and unim-
peachable integrity, who proffered a bet in tens,
ponies, or hundreds.

"Will you do anything?" enquires the sprightly
Spleen, and stands aghast at hearing Dayrell say
he intends to give up betting; then he slinks back
into the crowd, concluding that Mr. D. has either
no more money to lose, or that he will change his
mind next week.

"You may have the favourite against the field,"
says Bunton, the grey-headed layer of short odds,
the *soi-disant* commissioner of a marquis, and ever
on the heels of speculative *youth*. "You must win
of me," he adds; "I am so unlucky this meeting.
I have only won 15*l.* on the week's balance"—an
announcement that did not, it is needless to add,
induce our hero to change his mind.

The races are over; the Doncaster of 185— is
numbered with the things that have been. Noblemen, gentlemen,—"patrons of the national pastime,"
the newspapers call them,—hangers on to the Turf,
ringmen, and the indescribable οἱ πολλοὶ of the
race-course, hurry to the railway station, just as
anxious to quit the old Yorkshire town, as they

were to come. Dayrell is amongst the number who await the express-train. Ten minutes may elapse before it arrives; not an instant must be lost. Although the Leger is over—nay, well nigh forgotten, is there not a great handicap at Newmarket in a fortnight? On this the layers are occupied; they are offering the same odds nearly as yesterday, the names of other horses only being substituted. They never cease, never rest. The more the races, the merrier for them, for they know they must win in the long run. Hence with careless indifference they count up their losses, should they extend over a month, or even six months. Their turn must come; it is only a question of time and industry. The train arrives; they shut up their books, and take their places. But speculation is only scotched, not killed. A dozen boards are dragged from their hiding places by the railway guards: between this and London the ringman will not lift his eyes from the cards dealt him at whist.

Let the curtain fall on this the first act of the drama, in which the performers are not of high repute, or their mode of living *sans reproche*. Let us not, however, be too hard upon them. Let us remember that what they do is for their livelihood, and that of their families; that there are honest men in the ranks, and that this is the only employ-

ment *now* open to their talents. This necessary evil
or blot upon the pleasant pastime of racing must
and will flourish so long as " young blood " feeds the
arteries of the betting corporation. Until popular
opinion makes itself heard, and votes it *infra dig.*
for the better classes to consort and bet with men
whose social standing is far below their own, many
a mother must tremble for the fate of her high-
spirited son, when he launches into London life,
and has to run the gauntlet of this most perilous
and alluring pursuit.

CHAPTER II.

FROM the race-course to a lawyer's office is a wide
jump. What can be the connection between the
two? you ask. Wait a moment, and you will see
by following Dayrell to Mr. Tales' house in the
secluded and quiet county-town of ———shire.

But few lawyers have allowed modern innovations
to usurp the place of the ink-stained desk or table,
the well-worn arm-chair, the uncleaned windows,
and other seedy appurtenances of their council-
chambers. Should there be a carpet, it will, in
the majority of cases, be thread-bare; should maps
decorate the walls, they will probably be fly-blown;
should you look into the paper on the walls, the
original colour will hardly be settled to your satisfaction. Ominous parchments and be-taped deeds,
methodically arranged in front of the master mind,
are still the stock-in-trade that frighten clients as
with a nightmare. Some day, I suppose, we shall
have *fashionable* lawyers, living in the midst of
plate-glass and gilded cornices, and receiving us in

their drawing-rooms.   Liveried servants will take
up our cards, and, who can tell (?), perhaps a glass
of sherry and a pickled sandwich will close the
interview.   Members of other professions, mer-
chants, &c., emerging from their chrysalis state,
flit about in carriages, and attract fresh customers
by fine offices and grand houses at the West-end.
Why should the disciples of Coke and Blackstone
be behind their time?   Why should they have
gloomy chambers, over the entrance of which Fancy
may see inscribed—

"Abandon hope, all ye who enter here!"

Tales' habitation was furnished after the ancient
model; it had all the gloomy air of its fellows.   Its
windows were dirty, and its pigeon-holes were full
of dust; its carpet was well-worn, and its table was
ink-stained.   There was but one redeeming point
in that room, one bit of Nature amid all that mass
of musty, dusty paper—a few flowers on the mantelpiece, placed each morning, from time immemorial,
by the old housekeeper in a cracked jug: wall-
flowers in spring, China roses in summer, and two
heavy dahlias in autumn.   They bloomed and faded
by old Tales' almanack.

Dayrell arrived in the "dahlia" season, and for
him the old house was full of memories.   Here was

the room where the senior partner (now deceased)
met him, a white-trowsered and blue-jacketed boy,
with the extended hand of friendship, and let fall
a perfect avalanche of sixpences. Munificent act!
heirs to good clients do meet with such slices of good
luck. On the left was the hall-table, whereon he
had once espied a mutton chop, or rather, the bone
of what, at one P.M., had been an underdone specimen of its kind, picked as clean as knife and fork,
and teeth, could effect. Thus spake his aged friend
on that occasion : " Do you see it ? That is the way
a lawyer does business. He never leaves the bone
till every morsel of meat is removed ; then the value-
less remnant is cast out of doors."

Again, when released from the comfortless waiting-
room, he was ushered into "the presence;" more old
familiar friends were ready to greet him—" Jorums'
securities," as the letters on an iron safe record, still
occupied their ancient niche. " Easy's Trust " was
still in that japanned box, and carried Dayrell back
to the days of pinafores, when he curiously peeped
into it, and, in place of deeds, found only a paper of
seed-biscuits, probably intended for Tales' luncheon.
His faith in outward appearances suffered much by
that discovery. " Estate of Crabtree," " In re Bla-
zer," " Spendthrift's Mortgage," would fain renew
their old acquaintance, and appear to be sitting round

the room, in solemn conclave, to hear what their old
comrade had to say. And Tales, the mainspring of
of the whole, greeted him in his own frigid, quiet
way, scarcely changed himself these five years, in
garments, manner, or face. Those pepper-and-salt
trowsers of his, dated from remote ages; those shoes
could have told a tale of many a weary mile "traversed." We could make an affidavit about that
blue coat with brass buttons, we could select it out
of a thousand in Mr. Nose's emporium. In antiquity
it could give many years to the hat and leather
gloves, to which latter it would be more difficult to
assign an age than to any maiden aunt of our
acquaintance. Tales, however, was a great man of
business. Leave matters to him, and he will pull
you round. It is his repelling manner, his forbidding frown, and somewhat sarcastic conversation,
that make us lament the necessity of paying him a
visit. Meet him, as Dayrell did, one first of September, in the stubbles and turnips. What a trump
the old boy was then! How he mowed down his
doubles with unerring accuracy! How, when under
the influence of the nut-brown ale, he actually
smoked Haycock's black pipe, totally regardless of
the internal inconvenience it afterwards occasioned.

"Punctual to a minute, Mr. Tales," said Dayrell,
glancing at his watch. "If punctuality is the soul

of business, I ought to succeed in anything I undertake."

The lawyer's bow and smile gave but a qualified assent to the assertion. He, however, said nothing, but, somewhat impatiently, demanded the object of his client's visit.

Dayrell, without any circumlocution, entered into the details of the Doncaster catastrophe. He mentioned his settlement of all minor claims on his purse, and gave the names of three or four persons to whom he owed large sums, but who consented to wait till it was quite convenient for him to pay. He reminded Tales of certain securities on which money might be raised, and finished with a sketch of the mode of life he intended in future to pursue.

"I have made up my mind," he said, "to abjure gambling. The last two days at Doncaster I did not make a bet." (Smile on Tales' face.) "And, if my debts are paid, I will begin life again, and in quite a different manner. I don't think I am deficient in talent; at all events I understand addition and subtraction, and can write as well as the clerks in your office, for instance. I intend entering some line of business in which, if there be no chance of retrieving my fortunes, there will be a certainty of earning a fair competence."

The lawyer nervously turned his pencil round and

round, and listened to his client's plans, with incredulity written on his face.

" I am glad to hear," he said, " that you have made such good resolutions, and hope you will be able to keep them. But your present liabilities are the first objects for consideration. I must tell you candidly, that I do not think your securities sufficiently good for me to advise any of my clients to advance money. And, although your word may be as good as your bond, I am afraid nobody will be willing to take that as a basis for affording you the required relief."

A long conversation ensued. Papers were examined; residuary estate and reversionary interest valued, and calculated, without arriving at any solution of the knotty point. After many *pros* and *cons* it was agreed that Tales was to have time to reconsider the question, and that Dayrell was to use his best endeavours to pacify his creditors, and to retire to some quiet spot, where, by studious economy, he might be prevented from making matters worse.

At that date, "the advantages of a cheap and comfortable home, combined with the amusement of sporting over an extensive domain, and fishing in a celebrated and unnetted (?) river," attracted the attention of those who perused the advertisements in the weekly newspapers. "The comfortable home" was at Aberdovey, in North Wales. The Torpid

Arms was the actual residence, whose landlord proffered his generous hospitality to the public at the
moderate rate of thirty shillings a-week. There was
also "a carefully selected assortment of foreign wines,
spirits, and cigars," awaiting the stranger who might
drift so far west. "The very thing," thought Dayrell. "Twice thirty make sixty, and twice sixty are
one hundred and twenty, and one hundred and twenty
shillings make 6*l.* a month ; economy and shooting,
fishing and saving money ; I will start at once."

Theory, however, is one thing, and practice another. There certainly was an extensive domain to
shoot over in the vicinity of the inn, but there was
no game. The landlord *thought* it had been a bad
breeding season for the " birds." There was a river
near the house, and another three miles distant, but
very few fish. In fact, although a woodcock, a few
snipe, or a wild duck, might occasionally be bagged,
the sporting was a dead letter. Dayrell had a companion in the sanded coffee-room—a fellow-sufferer,
from impecuniosity—one Crippleby, an old gentleman,
whose declining years were dedicated to the extinc-
tion of fowl and fish. Not that he did much either in
that way ; for his movements were slow, and his aim
uncertain. Dayrell once watched him kicking tufts
of grass to find a jack snipe that had alighted in the
next field. He found it, and great sport he had with

that bird.   He bagged it at two P.M., after an exciting
chase of three hours and fourteen minutes. Crippleby
was a man of few words, and slept in his chair after
dinner, with his gin and water untouched before
him, and a long churchwarden pipe, at one moment
slipping from between his lips, and recovered at the
critical moment by a convulsive start of the sleeper.
Beau camerade this for Dayrell, accustomed as he
was to the fun of the " Rag" and the jokes of the
" Garrick."

Weeks rolled on in the dull routine of shooting,
when the weather was fine; smoking, or playing
billiards with four coloured balls, when it was wet,
and adding but little to the register of game killed
and wounded. A Christmas ball was given at
Aberystwith. It was opened by the county members
" stepping" it in a quadrille. It was enlivened by
pretty Miss Jones and coquettish Miss Williams,
who polkaed with one-ball-a-year energy. Those
young ladies' papas asked Dayrell to dine at " the
Warren" and " the Retreat." Alas, even bright
eyes and fair complexions could not persuade him,
a second time, to face the perils of the road. Twelve
miles in an open chaise is no joke, especially, if the
quadruped objects to cross an overflowing torrent,
but sniffs at it as suspiciously as a Frenchman does
a cold bath. Spring time arrived, and Crippleby

impaling the ruby worm, cast it hopefully into whirling torrents, while Dayrell threw a fly, but seldom persuaded a fish to look at his feathers.

Rain is not a thing unknown in Taffyland. For days together, at times, will the clouds roll down the sides of Cader Idris and deluge the plains with water. It was during one of these playful freaks of "the clerk of the weather," when Crippleby had gone to read, for the fiftieth time, in the pages of the Sporting Mag., what "Hoarey Frost" had done in the fens and Linton in German preserves, when Dayrell had rejected the county newspaper, eight days old, and the Welsh guide-book—sole literature of the inn—as stale and unprofitable, that an idea struck our hero. Yes, through the smoke, as in rings and curls it ascended ceiling-wards, he saw his way to a "good thing;" and he pondered, and struck out a path. In that smoky room, and when looking on the rain-bespattered tiles, the future suddenly partook of *couleur de rose*.

He remembered a certain evening spent at that princely establishment, the "Bedford," at Brighton, when the claret of '44, owing to quick consumption, did not long sparkle on the board, and when a particular friend retailed a story about his model nephew. "I tell you, sir, he was a good boy, a brave boy;" and the old veteran's eyes sparkled.

"He was in difficulties, and he was in debt. He went abroad; he lived in a garret—'pon honour, sir, he denied himself all but the necessaries of life; returned here, and paid his creditors with the money he had saved."

"Why should not I do the same?" thought Dayrell. "Bother this country; if it does not rain it blows a hurricane, or *vice versâ;* abroad, I am sure to have fine weather. As to living, that is even cheaper than at the 'Torpid Arms.' Upon my word I'll try." And he puffed more furiously at his pipe, and suddenly recollected a tale that a chronicler declares to be true—far be it from me to assert the contrary—how a stranger, by a well-timed piece of civility to an old lady in a railway carriage, was taken into her confidence, and ultimately rewarded by a munificent bequest. And how, again—and this is a fact—an old gentleman dined one evening at Meurice's, in the company of fifteen Englishmen, all unknown to him; and when the dessert was put on the table, the old man got upon his legs, and made the following announcement:—"Gentlemen, my carriage is at the door—(great silence)—I am going to Marseilles to-night; whoever will accompany me thither shall live, and be brought back to Paris, free of expense." There was no answer, till a young man at the bottom of the table, thinking he might as well go to the south as stay in the capital with fifty francs in his pocket, said he was ready to go. The proprietor of the carriage was taken ill at Marseilles, and was nursed by his companion, to the best of his ability, for three months, when he died. The will was opened, and young B—— found himself the heir to 20,000*l.*, " as a return," the document said, " for kindness shown to a friendless old man."

"Why shouldn't I meet with some such windfall," thought Dayrell. " I'll start next month—I'll go to France," when his meditations were disturbed by rosy-cheeked, slipshod, slatternly Betty opening the door, and announcing that the boiled leg of mutton and trimmings, the oft-recurring *pièce de resistance* of the " Torpid Arms," was ready.

CHAPTER III.

The exile has ever been a favourite subject for historians and rhymers. When bidding a long farewell to the land of his birth, touching and pathetic words have been put into his mouth. The pious Æneas—hardened sinner, though he afterwards proved himself to be *in re Dido*—wept, we are told, on quitting burning Troy. Caius Marius, balancing himself on a hillock, looked back on Rome, and told its unconscious citizens that they would "want" him some day. Even Bill Styles, the convicted pilferer of watches and handkerchiefs, the ballad tells us, leaned over the taffrail, and made a gushing appeal to the sea-gull to lend him her wings, and waft him back to the arms of his "Polly love." But the gentleman in Queer-street—the gentleman with six children and a scolding wife, in search of a foreign clime and mutton at 4*d.* a pound—has somehow been forgotten. Surely, their feelings at leaving the white cliffs of old England might be made a theme by some sentimental pen. Take the hint, authoress of the "Bleeding Heart" and the "Washerwoman's Lament;" yes, see what you can do.

Dayrell was quite as sad and lugubrious as any of those we have named when on board the good ship "Seahorse," bound from Newhaven to Dieppe. It was one of those days in early summer when the winds, for once, are hushed, and a landsman would pooh-pooh the idea of making harbours of refuge. A shadowy haze enveloped Mr. Ainsworth's much-loved Sussex downs, and the clumps of trees that nestled in the valleys, each in turn becoming small by degrees and beautifully less, as the engines, performing I-dont-know-how-many revolutions a minute, propelled the steamer on her course. Pleasant day for you passengers, who fear the sea, and the malady that will, in spite of libations of pale brandy and water, affect those who venture to cross it. Happy are you (apparently) unprotected female, who, in be-nailed Balmoral boots, imitate on deck the sailor's short walk, so unlike your usual sweeping stride on "the slopes" of Brighton. Lucky are you, Frenchman of the yellow and bilious visage, who need not wrap your face in a pocket handkerchief, groaning, "*Mon Dieu, Mon Dieu*," but art able to light thy cigar—mind, on this side the funnel—and wistfully watch for the

low shore of your beautiful country. Rejoice, ye
occupants of the tarpaulined sheds on deck, that
you are well enough to ask questions about the
sea-birds as they skim past, and the probable length
of the passage. Even yon poor lady's-maid smiles,
and has not to lay her aching head against the
bulwarks, and wish herself in a premature grave.

It signifies little *where* a man travels. If he has
been at a public school, or one of our universities,
and vegetated afterwards in the metropolis, he will
meet men he knows in all parts of the world. Is
it not a fact, that Duster, who we remember at
Corpus, is chopping wood at this moment at Bal-
larat? Should we not find Dumpling, of Brasenose,
wielding the managerial bâton if we went into the
mines at Alten? Can we visit a German watering-
place without meeting Choperkin, late of the Blues,
or stay in Quebec an hour without rubbing shoulders
with the notorious Starter? Shall " auld acquaintance be forgot?" We meet and ask them, " How goes
it," and pass on, wondering, Who next, and next?

Just so, when Dayrell had finished his observations
on deck, a well-known face appeared on the top of
the cabin stairs. " Limmer it is, by all the powers!"
ejaculated Dayrell, and, in two minutes, the pair
were deep in Oxford reminiscences, and pacing the
deck in all the pride of university clanship.

Limmer was one of those men whose destiny it appears to be to fall into numberless scrapes and difficulties, to extricate themselves no one knows how, and reappear on the scene without material loss of reputation. Of his early life no one knew anything; even his exact place of residence, when at home, was a mystery to his friends. What brought him prominently before the public occurred during his second term at Oxford. At that time "the drag" was in great favour; the highest honours awaited him who came in first in those cross-country events. Of the winner of the "Wet Waterperry" fast men spoke with reverence; and reading men have been known to sit down, at twelve o'clock at night, and write an essay for the "first past the post" in "the Wheatley." To make a long story short, Limmer, one afternoon, in the tightest of buckskins and most slovenly of boots, slipped away from lecture to the meet. He rode one of Symon's hacks with unquestionable pluck, was the first to catch the eye of Judge Anisced, and was forthwith invested with the Oxford Victoria Cross. He was not the man to let such an opportunity slip without further improving his position. He could talk fluently, if not wisely, on almost any subject. From the prestige he had acquired, youth listened, open-mouthed, to his stories, and did not care to question his veracity. What, though his need of ready money should have become proverbial? though his well-worn purse never carried anything more valuable than a sixpence and a rusty key? Are not poole (at which he was a proficient) and betting (at which he took long credit) specially provided as instruments for replenishing the purses of our modern gownsmen? True, he had a rich uncle in the far West—a sort of Mrs. Harris—often mentioned, but never seen. Some such person must have befriended him in the hours of his direst need.

One episode in Limmer's life, as bearing upon his character, we must give. It was the day on which the greatest match of modern times was decided, that a party of undergraduates had assembled in a room to await the telegram announcing the result. He had backed the Richmond, the others the Middleham horse; Limmer suggested that they should hedge. "Put down five shillings each on the table," he said, "and I will cover them." When the news arrived that Middleham had won, the unblushing Limmer swept all the money off the table, so doing a clever stroke of business. He had realized a small sum, *but* it was *ready money;* he had lost a larger, but that payment *might* be postponed.

In spite of his talent, great grief awaited him in London; and, of his career in Paris afterwards, report did not speak favourably. Still, neither the one circumstance, nor the other, prevented his obtaining a commission in a colonial regiment; nor did the lessons he had received prevent him initiating his fellow passengers in the mysteries of roulette. His next appearance in England was as a cheery subaltern in one of her Majesty's line regiments. But time had made no alteration in his manners or habits; if anything, it had rendered him more indifferent to public opinion and prejudice. Some intricate money affairs—a regimental fracas—had compelled the colonel to request him to exchange; whereupon, glad enough to receive four months' leave, he left the matter in the hands of his agent, and started on this speculative continental trip.

So here was this hero of many a drama in public and private life—the reckless, unchangeable Limmer of other days—in person *redivivus*. Dearly bought experience—no, we can hardly say dearly bought, for the avuncular Mrs. Harris, not he, must have paid—has not checked his ever-rolling tongue; on the contrary, his travels, adventures, and all the events of his past life seemed to add fuel to the flame.

"I know Dieppe very well," he said to Dayrell, after listening to the plans of the latter. "I can show you where you may live economically. There are two hotels: one I call the aristocratic, the other democratic. The former is kept by Mr. Horgan, about whose birth and parentage some mystery exists." Here Limmer winked his eye. "He was confidential valet to some nobleman: hence the reason why rank and fashion patronize his establishment. Unless you are anxious to pay ten francs for cutlets, and five extra for looking at the waiter, we won't go there. We will visit *mon ami* Blossom, whose hotel is on the quay. He is a real good fellow; you should only hear him talk about Horgan—*pauvre enfant*, he calls him—and see him shrug his shoulders when he compares his rival's means with the trifle in the funds, the horses, and the house in the country, of which he is the proprietor. Still, both the hypocrites are most polite to one another, and elevate their hats to an angle of ever-so-many degrees when they chance to meet in the street."

Dayrell agreed to Limmer's suggestions, and, now that the chalky cliffs of Dieppe were in sight, began to prepare for disembarcation, Already the scent of the new-mown hay was wafted across the water. Already the sea was dotted with herring boats, their

sails flapping against the mast, and their sides disfigured by a capital letter and number. Already
upon the faces of the passengers smote the hot air,
driven thither by a thunderstorm that had burst
over the town, and sorely perplexed an old lady on
board, who believed—and was strengthened in that
belief by Limmer's assertions—that the steel beads
in her bonnet would prove lightning conductors.
"Ease her," cries Captain Bunting from his perch.
"Ease her," re-echoes the cabin-boy, as the "Seahorse" enters the harbour. "Stop her," and the
paddle-wheels, ceasing their revolutions, drive forward a great wave over the hitherto tranquil
surface. The rain, descending in torrents, deterred
the English and French loungers from witnessing,
as is their wont, the disembarcation. The *com-
missaire* of police, in his frock coat and Legion of
Honour decoration, was alone there to greet them,
and slipped, like an evil, yet affrighted spirit, down
the ladder. Safe from the wet himself in the cook's
den—by courtesy, I suppose, called a cabin—he and
his subordinate took notes of the passports. Unfortunate passengers, however, were grouped outside
—old and young, men and maidens, healthy and
strong, sound and unsound—in close proximity to
the chimney, which dropped its blacks in profusion,
near an engine-room that emitted rank odours of

oil and grease, and "*sub Jove*"—in this case truly *pluvio*—subjects for pity, almost to the stoker, the only man who, for pleasure's sake, balanced himself on a rail, and cooled his smoke-begrimed and heated brow in this summer bath.

Come hither, man of the wondrous name—Grandguillot, and any other subordinate of the newspaper called the *Constitutionnel*. You may be past the middle age, and, if so, probably are rheumatic. Try the effects of fifteen minutes under a black cloud, awaiting the official ticket-of-leave to enter free and enlightened France. In your next number, perhaps, you will be kind enough to give us your experiences of the system. I think you may draw in your horns, or, at any rate, talk less confidently of that "useful, necessary (vide *Constitutionnel*) and harmless protection for society."

"*Votre passeport*," demands the gensd'arme, and reading Mons. Lèmàre (as he pronounced it) and Madame, asks, "Mais, ou est, Madame?"

"*La voila*," answered the ever-ready Limmer, pointing to a nice-looking English girl, who stood next him, shivering in the rain, and awaiting her turn.

"*Bien, Monsieur*," said the gensd'arme; and Limmer in two minutes had transported the young lady out of the wet into the luggage-room, to her

own momentary gratification, but to the horror of
her mother, who, separated from her by the crowd,
helplessly wrung her hands upon deck, at seeing
her daughter carried off in this summary manner.

Quite a master-stroke of Limmer's, just such as
his complete *savoir-faire* enabled him at any minute
to accomplish. Miss Emily is seated in the shed
allotted to short-haired douaniers, passengers, and
piles of luggage. Then, from not seeing her mother,
she remembers the isolation of her position, and,
like a good daughter, expresses great anxiety on
the subject. Limmer disappears, and presently returns with that breathless but not over-pleased
matron, whose displeasure, however, is but momentary. In the face of custom-house officers, who look
as if they would rummage the boxes to the last pair
of socks, and with servants who cannot speak a word
of French, the services of a polyglot like Limmer
cannot be cast aside. Nobly does he do his duty.
By means of a five-franc piece he gains first *entrée*
to the sanctum. Hat in hand, and with the politeness of a Chesterfield, he addresses the head official.
In fifteen minutes the family boxes are upon a truck.
The search has been nominal—unruffled silks and
crinolines are on their way to the hotel.

But who and what is the young lady ? 'Tis Emily
Trelawney, well-known at Cheltenham, as young

ladies generally are at any place if they happen to be good-looking, and have money of their own in that noble institution—the Three per Cents. More than one hopeful individual had lingered about a certain house, with a green verandah and well-kept garden, not a hundred miles from Pittville. More than one had waited for a glimpse of a muslin dress, when its owner should please to come out and " do" the daily watering of heliotrope and nasturtiums. People did say that certain Irish adventurers, with more brains than money, had sworn fealty after a very short acquaintance, and been summarily remanded. At Tenby (where ladies are rather scarce) she was voted a belle the summer after she came out. Old Staggers, the horse-dealer, made quite a fortune out of the officers at Pembroke Dock, so many dog-carts did they require to take them to that western watering-place. As to Ensign Noodles, aged nineteen, he refused to be comforted with bitter beer and vingt-un, but was so terribly hit that he never left the esplanade for three whole days and nights, and would have been there now, perhaps, had not his superior officer put him under arrest. The year preceding this the young lady had visited Dieppe ; and we all know how Frenchmen will, even without encouragement, prostrate themselves before gilded beauty. This time it was Bellegarde, the Prefet's deputy, who was the devotee. That elderly gentleman—the wags called him the "dissipated crow"—ought to have known better. Thrice he seized opportunities to drop upon his knees, and ask her to become Madame La Comtesse. She refused the honour in the kindest manner. Undeterred by failure he came again, and, in impassioned language, besought her to change her mind. Emily was vexed at his persistence, and replied, rather harhsly, "Monsieur Le Comte, I am astonished that you have asked me a fourth time to do what I never will do. I really thought you were old enough to know better." Bellegarde after this went "on leave," and Dieppe knew him no more; and, pleased with their first visit, Emily and her mother intended to spend a second season amongst the Dieppois.

But we have landed on a foreign shore; we are amongst the gabled ends and the quaint old houses, the gamins in blouses and the red-trousered "*infanterie terrible*," the be-capped and be-ribboned shopgirls, and the old ladies with towers of laces upon their heads. We meet Frenchmen (in the season) from all parts, and stumble on our countrymen at every corner—residents, visitors for the day, the week, and the month; and, before we continue our tale, have a word to say about English society on the Continent.

Dieppe, patronised though it is by our countrymen, is not like some English colonies in provincial
towns of France—those stagnant pools, which no
clear, fresh stream of Life ever enters and purifies—
those strongholds whither flit the gay spirits of bye-
gone days to escape the inconvenience of poverty,
debt, or some *faux pas*. If, as is often too true,
there be a "history" attached to individuals residing
in the latter: if there be a stain on their escutcheon,
such as time can scarcely wipe out, one would think
that such a fact would render all more kind and
charitable to their neighbour's faults and short-
comings. On the contrary, nowhere is the war of
scandal and back-biting so actively carried on;
nowhere is the hand of each so perseveringly raised
against his friend, to tear away the last shred of
character he may still retain. Elderly ladies, will
nothing induce you to put on the cloak of Christian
charity? Gentlemen, young and old, are your antecedents and present mode of life respectable enough
to justify you in throwing the first stone? Are you
to be the self-constituted judges of others?—you,
who, some with the bloom of youth on your brow,
some in the very prime of life, are dragging on an
aimless, hopeless existence? Was it for this that
the talent of masters and a university education were
lavished upon you? Was it for this that parents

denied themselves, and struggled to give you a fair start in the world? True, on your first arrival, you bore up against the *ennui* and demoralization which surrounded you. Still your fall, though slow, was sure. By degrees you dropped into the dull routine of billiards, cards, and brandy-and-water. By degrees you became more negligent in your dress, more careless of shaven locks and beard, more deaf to what the world might say, and more oblivious of self-respect. Not many months elapsed ere you had inherited the listless, jail-bird air of your fellows, that now seems to sit upon you quite naturally. How are ye fallen, ye " good fellows" of other days! You, who, at your midnight gatherings, are content to listen to the oft-told, dreary tale of scandal, or the stale anecdotes of some quondam fast man, in whose muddy brain the reminiscences of demirep triumphs, and perhaps racing robberies, still hold high place. And yet in your social degradation, you, the Toms and Harrys of your respective circles, must sometimes sorrowfully remember that you are the objects of yearning solicitude to a mother in old England, who, unknown to her husband, deprives herself, good woman, of her last five-pound-note to save her son from the consequences of low extravagance.

Nor are these transmarine republics free from

E

occasional " *émeutes*," innocent indeed of bloodshed,
but safety-valves for such bad feelings as inveterate
idleness engenders.   Let us state an instance: an
individual and his wife, owners of a good English
name, and tolerably well off, arrive.   Straightway
flock the little society to their gate, drop their paste-
boards, and strive to be on good terms with people,
whom, in their heart of hearts, they consider to be
in a better social position than themselves.   Anon,
whispers begin to circulate, and, forgetting minor
squabbles, people gather together to discuss certain
vague reports.   By degrees the spark is blown into a
flame, and the individual, so lately courted, meets
with cold looks from former friends, yet cannot help
smiling at the solicitude of mothers, who, like hens
do their chickens, gather their daughters around
them, when lo! the monster appears.   Explanations
are demanded, and society sends forth its champion
to a conference.   There is a strong altercation, a
production of marriage certificates, a fierce rally, and
the old talk about pistols, to which every one with
little honour must appeal, but which, like the pica-
dor's red flag, are but a mockery and delusion, only
intended to frighten one of the belligerents.   Next,
society, trumpet-tongued, proclaims its victory.   It
has established the paltry fact, that the stranger's
wife once gained her livelihood on the stage, and

accords her champion a trumph, for, I suppose, the
same reason as the Roman senate of old accorded it to
one of her consuls, "Because he had not despaired of
the Republic." O society of little mind and cramped
ideas, when will you be less exacting and unkind?
When will you learn to imitate the example of your
clergyman, who lives in peace, and shows good-will
to all his neighbours? When will you, like some
brilliant exceptions to the general rule, devote your-
selves to your families and household duties, and
forbear to meddle with other people's affairs? As
at present constituted, you well deserve the rebuke
of a celebrated authoress, administered by her
through the columns of the *Court Circular,* when
she gave her "reasons in writing" as excuses for
a lengthened residence amongst you.

There are 66,000 British residents in France,
(*vide* "Murray"). We are not sure about the
page, nor can we tell into how many brigades or
"colonies" that number is divided. This we do
know, that there are some amongst whom, the
plague-spot we have just denounced, seldom breaks
out, or, if it does, only in a mild and harmless form,
and that the Dieppe colony is one of the number.
Thanks, perhaps, to Mr. Maples, promoter of steam-
boats constructed on the wave principle, or to the
railway that brings such hosts of passengers, society

changes every month—nay, every week. People come, stay for a few days, and hurry on. Smith, with brass inimitable, dances with Miss Fanfare five times at one ball. On the morrow, he leaves without giving Miss Fanfare's mamma an opportunity of asking his intentions, or society time to invent some scandalous story. " Cui bono?" we ask, who know the impoverished state of Smith's exchequer, for the mother to put herself forward? His flight is best for both parties. Smith's departure, and that of other birds of passage, is soon forgotten. When we asked the Dieppe doctor about our friend Jones, a goodlooking, black whiskered man, who the preceding summer had stayed three weeks at Dieppe, and thrice partaken of the medico's hospitality, he had quite forgotten him. When pressed on the subject, he said, " Oh yes, Jones, Jones; let me see, a short, thick-set man, with red hair and spectacles. Oh yes, I remember." On which we had nothing to do but smile feebly, seeing the utter inutility of vindicating friend Jones' personal appearance, and pointing out his error to the doctor.

It is the same thing with the French; they have no time for gossip. They come to Dieppe for a dip into the ocean and " to be seen." At the end of three weeks the Mayor of Lisieux reads the riot act to his wife, and denounces this expensive place.

Adolphe, of the monied firm of Argent Freres, is summoned to Paris, ere he has sunned half the wide-awakes and salmon-coloured *bottines*,* that he bought in the Palais Royal to astonish the natives of Dieppe. For a short three weeks does Madame Tête-à-Tête occupy the post of honour at the table d'hôte, and talks "little nothings" with young France with the cold politeness of *la grande nation*. "Monsieur," repeated at the beginning of all her sentences, and all his beginning with "Madame," does not sound well in our ears. Whatever the French may do in private, their conversation in public is common-place enough. And Madame the Procureur Imperial's wife, comes from Rouen, bringing with her her forty changes of raiment. Never dressed two days alike, she flits about the promenades, and then returns home to tell her poor friends Marie, and Angelina, who could not go *aux eaux*, of the conquests she made, causing their poor hearts to rankle with jealousy at the new bonnets and dresses she has brought back with her.

---

* A French lady on a visit to a fashionable watering-place boasted publicly that she had brought forty dresses with her, so that she might never wear the same twice during her stay. Her husband, also, had an equal number of suits of clothes. If he had not forty hats, his collection of caps, smoking and lounging, certainly made up the average.

A late luncheon at Blossoms', and Dayrell and
Limmer did the promenade between the Pier and the
Etablissement. On the beach to the right are the
rows of sentinel boxes, whence issue figures male
and female, and who, even in the afternoon, clad in
variegated oilskins, pick their way daintily over the
shingle, and take a dip in the sea. Some float, some
swim, some converse by the edge of the πολυφλοις
βοιο θαλασσης, and not a few, even in the water, puff
their twopenny cigars. On the right are the walls
of the town, and between them and the shore is a
strip of grass.

" Well hit, run it out ;" and a cricket-ball descends
with a thud in the long grass close to where Dayrell
is standing. A smart leg-hit can be made even at
Dieppe, and is watched, though scarcely understood,
by coquettish nursery-maids, who look on from a
distance, and by knots of soldiers, who we have seen
receive a pretty hard blow from the ball with the
utmost good humour. " C'est drôle," remarks an
exquisite from Paris, with a glass in his eye; " mais
je n'y comprends rien." The pair arrive at the
Etablissement, in front of which the band discourseth
sweet music, and the crowd of fashionables sit on
chairs hired at one sou a-piece. The dandy leans
back dreamily on his chair, or taps his patent leather
boots with his cane; the ladies ply their crochet

needles; the merchant walks up and down and chat-
ters with a friend from the " woollen districts ;" and
the *epicier*, less proud than his neighbours, lifts his
flounced and furbelowed children on to his knee, and
gives them a halfpenny each to invest in Cerise's
choleratic pears. Should any of the company be dull
for a moment, they play at *toupie Hollandaise*, and
spin the top, whence the luckiest, after expending a
franc, will triumphantly return with a prize of the
the exact value of five centimes!

Here, too, is the billiard room, which they enter,
and watch the match between Carambole, champion
player of the Palais Royal, and an English captain,
whose strokes have often astonished the frequenters of
the " Cocoa Tree" and the " Rag." The game is this :
Monsieur Carambole has to make sixteen cannons at
one " break." Failing in this, he has to begin again.
His adversary, on the contrary, scores every cannon
he may make. This is the critical moment. The
Frenchman has scored thirteen : the balls are wide
apart, and it looks impossible to do anything more.
Still there is an air of confidence about Carambole's
cleanly-shaven face; there is something in the way
he chalks his cue that half tempts Dayrell to take the
tempting odds that the representative of the firm of
Paring Brothers is anxious to lay. Slowly, amidst the
dead silence that prevails, the master hand poises his

cue, then striking his ball on the lowest edge, sends it full against the red, and, as the term is, "screws back," without touching a single cushion. "Bravo" bursts from the lips of the bystanders as Carambole, with the greatest nonchalance, finishes the game in two easy strokes.

The band have returned their instruments to their cases: the chairs are deserted: and the beau monde has retired, some to their lodgings, some to *the* Café to do justice to well-cooked dishes and Cunningham's claret. Anon, in that balcony, will appear well-dressed figures, and the Bohemians of the street will gaze and wonder if all Parisiennes are fair like those. The professional beggar will take up a position opposite, and plead for sous; a wandering minstrel will collect a crowd of *his* admirers underneath, and so a gorgeous July sun sets upon life in Dieppe, to be renewed in another form an hour later in the ball-room, or perhaps in a small apartment, which we shall have occasion to visit presently.

"The Dayrell at his old Oxford games, making play with the heiress of the far West," remarked Limmer to his friend, as the two made the best of Blossoms' ordinary, rather than extraordinary, claret after dinner. "You followed up the first attack, and held your own, I will say, against all comers. More than one Frenchman would have willingly changed places with you," added Limmer, in his usual bantering way.

· "Of course I did the agreeable as well as I could, especially when you kept out of the way. You would not have a poor girl walk alone on the sands of Dieppe —I was going to say, 'by the sad sea waves," but that expression might be inappropriate this fine weather."

"Not at all," answered Limmer; "only I happened to hear Lyatt tell you that she was an heiress, and my own eyes bear witness to her good looks; so I put this and that together, and wondered how many *têtes-a-têtes* would bring you to your old state of matchless despondency. Then I thought I would give you a timely warning."

"How absurdly you talk," said Dayrell. "Just because I spoke to Miss Trelawney, and so whiled away an hour at Dieppe, I must be trying to marry her. 'Pon my word, Limmer, I think you are jealous."

"Not I, my dear fellow, I only wish to give you a bit of advice, which, like other wise people, you will of course reject. Now, don't make any mistake; she is far too clever to lose her heart to a man who lost his money on the last St. Leger. You will be victim number three or four, and be left in the same state as you were after the Traherne catastrophe.

Have you forgotten the lesson, my boy, you received
then, and how you made a bet that you would not
be married for ten years?   Do as I do.   Enjoy yourself, and leave the other sex alone."   And Limmer
drew himself back in his chair, his hands in his
pockets, and congratulated himself on the improba-
bility of any woman ever getting the better of him.

"Thank you much, but I am not so green as I
was in those youthful days.   There can be no harm
in my amusing myself with a pretty girl, while you
are playing billiards and ecarté ;—at the same time,
Limmer, it was hardly worth while referring to such
unpleasant scenes."

One retrospective glance at the love-failures of our
hero.   On entering into life—so, I believe, he inter-
preted his first assumption of coat tails—he met, at
his mother's house, a lady some years older than
himself, and destined to give him many a sleepless
night.   Her quiet demure face, and her good figure
artfully draped in blue, were generally irresistible ;
in addition to these charms, there was something
about her that made a stranger turn round and remark, "That is what I call lady-like."   Young
Dayrell was her chaperone in daily walks and rides ;
and, in appointing him as her guardian, I think his
mother acted foolishly.   Yet the latter might only
have been carrying out the idea of the sage matron,

who, when asked if she was not afraid of her son
going too far with Miss Flirt-by-night, replied, with
the greatest *sang froid*, " I will take care he does not
marry a person I disapprove, but will give him every
opportunity of *getting his hand into practice*." Dayrell was properly " paralysed" before he went back
to school, and the bystanders had occasion to remark,
with some truth but greater malice, how Miss ——
was making a fool of that boy. But the boy returned
to his college-meads, and knowing no better, indulged
in his day-dream, selecting as his confidant a comrade
bigger, but not wiser than himself. It was, doubtless, all very childish, but the sequel was very painful, when his sister wrote and told him that Miss ——
had married " some one from Liverpool," and had
expressed a hope that he would come and pay her a
long visit after the honeymoon.

Dayrell had plenty of time to recover from the
shock of his first disappointment. Enchantress number two did not appear on the scene till the middle
of his second year at Oxford. He had retired, *more
Oxoniensium*, to the country to read, and had selected
as his retreat the district famed, as Mr. Dickens tells
us, for hops, cherries, and pretty women. Duffers-
ville was slow—as most suburban localities in England are ; no wonder if he was on the look-out for
something to relieve its dullness. This came in the

shape of a Miss Wilson—the subject of Limmer's
rhapsody—who he met one afternoon in the fashionable emporium of Miss Bandoline. He was introduced, the following week, at the county ball, and
was duly entered on the list of her admirers. Of a
verity had he fallen into the hands of a " queen of
men," a flirt of the first water, whose lustrous brown
eyes, braided hair, and merry laugh drew to her side
the most impervious of the sterner sex, and whose
cleverness prevented her from indulging her love of
fun and repartee to such an extent as to make her
admirers break the silken cord, and retire immediately from the contest. People did say—" but
then," as the wise man remarked, " people will say
anything now-a-days, except their prayers "—that
she had refused more than one good offer—still, if
the report were true, the " No, thank you," must
have dropped from her lips with inimitable grace.

Dayrell fell without a struggle. The victress had
not need to stoop to conquer, or waste much time in
bringing this new fish into her net. Then followed
the usual episodes in a lover's existence,—the frequent morning calls at the counting-house, sedulous
attention at balls which Annie was expected to
patronize, the selection of Mary Johnson's most magnificent and high-priced bouquets, and swift pursuit of
her when she retired with her father to London fogs

and Wimpole Street. Dayrell's infatuation was at its height, when he travelled a hundred miles—the greater part on the outside of a coach—to the Lady Patroness's ball at Richmond, when laughing Annie honoured him with but two dances in the course of that long evening, and, on handing her to her carriage, would grant neither gloves nor floral sprig as a reward for his devotion.

In the ensuing spring Oxford met Cambridge on the old course between Putney and Mortlake. Dayrell, like a good patriot, took a ticket on board that swift steamer, the "Pride of the Ocean," and saw the race. But while lustily cheering for Oxford, when her boat came in three lengths ahead of her opponent; while laughing on his return to the "British" at facetious waiter James, who met him on the door-step and asked him if he was going "'Ome for the 'olidays"—a scene which friend "Punch" was kind enough to immortalize ; and while chatting with light and dark blue-tied undergraduates, who thronged that be-mirrored yet tarnished coffee-room, previous to serving as jurymen for the Chief Baron, or being addressed as "My dear boys" by the ubiquitous Mr. Green, an untoward event had happened in Wimpole Street.

"Master is at home," said the servant who answered Dayrell's summons at Mr. Wilson's door on the morning after the race; "but he can see no one."

"Is Miss Wilson upstairs?" asked he; "and disengaged?"

"Have you not heard the news, sir?" stammered out the old domestic. "How yesterday morning our young lady went out for a walk, and has never returned, and how they say she has eloped with a gentleman, a Mr. D——, who you may have seen here sometimes, and how"——

Dayrell heard no more. He received a shock that morning which it took many a weary month to heal. In few cases is unrequited love fatal, Mr. Thackeray tells us. We "come again" with feelings somewhat blunted, but, perhaps, the chastening we have received makes us all the stronger to receive the buffets Life has in store for us. After all, Annie was the greatest sufferer. She who, by her numerous flirtations, had hoodwinked her relations, had taken unto herself a new home with a penniless barrister— albeit, her first and only love—and who had been pensioned by an unforgiving father with a hundred pounds a year.

It was chance that led Dayrell, some time after this, to a small lodging not a hundred miles from Lincoln's Inn, whose penetralia a charwoman was scouring at mid-day, while from the kitchen ascended odours of unappetising cookery. How were the mighty fallen ! Poor Annie sat in an ill-furnished apartment, her whilom lustrous eyes so dim, and her look so careworn, as she toiled at some sketches which Mr. Etching would probably refuse to buy, and rebuked her children, who, with their prattlings, would fain hinder her task. Difficult, indeed, was it to recognise in that figure the pride of the ball-room, the belle of other days ! It was a painful and touching sight for Dayrell. Glady would he have dropped a five-pound-note on the floor as though by mistake, or left all his loose cash in some place where she might find it after his departure. But he was far too considerate to hurt her feelings by a gift. Through Mr. Etching came money for her drawings, and a request for more. In them that eminent printseller seemed suddenly to have discovered some intrinsic value. But we happen to know the person who created the demand, and we also know that the initials " A. D.," in the corner of each, were a *sine quâ non* with the purchaser, and hope that his disinterested kindness may some day meet its reward.

CHAPTER IV.

THE savans declare that gambling hardens, smoking dries up, and early disappointment in love withers the human heart. If so, there must have been an "*œs triplex*" about Dayrell's breast. Verily had he run the gauntlet of all three. How can Emily hope to find a hole in the breastplate, bring our doughty hero on his knees, and make him utter sentiments such as are fully expressed in the grand old motto, " Ich Dien?" A band, too large for so limited an audience, played in the Dieppe ball-room. Dancing, even in *la belle France,* is not in high favour during the dog-days. We beg pardon, we must except Sunday evenings, when French meets French, and make up for lost time by dancing till long past midnight.

The new comers—Dayrell, Limmer, and the Trelawneys—were present that evening, prepared, as good dancers ought to be, to make the most of the unlimited space allotted to the deux temps walses.

" Mamma talks of staying here three weeks, and

going afterwards to Ems," confided Emily to Dayrell
at the conclusion of their second quadrille. "The
doctors say that my chest is weak, and that I ought
to try a little German air, and drink the waters. I
am sure it is all nonsense. I can walk, ride, and
dance as well as anybody, but mammas always will
take such ideas into their heads."

"I cannot imagine that any great hole has been
pierced here as yet," answered Dayrell, innocently
placing his hand upon his heart instead of his lungs.
"I am sure there can be very little the matter, to
judge from the rapidity with which you executed
that last waltz under the auspices of that queer-
looking Frenchman."

"Don't abuse the Frenchmen, Mr. Dayrell; they
dance much better than some English I could name.
Still, I like to choose my partners; for some of the
former say very odd things at times. Fancy, one
day last year, when I told Monsieur Bracque that
his long-haired spaniel was not a gentleman's dog,
and that he ought to give it to some lady, he replied,
'If the prettiest lady in France offered to give me
six kisses, and the prettiest lady in England offered
to give me a dozen, I would not part with my little
pet!' Still, most of them are amusing, and if not
allowed to have their own way, can be kept in pretty
good order. But here comes the only Frenchman I

F

detest. I am sure he is going to teaze me to dance with him."

" Say you are engaged," said Dayrell. The next moment he of the pinched-in waist and short-cropped hair dropped back discomfited, and Miss Trelawney and her partner were embarked in a graceful mazurka.

" As you are a stranger, Mr. Dayrell," said Emily, when the music ceased, " I must make you acquainted with the customs and habits of Dieppe. This ball-room is lighted three times a-week for our special gratification. Yet the English do not attend, except when they can make up a party, and, even then, re-fuse to dance with people they don't know. Singular custom, is it not? But, then, insular we are by name and insular in habits. There was a silly little girl, called Kate Turner, here last year, who refused at first to dance with Monsieur Grandjambe, a man every bit as respectable as her papa; but when he said he was sorry such a pretty demoiselle *could not* waltz, she jumped up and spun round the room with him like a teetotum. You see that young lady with the cherry ribbons at the end of the room. That is Mademoiselle Galette, an especial favourite with all my partners. She presides over the refreshment department, and supplies us with champagne and soda-water. You have only to open a bottle of the former, and, having quenched your thirst, confide it to her care. At the end of the dance, you return to Mademoiselle, and she has a second tumbler ready for you. She is an obliging and good girl. Out of the profits she supports her infirm mother, and three brothers of tender age. Up stairs there is, they say, a small room, where they play écarté all night. I hope, Mr. Dayrell, you never gamble?"

"I have quite given it up, I assure you," answered Dayrell, "and I hope never to play again. I have good reason for making such a resolution," added he, with a sigh.

"I am delighted to hear you say so. I cannot tell you how I dislike gamblers. Play makes you all so selfish and *distrait*, that you become quite unbearable in society. Besides, of the men you play with, so many are cheats. There was a very gentlemanly man here last season, and such a good dancer, who lost and won large sums of money every night. Most people thought him very rich, and so made private parties, at which even the ladies joined in a game called lansquenet. Of course there was a grand supper and champagne given on each occasion; and one evening the play was very high, or he very unlucky, but he left the table, having lost six thousand pounds. I was so sorry that such a young man should have been in the hands of people who play, if they do nothing worse, every night of their lives."

"Up to everything, as I live," thought Dayrell; "she has travelled to some purpose." "Then," replied he, "I must give a hint to my friend Limmer, who is hopelessly attached to all games of chance, and save him from the same untoward fate."

As this was not a gala night, the band left the orchestra at an early hour. Now, as Hansoms, four-wheeled cabs, or any sort of conveyance—with the exception of travelling-carriages under the guidance of jack-booted postilions—are unknown in Dieppe, ball-goers must follow the example of our ancestors, and submit to be lighted to their respective houses by lantern-bearing domestics. And a grand sight it is, at the break-up of a ball, to glance down the principal street at the lights moving hither and thither, and see white satin shoes daintily picking their way over uneven pavement and dangerous gully-holes. But Dayrell trod "the lantern-lit path of sentiment," when escorting daughter and mother to their lodgings. Emily had taken his proffered arm—her other being found sufficient to keep her ample folds of muslin off the pavement. Yet, had ill-favoured Brown or Smith awkwardly tendered her such assistance, how kindly she would have declined, with "Thank you, Mr. B., but I require both my hands to hold up my dress." What though mamma was a close follower behind, and the lantern-bearing servant was in front, they could not see that a fair round arm was pressed oftener than was necessary, giving correct emphasis to feebly expressed ideas.

"I hope you will call to-morrow," said mamma, as Dayrell shook hands with them on the steps; "we shall be glad to see you, and talk over the ball.—Good night." And Dayrell turned on his heel as their door closed. His white kids dropped into his pocket, and, after the manner of us moderns, the cigar-case was fished up, and our hero walked along the quay pensively thinking but furiously smoking.

"The very thing," soliloquised he, "pretty, agreeable, and has money. Yet people say that the three are never united in the same person. Bah! so much for what the world says. But what will the mother think—kind old lady though she is *now*—when I tell her that I am hard up, and that I have been unlucky on the turf? By Jove, it must all come out. Ah, never mind; I'll let things take their course, sail with the tide, and *vive la fortune!* It may, after all, turn out as Limmer prophecied. But that reminds me I must go and look for him;" and Dayrell with much reluctance quitted the open air, climbed a narrow staircase in the établissement, and entered a small room, hot, close, and full of cigar smoke,—of cigar smoke from thirty full-sized regalias in the

mouths of adventurers from every country in Europe,
and card-players of home growth.   Amongst others
the figures of Limmer, Tomkins, and Simpkins, loom
through the hazy cloud.   They are in high spirits, and
joking about the cards, the changes in the game, and
the quaint French characters.   They are very hard
upon one in particular, known to the brotherhood
by the soubriquet of " the mangey pointer."   Not
doubting the respectability of the members of this
establishment, they are throwing down their Napoleons, as though they were playing with capitalists of
almost European celebrity.   There is no good angel
to whisper in their ears, that one is a sharper from
Marseilles, a second a bankrupt manufacturer from
Lyons, a third a keeper of a Casino on the Italian
Boulevard, a fourth a ruined broker from the Bourse;
or that of those that remain a dozen are professional
gamblers who live at Dieppe and by écarté.   So
Limmer and Company play unconscious of the histories attached to their opponents.   Not that it is
probable that Simpkins would refrain from giving
his sovereigns away, or Tompkins forbear to hang up
his bank-notes in the money-changers' shops,* matu-

---

* A gentleman who visited Dieppe, and used to play at the rooms,
had a peculiar manner of folding his English bank-notes.   When
unfolded they retained the marks.   As the money-changers always
display their wealth in their windows, the fashionable world of Dieppe

tinal reminders of an over-night folly, if they knew all. The infatuation of gambling and the folly of such gentlemen is so great, that they will play till they have scarcely enough to pay their fare to England. More than that; the lesson they receive now will probably be forgotten a twelvemonth hence. With refilled purses they will visit one of the thousand foreign towns, so glad to receive the *beaux joueurs* of England. Again they lose, and return home ashamed of themselves, and afraid to register another vow that they will not be robbed a third time by foreign sharpers.

"You are new to this," said Lyatt to Dayrell, as he entered the room. "I don't think your friend, Mr. Limmer—that is his name, is it not?—can plead the same ignorance."

"I am so, and only a looker on," he replied. "I want to see how my friend yonder weathers the storm. Fortune does not seem to favour its Limmer to-night," he added, as that lover of games of chance rose from his seat discomfited, and took his place amongst the bystanders.

"You must let me initiate you into the mysteries,"

---

used to stop every morning in front of the shop to see how many notes Mr. —— had changed that day. It became at last the most important feature in the morning lounge.

said Lyatt. "'Gad, I ought to know something about the game, considering how dearly I bought my experience. When a youngster, I used to watch the Frenchmen in a kind of silent awe at the way they handled their cards. They seemed more like wizards than men. They knew what was in their hand by simply looking at the inside edges of the cards, Then I had heard of *sauter-le-coup*, bridging cards, turning kings, pricking fingers and anointing them with lemon juices, so as to make them sensitive enough to *feel* the difference between kings, queens, knaves, and aces. I believed that one of these tricks decided every game I saw played. I longed to discover an agile finger in an overt act; needless to add, I never did. Yet I know every one believes them to be guilty of such *faux pas*, whenever it is worth their while to practice them. I heard young Morton innocently tell a party of elders the other day, that he *thought* that Frenchmen, at least some of them, could turn a king when they liked, when Major Lanark took him up quite fiercely, and said, 'Why on earth mention such a stale old story? Don't you know that at Paris last month a man was turned out of a club, because, on an emergency, he could not turn a king!' My opinion is, that they are capable of practising such tricks, but are afraid of doing so in public. Every Frenchman suspects his neighbour, and watches him too closely to allow of any deception. In a private house they might exercise their talents, especially if playing with unsuspicious people. No, Mr. Dayrell, they have a much better system by which winning becomes a certainty. The rules of écarté at the club ordain that two players shall take the cards for one game only. When that is finished the loser vacates his chair, and one of the bystanders fills his place. The winner retains his, and, as it is technically termed, passes. Now at all games of chance, the luck follows one or other side of the table. For instance, the players on our right hand will probably pass twenty times, and their adversaries not more than three or four in the next two hours, because the vein appears to be with the former. Hence the backers of the right side will be winners in the proportion of four to one. Now, it is the special idiosyncrasy of the speculative Briton to support the losing party, either, I suppose, on the broad principle, that the weaker requires his assistance, or, that the run of luck will shortly change. A Frenchman, on the contrary, is prepared to bet heavily, so long as the cards are in his favour; if he finds matters going against him, he either retires, or joins the ranks of the winners. Thus, at some period of the evening, he must reap the benefits of one good

' pass ;' and no sooner has he realized that, and his champion has been vanquished, than, like a shade on the banks of the Acheron, he ' melts into thin air,' or betakes himself to supper and thin sliced sausages, leaving the unfortunate English, who have all along been staking their money on the losing side, to lament the absence of *capital*, when it is their turn to win. A happy notion this, Mr. Dayrell, is it not? It so completely realizes our idea of ' Heads, I win—tails, you lose.' "

" Upon my word it does," said Dayrell. " But, tell me, who is the little man, who sits at the head of the table, twirling his pencil, and looking so drowsy and uninterested."

" That is Descartes, whose business it is to make out a list of such as wish to take a hand, to prevent any one playing out of his turn, and to see that the stakes on each side are evenly balanced. It is his business also to prevent the frequent repetition of what they call ' *erreurs*.' In this he totally fails. At the end of every game, when the happy winners divide the spoils, there is always a deficiency of some ten or fifteen francs. A nice little harvest the robber must make. Supposing he sits out five hundred winning games in the course of the season, and takes up ten francs that don't belong to him on each occasion, he will net a snug income of two hundred pounds a year. That old colonel yonder, with the decoration, who sits by the money, is popularly supposed to be the plunderer-in-chief. Nobody ever saw him stake anything; still, at the end of every game he claims, and takes, ten francs, and the deficiency thus created is made good by the other winners. I asked Monsieur Le Bas, the other day, why somebody did not accuse the old gentleman of the robbery. The Frenchman simply shrugged his shoulders, and remarked, ' *Que voulez vous?* Do you think that any of us, for a few miserable francs, are going to run the risk of having three inches of cold steel in our sides to-morrow morning?' But look! your friend Limmer has just taken his seat. Let us watch the game."

The cards are dealt to Limmer. This, his first hand, is easy to play. Do what he will, he cannot lose the trick. The bystanders look over his shoulder, and in dignified silence watch the game. A moderate outburst of remarks as England scores one. Then Limmer deals, but gives himself a very different hand to the last, one that requires a moment's thought, and necessitates some hesitation before closing with his adversary's proposal to have fresh cards. Advice is freely tendered by everybody at the same moment. " *Jouez ça,*" says an old veteran who has grown grey in card service. " *Non,*

Monsieur, Jouez ça," implores a young clerk, who, beardless though he be, is no mean authority on a game that he has studied in bed and out of bed, in dressing-gown and evening clothes, since he was eight years old. Limmer is bewildered. Up go his arms spasmodically into the air. He shakes off the crowd of Frenchmen, as he would a swarm of bees buzzing about his ear, plays what he thinks best, and loses the trick. (Frightful crash of voices and Babel of bystanders' tongues.) Again the cards are dealt. Again Limmer loses, and retires to the back-ground to listen to the upbraidings of some, the execrations of others, and the consolations of nobody.

" Come away, Limmer," said Dayrell. " Take a glass of my champagne and then away to Blossom's. Your wide-awake is not destined, this evening at least, to be filled with five-franc pieces. Now, Mr. Solomon," added he, as they walked down the street, " who was the wisest man,—you, who were ruining your health in a hot, smoky atmosphere, and paying dearly for the precious indulgence,—or I, who had a dance, a pleasant talk, and now have a quiet conscience to go to bed with? *Allons*, Mr. Limmer, if I had not done the same thing in my younger days, I would read you a homily that you would not soon forget."

CHAPTER V.

THERE are few places so unsatisfactory for a court-ship as Dieppe. There are no special advantages in the shape of shady walks, sequestered arbours, or murmuring streams, whither a pair of wanderers can go and congratulate themselves on being un-molested and unseen. "Pleasant and airy is the pier," you say,—so it is; but the invalids and old gentlemen hold the same opinion, and taking their camp-stools thither, snuff the breeze from early morn to dewy eve, watching with obtrusive eyes any lovers who may chance to invade their sanc-tuary. There are objections to the promenade. For, supposing it to be, as yet, too early for the fair dames of Dieppe to turn out in their variegated plumage, one is safe to meet a host of bathers returning from their dip, or the blouse-clad *gamins* who everlastingly flirt with the nursery-maids. "Why not go into the country," you ask? Bah! and find nothing but dusty roads, and mutilated trees that give no shade, to say nothing of the chance of a stroke from the "sun's perpendicular rays." After such a trip, with the thermometer probably at ninety, Cupid himself might be expected to drop his wings, and feel his hair to be sadly in want of Mr. Marsh's washing and cleansing apparatus.

Enthusiastic mothers may "get up" pic-nics, but pic-nics, pleasant as they are, cannot be compassed every day. No matter how anxious Mrs. Hooker may be to give Captains Plantagenet and Fitz James an opportunity of "speaking out" to her Bessie and Margaret, she would be a bold woman to exhibit her daughters too often, and make the smitten admirer too conversant with their undoubted charms. Besides, should we wish oftener to partake of warm champagne and indifferently cooked potatoes under the wide-spreading beech-tree, appropriate spots for the purpose near Dieppe are scarce. True, the Castle of Arques is a delightful old ruin, but *toujours* Castle of Arques would become very stale. What is there left but the ball-room, and what we started from—the lodgings? The former, in the absence of balconies and conservatories, we summarily dismiss. The latter,—yes—something may be done there. But bear in mind, Mr. Adonis, mammas cannot always be leaving the room on pretence of rectifying some mistake in their dinner orders, or be continually

fetching scent or pocket handkerchiefs from a neighbouring apartment; nor run away with the idea,
that, in her absence, you are free from interlopers.
Spooner, in such a sanctuary, was interrupted when
approaching the most tender and touching part of a
lover's advances. At the end of the room there
was a glass door, veiled, in French fashion, by a
muslin curtain, which was supposed to prevent the
actions of the people inside being seen. A chance
glance in this direction assured him that two female
heads, belonging either to the domestic or family
portion of the establishment, were flattening their
noses against the glass, and attempting to fathom
the mysteries of Spooner's conference with his inamorata; and, although on being discovered, the
sight-seers scuttled off with marvellous celerity, and
Spooner regained his seat with as small an amount
of awkwardness as could be expected, it was a long
time before that bashful youth screwed up courage
enough to make a second attempt.

In spite of such local drawbacks, Emily and
Dayrell had frequent interviews. By occasionally
drifting on to the beach, where mamma certainly
sat hard by, but, immersed in the pages of a brown-
paper covered volume, was unconscious of the passing
scene, and by assisting at the balls and pic-nics, opportunities arose of which our hero took advantage.

Luckily too for him, Emily was mistress at home. She was an only child, and, what is of more account to those who love to have their own way, an invalid. If an honest professor of the art of healing, one of the tell-you-his-mind Esculapii of the old school, had been consulted about her bodily ailments, he would have abruptly answered, " Stuff and nonsense; she is as well as I am." But her relations had once been told that she was delicate, and having imbibed this notion, Mrs. Trelawney would have been untrue to the stubborn principles of her sex, had she refused to adhere to, and do battle for, the idea. Emily's wishes, therefore, were the law of the household. She could persuade her mother to do whatever she wished; but it is right to add, that she reigned less absolutely and tyranically than might be supposed. The exercise, however, of even a mild form of despotism tends to the production of a somewhat forward and precocious young lady. Not that this exotic, as a rule, fascinates the sterner sex. On the contrary, the peach-blossom cheek, the languishing eye, and the most milk-and-water conversation, will often wrest the palm from those who can think for themselves, and give an opinion which we Solons would be better for listening to. But Emily was not one of these forward girls. It was only when her advice was asked, that she showed she could speak to

the purpose; or when some young gentleman, in
over-joyousness of spirits, jumped over the traces,
that she could administer a rebuke. "Do your
friends call you 'mentor,' or 'menteur?'" slipped
out of her mouth one evening, in answer to a well-
known *raconteur* of stories and adviser of youth.

Thus Emily, being mistress of the household,
planned country excursions and walks, at all of
which Dayrell somehow assisted. Had Mrs. Trelawney been acquainted with his antecedents, and
the miserable state of his exchequer, she could not
have done otherwise than act the prudent mother,
and put a veto upon her daughter's arrangements.
But here Fortune befriended Dayrell. Stapley, who
knows everybody, and who, spring, summer, and
winter, is gadding about the watering-places, happened this summer to be at Dieppe, and, having
known Dayrell in his palmy days, gave flourishing
accounts of his resources and family, which, coming
in the way of friendly gossip to the ears of Mrs.
Trelawney, had lulled to sleep any natural feeling of
curiosity or suspicion. So pleasantly sped the days
for Dayrell, and in such good spirits did he write to
his sister, that she, good soul, guessed that there was
a lady in the case; and, balancing her foot on the
fender, and gazing into the fire-place, wondered
whether her future sister was fair or dark, tall or

short, and, in her answer, hoped "that everything would be for the best"—a general, not to say enigmatical, phrase, suggestive of further confidences. Nor were the warm summer evenings mis-spent. Often would Dayrell join the family circle, and, if not "hit" at back-gammon, or check-mated at chess, listen to the Spanish and French ditties for which Emily's voice was well adapted. Rare performer she was on the piano. Gladly did the old Dieppoise, as she clanked along the streets in her cumbrous sabots, stop under the open window, through whose muslin curtains the subdued lamplight struggled, and, hearing a favourite native air, muttered *c'est ravissant*, and stumbled off, a thought happier, to her confined, but old-fashioned garret.

One evening Mrs. Trelawney sat on the sofa toiling at yards of canvas, to be turned, albeit at some very distant date, into a border for her curtains. Kate was at the piano, and Dayrell stood by in the constrained attitude that a gentleman generally cultivates, when Mademoiselle sings from memory, and there are no music pages to be turned over. It was a Spanish air she was singing, in which a Seville girl was supposed to be standing at an open casement and lamenting the loss of her lover.

" Somebody in Dieppe must be doing this evening much the same as my Spanish heroine, eh! Mr.

Dayrell?" and Miss Emily slily glanced at him, and finished her performance with the customary run over the notes. "They say you are mixed up in it, if not the principal concoctor of the plot. I congratulate you on being able to keep a secret better than most people. Still I think you might have made *us* your confidants."

"So it is known already," he answered. "Well, I am prepared to meet my fate—even to be torn to pieces by the infuriated Mr. Sandes in the cause of disinterested friendship. Excuse me, Miss Trelawney, for my silence. However much I may admire a legitimate thirst after knowledge, I never could persuade myself to put a lady in possession of any important secret. Please don't frown. If you'll forgive my silence, I will now give you a true and correct version of the affair. You must recollect Captain Splice—a thin, good-looking man, with light downy moustaches—generally to be seen in front of Horgan's Hotel with an immense regalia in his mouth. He met Miss Sandes last winter in England, and followed her here from Leamington. They were a charming couple, just made for one another, I should say. It was quite affecting to see them making love, like a couple of doves on the eaves of a house. Neither said much, but the way they looked at one another reminded me of a little boy and girl, of the mature ages of nine and eight, exchanging timid sentimental glances at a juvenile dance. The only obstacle to their happiness was a stern father, who intended making over Miss Sandes and the 20,000*l.* she has on coming of age, to a youthful cousin. These family arrangements are all very well, but not viewed in the same light by my friend the Captain. He feels, Miss Trelawney, that the best feelings of his nature are being trifled with. If he could, he would, like a friend of mine, relieve himself by shedding tears; but his romance takes another turn. He preserves a dogged silence, and, the more unhappy he is, the more tobacco he consumes. Now, what advice would you have given to any one who came at midnight, told you he was in love, that his passion was returned, and that the only obstacle to his happiness was a crusty, unnatural papa?"

" In the first place, Mr. Dayrell, I would not have seen a person at that unreasonable hour; and, in the second, I would not listen to any one who hinted at rope-ladders, a chaise down the lane, and Gretna. Suppose I——"

" Wouldn't do such a thing for the world, Miss Trelawney. You won't see it in the right light. Just consider what are even a parent's wishes to blighted affection? What is married life without Love? And how miserable the poor wife must be

till husband number one is removed from this busy
scene. Besides, when the knot is once tied, the runaways can return to the parent, and the latter, when
he sees how useless all opposition and anger must be,
forgives, if he does not forget."

"What shocking ideas you have to-night, Mr.
Dayrell; and I am sure you must be quite wrong.
No one elopes now-a-days. Besides, thanks to the
spoil-sport electric wires, the blacksmith's occupation
is gone—at least they told us so when we passed the
Gretna Station on the Northern line last autumn."

"I must enlighten you on that subject, Miss Trelawney. There are Gretnas under another name,
where couples in a hurry can be expeditiously and
cheaply married—for instance, the loyal, free, and
independent states, as the inhabitants say, of Jersey.
With this harbour of refuge in my mind's eye, I
formed a plan for our gallant captain. A steamer
leaves this place every week for St. Helier's. I found
out that she was to sail on the day of the ball (yesterday), at 11 A.M. This would not suit my plans, so
I induced the captain for a consideration to delay his
departure till 11 P.M. Papa was in the habit of
playing two rubbers of whist at every ball; and if
any Englishman would cut in, and put up with his
mistakes, would sit out four or five games. This
task I undertook. I then told Splice that, when

he saw us comfortably seated at the table, he and
Miss Sandes might slip out, meet the servant who
brought her cloak, bonnet, and boots, and trot off to
the vessel with the utmost celerity. I, moreover,
hired a duenna—such an acid-looking monster—to
accompany them, and make it all proper. On the
night of the ball I met Sandes, and conducted him
to the whist-table. We cut, and I became his partner. Just as we were winning the second game he
made a revoke. Of course he was found out, and,
like most criminals when detected in such an act,
was horribly angry. 'I tell you, sir,' he said to his
adversary, a Frenchman of sinister and Barabbas-
like aspect, 'I did not play that card.' '*Monsieur
se trompe*,' answered Barabbas, quite affably, following up his remark with explanations far too profuse
and intricate to be comprehended by any ordinary
intellect. 'Then *bon soir*,' said Mr. Sandes, me-
nacingly throwing the francs he had lost on the
table; 'perhaps you will be able to play without
partners,' and he stalked away, and looked for his
daughter amongst the dancers. As ill-luck would
have it, Splice's scapegrace boy had been late in
coming with the necessary disguise. The anxious
pair were looking into the court-yard, when Mr.
Sandes burst upon them with, 'Why are you not
dancing, Fanny?' 'We were only looking at the

stars, papa dear,' answered the little deceiver; 'how beautiful they are to-night!' 'I am going home immediately,' said papa angrily, not because he suspected anything, but simply because the loss of thirteen francs annoyed him exceedingly. 'Go in and win,' I had just time to say to Splice, as he led Miss Sandes to the robing-room; 'tell Mr. Sandes everything;' but I could not add more without being overheard. They left the rooms, and I soon afterwards started for Blossom's Hotel. I went to bed and fell asleep. I had a dream. An object appeared to me, with hair scattered promiscuously over a manly forehead. A cigar protruded from the corner of its mouth. Evening clothes adorned its person, and a white tie, but the bows of the latter were twisted under the ear, not the chin, of the object. A composite candle, guttered by the draft from the door, flickered in its hand. This apparition stood at the bottom of my bed. 'It's all up,' I heard, and in the sepulchral accents recognised the voice of Splice. 'No I am not,' I managed to answer from between the sheets. 'I can see that,' he sorrowfully replied; 'but you soon will be, and ready to do me a favour.' ('Shall I?' I thought, thoroughly hating him for thus disturbing my slumbers.) 'I have seen Mr. Sandes myself, and spoken to him, but he will not give his consent. I start for England this morning. Will you go to Paris on my account?' 'Paris! I go to Paris!' I answered, starting up in the bed. 'Are you mad, or am I dreaming?' 'Yes, old fellow; I want you to go to Paris. It is no distance from here. You would be back in less than a week. You see, my plan is this. As soon as I arrive in England, I shall go to my uncle's, Sir E. Splice,—he is very fond of me,—always used to give me tips when I was a boy,—I shall ask him to write a letter—a proper letter, you know, all about our family and connections—to Mr. Sandes; this I will forward to you at Paris, and if you will give it to him, and in a quiet conversation talk of me as an exemplary character, or throw out hints about a slate quarry or coal mine that may be my property some day, you will render me a service I never will forget. Then, if Sandes receives the proposition kindly, telegraph to me, and I will be in Paris in twelve hours.' A cool proposition, was it not, at that early hour of the morning?"

"And what answer did you give?" asked Emily.

"He bothered me so, that in a weak moment I assented."

"I thought we should have had the pleasure of your company as far as Ems," said mamma. "You said, the other day, you should like to see that part of Germany."

"Indeed I did," he answered; "and, upon my word, if I had a shilling about me, instead of these shabby franc-pieces, I would make an affidavit, as Paul Pry says, never to do another good natured thing as long as I lived, much less attempt to run a young couple into matrimony. But when poor Splice is *in extremis*,—when pretty Miss Sandes is in the depths of anxiety and misery, and I have given my promise,—how can I retract?"

"You might go to Paris, and join us at Ems," suggested mamma.

"Yes, I might," replied Dayrell, hardly satisfied with the solution of the difficulty.

"But not till after the races, mamma," said Emily. "Mr. Dayrell promised the Prefet he would take us to the course."

"That is a prior engagement, and shall be faithfully kept," he replied. "Splice cannot command my services till the end of the week. But I think I have interfered sufficiently with your night's rest—I will only add, good night, and may we have a fine day for the races."

"Am I dreaming, or is it all true?" thought Dayrell, as he left the house. "Can it ever *be?* She was indeed anxious about my trip to Paris, and mamma invited me to Ems. Can I reasonably hope? Bah! They must have made some mistake—been led astray

by some report of a fortune that I do not possess—
take me for my rich cousin, perhaps—yet, after what
I told them, they could hardly be so foolish. How
am I to face the *exposé* of my affairs? How present
my *nil in presenti*, and not too much *in futuro*, to the
scrutiny of an inquisitive mother, or the Argus eye
of an own-brother-to-Tales? And the consequences!
rejection with ignominy; proved to be an impostor
by my own showing; turned off by mamma, and forgotten in a week by the daughter. By heavens——"

"Walking into the sea with the calm deliberation
of a blind man," uttered the well known voice of
Lyatt, from the opposite side of the street. "Am I
to be an eye-witness of a suicide, and be the first to
carry the harrowing news to the Rue St. Martin?"

"Where it might be received with more com-
posure than you imagine," replied Dayrell. "What
made you mention the Trelawneys, just as though
I had the slightest chance of succeeding in that
quarter?"

"Another bashful specimen of humanity," said
Lyatt in tones of pity, "discovered by accident, not
to say, by moonlight. For you, the envy of the
Frenchmen, and the subject of conversation for the
loungers of Dieppe, to tell me that you have not the
pluck to carry off the heiress of this and the last
season. 'Gad, Dayrell, at your age, you ought to be

ashamed of yourself; you, who cannot be numbered amongst the juveniles, the

'Fortunati nimium, sua si bona norint;'

the happy but timid youths, who, in excess of modesty, block up the doorways of ball rooms, and gaze with longing eyes at heiresses and beauties, yet are afraid to speak to them. Look at me. I am not rich, you know that; I am not good-looking; I am not young; I am not strong in conversation, though I may be blessed with a certain amount of impudence. Still, if Mrs. Lyatt were removed from this sublunary sphere, and I happened to meet such a good *partie* as Miss Trelawney, do you think I should shrink from speaking my mind? Why I would propose, and be accepted, before you bashful nondancers had made up your minds to solicit the honour of the next quadrille."

"Talk on. It's very easy to say what you would do. But tell me, supposing you were accepted, how are you going to multiply the great round 0 into something substantial, when the lawyers are called in and settlements have to be made? Besides, you don't know how I have been taken in on other occasions;" and Dayrell's thoughts reverted to his previous failures.

"Poor boy!" said Lyatt, mistaking Dayrell's

meaning. "Do you imagine that I am a convert to
Lady Scattercash's logic, 'if she has nothing, and
he has nothing, nothing could be better?' That
would not suit my constitution. No, if I were in
the country I should take the train; if in London,
a Hansom cab; and by proffering a shilling to a
guardian of last wills and testaments, should become
the momentary possessor of a parchment, whose contents would inform me how much a father did be-
queath unto his much-loved daughter, and under
what conditions. But you may keep your shilling in
your pocket. Miss Trelawney is an heiress. Take
my word for it."

"Granted; but that is not the point. I want to
know how to parry the usual enquiries made by an
anxious mamma on the morning after the proposal.
I don't mind telling you, Lyatt, that any letter addressed to my lawyer, asking for information respecting my pecuniary resources, will be shortly,
nay, curtly, answered."

"Is that the difficulty?" answered the mentor.
"It was you that gave such excellent advice to Splice
the other day, surely the same is applicable to your
case."

"Not at all. His was quite different. He has a
rich uncle and relations who might help him."

"So have you, doubtless. Write to them—give

them full particulars, and a mother and a sister will manage it for you. Stay, it will suit you better to inveigle the Trelawneys across the Channel. Let them meet your family. Let mamma meet mamma Let a sister pour her gushing experiences into Miss Emily's ear. Let them talk for a week, if they will. I'll answer for the result. Do you still say no, and shake your head? I understand it now—you have been too long in the same society. You want a change of scene—a few of those cobwebs swept out of your brain. Come to the écarté room, back Limmer's hand, distract your thoughts by winning or losing a few Napoleons. Wonderful results have sometimes flowed from such a chance visit to the tables."

"Perhaps so," answered Dayrell; "but not tonight. Here is my hotel, and I shall retire upstairs. Thanks for your advice. Till the races, adieu!"

  *   *   *   *   *   *

Limmer, in the meantime, had not been idle. A few pages back his gift of eloquence was fully recognised; and, as he spared not the flower of his rhetoric when conversing with his inferiors, besides being liberal in *promises* of future douceurs, it is not to be wondered at if he was very much "thought of" by the uneducated masses. Landlord Blossom, albeit ofttimes bitten by plausible adventurers in the matter of his bill, succumbed in forty-eight hours, and in glowing terms described him to his wife, as "*le brave garçon Anglais.*" But Limmer, as he took his candlestick and retired to his room, after making this impression on the facile heart of Blossom, winked knowingly at himself in the glass, and had already decided on turning it to his advantage.

It happened that, in the stables of the hotel, there stood an Irish horse—ugly and ragged hipped, 'tis true—but of great size and power. It caught the eye of Limmer in his first matutinal ramble. He prosecuted enquiries, and received answers in the flowery language in which ostlers of every country are wont to indulge.

"Can he jump?" enquired our speculator.

"*Oui, par exemple, haut comme ça,*" replied the glazed-hatted attendant, flourishing his fork a yard above the corn-rack.

"Can he gallop?"

"*Oui, Monsieur,* like the wind." But we need not stop to ask how that element performs such a feat.

Then Limmer leaned his chin on his hand, and took counsel with himself touching this noble quadruped. Buy? No; he would not buy—perhaps, we might add, he could not, except by a bill at six months, a species of payment not exactly suited to the tastes of our lively neighbour the Gaul. Besides, experience had shown him the folly of investing in such uncertain property as horse-flesh. As hiring or borrowing were the only other means at his disposal, he had an interview with Blossom, the owner, the result of which will presently appear.

" *Chacun à son goût,*" said Limmer, as Dayrell and he sat one evening after dinner discussing their wine, and the former concluded the account of his adventures in the Rue St. Martin. " Since you have given me the details of your proceedings, perhaps you would like to listen to mine. You will be sorry to hear that, owing to sudden creditorial pressure, the Honourable Mr. Fakenham has been obliged to leave Dieppe. But Blossom did not allow him to depart without leaving some security for his 'little' bill. In the place of money, the hon. gentleman left his famous horse, Casse-cou, intended to start and win the Dieppe Steeplechase, and now under the control of me, Limmer, surnamed 'the Lucky.' Blossom's knowledge of horse-flesh is very limited; his management is worse. Casse-cou was allowed his full feeds of corn, but was seldom exercised. Casse-cou, in the exuberance of his spirits, kicked the ostler. Casse-cou was harnessed to the landlord's gig, and kicked it to pieces. Then Blossom's heart was sad; Mrs. B. was visibly affected unto tears, and urged

her lord and master to make away with *ce vilain
monstre.* Then I came to Blossom as a saviour;
rescued him from the slough of despond, by taking
the whole care and responsibility of Casse-cou, and
am to pay fourteen francs a week for his keep. Fur-
thermore, we have agreed that the horse is to be
entered for the gentleman's race; that if he wins,
the stakes are to be divided; and if he loses, he is to
be again under the care of Blossom. I assured him
that the horse must win, and some rich Parisian
would give a thousand pounds for him. 'A thousand
pounds! how many francs is that?' he exclaimed,
as the commercial mind of Blossom expanded. 'I
will send the receipt to Monsieur Fakenham to-
night, and I shall gain the whole thousand pounds
for myself.' Thus, I have not spent any of that
precious commodity, ready-money; I am the quasi-
owner of a horse; I may win a great race, and as
much money as your gaudy wide-awake will hold.
Shake hands, Dayrell, order another bottle of Mouton, and drink to my success."

" A remarkably nice boy you are, Limmer, not to
say clever. But this time you may find that you
have overreached yourself. Do you believe, for one
instant, that the French will allow an Englishman
to win one of their races? If you come in first, a
distance a-head of the others, they will prove you to

have gone the wrong side of a post; and if you win by a length, obliquity of vision on the part of the judge will give the victory to the second horse."

"Never fear, Mr. Dayrell, I know all about that; I didn't attend La Marche races for nothing, and see the English-trained, English-ridden horse, the Curate, proclaimed the winner, though, to my certain knowledge, he was not the first to pass the post. The man in the judge's box was not a genius, like our Mr. Clarke; he was only an amateur, and was terribly flurried by 'a near thing.' So half-a-dozen confederates assisted him to form his judgment by shouting under the box, as the horses passed, 'Bravo the Curate! the Curate!' and, strangely enough, up went the Curate's number. It is as well to be prepared for all contingencies. Perhaps I shall be, perhaps not;" and here Limmer chuckled.

"Allow me to say, Limmer, that in a parliamentary sense, you are nothing better than a robber."

"Don't flurry yourself, my dear fellow," said the other, noways disconcerted at the compliment. "I was only talking of what was done at La Marche. I shall win without any assistance of the kind. It is only in case of accidents," and here a succession of winks closed Limmer's sentence.

From the date of this conversation up to the morning of the race, it would be difficult to say when Limmer took his natural rest. His training summoned him twice a day to the race-course. There, on Casse-cou's back, he galloped at a furious pace, standing up in his stirrups, and shouting to the workmen to get out of his way. "*Diable*," muttered the natives as he passed them at full gallop, and strained their eyes, expecting a man who did not sit down in his saddle to fall off any moment. Notwithstanding all this, his *séances* at the écarté table were not foreshortened. He even found time for further schemes in connection with the race.

There was a spice of romance about the ostler's summary of Casse-cou's capabilities. True, he could jump a fence of any reasonable height, but he lacked the quiet "on and off" of the accustomed steeple-chaser. He could "stay" for ever, but he was deficient in pace; a failing that in winter might not be of much account, but in summer, when the ground was hard, would materially interfere with his chances. Limmer soon discovered this defect in his horse, and hit upon a plan for remedying it. He obtained an introduction to the race committee, and singling out more particularly that working member, Monsieur Paille-foin, inundated him with so many compliments, that had not Limmer, from motives of his own, declined the honour, he certainly would have been elected honorary steward.

"Really, Monsieur Paille-foin," said Limmer one morning on the Place, "the fences now-a-days on the steeple-chase courses are simply ridiculous; there is not one on ours that I could not hop over. I am sure your grey mare would not stop to look, but take them all in her stride. You remember our Leicestershire gates and timber jumps; you should have one or two like them, and, depend upon it, your mare, who is such a splendid fencer, would have a better chance of winning."

"I have seen Leicestershire myself,—I know it well, Monsieur Leemare," replied Paille-foin, who, in a *railway carriage*, had once travelled through that country, and was therefore a competent authority. "I think it will be as well to make some alterations. I will give orders to the workmen to make some of the fences stronger and higher."

Which no doubt he did. But, to make assurance doubly sure, Limmer changed a five-franc piece, and distributing the smaller coins amongst the peasants, caused two or three superlative "obstacles" to be reared and propped up with extra stakes and palisades, so that the committee, should they change their minds, might be hindered by the trouble of reducing so formidable a barricade.

O, Limmer! well may you look at yourself in the glass with satisfaction, on this, the eventful morning of the race. Well does the Oxford-blue jacket sit upon you; well do the shining tops and Barclay breeches adorn your little short legs. Does the complacent smile upon your countenance forebode success, or is it only one of satisfaction at your elaborate "get up?" You deserve to win; you, who in a business and commercial point of view, have left no stone unturned, and have risked much capital on the result. We saw you in conversation with members of the Jockey Club, and the gentlemen riders from Paris. You knew that no accommodating ring would offer you the chance of winning money, so you depreciated your equestrian talents; you spoke with modesty, and they fell into the snare. We looked over your book, and saw the entries on the second page, and we have been credibly informed how many hundred francs Mr. Dayrell has invested for you. All honour to your talents, but we cannot help thinking how sadly they are misapplied.

"What a funny race course," exclaimed Miss Trelawney to Dayrell, as, under the guardianship of mamma, they drove up in their carriage. "They have marked out the course with soldiers instead of flags. What can they want with their guns and bayonets? Not to make the horses jump better, I hope."

"No, no, Miss Trelawney," replied Dayrell. "They

are there to prevent the country people being ridden over; in fact, to keep the course clear. There is your friend the Prefet in the stand, in cocked hat and official coat."

"Is he the judge, Mr. Dayrell?"

"No, he only distributes the laurel crowns to the happy winners. I must tell you that the promoters of races in France being classical scholars, have read of the Isthmian games, and imitate the Grecian practice of decorating the winner with a floral trophy—so much honour for the animal. For the owner, or rider, there are a couple of bags full of coin. It will add much to our amusement, if Limmer should win, to see him carrying his bags of metal to the town; for his proverbial craftiness will prevent him entrusting them to any one else, and I suppose Mrs. Trelawney will not spoil sport by offering him a seat in our carriage."

"I am quite ashamed of you, Mr. Dayrell; I am sure mamma will behave better than that: if she does not, I shall myself ask the poor man to come back with us."

"Then I shall tell him you intend to commit a petty larceny. Ah! there is the trumpet. Act the first, scene the first—two horses upon the stage, and both horses belong to the same stable. You may choose which you like for six pair of Pivet's gloves—

Yes—you have selected the right one—yellow jacket and black cap. Now, Mr. Yellow Jacket, do your best; you are carrying Miss Cæsar and some of her fortunes."

"How very stupid!" exclaimed Emily, as Yellow Jacket trotted in, a distance a-head of its opponent. "If I had been the Prefet, I should have been ashamed to put a collar of evergreens about that animal's neck. How foolish too it looks—even the Prefet is smiling. Why don't they take the poor creature to its stable, before everybody dies of laughing?"

"If they couldn't raise a cheer for the winner, they might have hissed the loser," said Dayrell. "I remember, when I was an undergraduate, our college started twenty-one horses in an amateur race on Abingdon course. The proctors heard of it, and sent an emissary to take the names of the riders. 'Bravo, Stunner! Stunner wins!' shouted the crowd, as the gentleman, rejoicing in that soubriquet, went first past the post. 'Get away home, Lobbs! Ah, ah, Lobbs!' they exclaimed in derision, as that unfortunate undergraduate toiled in last. The names of Stunner and Lobbs were duly reported. But Stunner, the winner, could not be traced;—there was no person of that name. Lobbs only was discovered, and rusti-

cated for the heinous crime, the University face-
tiously remarked, of being *last* in a race."

The Gentleman's race stands next on the card.
There is a stir amongst the crowd in front of the
stand, as the horses are led round. Gentlemen rider
and their friends fill the weighing tent, and chatter
about kilogrammes as they sit down in the scales,
and about the fences. When the official has declared
them "all right," La Belle France simmers up into
a kind of enthusiasm, more particularly the ladies,
who have come to see their particular fancies ride.
Their faces are somewhat paler than usual, at the
sight of those formidable posts and rails. Mademoiselle Delahay's merry laugh—such as she in-
dulges in when she trips into the sea—is suddenly
hushed. The fate of Baron Longchamps is in the
balance. Perhaps, she thinks, he is taking off his
white coat for the last time. Mademoiselle Millefleur regrets she ever came—only think, should her
wealthy *fiancé* be brought home on a hurdle, where
will be her *trousseau,* her equipage, her opera-box
next season? At the same moment the object of
her thoughts gallops past the stand, charges the hurdles, and scarcely saves a fall by clutching the neck
of his astonished horse. A little shriek is heard in
the stand, but Monsieur Lupin recovers himself, and
walks to the starting post. Limmer is the only one

who starts uncared for and unwept—a circumstance somewhat in his favour, as removing all cause for nervousness.

The bugle sounds. "They're off!" exclaimed the English in the stand.

"Which will you have for a dozen pair of gloves, Miss Trelawney," cried Dayrell? "England or France?"

"England," Mr. Dayrell.

"A patriotic selection, but the odds are seven to one against you," he replied.

The horses started at a moderate canter. The first jump was a flight of hurdles bushed with furze, a rood of which Lupin's horse knocked down, and the others followed through the gap. Limmer puts on the steam, and clears a brace of fences without accident. They are approaching the rails that caused such terror to Mademoiselles Delahay and Millefleur. Limmer sits down in his saddle, and shakes old Casse-cou. "Bravely done! bravely done!" shouted Lyatt in the stand; and the feelings of the crowd found vent in a buzz of applause, as horse and rider landed safely on the right side.

"Get on—don't look back; please don't look back, and throw away the race," cried Lyatt imploringly; as though the distant Limmer could hear him. Limmer did not hear, but did look back, and,

doubtless, chuckled at what he saw. Flourishing
his whip, and muttering between his teeth "Allez,
villain, allez," Lupin upset his horse, who, if left
alone, might have done well enough, and had a
stunning fall. Luckily for her, Mademoiselle did
not recognise the colours, till the unfortunate Frenchman had picked himself up, and mounted his animal,
which had been caught by one of the soldiers. The
hesitating Longchamps came next. Feebly he put
his horse at the stiffest part of the fence; but that
sagacious animal, knowing that greater pluck and
pace were required, stopped suddenly on the taking-
off side, and shot the Baron on to the green turf
beyond, a *contretemps* that, of course, made the
others refuse. By the time that three or four had
scrambled over, Limmer was a quarter of a mile
a-head. A little further, and he disappeared from
the sight of the occupants of the stand, yet hotly
pursued by the mare Penelope and two others.
Four minutes elapse and Limmer re-appears, still
with a commanding lead.

"He must win, I tell you; he must win," cries
Lyatt; "it is all over, and they never can catch him."
Wait a minute, Sir, do you see Penelope creeping
up, and she *has* a turn of speed, and is taking the
smaller fences in gallant style. One field from home
Limmer is still leading, and Penelope drawing nigh.

Over the last hurdles flies the former, flourishes his whip, and sits down in his saddle for the finish. "Casse-cou wins!" shout the English; "Allez, Penelope!" shriek the Frenchmen. But the latter stumbles, as she lands over the last hurdle,—she comes again, but too late to prevent her rival passing the chair, a winner by two good lengths.

One hat flies into the air—a peculiar hat, one with a broad brim, evidently the property of an elderly gentleman, who ought to know better than to be so reckless. One voice is heard above all the rest,—"One tousand pounds! *je le vendrai*, Mons. Leemare, I will sell, I will sell," and we recognise the hatless head of Blossom, as he leads back his horse to scale. "I will sell, I tell you," continued the landlord, flourishing his arm, and the crowd fell back, awed by his gesticulations, or the evident desire of Casse-cou to lash out and damage a by-stander. "Oh, but he is a good beast, and worth one tousand pounds," contined Blossom, patting, and almost hugging, the old steeple-chaser.

"So he may be, man; sell him, if you like, but don't make such a fuss about it," said Limmer, as he returned from the scales.

The auctioneer posted himself in the front of the stand. A circle was formed, and Casse-cou led round, exposed to the gaze of the multitude. The

conditions of the sale were read,—" What price shall
I put upon this celebrated horse, *pur sang Anglais*,
winner of the last race? *Dix mille francs?*" asked
the auctioneer. "One tousand pounds," muttered
a voice by his side. "*Cinq mille* for this valuable
animal; a gentleman says *cinq mille*." "He is
asking nothing for my horse," muttered the same
voice. "*Six—sept—huit*," continued the auctioneer.
"*Allez bon homme*," exclaimed the voice; but the
bon homme would not bid more than *huit mille
cinq cent francs*, and at that figure the hammer fell.

A note was put into the auctioneer's hand, which
he read, and look perplexed.

"Is this your horse I have just sold?" enquired
he of Blossom, who was standing near.

"*Oui, Monsieur.*"

"Will you have the goodness to read this?"

Blossom read,—"Mr. Fakenham presents his compliments to the auctioneer, and requests him to keep
the amount realized by the sale of *his* horse, Casse-
cou, till he has heard further from Mr. Fakenham."

"*Je suis volé*," exclaimed Blossom. "I am robbed!
Where is that perfidious English? He owes me
money,—he gave me the horse,—he would rob me
of my own:" and Blossom's abject state of misery
was piteous to behold. But suddenly recollecting
himself, he cried out, "Where is Mons. Leemare?

He is my witness; I will bring him to prove it;"
and poor Blossom left the stand to search for Limmer. 'Tis needless to add, without success; for,
disgusted with the landlord's greedy rapacity and
eccentric behaviour, Limmer, to avoid further scenes,
had left the course while the auction was going on.

And ofttimes of a summer evening, when smoking his pipe under the gateway of his hotel, has
Blossom recounted to chance strangers his romantic
tale, and as he comes to the end, he smiteth his leg
vehemently with his right hand, and calls to witness
the disgraceful conduct of that *canaille Anglaise*
Fakenham, who paid him the amount of his bill out
of the proceeds of the sale, and, as an Irishman
would say, "sarra a rap beside."

As a matter of course, after the races there was a
ball, this time worthy of the name. The crush, the
dresses, the heat—three criterions of excellence—
were unparalleled. The French came in a body,
and as it was not Sunday, the English also. Dancing
was almost out of the question; and chaperones,
once separated from their charges, might look for
them in vain. For once the scandal-collectors were
at fault, as the crowd limited the area of their observation. Even Belle-garde, had he been present,
might have bent the knee for the first time, and
escaped the notice of all but his nearest neighbours.

It is high change with Mademoiselle Galette—lemonades, ices, cakes, all quickly disappear. The frequent pop of champagne corks bear witness to an unparalleled consumption. She 'll win, not her spurs, but her cherry ribbons, and we shall see her, *decoré* with that harmless finery, on her way to St. Jaques next Sunday morning.

"Will you take me to mamma? I should like to go home. No, I am not ill; it is only the heat—and—and—I feel very tired after the races; and, Mr. Dayrell, please, find mamma, I cannot stay in this room any longer."

"I want to go home, mamma dear," continued Emily; "Mr. Dayrell was kind enough to find you in the crowd, and, I am sure, will excuse me for leaving so early."

"If I may only have the pleasure of seeing you quite recovered to-morrow," he answered.

"But you must not escort us home to-night; the servant is here with a light," said Emily. "Mamma will see you to-morrow, and perhaps I may be at the station before you leave for Paris.—Go back to the ball room, Mr. Dayrell; you will, I know, if I wish it."

Dayrell stood as one entranced on the steps, watched them until they turned the corner, and then re-entered the ball-room. No wonder he was restless and uncomfortable, roaming amongst the dancers without a fixed purpose, and not even making an attempt to engage one of the "talents" in the waltzing line. While the quadrille—the most crowded one of the evening—was going on, he had proposed to Emily, not in the sentimental high-flown language of the modern novelist, but simply asking the question "Will you?" To which the reply might have been equally short and explicit, had the scene not been in the second tier of benches in the ball-room, where dowager ladies were within earshot, and their eyesight confined to their own immediate neighbourhood. But there happened to be a French lady on the bench above them, whom nobody asked to dance, and whose dress nobody admired, and to whom scarcely any one spoke, although she ofttimes rattled her sandal-wood fan, and attempted to attract to herself one of the passers-by. Her eye lighted on Emily and Dayrell, and though ignorant of the English language, she instinctively guessed the subject of their conversation. Emily started on finding that sinister look directed towards her; she felt that her secret was in another's keeping,—in the keeping of one who had envy and malevolence written in her face; so she rose hastily, asked to be taken to her mother, and left Dayrell without giving him a definite answer.

"I cannot stand this any longer," said Dayrell to himself, after three or four rounds of the ball-room, during which he came in contact with half-a-dozen couples starting in a waltz, and was set down at once by the French as a rude, unpolite Anglais. "I will leave Dieppe to-morrow; but I will do one good act first—take Limmer, if possible, from the écarté-table. I wish it could be for ever."

There is a great crowd in the card-room. The habitués are lost in the vast influx of fresh faces. Strangers range themselves on both sides of the table, and invest notes and gold in place of the accustomed five-franc pieces. Descartes no longer sleeps, or mechanically puts down the names of the players. His eye is on the notes, and gloats over the pile of gold on either side of him. "*Erreurs*" to-night are of no account. The winners settle them without a murmur. Time is precious, the loss of a few francs a trifle to the winners of hundreds. A dead silence prevails as Dayrell enters the room. Limmer holds the cards that are to decide whether he passes for the sixth time. There is the old smile of confidence on his face, such as he wore when making the last stroke and winning a hundred pounds in his match with Carambole, or when he cleared the Aylesbury brook on the redoubtable Nimrod. "Quatre a," is all the anxious spectators

can exclaim, and draw a long breath while Limmer
shuffles the pack for the last deal.

"Trois a vous," says Limmer. "Trois a moi;
deux a vous; deux a moi; et, monsieur, je vous
salue. Le roi."

Limmer has won again. He carries all before him
to-night, and pursues his triumphant way. Are you,
Dayrell, going to warn him when in the heyday of
luck and good fortune? What folly, what presump-
tion for you to think that a gambler when winning
will do aught but laugh at your advice. If in a vein
of ill-luck, he might listen, he might be decoyed from
the table, though oft-times then the tempter would
whisper, "Remember your success last year: this
bad luck must change some day." No greater curse
can befall a young man than to win. Better to lose
half a fortune, while youth sits lightly on the brow:
better to receive some hard knocks on a race-course
before sitting down to the hard business of life, than
be induced by a transient gleam of sunshine to
gamble on, until, sinking deeper and deeper in the
mire, he falls into that abyss whence there is no
recovery—no resurrection.

CHAPTER VI.

ONCE more on the wide world—cut off again from the civilizing influences of a domestic circle—in an express train moving at the moderate rate of twenty-five miles an hour, sits, must it be owned, the miserable, disconsolate Dayrell.

Why so miserable?—with the pace for France considerably above par, with soft, luxurious cushions to loll in, with warm bottles for the feet, with permission to smoke granted by the one other passenger in the carriage. As times go, such travelling is not to be despised. Compare it with a trip in a yellow-panelled diligence fifteen years ago. In very truth that was a weary, dreary voyage. The dusty roads, the jolting pavement, the walks up hill and the "shoots" down inclines, the delays while postilions tinkered the rope harness, the crowds of loathsome beggars at the relays, the interminable lines of poplars, and the cramped position even in the coupé ; the infamous dinner at Abbeville, and the still worse breakfast at Beauvais, and the arrival at the Porte

St. Denis, tired, bilious, with a fearful headache, thirty hours after leaving the inhospitable Calais. Compare that with the rapid, comfortable railway, with no stoppage between Calais and your hotel in Paris but what the octroi choose to impose. What if the latter do want to look into your portmanteau for a defunct rabbit or a slimy John Dory? They will only keep you a minute. Let us be thankful for being let off so easily.

But Dayrell had been spoilt in the last month. He had tasted the sweets of domestic life. The contrast came too suddenly, and at an inopportune moment. So his fellow-traveller—a *commis-voyageur* —receiving but curt replies to his questions, slunk back into his corner, and endured the torture (to a Frenchman) of a prolonged silence. Doubtless, when he joined the circle of admiring comrades at the café that evening, he told a terrible story about *ces bêtes Anglaises;* and, perhaps, concocted an artful tale about the scene he witnessed at the Dieppe station, of which he made himself the hero, and a heroine of the pretty English girl kissing her hand to him! When does a Frenchman not believe himself the centre of attraction to woman's eyes?

" Hotel des Juifs," said Dayrell to the driver of a Parisian cab; and as that model conveyance rattled over the pavement, by the lines of tall, gloomy houses, his thoughts reverted to Splice and his reasons for visiting Paris.

Lyatt must have made some mistake. He never could have meant me to come to such a gloomy place as this. Is it the Hotel des Juifs? Yes, there is the name, and here the porter. "Hallo! Sir," he exclaimed to that aged Israelite, as he sulkily emerged from his den, "what is the fare from the station here?"

"*Quarante sous*," was the reply, with a strong emphasis on the last two syllables, and the old man fell upon Dayrell's luggage, and bundled it within the gates, which he carefully closed on the new prisoner.

The bell was answered by a Hebrew maiden, whom some might called ill-favoured, and every one vote unclean. From the rack on the wall, she selected one of the 160 keys. "Allons," she said to Dayrell, and led him across a dreary courtyard, where no life was seen, save when a slipshod waiter, with the strongly marked features of the despised race, flitted from one side to the other, through a gloomy quadrangle of curtained windows, suggestive of robbery, if not the murder, of the last tenants—up the old oak staircase, and along an echoing corridor, till she came to No. 65. Then the key turned gratingly in the lock, the door opened, and an odour of "unoccupation" saluted the nose of the visitor.

"*Le voila*," said the maiden, showing Dayrell his
room, and unprepared for the assault he made on the
windows, so as to bring a little air and light on the
bed in the recess, the gorgeous, but fly-blown, mirror,
the cold marble-topped table, and the pie dish for
washing, execrated by tourists, and every man who
has ever put pen to paper.

"Is there any one in the hotel?" he asked, seating
himself at the same time on his portmanteau. "The
rooms look empty on both sides of the courtyard."

"There is scarcely anybody," said the girl.

"Where 's the landlord?"

"In the country."

"Is there a table d'hôte?"

"No; but you can have some dinner."

"Can I have a bath? Here, I mean."

"Monsieur!" ejaculated the maid. Her mouth
opened, and she stood aghast at the idea of her
polished floor being soiled. But suddenly changing
her mind, she thought there was one down stairs that
would suit Monsieur. For an instant she disappears,
and returns, bearing in triumph a tin vessel, twelve
inches in depth and twenty-eight in circumference.

"Is that what you call a bath?" asked Dayrell, in
disgust. "Take it away. But stay; you may as
well tell the people of the house that I don't dine
here to-day;" and he descended the staircase with the

comfortable Café Anglais in his mind's eye, and wishing every thing but long life to the present dynasty of the Hotel des Juifs.

To the gain of the Bordelais (there was a great vintage that year), and the detriment of fair complexions, the heat during that summer was more than usually oppressive. In Paris, the glare of the Boulevards made the eyes ache; the asphalte pavement melted, and waved under foot; the leaves in the Champs Elysées changed colour before their time; and even the maize in the country became sickly from the continued drought. Paris—*i. e.*, monied Paris— every one who could scrape a few francs together —had retired *aux eaux*. Shopkeeping, mendicant Paris, with a few visitors, had it to themselves. Jean Racine, of the cropped head and obese figure, who is serenely smoking in front of his shop; Baptiste, *ainé*, who is wrangling over dominoes, and gathering inspiration from *eau sucré* (O, printer, beware lest thou change a vowel of the French adjective); and Adolphe, who spends five hours at his café for one in shaving chins, would have all departed, had the god of trade been kind. Passing these philosophers of the Italian Boulevards, our hero strolled into the Café Anglais.

The proprietor of these whilom comfortable quarters is also taking advantage of the dead season. Painters ply their brushes on the outside of the edifice ; the oily perfume sneaks through the folding doors.   But half the tables in the dining-rooms are covered with the snow-white linen; pyramidically-shaped *serviettes*, and cool-looking water bottles, attract no guests. The waiter, who has not leave of absence, sleeps, with his head on a table, and dreams of Mabille, or perhaps a square-shouldered sabotted paysanne, far away in a snug valley of the Côtes d'Or.   But he awakes at the oft-heard summons of *Garçon*. He hurries with his *carte*.   His "*bien, Monsieur,*" follows each selection of a dish; and he quite respects Dayrell for doing something different to his countrymen, *i. e.*, ordering three French dishes in the place of the conventional *bifstek aux pommes;* while Jeanette at the buffet, astonished at the unwonted order, lays aside her crotchet, and produces a bottle of Chambertin.

"Monsieur is a stranger in Paris," begins the waiter, with all the volubility of his clan, on receiving some encouragement to converse.   "He will find it very *triste*—everybody is absent—the operas are closed—and the cafés-chantants are *vilains ;*—but the Cirque Impériale—Monsieur has never been? ah! never seen Mademoiselle Caracole ride twelve horses, jump through twelve hoops, and fall again light as a *soufflé* on their backs.   Oh, but Mademoiselle is wonderful!"   And he threw up his hands, twisted his mouth into strange shapes, and indulged in gestures indicative of intense admiration of that talented lady. Luckily for him, we might imagine, that Marie of the Côtes d'Or is out of hearing.

So Dayrell finished his Burgundy, lit his cigarette, and went to see this equestrian phenomenon. There was no difficulty about a seat, most of the benches were tenantless. He selected one near the arena, and looking round, watched the arrivals with the critical gaze of an English occupant of a stall.

Three officers, in lancer uniform and extravagantly bandolined as to their moustaches, four bright-eyed wives of well-to-do bourgeois, one gens-d'arme on his own account, and another on that of the government, with as much business on hand as a Belgrave Square policeman in September, arrived. Next, a female figure delicately descended the steps; it hovered for a moment, uncertain where to place itself (here the gens-d'arme on duty winked to his comrade), and finally dropped into a seat near Dayrell. Like a partridge, when it has fled from a sportsman and alighted close to an enemy armed also with a gun, it started and cowered in its timidity as it recognised him. But shortly recovering itself, it carefully adjusted its crinoline, and, by its movements, invited him to a conference. It was Miss Sandes' maid, or bodyguard, and of course she recognised Dayrell. Often, at Dieppe, had she dropped in to tea with her fellow-servant at Mrs. Trelawney's, and discussed, with true spinsterian fervour, the wedding that was to be; the more so as she herself, although of unprepossessing appearance, was embarked on a like speculation, and did not despair of bringing to book one "James," confidential valet to a baronet, and expected by her this evening at the Cirque.

"I hope Miss Sandes is well," said Dayrell, luckily recollecting the lady's-maid's face, and unhesitatingly jumping into the breach.

"Very well, Sir; that is to say, pretty well," answered the abigail, not knowing how far she might unburthen herself to a friend of the family.

"And Mr. Splice; have you seen him lately?" he asked, with well-feigned unconcern.

She looked at him searchingly for an instant. He did not wince. She banished all reserve, and told her piteous tale, beginning with the failure of the Dieppe scheme "of which master had heard, and was owdacious angry," down to their arrival at Paris. "And you can't imagine, Sir," she added, "how my poor dear missus do take on; it makes me quite unhappy to see her, it does."

"You would do anything for your mistress?" he asked.

"Anything, Sir."

"And you are not afraid of your master?"

"Me, Sir? O no, Sir; I hate him; he is a monster. He never lets my poor dear missus go out. He has nothing but bad words for her and me. I'll give up my place soon, if he goes on so much longer."

"Perhaps I can help you. I shall be at Mr. Sandes' to-morrow, or the next day; call on me the same evening at the Hotel des Juifs, and I shall have something to tell you." Here he dropped a piece of gold into her hand, in nowise reluctant to receive it. "Remember, not a word to anybody, unless you wish to hurt your mistress and yourself."

By this time the three mountebanks, rejoicing in the names of Achille, Hercule, and Samson, respectively, had mounted on each other's backs, and, in the form of a perambulating pillar, had disappeared through the curtain. Our abigail, too, waxed uncomfortable lest "James" should find her conversing with a stranger, so she turned uneasily in her seat, and glanced at the door, as a sign to Dayrell that the conference should be at an end. He dropped into his former seat just as the popular idol, Mademoiselle Caracole, glided into the sanded arena, and treated her enthusiastic admirers to a curtsey and a smile.

But Mademoiselle, though in her gauze and wings supposed to represent an angel, is, after all, but

mortal. Naturally good-looking, she must borrow
something for stage effect. There is the rouge upon
her cheek and the puff-powder upon her brow, of
which the departing daylight is an unfavourable ex-
ponent. And although with lightsome foot she
dances to a wild Hungarian melody on the back of her
piebald, though she jumps through the twelve hoops
with astonishing accuracy, the heat tells upon her
borrowed colours, and gives her a sad, jaded air as she
sinks exhausted into her saddle. But the Faubourgs
are pleased. Hands are clapped, and an encore demanded, the latter followed by a shower of bouquets
—a signal to the poor old piebald to stop and nibble
at the nearest, till, detected by the "master of the
whip," he receives a notice to be more careful for
future.

"Good night," said Dayrell, softly, as he passed
the lady's-maid, now deep in conversation with
James of "the loving 'art," as that confidential valet
described himself. "Mine, Mary Ann, is a loving
'art," he whispered, and skilfully wormed himself
into her affections. It was not till her assets at the
savings' bank were found to be small that the heart
forgot its affectionate character and clung to another
—behaving shamefully to our abigail—a record en-
dorsed by many Marys and Susans in an English
servants' hall assembled.

On leaving the Cirque, Dayrell returned to his
hotel. In deep thought he paced up and down his
room, occasionally stopping at the open window, but
oftener opposite four queer daubs upon the walls.
Their subject matter seemed to fascinate him. Picture I., scene 1 : Genevièvre, happy child, distributes
spare half-pence amongst the poor ; castle in the distance; peasants in the foreground, clad in green,
yellow, and red night-shirts, holding out their hands
and begging. Picture II., scene 2, is the same
maiden bivouacking in the forest, tended by stags
and other wild animals. Subaudito, stern father has
told miserable G. to marry a bearded marquis she
does not like—hence her escape from the paternal
mansion. Picture III., scene 3, is G. discovered by
her true love, when hunting, after his return from
India with boxes of sovereigns. Picture IV., scene
4 : Happy marriage of G., and intense delight of the
parties in red, yellow, and green night-shirts; papa
relents, and points to the castle in the distance, evidently meaning to give it as a dower to the injured
Genevièvre.

"Good omen for Splice," said Dayrell, chuckling
over the moral of the painter. "Spite of papa, he
shall marry his Genevièvre. As to his bringing the
boxes of sovereigns, like that baron in the picture, I
doubt it much. Uncles are kind sometimes, but

would sooner promise a reversion than part with
R.M.D.—ready money down.   To-morrow, however,
I shall know all."   And he went to bed with many
plans and schemes revolving in his brain.

"Senior partner at Vichy—junior at Eaux Bonnes
—head clerk out," answered the boy, left in charge
of Messieurs Viguerie's well known firm, in the Rue
St. Honoré, to our hero's enquiry.

"Is there a letter for me? Dayrell, Anglais. You
understand."   But the youth would not, or did not
understand; and Dayrell left the house, fully impressed with the worthless character of French gentlemen of commerce, to spend an hour of idleness till
the clerk might return.   "Call them men of business," muttered he, "and not to be found at *this*
time of day.   Why, in England——."   Well, Mr.
Dayrell, and what would you find in your model
father-land?   Not Mr. Lappin and Mr. Toole in
their respective emporiums at the end of August.   I
rather expect that the former is leaving his card on
Monsieur Mocquard at the Tuileries, and the latter at
Winslow, is looking over his stud, and settling what
horses he shall keep, and what he shall dispose of
before the hunting season begins. So do the "Johns"
of French extraction leave their desks and counting-
houses, and flit where mineral waters bubble, and

where the provincial " Place" collects a crowd of
jabbering, coffee-drinking, holiday-makers.

" Here they are at last," said Dayrell, an hour later,
as he tore open a packet the head clerk gave him.
" Here is a letter in an elderly gentleman's hand for
Mr. Sandes. I understand. Splice and his uncle
mean business. Here is my letter. Now for particulars, and a convenient bench."

" Cool hand, Splice—remarkably cool," he muttered, on coming to the " Yours for ever, sincerely,"
of the letter. " So, I am to be his ambassador.
Why not come himself? He tells me his uncle received the news very kindly—all the more reason for
him to throw himself at the feet of the obdurate
parent to confess and be forgiven. And I am to
telegraph the result. By Jove, he will be on tenter
hooks until that arrives. Well, I'll do as he wishes
—beard the lion in his den. It may be great fun
after all." And Dayrell, letter in hand, went to
Mr. Sandes' house in the Rue Vivienne.

He was shown into a room. Splice's beloved had
but just left it. Her workbox was open on the table.
" I wonder," thought he to himself, " if there is a
lock of hair inside. Splice's ' hay,' as it was igno-
miniously called at school, would look funny with a
piece of blue ribbon round it. I should like to see."

But the search was frustrated by Mr. Sandes, who entered the room, looking quite the reverse of the affable, agreeable English gentleman.

" May I know the object of this visit," asked the elder, repelling any advances, and neither offering his visitor a chair, or taking one himself.

" A letter, Mr. Sandes, that I was to deliver into your hands, and ask you to read. I would not intrude, only I was to be sure that you received it."

Sandes looked at the writing suspiciously. " Has it anything to do with Mr. Splice ?" he asked.

" You had better read it," replied Dayrell, taking a position near the mantelpiece, his attention being equally divided between the contemplation of his hat and Mr. Sandes perusing this missive from Splice's uncle.

" You know the contents of this," said the elder, carefully folding the epistle.

" By Jove, I don't; the seal was not broken, was it ?"

" No trifling with me, Sir," answered Sandes. " I ask you, if you know the object—contents, if you like—of this letter ? Further, I wish to know, if you and Mr. Splice intend to continue this persecution of my daughter and myself? For, I'll put a stop to it, mark my word, if I do not. I'll have no more of your Dieppe scheme and plot—yes, Sir, your plot. You need not trouble yourself to deny it."

"Mr. Sandes, listen to me for an instant; I will speak." And he commenced an oration, the remembrance of which caused him many a laugh in after days. "I don't wish to deny anything. I will confess as much as you like—confess that Splice is foolish—yourself in the wrong" ("Thank you for nothing," from Mr. S.), "and myself foolish; oh! horribly foolish. This was, as you justly observe, *my* plot; it was my intention to make two people happy; it was my idea to bring the couple back to a certain parent, and ask his forgiveness. Blame my exuberance of spirits and inventive brain; but do not give Splice credit for taking the initiative in a plot; his talents, Sir, I assure you, are of a different order. He is the good fellow of social life, the man to be appreciated in the domestic circle. As to his morals, they must be good. Since he was introduced to your daughter, I know he smokes less every day by two cigars. Then, he is no bad match—good looking, has some money (Oh, fie, Dayrell), has also an uncle, a *bonâ fide* uncle, with slate quarries, a saving disposition, and the ripe old age of 74. Let me make it up between you both. Let"—here he waved his hand in the air,—"the telegraph carry the olive branch——"

But further confusion of metaphor was avoided by the hasty interposition of Mr. Sandes.

"Confound your impudence; if you have nothing

further to say, you may leave this room! You come here to talk about 'making it up' and 'olive branches;' I'll olive branch you,—I'll—I'll horse-whip you, Sir!"

"Have a care, elderly gentleman; don't, please, lose your temper," said Dayrell, laughing in spite of himself, but at the same time moving towards the door. "Don't put yourself into fighting position; youth must win if it comes to blows.—Good morning, Mr. Sandes—poor Mr. Sandes. To our next meeting, which I have a melancholy foreboding will be a second Philippi."

"Show him out—I mean, turn him out," said the frantic old gentleman, as Dayrell emerged on the landing.

"Don't trouble yourself," returned the other; adding in a louder key, for the benefit of a young lady whose crinoline had just disappeared round the corner,—"Send to the Hotel des Juifs if you want me; this evening, if you like:" but any answer Mr. Sandes may have given was lost upon Dayrell, who had descended the staircase and gained the street.

"A nice kettle of fish," said Dayrell to himself, as he puffed his after-dinner cigar in the ante-room of the hotel. "I've done my best, however, telegraphed for Splice and his special license. This is his last chance; the wedding may come off in spite of that

rusty old governor. He is a good plucked one, nevertheless. Wanted to horsewhip me, eh! and I am
not a baby. I wish he had tried. I wonder what
Emily will think of this. Like it immensely, I'll
be bound. Women like an *émeute* got up for the
ultimate benefit of one of their sex."

" A lady wishes to speak to you, Monsieur Anglais,"
said a grinning waiter. " Shall I show her in?"

"Yes, directly," answered Dayrell, throwing his
cigar into the grate. "The plot thickens," thought
he to himself.

The waiter placed a chair for the new arrival,
withdrew for a moment, and returned with Miss
Sandes' servant, mysteriously disguised in a thick
veil and cloak. He officiously offered his services as
lady's-maid, but, on being rebuked by Dayrell, reluctantly glided out of the room.

" Now that impudent man is gone, let me hear
what you have to say. You are not ill?" he added,
as the abigail lifted her veil, and disclosed a pale and
sallow face. " Let me order some *lemonade gazeuse*,
or some coffee; or would you like anything else? I
suppose we can get what we want in the hotel?"

" Nothing, thank you, Sir," she answered; " I
cannot stay long. I only came to tell you about my
poor mistress, who is in such a way, and so unhappy
about you, and your visit to her papa. He has been

K

so unkind to her, and was so rude to her at dinner,
that she came crying to her room, and told me to
come here and ask you to leave Paris. And you are
to tell Mr. Splice not to think of her any more, and
that she would rather he did not come to see her;
and oh! Mr. Dayrell, she cried, poor thing, as
though her heart would break."

" She won't do so any more, when she hears Mr.
Splice is here," he said. " Listen to me; you must
cheer your mistress. Tell her that better times are
coming; and, remember, the *when* depends upon
you."

" Upon me !"

" Yes, you."

" Tell me how."

" You are fond of your mistress, are you not?
You would do anything for her?"

" Yes, Sir."

" You can't bear your master, and you said the
other night you would be glad to return to England.
Somebody else is going back there. Ah! well, you
need not blush. Now will you go to England with
your mistress?"

" Alone?"

" No, with Mr. and Mrs. Splice. It all depends
on you, whether he marries her before the end of
the week. You must see your mistress this evening;

you must cautiously break my plan to her; persuade her to run away with him, and tell me to-morrow the result of your conference. Leave the rest to me; this time there is no chance of failure." And Dayrell straightway unfolded his plans, which, after a long lesson, the lady's-maid learnt by heart, and agreed to do her best. "You had better return home now; and remember, you will not be forgotten," said Dayrell, significantly touching his pocket.

So the servant departed on her errand, thoughtfully, as became the guardian of a great secret, but with a mind more at ease than when introduced into that room.

"Awful night this, Stretcher; just the one for a runaway match. Jingle was not more befriended by the weather in his evening excursion with the spinster aunt, eh! There's a gust of wind! How the old casement rattles," said Dayrell, as he peered into the outer darkness, rendered more visible by the flickering lamps, while the person addressed, a clergyman and old Oxford friend, looked first at his watch, and then at his thin boots, with a melancholy presentiment of a wet walk home. "Does it not seem like a dream?" continued Dayrell. "Only four days back I telegraphed to Splice. In the interval he has, he tells me, drained poor Cox to the uttermost farthing, bought his license, come to Paris, and is at

this moment awaiting 'the veiled female form' of
Miss Clara in the Rue Vivienne. Give me some
credit, my jolly parson; haven't I arranged it well?
Sandes, I was told, went every evening to some club.
Mademoiselle and her maid are to take advantage of
his absence to-night, slip into a cab that Splice has
ready, and drive here. I have a travelling carriage
engaged. In it they are to drive to the first station on
the Northern Railroad; the six o'clock train will
pick them up,—at which time may Sandes, the
governor, still repose unconscious."

"What will you do?" asked Stretcher.

"That is the question. Methinks, retire with a
brisk and airy step. I cannot visit that irascible old
gentleman again; still I have a presentiment that we
two must meet once more."

"Are you quite sure," asked the divine, "that this
marriage is legal? Ought they not to be married at
the Hotel de Ville, and sign the papers in the presence of the Mayor?"

"Not if they have a special license; I have asked
about that."

"I have my doubts," said Stretcher; "but that is
not our affair. But what's that?" he exclaimed, as
the rumbling of wheels in the court-yard was heard,
and Dayrell disappeared down the staircase two steps
at a time to reconnoitre.

"Only the travelling carriage come too soon. I have spoken to and tipped the jack-booted postillion, a politic measure such a night as this. I hope the runaways will soon be here. She cannot have declined at the last moment."

"Here, Stretcher," he continued, "bear a hand. Let us make this room look more like a bridal chamber. You used to have good taste; your rooms at Oxford were admirably furnished. They only wanted a Rosa Bonheur or two, in the place of those Farebrothers and Ceritos, to have made them the gem of our 'quad.' Let's first make the place a little less gloomy. Where shall I put the candles?—the paper won't light up. Move that sofa, and put the easy chair on this side, convenient for the bride to drop into should she wish to faint. There, that's better. Now for our visitors."

An anxious quarter of an hour elapsed, during which Stretcher looked alternately at his watch and his companion, who paced the room uneasily, in fear lest his plot had miscarried. Presently there was a stir on the staircase; the door opened, and Splice rushed in. "They will be here directly," he said, shaking both their hands at the same moment. "It is all right." An announcement followed by the entrance of two females, so lavishly veiled, as to make it difficult to distinguish mistress from maid.

To prevent Miss Sandes feeling the awkwardness of a sudden introduction to strangers, Dayrell, in his capacity of master of the ceremonies, marshalled bride and bridegroom into their places, and handed the book to Stretcher as a hint for him to commence the service.

Bravely did little Clara perform her part; her conduct on this occasion deserves a passing word. Barely twenty years of age—just escaped from her father's roof—in a foreign city—with none of her sex about her, with the exception of her maid—she stood at the table, and unhesitatingly responded, "I will." No emotion was visible in that pale face. No sign of timidity in that compressed lip; her mind once made up she took the final plunge, without, so to speak, a shiver on the bank. No use now for the father to forbid the banns; the irrevocable words, "let no man put asunder," have gone forth. And Splice, you are a lucky man; with that little heroine by your side you may go bravely through the world. Little did you think, the evening you met a shy timid girl at the Leamington ball, of the pluck and courage that lay concealed in the bosom of the embryo Mrs. Splice.

The service ended, there was but little time for congratulation.

"Cut it short, old boy," said Dayrell, as Splice profusely poured forth his thanks. "One glass of champagne all round, and you must go. By Jove, if that isn't the governor!" he exclaimed, as a well-known voice was heard on the stairs. "Lock the door, Stretcher—take your wife, Splice, through these folding doors, cross the *table d'hôte* room—mind the chairs in the dark—you'll find a staircase—and get away as quick as you can. I haven't a slipper, or I would, even now, throw it after you both. I'll entertain the gentleman till you are out of Paris; leave him to me. Good-bye."

"Open this, or I'll break it down," exclaimed the angry voice outside, and at the same time certain knuckles descended on the panels with alarming violence.

"Hallo!" exclaimed Dayrell. "Who's there?"

"It's me, Sir. I will come in. By heavens—" and other thumps descending on the unfortunate woodwork, drowned the rest of his speech.

"You are a nice sort of person," said Dayrell, opening the door, "to come and interrupt a gentleman's repose at this time of night."

"Where's my daughter?" gasped the other. "I have traced her here; the porter saw her come in. No prevarication, Sir; answer that question. I will find her."

"Will you," said Dayrell, as his quick ear caught

K 4

the sound of departing wheels. "Pray search the cupboards, look under the sofa. You might find her under the table," he added, seeing his visitor glance at that light piece of furniture.

"You may talk," said Sandes; "but only let me find him-- your friend—that villain, Splice."

"You are a nice specimen of the Christian parent," began Dayrell, rightly supposing that the happy pair were by this time out of the house. "Do you know, Sir, what you are saying? Do you know that Mr. Splice is your son-in-law, and would you take his life? Yes, they are married, and far enough away by this time. Run down to Bordeaux, you might catch them; but let me tell you one thing, you are too late to prevent the marriage;" and he snapped his fingers at Sandes.

"Be quiet," said Stretcher to Dayrell, and, turning to Sandes, attempted to soothe him. "Stop a minute," he began, "and I will tell you everything. Mr. Dayrell has told you the truth; they are married, and out of your reach. It is no use being in a passion; what is done, cannot be altered."

"Who are you?" furiously interposed Sandes. "Are you in this plot too? I'll make short work of this. I'll call in the police."

"Who will turn you out of this hotel, and, perhaps, lock you up as a disorderly character," an-

swered Dayrell. " No wonder you are in a rage,
you who wanted your daughter to remain unmarried
and keep the money yourself. Splice will have it,
and he is a good fellow—much too good to be your
son-in-law."

" I 'll prosecute you both," exclaimed Sandes. "If
there be any justice in England, I will have you up
for—for—a libel;" and, seeing Dayrell laugh at such
a notion, added, " You may laugh, Sir, now, but you
won't when we meet again."

" At Philippi?" asked Dayrell; but Sandes did not
hear him. He only closed the door with a noise that
electrified the domestics who clustered on the landing, and went down-stairs breathing vengeance.

" You have put him on the wrong scent," remarked
Stretcher. " I hope he will start for Bordeaux by
the early train, and not for Calais. If he went to
the latter place, he might catch the fugitives and
create a scene."

"I cannot help it if he does," replied the other;
"I think I have done enough for friendship's sake.
So now for packing, and my journey to Ems."

CHAPTER VII.

"WHAT will Emily say when I tell her all?" was
uppermost in Dayrell's mind, when, leaving Paris on
the following day, he reviewed the incidents of the
past eventful week. But ere the train had reached
the second station on the line, his thoughts had wandered to a point which up to this time he had forgotten.

Mon ami lecteur will remember that the offer had
been accepted at the Dieppe ball, and ratified next
morning at the interview witnessed, and rashly com-
mented upon, by the *commis-voyageur*. But nothing
further had transpired. I mean Mrs. Trelawney
had not invited him to a "morning sitting," or
hemmed the conventional pocket-handkerchief, while
he broached the subject of £. *s. d.* I doubt, even, if
the inaugural kiss had been given, previous to which,
Lovelace tells me,—and he ought to know, seeing that
his experience extends over unnumbered props.,—
it would be idle to ventilate the topic of finance.
Not that the having given or taken the " pledge of

love " will influence a parent when monetary matters
are discussed. For the, as yet, unmarried Lovelace
goes on to complain that, " often as he has arrived at
that happy Thule of his wishes—a kiss—it had never,
never done him any good—never made a parent over-
look the emptiness of his exchequer. His inamorata,
spite of the kiss, was again in the market to be sold
to the highest bidder." Dayrell, then, had paused
on making the tender prop.—had postponed the
financial dénouement till his arrival at Ems.

Now, as he sat in the express train, occurred to
him, in full force, this difficulty. How was he to
break his impecuniosity to his intended mother-in-
law ? " If," thought he, " Emily's parent had been
of the male sex, my task would have been comparatively easy. Men, I am sure, are not so ambitious as
the ladies ; they place less value on the pearl of their
domestic circle. ' Let them settle themselves in life,'
papa says; and adds, perhaps, *proh pudor*, ' better
take him for a husband than none at all.' To papa,
certainly, I should have to confide my financial secrets.
But I would choose my opportunity. I would begin
my tale when the third glass of ruby port warmed
the paternal heart, when his walnut cracked comfortably, and his fire burned cheerily. Then would
I talk glibly about reversions, and hopefully about
' life interests'—mere temporary stumbling-blocks, I

would call them. I would sketch a pretty story, throwing in here and there a bit of colouring—such as family interest, and the like—and by the time I broached the dangerous topic of 'expectations,' which might—and it is a *might* with a vengeance; what would Quilter and Ball say to them in a balance-sheet?—ten to one the paternal face would brighten, the paternal fist (if he was a pleasant old gentleman) would find out my fifth rib, and the paternal voice would congratulate me with, 'Take her, Dayrell, my boy; I hope it will be all right. Let's shake hands, and join the ladies.' When the right time arrived for the admission of a Tales to the conference, a dark cloud or two might darken the horizon. But then the game is my own. Pater-familias would see what the lawyer meant, but would think the affair had gone too far: it would be better to smooth over the difficulty than break off the match. The other sex do not offer us the same opportunities. Mammas do not generally drink port wine—certainly not more than a glass or two at a time. Lovelace used to sigh and wish they would have a fête on the evening of the proposal. But in real, sober earnest, the mothers have an awkward habit of putting too high a value on their daughters. Mary Ann, aged seventeen, although her hair may have more than a slight tinge of red, must marry a

baronet at least; and dear Clementina, who ever
since she was a baby has been told every day not to
stoop so, turns up her nose at anything under 4,000*l.*
a-year—excellent ideas, but seldom carried out. Far
oftener do Mary Ann and Clementina descend from
their high pedestals, in their sixth and seventh seasons respectively, and, without breaking bone or
heart, take a quiet parson, or some one who (in equi-
vocal language) is said to be not-such-a-bad match.
Then a mother's knowledge of business is limited. If
I tell her I have a thousand a-year in the Three per
Cents. she can understand; if I mention reversions
and residuary estates, I talk a language not understood by the British matron. This is in my
favour, you would say. Pardon me, it is the contrary. For woman is by nature curious. What she
comprehends not herself, she asks others to investi-
gate, and to explain in very dreary prose. This, in
fine, is her ignoble method of probing the financial
wound. Premised that the suitor has unburthened
himself of his secrets, and been dismissed from the
maternal presence with gracious smiles—mamma now
pondereth for a while, then sitteth down to her desk,
produceth her cream laid note paper, and draws the
prospectus of a kind of 'Limited Liability Company'
in this fashion. Herself, she appoints chair-woman
of the new Co. Members of her family—say, an elder

daughter or two are made *directors*—maiden aunts and
female relatives at a distance constitute the 'working staff.' I, Dayrell, am the mine. Given, as they
say in Euclid, me, the mine, it is required to find my
value. Working staff receive instructions to prosecute enquiries as to the quantity of ore the mine can
produce now, and how much *in futuro*. Chair-woman
reposeth till answers arrive. One sunny morning she
calleth a special meeting, and lays the correspondence
before the board.

"Answer No. 1, is from an old friend of the
family, acknowledging the receipt of company's commission, with congratulations relative to taking possession of the mine.

"Answer No. 2, is from an energetic maiden aunt.
It says, 'We have not yet come to the vein; but we
think it will turn out profitable. We intend to sink
the shaft lower, and report in our next.'

"Answer No. 3, is from a married aunt, who lives
at a watering place. It says, 'We have discovered
some valuable quartz, (this is my more venerable
than venerated uncle. Query; are they going to
'crush' him?) which, some day, should supply a fair
amount of gold'—or, No. 3 is unfavourable, and
says, 'This mine has been worked before, and aban-
doned. You had better put up with a small loss and
leave it.'

"Dropping all metaphor, I shall be made over to the tender mercies of divers old ladies, who will glean the history of my past life, and detail it with much unction to my intended mother-in-law. Slangley, when on the point of winning a 30,000*l*. prize in the matrimonial lottery, was treated in the same way. His *fiancée's* aunt gathered some particulars respecting his scapegrace 'doings,' and the match was, in consequence, broken off. 'Sir,' said the stern Mrs. Chamfront, when Slangley demanded explanations, 'I only did my duty to my relations. I would not allow an impostor to enter our family.' To which Slangley replied, 'It was a pity, madam, for such a good woman to forget her duty to her neighbour.' There Slangley was wrong. He should have avoided the interview. It is no use complaining when the game is over; no use dashing the cards upon the table when the rubber is lost.

"How am I to get over the difficulty? Which of my relatives will assist me in the matter of an ante-nuptial settlement—put a twenty thousand pound cheque under my breakfast-plate—or even give me the reversion of it? and, echo answers, who? My aunt Fan, owner of the oft-persecuted tabby, also of the room redolent of tobacco (she says) since I slept there, won't do anything for me. Uncle Thomas cannot, and my cousin will not. Yes; I have solved

the difficulty. How stupid not to think of it before.
I will write to my mother when I reach Ems, and
tell her all. She is the proper person to undertake
such a business. She must enter the breach: when
woman meets woman—no, that quotation is inappropriate—when women are made ambassadors in a love
affair, they vindicate their character for diplomatic
talent. It is their mission——"

"*Place pour un Monsieur,*" said the guard, interrupting Dayrell's conclusions about woman's special
mission, and opening the door for a gentlemanly
Frenchman, who, with a bow, and profuse apologies
for disturbing him, took a seat on the opposite side
of the carriage. Unlike that eminent sportsman, the
Baron de N., who went to Angoulême on a shooting
tour with only a gun and a few shirt collars in a hat-
box, or our Breton Chevalier, who started on his
travels with no further impedimenta than his pipe,
the new comer had luggage and coats in abundance.

"*Pardon, Monsieur,*" said the Frenchman, "will
you allow me to put that bag under the seat. *Merci,*
I am obliged," he added, apologetically, "to travel
with many packages, because I may not return to
Paris for some time. I may go to your country.
Will monsieur take a cigar?" proffering his case.

"Who can he be?" thought Dayrell. "A government victim, perhaps, recommended to travel for his

own and his country's good. Still, if that is the case, he is a happy exile." Stranger becomes more cordial, and praises England and the English. " I only hope he mayn't be a sharper," thought our suspicious islander, "going to ask me to play at lansquenet or écarté. Does he look the sort of man to have four kings inside his hat or concealed in his sleeve ?" and Dayrell looked very hard at his neighbour, who, nowise disconcerted, continued the conversation.

" I am delighted to hear you are going to Ems. We must travel together. I know the road. We can go by Cologne and Coblentz. But you would, perhaps, like to hear what takes me so far. Ah, Monsieur, it is an affair of the *heart*. You shall know all some day ;" and he threw himself back in the carriage with an air of sorrowful resignation.

His words struck a chord in Dayrell's breast, causing him to warm towards the stranger. He was too polite, however, to enquire further, but changed the conversation.

" How pleasantly," he said, " we travel in this express train. I remember, when a boy, going from Paris to Brussels in the diligence ; such a thirty-six hours torture I never underwent before. I was in the *interieur* with four ladies. One of the latter was a strong-minded governess ; another, a little girl under her charge. The former was wakeful during

L

the night, like Sir Walter Scott's hermit, but instead
of minding her beads, she told stories—told them,
too, in an undertone far more aggravating to a drowsy
person than the loudest conversation. I awoke out
of my first sleep as we entered Cambrai. It was
not the town, but the governess who disturbed me.
She was improving the occasion by telling the young
lady some long story about Fenelon and Charles V.
Where she had heard it I don't know; I am sure I
never met with it in any old history. I dozed, and
was just becoming oblivious of the regal and Fenelon
tale, when the cold air of the Peronne marshes
struck me. Again I awoke, and heard the same
voice. This time it was prattling about 'La Pucelle,'
and the death of the British guardsmen during the
siege in 1814. Little girl became excited, must tread
on my toes in order to get to the window to see the
fortifications by moonlight. 'They are not nearly
so big in our church-yard at home,' she remarked,
mistaking the earthworks for the guardsmen's graves.
'Now go to sleep dear,' said the preceptress, as the
diligence rumbled out of Peronne. Voices were
hushed for a time; but sleep! no, I could not,—the
shaking and jolting were positively awful. At Valenciennes, benumbed and cold, we had to get out of
the *interieur*, and go into a fireless vault to be inspected by gensdarmes. Everybody was very jaded,

except that governess of the iron constitution; she was as fresh as paint, and came up smiling, till the gensdarme, turning to her, read a name in the pass-port, and insisted that she was the *femme-de-chambre* described in that document. She fired at this, her colour went and came, but the gensdarme shrugged his shoulders, continued his writing, and when she commenced a speech, told a subordinate to show her into the diligence. Another quarter of an hour's travelling, I was just going to sleep, when she began another homily. This time the subject was rather personal. 'French politeness! Is it not a mis-nomer?' Here we are at Valenciennes—as gloomy looking, as on that eventful morning fifteen years ago."

"*C'est bien triste,*" replied the Frenchman, as he shrugged his shoulders, and talked contemptuously of its *epiciers,* that abomination to Frenchmen of any rank or position in society. "Nevertheless, I once passed a pleasant three weeks in a chateau about ten kilometres from here, belonging to a friend of mine. A curious incident happened, which nearly brought him into trouble. They smuggle, as perhaps you know, a great deal along this frontier. To carry light contraband articles dogs are used. A man takes five or six with him into Belgium; the articles are tied to their necks, the animals are turned loose at night, and run home as fast as they can. My friend had half-a-dozen dogs, and one especial favourite, called Castor. Castor had made many journeys, the custom-house officials knew him well; but although always on the watch, could never catch, or rather shoot, him in the act. 'I expect Castor to-night,' said my friend, as we sat smoking after dinner. 'We shall hear him scratch presently at the door. There is the plate of bones on the sideboard; how the old dog will enjoy his well-earned reward.' He had hardly spoken when we heard the report of a gun. My friend left his seat, and opening the door, let in poor Castor, who, dangerously wounded, could scarcely crawl into the hall. The parcel that had cost the dog his life had hardly been concealed, when the douanier arrived to make a search. My friend was so annoyed at his loss, that he entered a *procés*, and claimed large damages from the douanier. The case came before the justice of the peace, who said to my friend, 'You seem to put a high value on your dog; what use is he to you?' 'He is a good dog, and a great favourite.' 'But for what purpose do you keep him?' 'As a guard for my house.' 'And you describe him as such in your tax-paper?' 'Yes.' 'Then, according to your evidence, you kept this animal to secure your premises against robbers. A douanier met him one night in your grounds. The dog took no notice of one who, if not a robber, was certainly an intruder. What use could such a dog be? he was no guard to the house. I cannot award damages to the plaintiff, or even the costs of this action.'"

Thus beguiling the time, they sped through the dreary fog-enveloped lowlands of Belgium—past the flag bearers, who stood at attention in the cross-roads, and looked so woe-begone, poor fellows, and so wistfully at the carriages as they rushed by. Their ideas of what those trains carry must be like those of the man who drove the Morlais malle-poste for fifteen years. "It is no use, Monsieur," he said, drearily, "to ask me where such and such a place is, or such a house was, I know no more of the country than yourself. Long as I have driven this cart, it has always been by night—*Cré Dieu*. By *daylight* I should hardly know the inns where I stop to change and refresh my horses. No man living sees less of the country and the sun than myself!"

The ugly flat plains, however, made no impression on the Frenchman. His soul rose superior to the influences of scenery. It was a *mauvais goût*, he thought, to go to Chamouni and Switzerland, and hide oneself amongst barbarians, when it was so much more easy and pleasant to visit Dieppe and Paris, and promenade amongst the *belles femmes*.

Great emphasis, mind, he laid on the last two words. Although forty-five, he was still the lady-killer, the irresistible; and, as an echo to the sentiment, he sang the refrain so popular amongst the blouses of the west, recording the successes of the owners of a few sous amongst the fair denizens of the Faubourgs, in the last line of which the patriotic usurps the sentimental element :—

> "Je suis Français—mon pays, avant tout."

" How ugly they are ! " he continued, as the train stopped in the station of Liege, and the girls brought their baskets of peaches to the windows of the carriages. " Here is one not so bad," he said, alluding to a square-built Flemish damsel, owner of a pair of twinkling wicked eyes. " Not so bad," he reiterated, chuckling her under the chin. Wicked eyes looked slily at the Frenchman, and read his character at a glance. Turning to another peach-seller, she said loud enough to be overheard, " *Comme il est beau, ce monsieur la.*" Silver coin is dropped into the peach basket. Wicked eyes retires well satisfied with its reward. Frenchman shrugs his shoulders, and looks at Dayrell, as much as to say, " We *are* irresistible; it is always so."

Elated with this victory, the Frenchman's spirits rose. First with stories, then with snatches from the new opera of Orphée, he beguiled the tedious journey, till, fairly tired, he sunk to sleep in his corner of the carriage. It was late in the evening when they arrived in the " scented city " of Cologne. They went to the same hotel. Mine host gave them but a sorry dinner. A bottle of Moselle, however, made some amends for the scantiness of the repast.

" Monsieur will come to the café," asked the Frenchman, " and have ' a grog?' "—a curious expression, and one of the few Saxon words engrafted into their language. The name even of the Thunderer is changed. In the word " teems" no one would recognise the name of his favourite paper. But " grog !" " grog" is French. Future dictionaries must mention it, more especially, if what a distinguished English traveller says be true, that under its genial influence only does the *entente cordiale* blossom.

There was but a " summer" attendance at the café. The gay world, young Germany, in fact, were in the suburbs footing it to Strauss' last walse ; only a few of the old stagers remained to smoke their pipes, and work out intricate chess-problems. Even the billiard-room was deserted, and the three balls bivouacked together in the top pocket. Josephine, fair dispenser of coffees and grogs, in the absence of victims to her killing glances, was busy knitting; and the waiter, having attended to the few wants of his guests, slunk

back into his corner, and gloated over a dirty
dog's-eared copy of the German "Dame aux Came-
lias."

The Frenchman, in his character of *host*, behaved
well. He ordered the "grogs," and when they had
disappeared, he ordered a second relay. But the
genial lemon, or sugar, or spirit, had lost its power.
In fact, the Gaul was miserable. No longer chanting
the refrains from Orphée, or boasting of the successes of his youth, he moodily smoked his cigar,
and replied in monosyllables only to Dayrell's queries.
The latter thought that the absence of "movement"
had demoralized his companion, and attemped to
draw him into conversation by telling him the names
and histories of certain titled dames that he would
meet at Ems.

The Frenchman listened as though he heard not,
till suddenly interrupting his companion, "You have
not guessed the reason of my low spirits," he said.
"It is here, Monsieur," he added, holding up a letter.
"This has been re-directed to me, Poste Restante,
Cologne. It is the same that I wrote ten days since,
to the most beautiful—the most *ravissante* of your
countrywomen. Here it is, I say, returned to me.
But by whom?—ah! that is what annoys me—by
her mother! *Cré Dieu!* that woman has always
thwarted my plans; and inside the envelope asks me

never to write to her daughter again. *Ma foi!* am I to submit to this, when I know by a thousand signs she loves me. I could tell you, but I won't, how that girl encouraged me. I will see her, when I reach Ems; and I will marry her. They shall not laugh at me again at Dieppe——"

"At Dieppe! You were at Dieppe?" exclaimed Dayrell, as an idea struck him.

"Yes, Monsieur, for many months."

"And your name is—is Bellegarde."

"The same," replied the Frenchman with a bow.

"Good heavens, is it possible!" thought Dayrell. "How, in the name of fortune, have I managed to stumble on this old driveller; hear his intentions from his own lips; and be engaged to travel—perhaps, in the same carriage—with him to Ems, where he must be a source of annoyance to Emily and myself. The conceited fool, to boast of the thousand signs; but, at the same time, so like a Frenchman, to put an affectionate construction on mere commonplace civilities. Bother the man! What am I do? Tell him the true state of the case? That I would, if I had settled the financial question with Emily's mother. Would that I could leave him, or drop him into the river, or remove him gently—ah, well, the case is hardly desperate as yet. Let me try and convince him that his errand will be fruitless."

"Do you know," he said to Bellegarde, "that Miss Trelawney is going to be married?"

"So I have heard, and to a young Englishman; but my friend at Dieppe tells me quite a different story."

"Hoaxed he is, as I'm a sinner," soliloquised Dayrell, "this is really too ludicrous." "Let me tell you, Monsieur Bellegarde, that your visit to Ems will be profitless; that Miss Trelawney is engaged; and that by going there you will only annoy her."

"It is very kind of monsieur to tell me this," answered Bellegarde. "Monsieur will, perhaps, read this letter," he added, handing one out of a packet he held in his hand.

"I can't read this," said Dayrell, petulantly; "it begins with *mon cher*, but the rest I cannot make out. Your French MSS. are abominable."

"Listen then to me," said the Frenchman, and he read out one of the most unblushing epistles ever penned. Young Terranova, the writer, knew the Count's foibles, and had artfully mixed the cup of flattery and romance. "The Trelawneys had left Dieppe," it said, "so soon—much sooner than they intended. Ah! why did the belle Anglaise leave? Monsieur Bellegarde could understand. The poor girl was low-spirited, and had refused to dance with any one; and why, oh Bellegarde? Bellegarde, why were you absent from Dieppe? But go to Ems," the writer continued, "where success awaits you; where the heiress is ready to throw herself into your arms; and where you have the good wishes of your friend Terranova." "What do you think of that?" asked Bellegarde, triumphantly.

"That you are deceived and taken in by your friend."

"Deceived! he had better not attempt that. No, Monsieur, it is not, I tell you, it is not so. I know that this is all true; and that before a month is over, there will be many to wring their hands and be jealous of the grand success of Bellegarde."

"Good night," said Dayrell, utterly disgusted, and leaving the café. "It is no use trying to pierce the rhinoceros hide of that man's conceit. Most people would have thought a 'returned' letter a broad hint to retire from the contest. But a Frenchman! faugh! a hint is lost on him. Let him revel in his absurd fancies. He will change his note before the end of next week."

Although a foggy morning, the real pilgrims of the Rhine mustered strong on board the Coblentz steamer. From every street that led to the quay they came in ones, and twos, and threes; some struggling under the weight of heavy coats and bags, some half washed, and some half shaved, all unbreakfasted,

and consequently very cross. Comes Briefless, bravely
walking, stick in hand and knapsack at back; Briefless will blister his feet, but he'll save his money and
gain information. Comes our Bagster, of the Foreign
Office, on his way to Homburg, with that five-and-
twenty pounds he borrowed from the mess waiter of
his club for (must it be owned) a losing flutter at rouge-
et-noir. Absent is the genuine chieftain of the hills,
but present the mock ditto of Cheapside, in a tartan
kilt unowned by Highland clan. Treading the
ground delicately, with the air of languid swelldom,
comes Noses—our old friend Jedadiah Noses. Take
off thy thistle-adorned bonnet, Noses; that deception won't do, for we know you. Why try to pass
for a Highlander, thou scion of an unloved race?
And poet Jones, quiet Jones, dreamily passes to the
bows of the vessel; he, whose brain is already at
work, and who at one P.M. shall produce the four
lines that will astonish, nay, move unto tears, susceptible maternal Jones. Forgive us, Jones, if we mis-
quote them, but to the best of our recollection they
ran as follows:—

> "I love, I adore thee, thou peerless Rhine,
>   From Mayence to Drachenfels
> I'll sit on this deck, and I'll quaff thy wine
>   Regardless of dinner bells."

"I hope he will be late—there is the second bell

—three minutes more and they will cast off," said Dayrell, to himself, as he stood near the paddle-box of the steamer, and anxiously scanned the last groups of pilgrims hurrying on board. "Alas, here he comes, with his light coats on his arm, and the inevitable bag slung round his shoulders. Ah! he has a squabble with the porter; he may yet be left behind. No, he has settled with that sleepless man-of-all-work, the night-hawk of the hotel, and steps jauntly on board."

"*Bon jour, Monsieur Dayrell*, I say that man is a robber; he has charged me forty sous for carrying my little packages to the steamer. It is too bad," exclaimed Bellegarde, in his anger at manners, customs, and all things Prussian.

But Dayrell, in his disappointment, returned no answer. He looked at Bellegarde with much the same disgust as Pickwick did at the ungainly quadruped he was compelled to lead along the dusty road. "To be tied to that man," he thought, "is something awful. I must be rid of him. If he would simplify matters, by dropping into one of those boats that come from the shore to meet the steamer, be carried to a village at the top of the mountains, or be locked up because his passport was not strictly *en reglé*. Alas! no such luck for me. I must listen to his nonsense; I must travel with

him as far as Coblentz; I must be a Sinbad, a victim
to that man of Gaul. Jones is at liberty to ponder
with his elbows upon his knees, and his head between
his hands, while gazing on the picturesque Drachen-
fels, and be unmolested. Noses enjoys himself, sipping Johannisberg, price two thalers a bottle. His
sorrow is only temporary, when the waiter, who
guesses that Noses is no tip, brings him the drum-
sticks of a fowl, and explains, 'For you, for you, ver
goot, ver goot.' Even paterfamilias, though his coat-
tails are pulled every five minutes by his daughters
wanting to know the name of some tower, can find
a refuge amongst the smokers at the bows of the
vessel. But for me there is no escape. The steamer
is small. Bellegarde follows me everywhere, even
unto the confined and dinner-scented cabin."

Never had Dayrell passed a longer day—never
been so thoroughly bored. Cost what it might, he
had determined to be rid of the Frenchman. He
had no notion of travelling to Ems in such company.

Now Hermitage is a strong and soporiferous liquid;
more especially the "vintage" which mine host at
Coblentz brought from an inner crypt for Bellegarde
and Dayrell's dinner. Vachette's ten sou cigars are
black, new, and strong. It was of these the Devon-
shire parson spoke with much unction; "They are
thick, they are strong, they get into my head, and I

like them." Bellegarde would have one out of
Dayrell's case; he would smoke it on the bridge of
boats, and with flushed face, and somewhat unsteady
step, he repaired to that sub-Jove smoking-place. The
sun went down. The fortress of Ehrenbreitstein was
the last to profit by its rays. The twilight succeeded.
One by one the lamps were lit along the quay. The
tea-gardens began to fill, and the merry voices of the
peasantry were wafted across the broad surface of
the Rhine. Then, from behind Stolzenfels, arose
the moon, putting the lamps to shame, silvering the
old gabled ends of the houses, and throwing long
shadows over the swift running stream. True to its
character for strength, the Hermitage had done its
work, and mounted to the Frenchman's brain.
What the wine had begun, the cool night air and
the strong cigars finished. Fain would he have
visited the dancers, but his step became unsteady.
He was tired, he said; he would return to his hotel.
So a candle and key were put into his hand, and
door, No. 76, closed on the partially intoxicated
Bellegarde.

Dayrell lingered some time by the river, smoked
another cigar; then conversed with the landlord,
and finally ascended to No. 75. He listened at the
Frenchman's door. Nasal sounds, deep, but irregular,
proceeded from within. The moon shone through

the casement on Bellegarde's patent leather pearl-buttoned shoes, and the be-labelled key. The temptation was too great. Dayrell turned the latter noiselessly in the keyhole, opened the window—a water-butt stood underneath; into it fell, with little splash, key No. 76. Then in each enamelled shoe he put a stone. Both descended swiftly to the same bourne, much to the comfort of the frogs, who, doubtless, bivouacked that night in a pair of real Parisian bottines. Everything still, quiet, save the irregular snore of the Frenchman, Dayrell retired to rest, delicately, and in much comfort.

It is morning, and seven A.M. There is a disturbance in the upper regions of the hotel. Chambermaids, with dusters and brooms, flock about Carl the blubbering, Carl the wounded boots—partly curious, partly with a view to consolation. Carl relates his short but moving tale: how, instructed by the recording slate, he had been to call No. 6—76 it was originally, but the 7 had been erased by Dayrell. No. 6, a commercial, but choleric Englishman, had retaliated by hurling a perfect avalanche of weapons at the intruder. Carl, wounded on the side of his head, and with china candlestick broken in his hand, is in full retreat, about to go downstairs and report the case to landlord. All this time Frenchman—our Bellegarde—in No. 76 snores unconscious.

Malle-poste is on the point of starting for Ems. Dayrell, clean-shaved and breakfasted, knocks at No. 76. Frenchman, unconscious of locked door and key abstracted, warbles cheerfully as he tumbles out of bed. Dayrell takes his place in the coupé, and is at least half a league from Coblentz, amidst the vines and on the right of the placid Lahn, ere Frenchman finds that he is a prisoner, and vociferates through keyhole, in tones at first angry, afterwards plaintive.

CHAPTER VIII.

Ems, August 14th, 185—.

My Dear Mother,

Thus far have I travelled. When you have finished this letter you will say, " I might have gone farther and fared worse." Annie must have already told. you that I met a Miss Trelawney at Dieppe. Without any circumlocution, I have to inform you that I am engaged to her "conditionally." She is beautiful—a pleasant thing *at* the breakfast-table; has money, which will put something *on* the breakfast-table; and a good temper, so she will not blow me up *over* the breakfast-table. You will ask what I mean by " conditionally?" You see, my dear mother, I had an interview with Mrs. Trelawney to discuss the topic of finance. I admitted that my *æs in præsenti* was of ridiculously small amount, but hinted that my *æs in futuro* might be large. She did not express any decided opinion on the merits of my rambling statement—I wish she had. She only desired me to write to you. She will not correspond with her relatives till your answer arrives. She cannot with Tales, *till* I give her his address, which may I not do till the last moment, lest that man of best intentions—but unable, like Micawber's boy, to carry them out in any way whatsoever—should send a dry and depreciating answer to Mrs. Trelawney, and, perhaps, in his enthusiasm for legal phraseology, should add the heading, "*In re* Dayrell." Mother, neglect not this opportunity of settling your son. Smooth away all difficulties in your letter to my intended mother-in-law. A subsidy paid annually to the young couple would settle the question. Even this you may be inclined to do, when you remember that most men have but one chance in their lives of bettering their condition. This, my dear mother, is mine. Hoping and expecting,

I am,

Your affectionate Son,

E. W. DAYRELL.

P.S.—Beware of two female relatives of the Trelawneys—known in fashionable circles as the Kilkenny cats—and who live near you. They must be unfriendly, Emily tells me, as they have settled that their niece is not to marry any one under the rank of viscount.

This letter, still preserved among the family ar-

chives, Dayrell sent to his mother the day subsequent
to his arrival at Ems. One remark we who are behind the scenes have to make—namely, the writer
was a bad judge of woman-kind, and had failed to
notice the disappointment his confession had inflicted
on Mrs. Trelawney. The vague reports that had
reached her ear at Dieppe had led her to suppose
that our hero was a most desirable party. True, he
was gentlemanly, of good family, might be well off
some day, and would probably receive assistance from
his mother now. But her daughter Emily, she could
not help thinking, might have done better, or, before
the affair had gone so far, might have learnt more
about his actual position. Congratulating herself,
however, on her residence in a quiet place, far from
her friends and relatives, who would otherwise have
seen, heard, and, perhaps, maliciously circulated news
about her daughter's courtship, she determined to
await Mrs. Dayrell's answer before she gave her consent. For the nonce, she dropped all idea of forming
a Limited Liability Company. She would wait, and,
in the meantime, warn Emily to be cautious, and not
go too far with Dayrell. But in this she was out
of her reckoning. Her daughter would not take the
hint. Miss Emily had always had her own way, and
she intended to have it now. With her, it was
" *Dayrell aut nullus*," although she did not say as

much to her mother in either Latin or English. The victory over Sandes and the discomfiture of Belle-garde were bearing fruit. It is not the first time that enterprise and pluck are favourably weighed in the balance against rank and the English Fetah—money.

A few words about Ems, the quiet and secluded; Ems nestling amidst wooded hills, the sun-scorched, the paradise of flies. Ah me! but the latter are hardly less troublesome than our old enemy the mosquito. This little village is not aristocratic, like Carlsbad; nor a nest of gamblers, like Homburg; nor mobbed, like Baden; nor a refuge for invalids, like Kissingen; nor ugly, like Wiesbaden. It is essentially a lady's watering-place, and generally quiet, its gaiety or dullness depending mainly on the characters and purses of its visitors. There is a kursaal, and there is a band; there is a gambling table, and there are balls, and immemorial custom has established for its visitors a programme, like Median law, unchangeable. At one P.M. the Germans and fashionables of all nations (our record has nothing to do with the legitimate water-drinker, whose muffled figure at exercise we have seen from our window a dozen times since day-break) make their first appearance at an early dinner. At three P.M. on the promenade, but in the shade, the German settles to chess and coffee, not disregarding the ubiquitous meerschaum. English lions, male and female, repose after heavy dinner near the fountains, for the nonce insensible to donkey-boy jargon of "ver goot, ver goot,"—the epithet the native applies to his sad-eyed animal. Four P.M. sees donkey-boys trium-phant, and pursuing their weight-carriers with shouts unearthly. Stumble not, pony of Jerusalem; lag not, there is a rod in pickle for the offender; whack, whack, we hear it afar off descending on the culprit's back. At six there is the grand promenade of rank and fashion on the Place. At eight the world attends a ball or a concert, or crowds about the roulette table. At eleven the curtain falls on the legitimate drama, the majority of the strangers leave their boxes and go home. A *farce* (as we shall presently see) may follow, but it will be played to a select audience.

In this routine the quasi-engaged couple took little part. They opined that the general public regarded love-making in the light of a bore, as of course that general public does, who, when the excitement of watching the flirting campaign is past, when the offer has been accepted, and the what-he-has-got has been ventilated, look out for the next victim on the high road to the hymeneal altar. "*Le roi est mort*"—the public says, "*Vive le roi.*" Our

king, however, was not dead, but, in spite of Mrs.
Trelawney, who insisted on making one of the party,
fled with Emily every morning to the other side of
the Lahn. We say fled, for Bellegarde had already
arrived at Ems. From early morn to dewy eve the
Frenchman might be—nay, was—seen by Dayrell
"persecuting" the Place, and performing sentry's
duty opposite the hotel, in animated conversation
with a compatriot. To avoid him required the use
of stratagems, only inferior in cleverness to those of
a debtor when watched by the myrmidons of the
inexorable lord of Cursitor Street. For some days
the pair had succeeded in preserving their incognito,
longer than that was impossible in so small a town
as Ems.

It was while wandering from the Place by a cir-
cuitous route that Bellegarde pounced upon them.
With self-satisfied smile, with cordiality bursting
out of every pore, with sweep of hat from head to
knee, he saluted Miss Trelawney and her mother.
He was so delighted to meet them. It was so long
since they were at Dieppe. Ems had appeared so
triste without them ; but now,—and he slapped his
padded breast, and looked theatrically happy. Then
selecting Mrs. Trelawney as the recipient of his
compliments, he told her of the news from Dieppe,
and how happy he was to hear of Mademoiselle's

engagement. "My little passion," he said,—"ah well, that is forgotten; we young men must sometimes suffer!" Then adroitly changing the subject, he prattled of Paris, and his imprisonment at Coblentz, ascribing his misfortune at the latter place to supernatural agency, as neither shoes nor key could be found. As to a practical joke, such an idea never entered his head. Bah! who would dare to play one off on him?

Emily thought him a strange creature, and laughed as of yore at his absurdities; but Dayrell felt grateful at being released from an awkward situation. So when Bellegarde asked Miss Trelawney to go to the ball that night, and confidentially informed her how utterly "desolate" he felt every evening amongst the ugly stupid people at Ems, she consented; and the Frenchman, having gained his purpose, retired, waving farewells with his hat, and smiling blandly.

One word to explain this change in Bellegarde's sentiments. The thirst after knowledge is as universal in Ems circles as elsewhere. The only exceptions are the Germans, whose apathy is proverbial. If Clara Smith returns from her ride a little after dusk, or Bagster entertains Josephine with the pearls of his rhetoric for an hour in the avenue of elms, all the world will know it next morning. Alas! the character of the former will not be worth an hour's purchase, and the latter, unless he elects to go to the hymeneal altar, will be said, by every dowager in the place, to have "behaved shamefully." But 'tis an oft-told tale, that of scandal being the marrow of existence to small societies. Even the waiter of the hotel (with an eye to his own emolument) adds to the general stock of information, and learns what the soi-disant colonels and captains are doing at the gambling tables. When from his friend the croupier he hears that Carambole is winning, and that Diddle's losses are considerable, and when the latter, not being of a taciturn disposition, or over wise, makes the chambermaids his confidants, the news, like sweet incense, ascends to the remotest boudoir, and the maid, as she brushes her mistress's golden tresses, tells the results of roulette, adding such trifles as an 0 to a 100, and so on, according as her fervid imagi- nation may happen to dictate.

Hence Bellegarde, ere he had been twelve hours in Ems, had heard the petty scandal of the place, and also of Emily's engagement. Such persons as knew not his character, would expect to hear of wringing of hands, of tearing of hair, or at least that the *spretæ injuria formæ* would have found vent in forcible expletives. On the contrary, he received the news like a philosopher, and argued with himself after the manner of the French school, that believes in nothing, and puts faith in neither man nor woman, no matter how serious the subject, how strong the protestation. "She is not a whit better," he thought, "than her countrywomen. She can walk and flirt with me. She can be amused with my stories, she takes my arm for the Lancers in preference to one offered her by a stupid English boy, whose forte is walking stiffly, and most shyly talking *pendente* quadrille. Yes, she even walks alone with me on the promenade, and straightway the *cercle* congratulates me on my success. Yet, after all, I am only her friend, her good-natured friend. Enter some fine morning one of her rich but unamiable compatriots. Once in a way he opens his mouth, asks her to marry him, and is accepted. Of no account in the balance are good looks, sprightliness, and devotion,—all is forgotten when weighed against the one thing needful—money! *It is a nation, that England, very philanthropic, they say;* I would rather call it by a name signifying love of money. *Cré Dieu!* but I should be angry if there were not as good fish in the sea as ever came out of it. This Mons. Dayrell is rich, is he? On that account he is preferred to me? *Eh, bien!* let us see if fortune will always stand his friend."

When Bellegarde talked of "a ball to-night," he spoke figuratively, and simply alluded to one of those assemblies held twice a-week at the Kursaal. Here, at that date, met *convivæ* of every grade, not decked in suit of sable or cloud of gauze, but in the matutinal high dress, the frock and morning coat of diverse pattern. In spite, however, of such indifferent toilettes, the saloon looked well. Gloriously refulgent were the lamps, full was the band, and peremptory the master of the ceremonies in keeping the circle clear for the waltzers, and preventing enthusiastic Smith and Company from gyrating out of turn round the spacious room. It is said that, since the family of Smith, Brown, and other time-honoured English houses have dropped like a cloud of locusts on the scene, the waltzes are mobbed, the quadrilles impassable, and that the polkas form a confused mass of dancing matter, like unto what we, in our younger days, used to witness on a Derby night at Vauxhall.

It is regulated by Kursaal decree that ladies must dance with the first partner who claims their hand. Very pleasant rule for Ellen, plainest of the plain, and Jane, pronounced heavy in hand by her not over-indulgent countrymen, a pair who thirst for waltzes, and are only anxious to be seen dancing, no matter with whom, without an eye to, or a thought of marriage. To them is the simpering Fritz, with hair parted down the middle, and on good terms with himself, most welcome. He whisks them round the

magic circle, and talks over his beer afterwards, as
we have ourselves heard, of the gushing truthfulness
of those English maidens. But by Emily, disturber
of hearts, and Edith, usually engaged ten deep, is
the rule ignored. What? Lower their banner to
some German shopkeeper, be whisked round the
ball-room by the possessor of some 30 roods of vine-
land. No, thank you. A belle of Bourbon-Vendeé
may have been sent to a kind of dancing Coventry,
because she refused to waltz with the indignant
οἱ πολλοί. Our Ediths and Emilys fear not such a
catastrophe. They know that one glance—one wish
expressed—will bring a score of Englishmen to their
aid.

Thus was Emily beleaguered by the foreigner on
the first night of her appearance. Carl, of length
of limb interminable, the straddler in the noble
waltz, hovered on her flank. Rochow, the pensive
painter, took her measure from a distance, and waited
for the first bar of music, etiquette forbidding him to
make engagements beforehand. There was Von Dandelsen, known in select circles as the falling tower
of Pisa, so much out of the perpendicular did his
body incline during the waltz, conversing with two
companions, and looking askance at the fair English-
woman, prepared at a moment's notice to swoop like
an eagle upon its prey. There was yet another on the

watch,—Bellegarde, who, at the first wave of the conductor's baton, stepped forward, and offered his arm. Emily hesitated, and would have declined the honour, but recollecting the customs of the country, she took a place with him in the quadrille then forming.

The Frenchman plunged into conversation with truly national ardour. " Mademoiselle," he said, " will make conquests to-night. She will not be allowed to sit down during the evening. If she only knew how the *jeunes gens* panted to dance with the prettiest *Anglaise;* not that they perform well, or are practically safe. Oh ! no ; Monsieur Rochow is the wildest waltzer in Germany, and the day of Monsieur Dandelsen's fall cannot be long postponed. Command my services, Mademoiselle Trelawney ; use my name, if you wish to say that you are engaged."

" Thank you," said Emily, smiling; " I shall not require any one's assistance; I have a headache, and intend to leave early—after the next waltz, probably."

" It is too early to go to bed," suggested Bellegarde to Dayrell, when they had escorted the ladies to the hotel, and bade them good night. " I have a supper in my rooms at twelve—you must come— till then we can smoke a cigar, or go back to the ball-room, whichever you wish.

They re-entered the Kursaal. Most of the dancers had adjourned to the saloon and the table, where the

croupiers were reaping an unprecedented harvest
from roulette.   An Englishman had just arrived.
He threw a thousand franc note on the table, and
calmly awaited the result.   The wheel, surmounted
by a cross, typical of pain created, revolves: the ball
jumps hither and thither, strikes the sides, and crack,
crack, flies off at right angles, till gradually exhaust-
ing itself, it looks into one or two pigeon holes
longing to receive it, and finally reposes in No. 28.
One lynx-eyed, green-shaded, yellow-visaged croupier
monotonously calls the colour and the number. Two
of his brethren rake up thalers, or pay the small fry
their winnings with nonchalance inimitable.   Senior
croupier's hand dives into a strong box, fishes out a
yellow note, which he hands to the successful Englishman.   Again the wheel revolves to the old chorus of
the lynx-eyed; at first the ball runs fiercely, then
demurely, till it languidly drops into the red.   From
small fry arises a mingled murmur of astonishment
and inquiry.   " Won three thousand francs ! who is
he ? "   Answer, " Sare Robare—Sare Pale," so they
pronounce the name of a sporting baronet.   Small
fry forgets to stake, and concentrates its attention
on the three yellow notes again staked on the red.
" He has won again.   Oh, Sare Robare—Oh, Sare
Pale," bursts from the excited multitude; "he is
the luckiest man in the world."   Previous murmurs

break into a mingled roar of astonishment and congratulation, when for the sixth time the colour is red, and the Englishman wins. There is a shuffling of feet, a confusion of voices, an uneasy wriggle on his stool on the part of the lynx-eyed. When the excitement has partially subsided thirty heads bend forward to see what the owner of the yellow notes will do now. But where are they, and where is he? Oh! Sare Robare—Sare Pale—has left with his winnings during the confusion. Did anybody hear of such luck? "*Faites le jeu,*" calls the croupier; the ball jumps as lively as ever, but the mob have not recovered the shock; there is scarcely a thaler this throw upon the table.

"Not so bad, my friend; we have won some Napoleons," said Bellegarde to Dayrell, both of whom had followed the fortunes of " Sare Robare." "The play is nearly finished for to-night; let us go to my rooms for supper."

Dayrell had broken his vow, but the coin jingled pleasantly in his pocket. Just this once can do no harm, he thought. At twelve o'clock at night any excuse will set a man's conscience at rest.

To Bellegarde's supper had been invited such a motley party as only Baden Homburg or Ems can produce. The majority of the guests were English, some of them titled, and all owners of good names; but for different reasons tolerated rather than wel-

comed in continental society. Their presence in
foreign parts is easily accounted for. Some, England
loves not well; others it loves, but somehow the
subjects of its yearning slip from the maternal embrace, preferring the air of liberty to that of Her
Majesty's Bench. Of course if we were to hint at
their compulsory absence, the notion would be received by them with derision and rejected with scorn.
Their manner of living is extravagant, and their
carelessness about money proverbial; but we who
are behind the scenes, remark that a display of
Napoleons is only consequent on luck at the tables,
or the arrival of allowances from home, at the beginning of each month.

Included in the party that evening were those distinguished characters Sir Henry Fireworks and Mr.
Baillie. The baronet, a wanderer on the Continent
these twenty years, was a chronic sufferer from insolvency and a quick temper. One outburst of the
latter they talk of to this day in Paris. Sir Henry
was staying at Meurice's Hotel. To that world-
renowned hostelry flock every morning such English
as happen to be in Paris, to make plans for the day
or to read the papers. On one occasion Sir Henry
left his bedroom at a late hour. On his breakfast-
table in the coffee-room there was no copy of the
Times. "It is engaged," the waiter said, pointing

to a youth who sat near the fire, devouring its
contents. That boy, unconscious of his crime, had
revelled in the leading articles, calculated what income 30,000*l.* invested in " Canadas" at 114⅝ would
bring, and impartially reviewed the decision of the
worthy magistrate in the matter of Mr. Babbage
and the organ-grinder, when happening to raise his
mild blue eye, it encountered the glaring optics of
Sir Henry. "Would you like to see this?" sim-
pered the youth, offering a portion of the paper.
" What on earth do you mean by keeping it?" cried
the irascible baronet. " Do you know, Sir, I was at
Waterloo before you were born?" Baillie, on the
other hand, was the reverse of Sir Henry, a quiet, but
eccentric old gentleman—a veritable Bedouin. He
had travelled and played in every European capital,
cheerfully risking his money when he had it to lose,
borrowing from others when he had none himself;
and, in the absence of sovereigns and lenders, watching the game for hours in a blue military cloak,
sole relic, people said, of his Waterloo campaign.

Most Frenchmen would have provided sparingly
for their guests in the matter of wine for supper. A
little Chablais with the oysters, a bottle or so of
Jullien dispensed in tumblers, with a thimbleful of
Burgundy or champagne to conclude the banquet,
would have been followed by a throwing aside of

napkins and a lighting of cigarettes. But Bellegarde produced the different vintages in profusion, and, believing it to be the English fashion, proposed the health of his guests in what the papers would call a neat and appropriate speech. The party was gradually becoming noisy—Sir Henry was, in fact, uproarious, when Baillie's clear, ringing voice, the only part of his battered frame uninjured by the destroyer, silenced the others—the tone and manner of the narrator indicating how sincerely he believed what he was telling them.

"You have asked me for that story, and I will tell it you. I was at Vienna in the year 1825. I was a young man then, and stopped there solely for pleasure. One night I had a dream. I dreamt that a figure, which I took for John the Baptist, appeared to me, and, calling me by name, asked me what I should like to know? I answered promptly, 'The year of my death.' The Spirit said, 'Follow me.' I was carried through the air, and presently found myself in a vault in which were three coffins, with names and dates inscribed in letters of fire. On the two lowest I read the names of my nearest relations : on the uppermost I read my own, and the year 1832. I turned to John the Baptist, and said, 'What so soon?' He answered, 'Look again.' I did so, and read 1852 ; and again said, 'What so soon?' He re-

plied your eyes are dim, look once more.' This time
I read 1872, and, turning to the spirit, said, 'I am
content.' The dream passed away. I own I was
alarmed in 1832, and very nervous in 1852; but in
1854, I was convinced that what I had seen would
come true. I went to England that year to attend
the funeral of one of my relations. It took place at
Kensal Green Cemetery. The service over, I went
into the vault and saw my dream partially realized.
There were the names of my two relatives and the
dates of their decease on two coffins, and there was
a place vacant. Gentlemen, I shall fill it in 1872."

" Let Mons. Baillie live till '72," exclaimed Bellegarde, amid the general silence that followed the
story. " You all seem very dull," he continued.
" Who will say yes to a game of baccarat? You
cannot play, Mons. Dayrell. That makes no difference: it is the easiest game to learn. Sir Henry
says he will make a bank with you. Beginners
always win. I envy him his partner."

Now, to the uninitiated, baccarat seems to require
less skill on the part of the player than any other
game of cards, blind-hookey excepted. But the cool,
wary speculator knows better. To him its apparent
simplicity is a mine of wealth. While young Reckless declares that " It is all luck," and, without consideration, throws his Napoleons on the table, the

practised player knows by instinct when to increase
his stakes and when to stop.   The game has been the
ruin of many.   When we asked the other day the
reason why Mons. T—— and the Count de V——,
the cheeriest and pleasantest fellows in Paris, had disappeared, we were told that " they played nothing
but baccarat, and that only for three years."

Fortune has been at times a cruel persecutor, but
never more so than on this occasion.   The ill-starred
bank couldn't, you might almost say, wouldn't win.
If the pair played prudently, and in their deal
amassed something trifling, a *fatal* " banco " would
dissipate it before the cards were passed.   If Sir
Henry growled, and rashly bancoed against Bellegarde, the latter would take the announcement with
much the same defiant air as a Finisterre cliff receives
the rolling wave of the Atlantic, and turning the
right card, invite the chafing baronet to " banco "
the whole amount just this once—only this once.
At the end of the fifth round Sir Henry was furious,
and his last Napoleon was swept away.   " I 'll have
my revenge another night," he said, gnashing his
teeth, as he left the room.   " You had better come
with me, Mr. Dayrell," he added; " you will lose all
night, mark my words, if you stay."

Dayrell not only disregarded the advice, but hoping
to regain a portion of his losses, borrowed from

Bellegarde, and continued his set. Only introduce the credit system at play, and the end is certain; namely, a heavy loss for one of the party, and (probably) a long-deferred settling. Baillie had up to this time played mildly, but certainly with the luck rather against him than otherwise. His *pose plastique* in the military cloak, his solitary hover about the tables for the remainder of the month, was, after a manner, predestined. But now, on hearing Dayrell use the words, " borrow," and " that makes so much," his eyes glistened; he felt his time had arrived. To tell the plain truth, people who knew Baillie well were shy of taking his I. O. U.'s; but strangers could not resist the winning address of the gentlemanly old man. So, when smiling affably, he offered to fill the vacant baronet's place, and bring Dayrell through in triumph by means of a system that had never failed, the latter unwittingly assented, and the old man chuckled audibly. The latter thought to himself, " if our banks wins, well and good; if it loses, it is a case of my giving an I. O. U. to one more stranger in the world; that is all." The system throve well the first quarter of an hour. Bellegarde almost regretted that he had given his guests their revenge, till Baillie, too confidently, covered twenty Napoleons set by the former and lost. From that moment everything went wrong with the firm. No matter

how they played, they lost every set, and at the end
of the *séance* two hundred pounds would not have
covered Dayrell's losses.   Two hundred pounds !
Where was he to get it ?   An awkward sum for him
to lose just now—very awkward, he thought, as leaving Bellegarde's rooms, he went out into the Place.
" What a fool I have been !   Confound that fellow
Baillie ;" when looking up, he burst out laughing.
There was that old gentleman; his appearance not
improved by a hard night and the garish light of
day, his wig awry, his complexion yellow, his teeth
chattering, his legs unsteady, determined not to give
in ; but chirping cheerfully about " better luck to-
morrow.   My new system, Mr. Dayrell, will win it
all back at roulette."

Six hours' sleep,—if that could be called sleep,
when shadowy forms of kings, queens, and aces
danced wildly in the air,—when the ears rung with the
exclamations of the players,—when the winning card
seemed to leap from the pack, but the stakes were
detained by some hidden power, or melted in the
grasp, the dreamer knowing not why or wherefore,—
when the body turned from side to side of the bed
and the head sought in vain a cool place on the
pillow—and when the sun shining bright, scarcely
dimmed by the white curtains, made the sleeper open
his eyes every quarter of an hour to close them again

with a weary, dreary feeling of disgust. Awake, but
with ideas misty and undefined, Dayrell saw his
watch unwound by his bedside, the hair chain re-
clining in the ash of a half-smoked cigar; some
small change, evidently emptied out of his pocket in
haste, and a paper, with hieroglyphics supposed to
represent figures. The last recalled, too vividly, the
scene of last evening.

"How utterly foolish I've been," he said, when
sitting up in his bed and sipping the coffee the waiter
had just brought. "How could I play at all, much
less lose such a sum? Here's Bellegarde's name.
I owe him 180l., and how am I to pay it?" He
thought for a few minutes, when he remembered
Baillie's parting words. "No," he continued, "I
won't write to Tales to-day, or apply to that good
mother of mine, until I have tried my luck once
more. There are still enough Napoleons in that
drawer. I will meet my creditors cheerfully—go to
the table to-night—try Baillie's system; and, hah,
hah, 'win it all back.'"

He might meet his creditors cheerfully, and make
them believe he did not care; but there was one to
whom he did not owe money, but something infinitely
more precious,—one who would examine more closely
the cause of his unnatural gaiety. Meet a pretty
girl, they say, for the first time at a ball, a dinner

party, or a pic-nic, and a man needs some power of
speech to make her a listener.   Let the same girl be
engaged, or let her merely have selected one on
whom to turn her heaviest artillery, and mark the
difference.   From that moment his every word is
weighed, his every look is watched.   He lives, so to
speak, in a glass case; a searching eye peers through
and through nature's bulwark—the outer man.   The
individual has yet to be born, whose *acting* can really
deceive the woman who loves.   Thus Emily perceived
instantly the change in his manner.   She felt there
was something wrong, and hoped by treating him
coldly to discover his secret.   There was something
between her love and him, she could not tell what;
but her altered behaviour did not elicit a clue to the
mystery.

A fête on a minor scale was celebrated that day at
Ems.   For it the country people came "to town,"
and in the absence of other amusements flocked to
the Kursaal and roulette.   The fashionable visitors
were also present.   Here was Bellegarde, and there
Sir Henry, the latter moving uneasily from group to
group like a troubled spirit, not playing himself, but
teazing every body that did.   Baillie, of course, was
there; but he had hoisted his signal of distress, to
wit, the blue cloak of Waterloo memory.   He had
not a thaler left.   But was he unhappy?   Not he.

He lived in hopes that he would yet break the bank with the very newest and the very latest system invented. The old man still wielded the pin of approved pattern, sharpened point, and malachite knob, with which, for six long years, he had registered the winning blacks and reds. He had kept a weekly, monthly, and annual account. No merchant's ledger was so neatly copied; and the result —a system infallible, only requiring a proper capital to work successfully. By the bye, nine of his systems had already gone the way of all flesh, and been discarded. The one he now cherished was built on the ruins of the Mortui; in it had the old prophet verily put his trust.

Baillie's hearty and cheerful welcome a man of a suspicious turn of mind might have misinterpreted. It savoured strongly of the art of borrowing, and Baillie, as all but the wilfully blind and deaf knew, was not above that. But in this case he aimed at higher game, viz., to persuade Dayrell to test his newest and latest system. To this end, it was first necessary to explain away the mistakes of the previous night. "You lost 200*l.* last night, did you?" he said to Dayrell, "and I the same, unfortunately. It was our own fault, we were too rash. It was not the game to banco the sixth time. It was sixty to one against our winning. But we shall do better

to-night. Monsieur Garcia at Homburg, and Madame
Adrienne at Baden, have discovered how to break
the bank three times a-week, and I know it. Yes;
we will do the same. For two million francs, the
proprietor of the Homburg bank sent to Paris to pay
Monsieur Garcia. We will be content with that,
eh? Some of these boys here learnt his system.
They tried it, and won for a time, but becoming im-
patient played rashly and lost everything. It is
thus ——" and Baillie commenced an exposition of
his theory, making frequent references to his printed
cards, and telling off his conclusions on his fingers—
most puzzling to a person not sufficiently sagacious
to discover the one wanting link. " Did you ever
see such luck ?" he said, calling Dayrell's attention
to the table; " the third time, upon my honour!"
A countryman had elbowed his way to the front.
On the single zero he had put a pile of copper coins,
representing the lowest stake allowed by the proprietors. The lynx-eyed raked together the coins,
counted contemptuously, and replaced them on the
round O. Ball revolved with energy more than
ordinary, dallied longer with pigeon-holes unwilling
to receive it, and finally bivouacked in the countryman's number. Pile of silver is thrust towards him.
" Again, the zero, if you please!" he cries, adding
a few words of playful badinage for the special be-

hoof of the lynx-eyed. Ball runs quicker than ever, hops, jumps, skips, and stops suddenly. Croupier has to stretch his hand, and check the inner wheel. It is in—zero. "Once more," calls the excited win-ner. Ball receives an extra push, rattles, threatens to take a fence, and land on the green sward this side the table, seems to spectators as though it never would stop, rolls in and out, in and out—slower, slower, till, for the third time, it glides into zero. Wriggles on his high stool, as his custom is, the lynx-eyed; countryman retires, gesticulating franti-cally, and receiving an ovation from the multitude, some of whom will presently borrow a gulden from him, as they will say, for luck.

From Baillie burst a sigh of regret, because he had reaped no advantage from such a remarkable coin-cidence. His melancholy was, however, quickly dis-pelled. His system was on trial, the interest evoked by that was all absorbing; but, as the theory is un-likely to be serviceable to future visitors of German baths, an elaborate detail is unnecessary. Suffice it to say—first, that Dayrell's capital was forty Napo-leons; secondly, that this was to be divided by eight; and, thirdly, that Baillie would select the numbers on which the quotient fixed should be placed. Once in eight times the right number would turn up, at least so said the prophet. The game proceeded : the

croupier worked his rake indefatigably—Dayrell's
money was being rapidly absorbed into the piles of
tempting coins representing the bank. His faith
wavered, and he looked at Baillie, who, spectral-like,
pointed with his finger to a number. "I won't do
it," said Dayrell petulantly; "these five Napoleons
are my last, and I won't do so." "Only this once,"
supplicated Baillie so piteously; "try it but this
once, it must come." But pleading was in vain:
Dayrell's Napoleons were thrown on the black. The
red won, the number came according to Baillie's
prophecy, and the rake brought to the bank the last
stake. The old man hid his face in his hands, he
groaned, and, if the fountains of his eyes had not
been utterly dried, for the first time these twenty
years he would have burst into tears.

Retribution follows swiftly on the track of the
gambler: sad is the morrow of the man who has left
his last thaler in the croupier's hands. His is the
deadening feeling that Life is a mistake,—when the
bright sky appears of a leaden hue—when the joyous
river and hill side form a dreary landscape—when the
distempered fancy converts a smile into a scowl—and
when champagne and claret, erst so gladdening, only
add to his gloom. At no moment of his life does a
man more earnestly long to "flee from himself." In
such a mood awoke Dayrell the morning succeeding the

affair at the Kursaal. Besides the loss of the money, which he knew not how to make good, he had other reasons for wishing the past undone. Emily had heard a version of the story, founded, like scandal generally, on fact, but exaggerated in detail. No sooner did his eye meet hers than he felt that his secret was known. He knew her horror of gambling, and the forced smile he had assumed on entering the room froze on his lips. " Shall I tell her all, and ask her pardon? or shall I laugh it off as a matter of no consequence?" he thought. He had not time to do either, for Mrs. Trelawney unluckily entered, and beckoned him into the balcony.

" It would not be right for us to conceal," she said, " what we have heard about you. They have told us a shocking story about the Kursaal," and she gave an exaggerated account of Bellegarde's party, and the roulette, and finished by asking point-blank whether it was true.

Although Dayrell was not in the best of tempers, when he came to the Trelawney's rooms, yet he might have confessed to Emily, and there would have been an end of the matter. But, when questioned by the mother in this way, his feathers were ruffled, and he answered, " That he did not see what difference it could make to anybody; that he certainly had lost a little, but it was a very trifling matter."

"But it is no trifling matter," Mrs. Trelawney broke in. "I object to it on principle, for I know what it leads to. Gambling ruined my poor brother, as it must everybody who has to do with it. I tell you, Mr. Dayrell, plainly, that Emily shall never have my consent to marry a man who plays at cards, much less one who haunts the public tables."

"You are quite unreasonable this afternoon," he said. "All the world play whist, and most of the people play roulette, at least, they do so when they come to these German watering places, and they are not all ruined. For the life of me, I cannot see any harm in a quiet game in another man's rooms."

"One leads to the other, Mr. Dayrell. You know that your *séance* may begin with a quiet game, but what does it end with? Ecarté, perhaps—lansquenet, not unlikely. I am quite sure of this. My brother told me as much, and warned me a hundred times against men who defended a quiet game of cards. You will think over what I've said; and mind, I expect you to give me a promise, never to play again."

"A promise!" echoed Dayrell, as he left the hotel, fuming at the bare notion of such a thing. "A promise to pay to Bellegarde is another affair; but to tell my future mother-in-law that I will never touch a card again; bah! nonsense. I cease to be a free

agent at once. I have a spy eternally set over me.
She will have an excuse for attending my afternoon
walks, and haunting the card-room afterwards to see
that her dear Edward does not transgress. Gad! I
might as well be tied to her apron strings at once."
Here Baillie, who was taking that modicum of air,
supposed by him to be sufficient to clear his smoke-
dried lungs, viz., a walk of 400 yards from his lodgings to the Kursaal, once per diem, happened to
meet him, and offering an arm, received Dayrell's
disclosures with the calmness of a man who lived
perpetually in hot water, but, somehow, always
managed to escape serious damage. "With regard
to the first point, you are done, my boy," said
Baillie, "if you give in to a woman. Let her once
get the mastery, and life will be a burden, that
lady's society a bore. This, in your case, is the
thin end of the wedge that they in such a hurry
always love to insert. You are not to do this, she
says, to-day, and you must not do that to-morrow;
you promise not to hunt any more, because it is
dangerous; and you won't shoot again, because you
might catch a bad cold; till, by Jove, Sir, on some
pretext, or other, you are deprived of every amusement, and they have gained their point—reduced
you to the level of an amiable sheep-dog, fit to
fetch and carry, fetch a cab in the middle of hail,

rain, and snow, or carry, like poor Meek the other day, a barrel of oysters from Temple Bar to the top of Regent Street, to the delight of the small boys, and the disgust of the cab-stand; for his wife, mind you, had made him *promise* not to incur the expense of an eighteen-penny ride. Bellegarde's case is different. There you may promise, and your promise will be as good as your bond." This was a long speech for the old campaigner; but he was on his favourite theme. He had thoroughly worked it out, and boasted that his advice had rendered many a hesitating juvenile proof against the persuasive as-saults of women.

The pair dined in company that evening, when the old man revelled in the past, telling stories, and shifting the scene from one European Capitol to another.

"It is nine o'clock," said Dayrell, returning his watch to his pocket. "It is time for me to go up-stairs. Adieu, till to-morrow."

"Good night," said Baillie, hobbling off; "but, remember, don't do it. Listen to an old man's advice—make no promise."

"He is right," said Dayrell to himself, as he left the dining-room. "I'll promise nothing." Fortified with this resolution, he was on the point of proceed-ing to the Trelawney's rooms, which were on the second floor, when he heard a shriek of the most thrilling, piercing character, and coming from the flat they occupied. He hurried upstairs. On gaining the landing, he met a figure so enveloped in flames, that its mortal identity could not be discovered, save by the waving of its two arms, and the hands clutching at burning portions of its dress. He took off his coat, wrapt it about the body, and with his hands tore off fragments of the gown. Others came to his assistance, some bringing druggets, some water, some blankets,—the first things, in fact, they could find; while more than one person went in search of doctors. In five minutes the flames were extinguished, the last vestiges of smouldering embers trampled under foot, and the poor victim carried to the nearest bed-room. The usual remedies were instantly applied, but without alleviating the intense agony of the patient. The doctors arrived, and during their ex-amination and consultation, the others left the room. "Ah, poor thing," they said to the groups assembled in the passage; "it must have been the candle which caught her sleeve, for her neck and shoulders are so dreadfully burnt; besides, we found it alight on her table, when we first went in." The doctors, their consultation over, looked serious, and declined answering questions. They only left instructions with the four ladies, who volunteered to watch, respecting the proper course of treatment to be used.

Dayrell, in the meantime, burnt and half-suffocated by the smoke, had fainted. They put him on a sofa in the adjoining room, and his attendants at first thought that his case was a serious one. For an hour he remained unconscious, when he opened his eyes, turned on his side, and struggled to collect his thoughts.

"Who is it?" he asked of the maid, who stood by him. "Who is it, I say? It is not . . . ." and the name seemed to stick in his throat.

"The doctor said you must be quiet," replied the maid, "and not excite yourself."

"It is her. I am sure that's her, I hear—I know it is," he exclaimed, starting from the sofa. "Here, dress these hands, put my arm in a sling—I will go and see." The maid, seeing that further resistance would be useless, did as he wished.

He entered the room during one of the paroxysms of pain that occasionally convulsed the sufferer. Two ladies were holding her in the bed, another had some medicine in her hand, and a fourth a basin of flour, which she was liberally applying to the burns. The paroxysm over, the sufferer relapsed into a sleepy, half-dreaming state, her heavy breathing being the only sign of life. Dayrell felt shocked, and sick at heart, the instant he saw the ravages of the fire, partially concealed though they were by the layers of wool, and her eyes so fixed and unlifelike— never closed even when she slumbered, but turned upwards, as if in mute prayer for relief. This feeling, however, the necessity for active exertion on his part somewhat mitigated. The pain again shoots through her limbs. He helps to hold her in the bed until, exhausted, she sinks back upon her pillow. Now her thoughts are wandering—she is in dream-land. She fancies herself in her native county in the north of England. She is walking with her governess by the banks of the Croquet; at that lady's request she repeats some lines, at first, glibly, then slower, then dwelling doubtfully on each word, as though memory was failing her, when a sudden twinge of pain recalls the fire. She springs forward in the bed. "Oh, put it out—put it out," she cries, and her struggles are fearful to witness. The ladies call her by name, speak soothingly, and administer medicine. Once more she is quiet, and in the land of dreams. "Will he come, do you think?" she asks, and her eyes glance round the room. "He did not play, I tell you,—I know he did not. What right had that deceitful servant to tell us so? But he will come this evening to see us; no, to see me. He will explain all, and we shall be so happy. Yes, he will

o 2

come. I hear him on the stairs, I said he'd come. Here he is to save me—to save me—from this agony. Oh, my poor head — oh, my poor head."

"You had better leave the room," whispered one of the ladies to Dayrell, "and return when she is calmer;" but he shook his head gloomily, and signified his intention to remain. Never did man pass a more weary night, when time moved so lazily, that minutes seemed prolonged into hours; when feverish anxiety, the throbbing heart, the sickening, suffocating sensation in the throat, combined to unhinge the whole nervous system. It would be difficult to say which was the hardest to bear,—the delirious ravings of the sufferer, or the deep silence, when the attendants, for fear of disturbing her, forbore to whisper. Hark! during one of these quiet intervals, there is a knock at the door. A feeling of relief succeeds. It is the doctor. He approaches the bed noiselessly, and examines the patient. The ladies converse with him in whispers, ask him questions in bated breath, and attempt to gather hope from some chance expression he may use. This visit for the nonce removes a load from each breast. The doctor retires, and the watchers again relapse into a melancholy train of thought. During those intervals how changed, how humbled, felt Dayrell. In that presence, and in that bed-chamber, the artificial crust of his selfishness was broken, his short-sighted views of life were dissolved. Selfish! Yes; worse than that he had been, to break his promise, to be only intent on the turn of a card, or of a number; when one loving heart bled for him, and only thought how she might best exonerate or forgive the act. How insignificant, how trifling did loss of money, reputation, did anything appear to the chance of having forfeited such love as hers. He had run that risk, and he positively loathed himself. He would have given all he had to undo the irrevocable past; but an accusing conscience has firm vantage-ground, and its punishment is more severe, because such a boon is denied to mortal man. A reaction, however, sets in—calmer, purer aspirations succeed. " If she is only spared," he thinks,—" and she will be spared," he mutters confidently,—" this lesson shall never be forgotten. I will make amends not by promises, but by deeds."

The first beams of the morning sun shine upon the blinds. The candles in very shame flicker in the sockets. The night-watch is at an end, and that of day begins. The faces of those who stand about the bed may be pale and haggard; dark rings may encircle their eyes; a tear or two may glisten beneath their eyelids; but the indomitable courage of woman

holds out to the last. What? give up the post of
duty to others. Not they. They will tend the poor
sufferer to the last, knowing not fatigue; they will
satisfy her every want, ignoring any inconvenience
to themselves. Heaven bless them for thus vindicating the moral strength of their sex. Bless them,
we say, who, when man is utterly prostrated by
the blow, step forward, and unhesitatingly fill the
breach. The light falls on this chamber of sorrow.
The curtains are drawn. The sun is just peering
from behind those wooded hills, and throwing deep
shadows as far as the opposite bank. Mist gently
disengages itself from the bosom of the Lahn,
covering the valley with transitory vapour. Nature,
in its own quiet way, is awake; but all Ems sleepeth,
save the devoted band in Hotel ——. Emily's
paroxysms become less frequent, and, as the morning advances, cease altogether. The uninitiated
believe this to be a good sign, but those in the confidence of the doctors recognise the beginning of
the end, the commencement of mortification about
to devour its victim silently, and inch by inch. As
the pain ceases, her consciousness returns. She
begins to talk a little, and she understands all they
tell her. "Move my bed nearer the window," she
asks; "it seems such a lovely day. I would like to
see our pretty valley once more," and she tries her

old cheerful smile, but it will not do; the attempt is feeble and sickly—it dies frozen-like upon the lips.

It is past mid-day, and a great change has taken place. Her colour is of deeper hue, the expression of her face is altered, foreshadowing the end. She is quite calm now : she knows the worst. They have broken it to her by degrees. She is out of pain, and the grim destroyer is stealthily entering the citadel, which may she vacate with all the honours of war. The clergyman has visited her, and left her in a peaceful frame of mind. She has but one more word to say—one more person to address. Her faithful attendants know this by instinct, and leave the room singly. Edward—her Edward—is alone with her, holding her hand in his, and, like a very child, unable to restrain his tears.

" Edward, dearest, you must not," she said slowly and softly; " you must not take it so to heart. I am out of pain now, and, with you, I feel so quiet and happy. Perhaps, dearest, it is better as it is—better for me not to recover; for the doctors say that the pain during my recovery would be greater than all I have hitherto suffered. I might not be able to en-dure so much. Besides, I should be so altered, so disfigured, you would hardly know me. Then, out of pure compassion, you might express the same re-

gard for me; but when you compared me with other
ladies, you might repent of what you had done ; and
that I could not endure.   No, Edward, it is better as
it is—better to part before we had quarelled, and
before we had found out our mutual faults.   If,
dearest, you should marry another—ah ! you say you
never can, and I am selfish enough to hope it too—
if you do, I only trust she may prove a better wife
than I should have made.   Don't make any rash
promise which you may repent hereafter.   Time and
circumstances will soften your grief, and then some
one may come worthy to take my place.   Yes, there
is one promise I should like you to make.   You remember the quiet corner I showed you last Sunday
in the churchyard, where the willow is; I should like
to be buried there, as it cannot be in England, and
you must plant some of my favourite flowers.   You
will do that, dearest, will you not ?   And now I am
beginning to feel so tired.   I should so like, as I go
to sleep, to hear you say a prayer for me ; you know
the one I mean, taken from the twelfth chapter of
the Hebrews."

And while the sands of life were running out, he,
with faltering voice, read as she wished.   Once more
she slept, and when next she awoke she must have
felt that her end was near, for she thanked the ladies

who had attended her for their kindness, and gave
them some of her trinkets as keepsakes. "It will
soon be over," she answered to one who suggested a
hope of her recovery. "I shall never see the sun
rise again. I am out of pain now, and you all know
how thankful I ought to be and am for that."
Poor Emily was right. Mortification had set in:
the Destroyer was already preparing for his last
assault. A torpor presently came over her: then
she sank into a deep sleep, but so peaceful and
noiseless that none of those, who with tearful eyes
surrounded her bed, knew the moment when that
meek spirit passed away unto Him who gave it.

On the day of the funeral more than half the
population of Ems joined the procession. Emily's
grave was in the corner of the churchyard, in the
place she had selected, and as the coffin was lowered
to its resting place, there was scarcely a dry eye in
all that crowd; and, as the earth fell with a hollow
sound on the coffin, and the clergyman uttered the
solemn warning words, "Earth to earth, and ashes to
ashes," the very foreigner seemed to catch their
meaning. They made the same impression as those
of Christopher Wordsworth once did when, in Winchester Chapel, he preached the funeral sermon of a
boy, who, in the heyday of youth and spirits, had

been carried off by fever. I can remember the regulated cadences of that impassioned voice, speaking
amid a silence almost oppressive, and before the
saints, who from their niches seemed to our heated
imagination to look down approvingly—when the
hand of the sacrilegious carver of his name on the
oak panelling was arrested—when the sleeper raised
his head from the reading-desk to stare open-mouthed
at the preacher—when the chorister ceased to turn
the pages of his anthem-book—and when a sigh of
relief broke from all at those words, " Earth to earth,
ashes to ashes, dust to dust." Moistened was many
an eye, we know, and touched was many a careless
heart, for those words haunted—yes, followed—each
boy from the chapel to the school-room, from the
school-room to the bed-room, and caused many an
improvised, but heartfelt, prayer to ascend that night
to the throne of the Creator.

On the right bank of the Rhone, near Avignon, are
the graves of two lovers, who, on their wedding-day,
were drowned in crossing the river. By a lake in
the Pyrenees they show the last resting-place of a
newly-married pair, whose boat upset, and both lives
were sacrificed sooner than that one should survive
the other. Both these are covered with *immortelles*
—gratuitous offerings of the peasantry, who likewise
take care that spring or summer there shall be no

lack of flowers. So about the stone, with the simple inscription E. T., the people of Ems have planted roses and evergreens. They will allow no weeds to grow, but keep up the little slip of garden, as though one of their own family slept beneath.

CHAPTER IX.

" You are always moping, my dear Dayrell; I never met any one half so *triste*. Isn't the play at Baden high enough, or isn't there a girl in all this crowd pretty enough for you? or do you want a change? The season here will soon be over, and then I'm off to my chateau in the Gironde. Will you come there? You will meet those young Parisian stars, Magnan, La Foix, and Latour, also D'Alençon, Colonel, and of Crimean celebrity, last, not least, my little nephew Villars, the best boy in our department. I am tired of this myself; tired of meeting old Baillie every day. He looks so mournfully at me, that is to say, when he does not avoid me altogether. You see,—mind, I tell you this in confidence,—he came one morning to my room, and told me that for six weeks he had tasted nothing but bread and water, that his wife and children in England were in great distress, and had written to him to come home; and that if I would lend him 500 francs, he would be so much obliged, &c. Flesh and blood could not resist such an appeal. I lent him the money, I really hoped that he would go home, and that we should see him no more. I suppose he has been trying one of his latest ' systems,' lost his money, and is again in his normal state of insolvency. But seriously, Dayrell, will you join us in a fortnight? There will be some shooting for you, a wolf hunt, a dance, probably, with native beauty—a novelty that, for you used-up men. Now, what do you say?"

"Accepted with pleasure, Monsieur le Comte. I am going to Pau for the winter, and shall be happy to take your chateau on my road."

More than a year and a half has elapsed since poor Emily's death. Dayrell has been half over Europe since then. He has been to Milan, Venice, Florence, Rome, Naples, and a hundred other places, partly with the view of distracting his thoughts, and partly because he didn't know what to do with himself. He has been staying at Baden for a few weeks, when he met an old friend, the Count d'Artois, and having received this invitation to visit his country-house, the wanderer packed his portmanteau, and left for France.

Now, when a man asks you to his chateau, you naturally expect to see something out of the way in residences. The mansion itself ought to be old, and should have the extinguisher towers of the fifteenth

century. There should be extensive wings, capable
of housing any number of domestics. There ought
to be an entrance-hall, hung with armour, or trophies
of the chase, and a curiously grained staircase leading to tapestried apartments, and the banqueting-
hall—never leave that out, please, in your calculations. Then the gardens should be stocked with
fruit and flower, swans also should breast the stream
in all the pride of feathery whiteness; or, supposing
the chateau to be a modern building, there should
be an old castle, keep, and moat handy, and a chapel
within which we might see the recumbent figure of
an old crusader or two, or of a knight, who fell
fighting manfully under the banner of his beloved
Henri, but who now slumbers under a marble slab
with some expressive epitaph, like " Fortissimo" on
it. But he who expects to see this, will, in the
majority of cases, be grievously disappointed.

The chateau of the Count d'Artois in the department of the Garonne was "a severe imposition."
Viewed at a distance, with its commanding position
on the side of a long low ridge of hills, its imposing
front, tall pointed roofs and towers, extensive wings
and outbuildings, it looked every inch a palace. A
nearer approach, however, revealed its many defi-
ciencies. At the entrance to the domain there was
no lodge and iron gates, but only two lichen-covered

pillars, to which were fastened a couple of wattles, which the stranger had to remove out of his way as best he could. Then the grounds were encumbered with straggling wood, hollow at the bottom, and hardly likely to pay for the clearing. Coarse grass waved on the lawn in the place of the green verdure of old England, and entwined itself so with wild rose bushes and hawthorns, that a divorce *a vinculo* seemed impossible.

Dayrell did not think much of his new quarters, as he drove his tired horse through the grounds and up the avenue (yes, we forgot there was an avenue, the only decent thing about the place), and still less when he entered the court-yard formed by the two wings of the chateau. There was the inevitable fountain in the middle, which, perhaps, threw up jets of water once on a time, but was now choked with weeds, thick enough to cover the image of a marine goddess, whom time or mischief had thrown from her pedestal into the basin. Sickly blades of grass sprouted from between the flagstones, and the very creepers bent towards the ground, in quiet despair of ever scaling the house without the aid of leather and nails. Then the wings of the chateau showed many signs of dilapidation. Few of the windows had curtains inside; most of them had broken panes of glass. " It is a queer establishment," thought Dayrell; " the best

thing I've seen as yet is the view to the south. If
that old waiter, who declared that he had not left
London these twenty years, and sighed in his hot
coffee-room for one 'bit of nature' before he died,
could have seen this, his life might have been prolonged beyond the three score years and ten allotted
to man."

"What are you thinking about, and why don't you
come in?" interrupted the cheery host, as good at
the English language as his own, thanks to a prolonged residence in England. "Three days after
time, and yet you stand in the yard and deprive us
still longer of the pleasure of your company. Le
Colonel D'Alençon, Messieurs Latour, Magnan, La
Foix, and my nephew Villars, let me introduce
Mons. Dayrell. Now come upstairs at once, I will
show you your room. By the bye, there are not too
many that are habitable in this house. Here we
are; large enough is it not? In your Leicestershire
language you will call it a forty-acred enclosure.
Now, no dress or ceremony; just make yourself comfortable, and, as you see we ignore those modern
inventions, bells, call when you are ready, and I will
conduct you to the state apartments of my chateau."

"Very hospitable; but who would have believed
that a particular man like the Count would have
lived in a tumble-down place like this? It is good

enough, however, for a shooting-box. If the others
are content to rough it, I am sure I am. The cook
too will, perhaps, make up for these short-comings,"
thought Dayrell, as he followed the Count to the
state room of the chateau, surnamed the Octagon.
But the *cuisine* was the rock on which the Count
more particularly split : it was worse than indifferent
—it was positively bad. How is such a thing possible in the land of cooks? Not easily explained,
unless it is because *chefs* are too volatile and extravagant for private establishments, and can only be
tolerated in public—still the fact remains. The soup
was thin—hot water with slices of bread in it—the
entrées were steeped in that abominable brown sauce,
and the joint was cold. The wine, too, at dinner was
ordinaire; the Chambertin and champagne being
kept for dessert, and when most people's minds were
set on cigars and cigarettes.

"A glass of champagne, and a welcome to the
chateau," said the host to Dayrell as the cloth was
removed. "Shall we all move to the fire and smoke
our cigars?"

"My uncle is going to tell the ghost story,"
whispered Villars to Dayrell.

"You don't mean to say the chateau is haunted?"

"Is it not?" replied little Villars. "Wait till
midnight and see."

"Everybody who visits the chateau," said the Count, "wonders why it is in such bad repair, and why, as it is our family place, we do not use it for something else than a hunting-box. To tell the truth, I have no affection for it, any more than you will, when you have heard a story I intend to tell you, and a tragical occurrence which happened in this very room seventy years ago.

"At the time of the first Revolution, my father was the largest proprietor, and the most influential, if not the most popular, man in the department of the Garonne. He made this chateau his home. He hunted and shot, was hospitable to his neighbours, and did much more for his tenants and the poor than was the habit of our forefathers. At such a distance from Paris, it was scarcely possible for him to hear all that was going on previous to poor Louis XVI being turned out of house and home. Consequently, the news of the king's imprisonment came upon him like a thunderbolt. He hoped, as others did, that his popularity would save him from the fate that threatened all who had a title, and who, in the neighbourhood of Paris, were undergoing every species of indignity and insult that popular caprice could inflict. For four months after the imprisonment of the king, my father and his young spouse (he had just married his first wife) lived in a state of uncertainty, but still very confident that the storm, like many others, would eventually blow over. The effects, however, of the Revolution began, ere long, to make themselves felt in even the far-distant department of the Garonne. First, the Count found his servants, one by one, dropping away without any reason; then, when he rode into the country, he was met by sullen looks, and even abuse, from some whose hearty *bon-jour* formerly greeted him. Then he received letters from Paris and the provinces describing the enormities committed by the *sans-culottes*, the permanent erection of the guillotine, the burning of chateaux, and all the other horrors that the blood-thirsty Convention let loose upon France.

"At the little town of Villeneuve, no great distance from here, lived my father's lawyer, a shrewd, bold man, who, seeing the turn affairs were taking, mounted the popular colours, and through his agents at Paris was nominated mayor of his *commune*. No sooner had he effected this object, than he proceeded to carry out a plan that doubtless had for some time been hatching in his brain. One day he came over to the Count, and with well-feigned appearance of regret, showed him a paper signed by the men in power, commanding him, Deslandes, to imprison and send to the capital any aristocrat that might be dis-

covered in his *commune;* at the same time, he repre-
sented how impossible it would be for him to avoid
the execution of his orders. My father was of course
thunderstruck at the intelligence, and, more than all,
astonished at the source whence this imminent danger
came; for he had on many occasions proved himself
a good friend to the notary, and even assisted him,
more than once, in the increase of his business.
Every argument was tried to change Deslandes's
resolution, but without success, until suddenly a new
idea seemed to strike the unscrupulous agent of the
national will. 'You perceive,' he said, 'that I must
act up to my instructions; but in doing so, I can
and will serve you, if you consent to follow the only
course by which I can reconcile my duty to the state
with my gratitude to the individual. You and your
wife must leave the chateau in forty-eight hours; you
must make your way to the sea coast, where a vessel
will be ready to receive you, and I will supply you
with a sum of money sufficient for your journey and
present maintenance in England. At the same time
you must make over your estates to me, and I will
transmit you, out of the receipts, an annual stipend.
Thus you will be more fortunate than most of your
other companions in misfortune, who have been only
too glad to escape with their lives.' In vain did this
new victim to the amenities of 'Fraternity' strive to

ward off the impending blow. Deslandes knew his power, and was inexorable. At last my father, alarmed at the representations made to him of total ruin, and perhaps of death to himself and his young wife, agreed to the proposal, and prepared to act upon it forthwith.

"By the influence and plans of Deslandes, everything was satisfactorily arranged. My father and his wife, after narrowly escaping detection in their journey through the country, safely embarked on board a small trading vessel, and were conveyed to England. During their long stay there, they only received one letter and one remittance from the notary, and neither threats nor remonstrances could ever induce that accomplished rascal to perform the most important part of his bargain; so that if my father had not received much generous aid and assistance from some English gentlemen (your health, and your countrymen's, Dayrell), he would have been reduced to the greatest penury and distress. Deslandes, in the meantime, continued to perform his functions as mayor of Villeneuve, and as an active supporter of the Revolution. He harangued the mob on every occasion, till he became, by his denunciations of the rich, and the great power accorded to him from head-quarters, the most dreaded agitator and tyrant in this department. For a long time he

kept aloof from the chateau, contenting himself with
the collection of the rents, until after the downfall
of Robespierre he found himself gradually more
secure in his position, and the country less disturbed;
he then, with his wife and daughter, left the village
of Villeneuve, and desecrated with his presence the
threshold of his injured benefactor. Mademoiselle
Deslandes was now a lovely girl of eighteen, inheriting all the national beauty of her grandmother,
an Irish lady, who had married a Frenchman at Bordeaux. As a child she was of course a great favourite
with her father,—in fact, was the only thing besides
money and power on which that worldly man lavished
his affection. The heart must have been made of
stone that could remain insensible to her beauty, to
judge at least from the portrait I have of her. You
shall all see the picture, and then you can form an idea
of the peculiar style of beauty she possessed. The
chateau, as perhaps you are not aware, has always
had the reputation of being haunted, arising, I think,
more from the noises of the horned owls, than
any supernatural agency; so if any of you should
hear anything strange in the night, you need not
start up and put a pistol ball through my windows
or walls. A few weeks after their domestication in
the house, Deslandes's two servants began to be
alarmed at hearing mysterious footsteps in the cor-

ridor at night ; their terrors were of course laughed at by the notary. At length, however, from a window in the wings, the servants declared they distinctly saw what they described as a spectre in white with a lamp in its hand, returning along the passage that connects these rooms with the suite opposite. Of course they raised an alarm, but as nothing could be made out of it, Deslandes was still incredulous, and simply procured other servants in the place of those who would no longer remain. The new servants, however, were terrified by the same noises; whereupon Deslandes, who was a bold man, determined to unravel the mystery. For this purpose he loaded his double-barrelled gun, laid it on a table before him, and took up his position at yonder fireplace, after the family and servants had gone to rest.

"At the time I am speaking of, there was no wall between this and the octagon room, the separation being made by drapery only, that could be pulled across, or left open, at pleasure. It was open on this fatal occasion, so that a good view of the second room might be obtained by the watcher. Deslandes might have waited there some three hours, and was already laughing in his sleeve at the absurd fancies of his servants, when he distinctly heard the sound of light footsteps in the corridor. He grasped his gun on seeing a figure in white with a light in its

hand enter through the doorway. He called out
first, and receiving no answer, pulled the trigger.
This must have missed its mark; but, quick as
thought, he fired the second barrel, and with a
scream the unfortunate somnambulist fell to the
ground. The notary rushed to the spot, and on
moving the drapery from the head of the figure,
recognised the features of his daughter, who, shot
through the brain, lay bleeding at his feet.

"A frightful scene ensued; Deslandes, on making
the discovery, had fallen down beside his daughter,
and was actually covered with her blood. The servants with great difficulty removed him to his room,
where for three days he raved in a delirium of
remorse and horror, when he gradually sank into a
state of melancholy madness, from which he never
recovered, but became the inmate of an asylum,
where he died. After the catastrophe the chateau
was shut up, and remained so until my father returned to France in 1814, and under Royal warrant
received back the large estates alienated from him
by the decrees of the Convention and the duplicity
of Deslandes. Neither he nor I ever had the courage to commence repairing the damage time had
inflicted on the old house. *Parbleu!* we are lucky
to have a few rooms that are anything like habitable,
considering how long they were left a prey to weather

and rats. You can see the mark of the first bullet fired by Deslandes in the wall opposite, but as an inspection of that after my story might disturb your slumber, you may as well defer it till daylight. Besides, you will all be called early to-morrow—four o'clock precisely. My wolf-hounds are going to draw some covers about fifteen miles from here, and if you want a decent night's rest, you had better follow my example and retire. *Adios ! Bon soir, Messieurs.* Punctuality, if you please, to-morrow morning."

CHAPTER X.

THE Leicestershire enclosure, as the Count called it, was not the room to put an early riser. The wax candle the servant brought made its gloomy recesses still gloomier; its acre-age was cold to the feet, and perplexing to the sleeper awakened. When Dayrell opened his eyes, and saw the melancholy dip, he turned on his side, slept for five minutes more, and then, with a hazy idea that there was something to be done that day, jumped out of bed. *Facilis descensus averni*, easy for him to get from his bed to the candle; *sed superare gradum*, very hard to grope his way back into darkness without breaking his shins over chairs, ottomans, or even his own boot jack; and harder still to see a thing, unless he happened on the exact spot where it was. He drew several covers before he found his socks, button hook, leathers, and gloves, and when he ran his tops to ground in a dark corner, his " who-hoop " was one of sorrow, on his foot coming in contact with spurs hidden inside. Such difficulties were all the more provoking, as he wished that day to astonish the French with the neatness of his toilet. He was in the hall, however, as soon as the rest, and better dressed and fresher than any; for Latour and Magnan had played picquet all night, d'Alençon had slept in a chair, and De Vismes looked unwashed, and was most certainly unshaved. Dayrell expected some coffee before their long drive, but none being offered, he took a light from the Count's regalia, and smoked like the rest.

The morning was so dark that the servant had to bring a lantern to light them into the break, and so cold, that nobody talked, not even Villars, the youngest of the party, who just before in the hall had whispered to Dayrell his determination of " cutting down" in the run that French triumvirate, of whom he further spoke in words disparaging, " They can't get over two fences, no, not if they are tied to their horses." But as the day dawned the party woke up, and by the time they had arrived at the inn where their hunters had been sent the previous evening, Latour and Magnan had rattled their r's in Gallic fashion, and drawn their hunting-knives across the throats of at least nine imaginary wolves.

The cover was about three miles beyond the inn. If drawing for a fox, the hounds would have been thrown into it in a body; but so true is the nose, so

good are the ears of the wolf, that if the same tactics
were pursued with him he would be in the next department before the pack opened.   So Chasseloup,
the Count's dapper little huntsman, worked craftily.
He learned from the peasantry where the animal was
likely to be found.   Thither he sent one of his
blouse-clad aides-de-camp with half a sheep.   The
scent of this attracted the wolf; he dined, and where
he dined, he slept.   This, Chasseloup repeated three
successive evenings; and on the fourth morning, he
came stealthily to the wood, where his gorged enemy
was.   He had only one hound with him, the remainder of the pack were coupled, their eagerness
being restrained by some *piqueurs,* who kept them
out of sight of the huntsman and cover.   The Count
was mounted on a clever bay horse.   When about
five hundred yards from the cover, he stopped his
"field," and impressed them with the necessity of
silence for a few minutes.   But in spite of him
Magnan, Latour, and De Vismes laughed, chattered,
and capered about the road on their weedy hacks.
What else could be expected of a triumvirate, who
went out hunting in blue shooting coats gathered in
at the waist, with fur aprons to prevent their legs
catching cold, with *conteaux-de-chasse* at the side of
their saddles, and French horns slung about their
shoulders, making them look like circus bandsmen,

who having blown their best on entering a country town, sling their instruments athwart their backs, and sit their horses as though tired of the admiration their efforts have excited. *Toujours* French horns no matter whether it is hunting or shooting they wish to celebrate. Frenchmen would even sound the trumpet after a hard day amongst the larks! D'Alençon, in his military trowsers strapped tightly under his boots, in his frock coat made for the Rue Rivoli, and spurs the very thing for the Champ-de-Mars, alone obeyed orders, for Villars and Dayrell were in animated conversation about the best point they should make in case they found a wolf.

"*Allez, Fontenoy,*" said Chasseloup quietly to his old line-hunting hound; and the old fellow topped the bank into the wood, and feathered up a ride close to where the mutton had been thrown the night before. Steadily the old hound worked upon the trail of the wolf, and never opened till he was quite sure, and close upon the animal. A signal from Chasseloup and the pack were uncoupled. It is all right; they have found, and in a couple of minutes are rattling him round the lower part of the wood in right merry chorus. In those two moments Dayrell, followed by Villars, had crossed the small piece of landes that intervened between them and the wood, had jumped the bank, and gained the ride near which the wolf had been found. The Count and the others declined the wood, partly through indecision, partly from fear of the bogs. "They're on him, now," cried Chasseloup, who, when hunting, used French and English phrases promiscuously, as the body of the pack swept across the ride, and crashed through the tangled underwood. "Mind the branches," exclaimed Dayrell to Villars, who was behind him, galloping down the overgrown path, "keep your arms before your eyes, and follow me. Hurrah! they're away," he continued, as his horse scrambled on to the rotten bank on the outside of the wood. "Come up, old boy;" and the apostrophized animal landed safely on the landes, across which the pack were racing with a scent tremendous.

These landes are uncultivated wastes—sickly grass and gorse are their only products. When the latter has been cut by the peasantry, the ground is good galloping, except where the uplands are drained by slips of marshy ground, which often prove a stopper to the uninitiated, and give them a dirty cold bath. The jumps are banks, seldom big, but with ditches on each side, varying in breadth and depth.

The hounds were well away; not a soul with them, but Chasseloup, Dayrell, and Villars, and they were doing all they knew to keep up with the tail of the pack. The two former rode their own line on and

off banks, and then, up in their stirrups, steered
across the uplands of the landes. Villars rode
pluckily enough, but rather "in the pockets" of his
leaders, and often looked back over his shoulder to see
if the others were behind. When in bonny Northamptonshire the best men of the hunt have sailed
over some frightful fences to shake off the crowd,
when the hounds and fox point for some far distant
covert, it is a terrible moment of suspense for that
gallant six, if the hounds are brought to a stand
still, and then sweep round to the right, as though
they had returned to the wood. "Is it to be?" is
plainly written on every face. The next instant the
hounds take up the scent a-head. "Forward, it is,"
shout those half dozen throats. They have ridden
for the run, and now have their reward in being the
only six *with* the hounds in one of the fastest bursts
ever known in the "shires." So when the French
pack, on reaching a long slip of marsh-land, swept
away to the right, it appeared as if the wolf had
returned to the wood.

"What a pity," said Dayrell, turning in his saddle
and looking back, when Chasseloup called his attention to old Fontenoy, who was working busily lower
down the swamp, heedless of the grey plover who
darted at and circled round his head, and of the
snipe, who went twit-twitting away from under his

nose. " Fo-orrard, it is," shouted Dayrell, as old
Fontenoy took up the scent on the opposite side of
the bog.

" Fo-orrard, it is," echoed the huntsman, piloting
the others over a piece of comparatively sound land.
" The old hound footed him across. I could swear
to it. Fo-orrard," he cried, as the body of the pack
took up the scent, and raced across the landes.
Chasseloup, good enough in the saddle for a short
burst, had his equestrian abilities put to the test in
the run that followed. Wanting the self-possession
of a thorough artist, he, in taking his fences, de-
pended on his bridle and horse's mouth for a firm
seat in the saddle. Hence his horse, when in
trouble from the severity of the pace, being pulled
at a bank, jumped short, and, the earth giving way,
left his fore-legs on the right side, and his hind-legs on
the wrong. Chasseloup, in consequence, was obliged
to dismount, and while he was extricating his horse
from his inglorious position, Dayrell and Villars
pushed on with the hounds. Twenty-five minutes
on a close day—the pace tremendous—found out the
weak point in the Count's horses, viz., want of condition. Had the ground been soft, the hounds would
have had it to themselves. As it was, by the time
they had thrown up their heads on the opposite side
of a valley, bleak, desolate, and covered with huge

boulder stones, Dayrell and Villars found their horses beaten, and unwilling to press them before they had recovered their second wind, sat helplessly watching the pack from the brow of the hill.

"It is well. Stay there," said Chasseloup, riding up at this critical moment. "I will cross the valley and set them right," and at the same time giving his horse a dig with the spurs, descended the hill by a series of short jumps and slides, dashing in and out of a small brook at the bottom, and was again with his hounds. The check was of short duration—scarcely five minutes; for Chasseloup, guessing that the wolf's point was the forest, made an excellent cast on his left, and hit off the scent. The hounds hunted slowly down the valley, winding in and out amongst the broken rocks, followed by the huntsman on the left, and our amateurs on the right side of the valley. The character of the country was now changed. Peasants had evidently made efforts to enclose the landes and to regenerate them. The fields were half-cultivated, and large banks had been thrown up and fenced on the top to prevent cattle straying into the corn. For a timid rider the country looked awkward. Chasseloup's eye wandered in search of accommodating heave-gates, as the hounds, leaving the valley, made across this uncompromising tract of country.

Q

"Send him at it hard, and follow me," said Dayrell to Villars, as, cramming in the persuaders, he sent his horse at the first of the banks, and with a scramble landed safely on the other side. " *Quelle mauvaise bête !*" exclaimed poor Villars, as his horse, pulled injudiciously at the moment of rising, jumped short on the bank, and fell on his head in the boggy landing, sending his rider into the mire with a thud that could have been heard a mile off. Villars, with a crushed hat, an aching shoulder, and an all-abroad feeling, gathered himself up, as well as a stirrup-leather that had come out of the socket, and staggered forward to Dayrell, who had caught his horse, and was leading him back. "This will never do," said the latter; " our horses are too beat for such a country, we must follow Chasseloup through the gates and trust to his knowledge." Poor little Villars again got into his saddle, and humbly followed his leader over a few heave-gates into a green lane, where, when joined by Chasseloup, the three galloped on, as long as the hounds ran parallel with it.

The broad line of the forest loomed in front. Not one of the three doubted but that the wolf had reached his home, and that this would close the day's sport. So the two eased their horses up the hill, content to arrive at the top about two minutes after the pack. Now they floundered in wet boggy rides, the soil readily receiving their horses' feet, and tenaciously holding them; now they trotted warily over an expanse of lately cleared forest-land, where the sharp stubs and piles of underwood stuck up in every direction prevented them from keeping up with the hounds; now they rode in Indian file through matted briars, with fine timber springing out of the midst—weary, tiring work for horses and men. Sometimes they were close to the pack, sometimes they were separated from them for many minutes. In the latter case, Chasseloup, whose powers of hearing rivalled those of an Indian, put his hand to his ear, listened for a minute, then struck down some small ride, and met his favourites as they pushed across a green oasis of the forest. The horses were now almost knocked up, and their riders would gladly have given in. But what was to be done? Chasseloup was obliged to keep on with the hounds for fear of losing them, and Dayrell and Villars for fear of losing themselves, if separated from the huntsman. The two were seriously thinking of stopping, and attempting to retrace their steps, when they came to a comparatively open part, where the hounds were running through a few brakes of brushwood and hollies at the same pace as at the commencement. In another minute hounds and horses were again on the landes; but this time, the country was hilly and rocky, and so barren that the peasants had never thought it worth while to enclose any part with the customary banks.

"He is gone to the rocks," cried Chasseloup, in great glee; "we must hunt him on foot, and walk home afterwards. *Allez-donc*," he added to his poor horse, who seemed anxious to subside into the mildest of trots. But neither his horse, nor those of Villars and Dayrell, could raise a canter. They were dead beat, and trotted on in the spiritless style of half-breds whose powers have been over-taxed. The hounds were leaving them behind, and carrying a splendid head through a belt of plantation on a hill-side.

"Farewell, you beauties, for to-day," muttered Dayrell, when—can he believe his eyes?—the pack suddenly turned, raced down the narrow belt, and, in the ditch below, evidently fixed upon the wolf. True it was, so Chasseloup found, as he struggled up on foot, and with his knife despatched the *vieux monstre*, as he called him. "Who-hoop," shouted Dayrell, as he tumbled over the bank into the middle of the hounds; while Villars executed a war-dance round the group, and threw up his crushed and mud-bespattered hat into the air, totally regardless of what became of that ill-used piece of property. This was indeed an ever-to-be-remembered sight in that primeval valley,—Chasseloup standing with one foot on the body of his prostrate foe, whose starting eyes and fixed jaw proclaimed the bitterness of the death struggle. Villars, whip in hand, and wielding it with unnecessary vigour, keeping the baying hounds at a respectful distance; Dayrell leaning over the wolf, and examining his paws, the state of which cleared up the mystery of the animal's sudden downfall. They had been completely severed at the joint by some sharp instrument, probably a scythe, left by the peasants (as their habit is) in the long grass of the landes, otherwise no old wolf, such as this one, would have so suddenly succumbed, not even after such a dance as he had this day led them.

The obsequies of a fox are quickly performed, the trophies hastily whipped off, and the remains quickly dispatched by the eager pack. But higher honours are always reserved for these old robbers, when chance brings them to hand. The skin (a work of time) must be taken off, and their heads preserved as the *spolia opima* of a not every-day victory. So, when the flask had gone round, and been duly emptied, when cigars had been lighted, and Chasseloup sounded as to the whereabouts of the chateau, which he reckoned to be about thirty miles distant, it was decided that their horses were too tired to compass so long a journey, and that the best plan would be to find their way to an inn and farm-house, which the huntsman thought must be in their immediate vicinity. Chasseloup therefore ascended the neighbouring hill, and blew his horn, to the sound of which two blouse-clad peasants quickly responded, prepared, for a consideration, to carry the wolf, and act as guides to the party.

The procession was formed, the wolf, slung between the two peasants, occupied the post of honour, Chasseloup and the hounds following; while Dayrell and Villars, leading their horses, brought up the rear. After comparing notes about the general features of the day's hunting, Villars said abruptly to Dayrell,

"Now, confess, was it not a run? Did you ever see anything like it in England?"

"I must say," answered Dayrell, "I never have; but then, you know, fox-hunting is very different to this kind of thing. It is not often that a fox strays so far from home as our wolf obligingly did to-day. Then the foot people and labourers working in the fields spoil many a good thing, by turning a fox from his point; besides, no animal, now-a-days, could live long before hounds which, in the majority of cases, are bred for simple racing, not hunting, and even then, fast as they are, are repeatedly overridden. It only requires straight running in the wolves to ensure a run, for, with the exception of the young ones, they will beat hounds in ninety-nine cases out of a hundred."

"Ah, I see," said Villars, "that France, or rather the Count's chateau, is the place for hunting after all. Give me hunting, and such runs as we have had to-day, and no Paris or Bordeaux for me. Don't you think, Dayrell,—and you have seen most things,—that there is nothing like hunting?"

"You are right," said the latter, "I have tried most things in my time, and though I feel the keen enjoyment of my youthful days a little blunted, I agree with you, that the love of hunting will never pall upon me, or, at all events, it will outlive every other pleasure. Fishing is a pleasant sport, when salmon take kindly, or even trout rise freely at your fly; but at the end of the very best day, there is a feeling of incompleteness, brought on, may be, by the recollection of fish larger, of course, than those on your gillie's back, having broke away, or of others that have disappointed you by 'rising short;' to say nothing of a slight feeling of jealousy if, after all your pains, a brother angler has topped your score. Again, a day's shooting on the moors or stubbles is splendid fun, but, on wending your way home, it is not pleasant to think of wounded birds that have escaped Dido, or of the good beat that you have

probably spoilt for another day; besides a kind of
difficulty in keeping up the excitement that numerous
points and clever doubles have caused throughout
the day.   I have heard from those who have been in
more than one cavalry charge, that there is no excitement equal to that which a man feels, when
riding at the head of his squadron; but they tell me
at the same time that the reaction is such as the
most hardened to such scenes can never forget.
Hunting alone seems to me to have no drawback.
A two hundred-guinea horse, a splendid run, and a
good place in it throughout, can never be remembered
without a thrill of delight, whether discussed that
same night, next week, or twenty years hence.
Listen to two old veterans, who have long since
relinquished high Leicestershire for some less dangerous country, as they talk over a Hillmorton, or
Barkby Holt day, in which, twenty years ago, they
held their own in the front rank through a glorious
burst over those fifty-acre pastures. Age cannot dim
their sparkling eyes, or the enthusiasm, kindled by
the reminiscences of a run, in which almost every
fence they charged, and every turn the hounds made,
is indelibly written in their memories. I believe,
too, Villars, that none once imbued with a real love
of hunting, no matter how long they may be prevented from joining in the sport, ever lose their

attachment to it, and that the words of Mr. Morritt's song are as true as any that ever were put to paper—

"'A foxhunter once, is a foxhunter still.'"

"Bravo, Dayrell," said Villars; "upon my word, when I come of age, I will have a huntsman, whippers-in, hounds, and all complete, and you shall come and live with me; when——I say, is this the inn we are to stop at to-night? Rather a tumbledown affair, is it not? And the landlady, what a guy she is!"

A wayside-inn in France is not an inviting halting place, either as regards its *cuisine*, or the general accommodation prepared for man and beast. Below stairs it is probable that uneven flags pave the floor; that a smoky wood fire will cause the tears, so bitterly complained of by Horace, to start to the eyes; while the chances are, that the landlady, in addition to other pledges of affection, will have a youthful stranger in her arms who has as yet learnt little else but to suck and cry. Above, there is probably an apartment with two or more beds for the benefit of travellers who may be compelled to stop and "be done for;" there is a fire-place in which, for the reason given above, you dare not apply a light to the wood; and rheumatic drafts enter freely through innumerable holes and crannies.

It sometimes happens that the aboriginal managers

of such hostelries can speak no language but their own semi-barbaric *patois*. "What are you to do then?" asked a young Cambridge man of his friend, a man who boasted that he had walked with his knapsack more miles than some people had ever travelled on wheels. "When I want to eat or drink," he answered, "I raise my hand to my mouth in piteous supplication; when I want to perform my toilet, I go through a singular pantomime of hand-rubbing my face; and when the drowsy god claims a willing votary, I simply begin to undress, and am bundled off to my dormitory with marvellous celerity." The bill of fare, too, at such establishments, is generally of the most simple kind (I wish I could say *simplex munditiis*), consisting of eggs and *crêpe*—a species of pancake, into the manipulation of which we had better not inquire. Lucky shall we be if the latter does not reek of garlic, the custom of using that odoriferous herb having long since crept across the Spanish frontier, and invaded the less civilized departments of *la belle France*. Cider, sour wine, and the worst possible eau de vie, compose a pleasant list of drinkables. The water, however, is likely to be both fresh and sparkling; so a health, "five fathoms deep," to Father Mathew.

Dayrell and Villars, after seeing their horses cared for as well as the resources of the establishment admitted, entered upon just such a scene as this. By dint of much blowing, the former coaxed a cheerful blaze out of the smouldering embers on the hearth; and the good-humoured expostulations of the latter induced the landlady to commence the preparation of a repast, of which our Nimrods stood greatly in need. Their endeavours to make themselves comfortable were somewhat assisted by the evident partiality the landlady showed for Villars. His good looks must have quite won her heart, so anxiously did she enquire if he was hurt,—so often did she call him her *pauvre enfant*,—so desirous to scrape off some of the red mud that still tenaciously clung to his person. As soon as dinner was ready, Chasseloup having fed his horses and hounds, came in, accompanied by Monsieur Michelet, the *garde* of the forest, a tall gaunt man, of about forty-five years of age. The latter carried the badge of his profession, in the shape of a game bag, across his shoulders, while on his arm rested a long single-barrelled gun, that looked as though it had been buried with its original possessor in case he should need it in "the happy hunting grounds" to which he had been removed, and sacrilegiously resurrectionized by its present owner. They all sat down in company to the improvised dinner, the quality of which did not prevent its rapid demolition; a consummation that was followed by a general move to the fire. In a minute the blue smoke from pipes and cigars curled upwards amongst the blackened rafters.

"*O dura Chasselouporum ilia,*" would the bard have sung with a grimace of sympathetic horror, had he seen our huntsman foaming up his sixth horn of lately-pressed cider, and pledging the company with all the easy freedom of the brotherhood.

"*Messieurs,*" said Michelet, "*au mort des loups;*" and Dayrell added, "May you never have a worse day than this."

The toast was duly responded to, and all the events of the run and the kill were detailed for the benefit of the keeper. In fact, the huntsman's tongue was fairly set going, he told many tales of other days, and amongst them, one rather singular story connected with his residence in England.

"Monsieur Dayrell, you will excuse me," said he, "if I dislike your countrymen for one little thing. I like your country; I like your gentlemen; I like your hunting; but I do not like you when you quarrel, and (putting himself in a most unscientific attitude, supposed to be one of self-defence) when you want to box. On my arrival in England I had plenty to do in the stable and the field, and after finishing my work used to go to the house for supper. The evenings would have been dull enough had I not taught

the other servants dominoes, tric-trac, and cards;
but, when they had learnt these games, I became
quite a popular character. While hunting one day,
a farmer, who had several times seen me nearly break
my neck over some big fences, came up to me, and,
laying his heavy hand on my shoulder, said, 'Dang
it, Frenchy, but you are a good sort of chap; you
stopped them all at that fence. Remember, there's
a horn of beer and a welcome at my house whenever
you like to look in.' After this invitation I used
often to go there in the evening, especially as the
farmer had a pretty daughter, who, I thought, was
likely enough to have his money some day. This
latter consideration made me desert the servants'
hall, and spend my time with Susan (that was her
name), who used to make herself very agreeable, and
seemed to take great interest in all I said and did.
My fellow servants were soon made aware of what
was going on, and became so jealous, that they determined to play me a trick, the results of which I
shall not easily forget. At the end of the hunting
season, our master gave a ball to his tenants; and,
amongst others, we were to be present in hunting
costume. 'Frenchy,' said one of the helpers to me,
the morning before the ball, 'never been, I reckon,
to a dancing party in England?' 'No,' said I;
'Why?' 'Nothing,' answered he; 'only you had

better do the same as other people.' 'And what is
that?' I asked. 'Why, only to find the girl you
like best, and kiss her, or else she will not dance
with you all the evening.' 'I'll do that,' I replied,
quite unsuspicious of any trick. 'There is nothing
I should like better.' I did not appear in the ball-
room till after the music had began and most of
the people were assembled, when seeing my Susan
standing by the fire-place, and her father talking to
some one who was standing near him, I walked up to
her. She held out her hand for me to shake; I took
it, and then kissed her on both cheeks. She screamed
out. I felt myself seized by the collar, and amidst a
shower of kicks, and many bad words, was pushed out
into the yard; where it was of no use stopping and
trying to explain through the keyhole, for they had
locked the door and had no intention of re-opening
it. Next morning I went in a terrible rage to the
stables, and seeing the helper who had been the cause
of all the mischief, began to abuse him, and call him
by every French and English name I could think of.
He put down the fork with which he was tidying the
straw, and said with a grin, 'Frenchy, can you fight?'
I rushed at him, but he gave me two blows with his
fist, that not only knocked me down, but fairly
stunned me for some minutes. When I came to
myself he was quietly raking up the litter as though

nothing had happened, and seeing me staring about, said, 'Frenchy, you have made a fool of yourself; you had better hold your tongue in future, or you'll get the worst of it.' Oh, Monsieur Dayrell, if I had known how to fight like one of our *roulage* carters, that helper would have regretted his attempt to box with me."

They all laughed heartily at Chasseloup's misfortunes, except Michelet, who did not see the joke of taking a man ·in first, and knocking him down afterwards; when Villars adroitly turned the subject.

"Michelet," said he, "you were talking just now about deer, do you think we could get one in the forest if we came and stayed here for two or three days?"

"There are very few left," answered the keeper; "the wolves have killed so many fawns, that I doubt much if you ever get a chance. I am always about the forest, and often don't see one for weeks together."

"Look here," said Villars, holding up a gold coin, on which the landlady in her chimney corner fastened her eyes, and, in order to obtain it, concocted a gigantic robbery in the matter of her guests' bill. "This piece of twenty francs is yours, if we kill a stag."

Michelet brightened hugely at the sight of money, and changed his tone. "I don't know but what we might do so, after the routing the hounds gave the forest to-day; besides, it has lately been disturbed so much by the wood-cutters. I think we might alight upon them—I am nearly sure we shall—that is if you let *me* show you the ground, and the way to set to work. At any rate, if there be a deer in the country, I flatter myself I am the man to un-harbour him."

"Very well, Michelet," said Villars; "that's settled. If you can show us the deer you win twenty francs, and as much brandy as you can stow away in a fortnight; and if we kill one, you shall have——"

"Stop, Villars, that will do," interposed Dayrell; "you have arranged the preliminaries, so come to bed. What do you mean, you young muff, by showing your money, and making such promises? Don't you know, that the more you promise the more such men as Michelet will want."

The landlady led the way to a drafty apartment upstairs—it was the only one she had—where Dayrell and Villars, rejecting the sheets, which smelt damp and musty, enveloped themselves in blankets, and in spite of all inconveniences soon fell asleep.

CHAPTER XI.

WHEN bad weather puts a stop to out-door amusements in England, a country-house, full of visitors, is by no means a cheerful residence. When the barometer has steadily fallen to 27½, and ominously points to " much rain," a most depressing effect is produced on the British constitution. The perusal of newspapers and letters may, haply, fill up two hours after breakfast; but even an elaborate report of one of Sir Creswell Creswell's trials will not stand more than a second reading. The matutinal cigar, and inspection of the stable, may wile away another hour; but no one, unless he is an extraordinary admirer of equine beauty, cares to listen, more than once, to the pedigrees and performances of his host's stud. Billiards and luncheon may kill time up to two P.M., when frequent walks to the window, and disconsolate glances at the falling rain, clearly indicate that the resources of the visitors have collapsed, and fallen with the glass. Two or three of the hardiest of the party may in despair envelope them-

R

selves in waterproofs, and walk out, unmindful of
the pelting of the unsympathizing storm, but the
majority of the party will be uncomfortable and
restless, and take their revenge by inflicting dull and
misanthropic letters on their friends till the dinner
dressing-bell rings, and puts an end to their *ennui*.
Truly, the hostess, should there be one, would
become a public benefactress were she jealously to
lock up the large chest containing Mudie's latest
works, and not allow its treasures to be ransacked,
until the rainy day arrives—that damper, in more
senses than one, to her unhappy guests.

Our neighbours, in France, when imprisoned in a
country-house by a similar stress of weather act far
otherwise. Wiser in their generation, they do not
look upon out-door amusements as the be-all and
end-all of life, but rather as the means of occasionally passing away an idle hour. So, when the deluge
descends, reducing every thing out of doors to mud
and misery, they bring forward their evening amusements into the day. If they cannot hunt or shoot,
they arrange the tables for whist, imperiale, écarté,
sometimes varying the proceedings with a bout at
fencing, or gymnastics. Throughout the live-long
day the same excitement reigns, as they reach " four
all," or some other equally critical part of the game.
The same old jokes are cut, and the same clattering

of tongues follows the conclusion of each set. No matter whether the stakes are 500 francs or 5, the novelty never seems to wear off. They are playing, and that is enough. It is, perhaps, a libel on Frenchmen to say, " Give them plenty of tobacco, and time to play cards, and they require nothing else." Still there cannot be a shadow of doubt but that these are the two most important items in the sum total of their happiness.

Dayrell, Villars, and Chasseloup had returned to the chateau, the splendour of their triumphal entry having been sadly dimmed by the rain, and their drowned-rat appearance. A committee of taste had deliberated at length on the ultimate destination of the skin and head of the wolf, and the Count had great difficulty in deciding whether he should make a rug or chair-cover of the old veteran's coat. The details of the run had been told all through, discussed bit by bit, and referred to so often, that the subject became a bore. Yards had been added to the breadth of brooks, and feet to the height of banks, that had been jumped by the successful horses, while the run itself was now set down at 50 kilometres from point to point! Magnan and the others, who were thrown out, chafed considerably at their misfortune, and threw the principal blame on the Colonel for leading them up the wood; to which the

Colonel good humouredly retorted, " That Magnan,
at least, ought to be grateful for his life being
spared, as he would inevitably have tumbled off at
the second fence. Not that my charity was quite
disinterested," continued the Colonel; "for, in the
event of a bad accident, I, as the biggest man of the
party, would have been expected to carry you on my
shoulders to some place where the carriage could
pick you up. Oh! the ingratitude of the world,"
sighed the Colonel; " I hope another time, Magnan,
you will better appreciate my kindness and solicitude
for your ribs."

For two days after the return to the chateau, the
rain fell in torrents, and the Frenchmen played at
cards. Dayrell and Villars took no part in the
games,—in fact, were only spectators, when the
evening put a stop to their occupations. For it was
vain to attempt fly-dressing by candle-light, or to
work out models of a boat intended for one of the
southern lakes. When the weather mended, the
Count and his companions, in all the severe panoply
of the French *chasseur*, and not unmindful of the
fancifully-worked game-bags, took the beagles to the
woods, whence they returned, perchance, with a hare
which the dogs had caught, and a couple of rabbits that
some of the party had shot sitting at a distance of
six yards, and nearly blown to pieces. Dayrell and

Villars traversed the whole country in search of woodcocks and snipe. The latter, under the guidance of his friend, was rapidly learning the art of "mowing down his bird," and was constantly repeating Dayrell's advice, "I am to fix my eye as quick as I can,—my hand follows my eye. I cut him down before he has time to mount into the air and twist and turn ;" to which his mentor answered encouragingly. " If you only continue to make the same progress, you'll beat the Squire of Hollycombe, in time, who reverted to a flint gun to put himself on an equality with his guests." The hounds, too, after the great run, had, of course, little rest. Young France burned to distinguish (or *extinguish*) itself in the saddle. But the fates were unpropitious. They did not always find, and when they did, on two separate occasions the scent was so catching as to prevent even a ten minutes' burst over the open.

But, if sport was denied to the chateau party in the field, great fun awaited them on the boards of Villeneuve. Subsequent to Dayrell's arrival certain cards of invitation had been sent, asking them to a ball the amateur musicians of the town intended giving on the fête of St. Cecilia—a lady—whether in the calendar, or not, I cannot say, but supposed to be the patroness of "instrumental movements."

" What fun it would be to go," said De Vismes.

"You, Colonel, will come, of course, and add one more to your fifty-two—was it fifty-two or fifty-three?—conquests over the fair sex. The belle of Villeneuve anxiously awaits you; you cannot say 'No' to her."

"De Vismes," replied the old beau, "when will you mind your own affairs? Let me tell you, that by the time you have got into a third as many scrapes as I have got *out* of, your hair will have become grey from vexation and trouble."

"Stop, Colonel," interposed the Count; "you are too hard upon your young friend. You shall not run the gauntlet of beauty this time. We will stay at home, and they shall have the carriage to-night and go to Villeneuve."

In the little village it was a gala night, for the good reason that it was the only night in the year in which the young ladies could put on white dresses, and figure in the *trois temps*. The music-hall was brilliantly lighted, and the white-washed walls, when decorated with festoons of laurel and paper flowers, lost much of their previous frigid look. On a raised dais at the upper end was stationed the band, composed of amateurs, and in close attendance lounged and conversed the stewards, with the well known nonchalance of the emancipated bourgeois. On each side of the room was ranged a double row of benches,

of which the lower was occupied by youthful aspi-
rants to matrimony, who laughed, and talked, and
smirked, as though accustomed to muslin flounces
and dancing every night of their lives. On the
upper bench behind, in grim array, like the old
Roman senators, sat mothers and duennas, who—
tell it not at Willis's, whisper it not at Mabille—
retained their long black cloaks all the evening,
—charity would suggest for a foil to their daughter's
dresses, malice would hint at a concealment of their
morning or walking robes. *Mais c'est l'habitude du
pays;* it is the custom at Villeneuve, and Villeneuve
is miles from Paris and civilization.

The music and dancing had commenced, when the
chateau party, in all the pride of sable suits, worked
shirt-fronts, and white ties, elbowed their way into
the hall, past half a dozen gens-d'armes redolent of
tobacco, and through a crowd of the οἱ πολλοὶ, whose
sabots precluded them from coming in. Such a
well-dressed party should have created a sensation.
On the contrary, with the exception of one or two
stewards, who addressed them with the easy affability
of Frenchmen, they were scarcely noticed by the
male sex. Every man here considered himself as
good as his neighbours, including the better-born
visitors from the chateau. *Egalité* far outstripped
Fraternité in the ball-room of Villeneuve.

"Les Messieurs will dance," said one of the French-men, who was better dressed than the others, for there were few present who could muster all the component parts of an evening suit. One perhaps had a black tail-coat and trowsers, but surmounted by such a variegated tie and waistcoat as would have effectually barred his entrance into Her Majesty's Opera House. Another, perhaps, had a tie of snowy whiteness and lengthy ends, but which hardly matched with a black shooting coat and green gloves. And so with the majority of the guests. If all the clothes there had been put in a heap, some nine or ten tolerably-dressed individuals might have turned out respectably for the evening parade.

"Les Messieurs will dance?" inquired the French-man. "The ladies await you; you should take partners for the quadrille:" after which piece of advice the steward dropped back into the crowd.

Oh the terrible solemnity of a first quadrille for the man who hails from old England, and has dined some hours previously, and having lost the confidence imbibed with 44 Lafitte, feels like fighting Bob Acres. Dayrell, to tell the truth, was more than awkward, as he led out a somewhat buxom young lady, while the "what on earth shall I say to her" feeling gave him a sort of a shiver. His reasoning faculties, however, being sufficient to point out that, if his partner was at this ball, she probably would like to hear something about similar *réunions*, he commenced a rambling account of a bachelor's ball, where, as manager, he had borne a conspicuous part. He descanted at length upon the decorations of the room, the performances of the band, and, warming to his work, was describing the supper,—yes, salmon and champagne, claret and clear soup,—when, on returning from the performance of a difficult evolution in La Pastorelle, his partner looked up in his face and said so naturally, " *Monsieur, ça vous coute bien cher.*" Dayrell was taken aback at the cost of the entertainment being the first object of consideration to youth and innocence, yet he had presence of mind left to answer, " *Rien, Mademoiselle, est trop coûteux pour les demoiselles.*"

The whirling waltz, the graceful mazurka, and the polka, not as yet obsolete in provincial circles, followed in quick succession, in each of which the chateau party performed with unflagging energy, as long as the violins and cornopeans held out. At the conclusion of each dance, there was a rush to the front bench, a disengaging of partners, a closing up of the ranks of *demoiselles* on promotion, and a general promenading of the male sex up and down the middle of the room. This unsociability was brought about by a law made and provided by the matrons of Villeneuve, and strictly adhered to in some other parts of France, to the effect that a stoppage in any dance for more than a second must be followed by an immediate return of the inexperienced flutterers to the parental wing. Thus the promenade of happy couples in search of cool breezes, refreshment, or conversation, after the music ceased, was rigorously prohibited.

While the evening was yet young, Dayrell and his companions had observed the anti-flirting regulations laid down by the black-cloaked conclave. They might have continued to do so till the end of the ball, had not opportunely arrived (by order) sundry bottles of Bordeaux wine,—a necessary step, for nothing but the mildest of refreshments were included in the invitation. The uncorking and general distribution of the wine caused a revolution in the state of Villeneuve. Under its genial influence the musicians became more vivacious, the cornopeans rang out a less lugubrious wail, the fiddle ran two notes into one with alarming celerity, and the whole band, at De Vismes' instigation, prolonged the waltzes to an indefinite length. Then was it refreshing to watch the airy movements of La Foix, to mark the adroitness Magnan showed in slipping through the serried ranks of slower dancers, and to see the pluck of little Villars, manfully struggling to turn his heavy partner. But De Vismes was the brightest star in the hemisphere of Villeneuve; he, whom even the Parisians applauded in Cellarian halls, when, dancing the *deux temps*, he described without an effort twelve small circles round one of the iron pillars, and afterwards completed twelve more in the " reverse turn " without a symptom of giddiness or exhaustion. No sooner did certain panting couples pause, than De Vismes, gliding across the room with his light and airy partner, performed evolutions in the mazy dance that made the whole company look on in amazement, and the musicians almost stop and admire. He was indeed a great dancer. Well might that young lady who had danced with him five times in succession, be proud of such a partner. Blushingly she allowed herself to be engaged for a sixth, quite unmindful of the presence of a moustached youth, who came to claim her hand for that mazurka.

" You are wrong," said De Vismes, " this lady is engaged to me ;" and, without further parley, swept off his Villeneuve belle into the mazy circle, and danced until, fairly exhausted, he as well as his friends were obliged to restore their partners to the charge of their respective chaperones.

" Have we had enough of this?" asked Magnan, moving to the stairs. " I see you all think so ; the carriage is waiting, let us bid adieu and retire."

They were descending the staircase, and De Vismes, in his conceited manner, was running his hand through his long black hair, when the youth of the shabby moustache, whom he had deprived of his expected mazurka, came quickly down, and addressed our dancing hero.

" Sir," said he, " I wish to speak to you."

" Very good ball indeed," relied De Vismes, not hearing what he said; " never enjoyed myself so much."

" Sir," said the jilted one, now fairly bubbling over, " you have insulted me—you are"——

" Very hot indeed," replied the other; " the heat was the only drawback to the pleasure of the evening."

" Sir, you shall speak to me," screamed he, raising his hand to De Vismes' shoulder. " I will prevent you leaving the place."

Dayrell saw the hostile movement, and, quick as thought, put into practice a little English science, and tripped up the irascible Frenchman. This gave time to the whole party to pass on to the carriage, and start before the disturbance could summon a crowd.

" Rather unfortunate termination to the ball," remarked La Foix, as they drove home. " We shall hear more of this to-morrow."

"Never mind," said the others; "let us wait till we do hear." And so these jovial spirits, dismissing the subject, went on to criticize the dancing and conversation of their respective partners.

If in England an aristocratic youth should hit, trip up, or otherwise scientifically dispose of an opponent, his punishment may be a fine and a damaged optic, requiring a coating of paint before he goes to Lady Turnabout's *soirée dansante*. Even the fine he sometimes escapes. A policeman has often in a street disturbance (at night), not a hundred miles from St. James's Palace, been known to take half-a-crown, and then act as bottle-holder and audience to the parties fighting. But in France, laying violent hands on a neighbour is a crime of the deepest dye. The law must be vindicated at once. Gens-d'armes immediately cock their hats in the approved ferocious style, pick up their swords, and serve the parties with *procès verbals* to appear before a judge, be fined, and imprisoned. So De Vismes was not surprised to receive a visit next day from the gens-d'armes, as also a notice that he must answer the charge of Mons. Cordon-noir, "universal bootmaker, but more especially to the inhabitants of Villeneuve," in that he, D. V., had insulted and injured the said Mons. C., for which injury the latter claimed 150 francs damages.

" I told you so," said the Colonel, glancing at the unwelcome paper. " Your troubles, De Vismes, are beginning. Don't forget to look in the glass every morning, or to tell us when you flush your first grey hair."

" Pay, and have done with it," suggested Dayrell. " It is only six sovereigns after all. The Colonel will subscribe one, I another, and so make the amount in five minutes."

" Pardon me," said De Vismes, " this is a criminal action, and we cannot compromise. If I am convicted, I shall have to pay, and go to prison for a week besides."

" You had better retire to Paris, De Vismes," the Colonel said; " or, suppose we have a mock funeral, and make the gens-d'armes believe the shock has killed you."

But while the Frenchmen spoke in language more forcible than polite, about the institutions of their country in general, and that of the law courts in particular, Dayrell and Villars made their plans for a start for the forest, thinking they would have time to kill a stag before their presence at the trial, fixed for the end of the week, should be required. So, after vain endeavours to induce the others to rough it in the wilderness, they put a stock of wine and provisions into one of the Count's carriages, and drove that afternoon to an *auberge*, where Michelet had been told to await them.

Bump, bump; jolt, jolt, over a road unstoned, and in ruts of awkward depth; swish, swish, through sheets of water that lay stagnant in the lanes all the year round, too deep for man to drain, or for the summer sun to dry; sometimes going at a foot pace, at other times absolutely obliged to lead the horse over a nasty place, where the carriage was within an ace of turning on its side, Dayrell and Villars made their way to the inn where they had slept after their day with the wolf-hounds. Not that they cared for the slowness of the pace or the chances of an upset. They were tired of the monotonous life at the chateau, and had not arrived at an age when the turning of a king at écarté, or holding the last trump at whist, are preferred to the results of twelve honest "right and lefts" in stubble-field and turnips. So they plodded on, making fun of their difficulties, and speculating as to the probable results of their expedition. Now they are near the forest, and the country ridden over by them a few days previous. They begin to form conjectures, albeit, far from accurate, about the scenes of their prowess in that ever-to-be-remembered run. In yonder valley they thought must be the morass, where old Fontenoy behaved so sagaciously, and, further on, the bank

that brought Villars to grief. Here must be the
spot where the hounds crossed the road and were at
at fault; and in that dell the morass, whence Chasseloup extricated himself and horse with the loss only
of a shoe. Dick Christian himself, riding through
the scene of many a Leicestershire scurry, could not
have summoned more cheery reminiscences than our
hunters did of their day with *the* wolf.

"You received our note, then," said Dayrell to
Michelet, who, pipe in mouth and hands in pockets,
awaited their arrival at the inn door.

"Yes," said that worthy, taking off his hat, and
commencing a long story about business in the forest,
with a view of impressing them with the magnitude
of the sacrifice he made in the cause of sport.

"Ah, never mind that; you shall be well paid,
Michelet. Here, take these cushions out of the carriage and place them safely upstairs," said Dayrell,
and followed himself with some more of the luggage.
That evening and night were spent by our hunters
much in the same way as by most people in a state
of expectancy. They made restless pilgrimages to
the yard, to see whether it was clear or cloudy over-
head, filling the intervals with speculations about
what they were doing at the chateau, and how the
trial was likely to end. The night they passed in the
old room; but, whether their weariness was not so

great as on a previous occasion, or the blankets were rougher, their slumbers were broken and unrefreshing.

Villars was the first to spring from his mattrass next morning to peer through the dirty window, and to look anxiously for the usual signs of fine weather.

"How looks it out of doors?" asked Dayrell from beneath the sheets. "Is Fortune propitious this time?"

"I hardly know," replied Villars, slowly. "The clouds hang about the hills, and there is a little rain falling; but Michelet said last night that mist in the morning is often followed by a hot day."

"I don't believe it, at this time of year at least," said Dayrell, dropping on to the floor from his lofty perch. "Still, no amount of rain must prevent us making a tour of inspection in and about the forest."

Michelet was waiting for his employers down-stairs, as well as a native of the country, to whose care was confided a dog,—a varmint but knowing cross between a lurcher and deer hound,—a handy aide-de-camp, that Michelet kept for a little quiet poaching on his own account.

"What are we to do?" asked Dayrell of the keeper, on going into the open air and seeing the fog still clinging to the mountain sides, and the drops pattering ominously on the flagstones in front of the

s

house. "I don't mind a wet jacket, but we shall lose ourselves in such a fog and mist as this."

"No fear of that, Sir; it will rain heavy in an hour, or clear up altogether."

"Then, Villars, let us make a start—shoulder rifles —forward."

"You might as well have left your rifles at home," remarked Michelet, when they had walked up the valley a distance of a couple of miles. "Should the fog clear away I cannot do more than show you the best parts of the ground. It would be idle to attempt to stalk a deer such a day as this. You ought to have been here last Monday; such a chance of killing a stag I never saw (just as they say in Paddy-land, 'if your honour had been here one week sooner or a month later, what sport you would have had.') One jumped up in a thicket not fifty yards from me. I was thinking of writing you word, but I knew you would soon be here. Then, four days after the hounds left, I saw two stags and five hinds on a hillside not two kilometres from Mons. Froment's farm, where they go at night to feed on his turnips and potatoes. How the old farmer hates them! *Parbleu!* he ought to give me a Napoleon if we kill one this week, and we shall if there is any power in your rifles.—*Mais pardonnez moi,*" he said, giving at the same time a sort of subdued whistle, as his eye

alighted on the rifle Dayrell carried, "but that cannot miss. *Par exemple!* that must have cost some
money."

"And your guns, too," chimed in Villars; "they
are the best I ever saw. Oh, if I could get such a
pair made for me in France, but I suppose that is
impossible."

"They ought to be good," replied Dayrell. "They
cost me not only money, but a great deal of trouble
into the bargain. When I made up my mind to
give a hundred guineas for a pair of guns, I thought
it was likely enough I should not be able to give so
much again, and that it would be as well to have
these made to suit me. Many a visit I paid to the
maker while they were in hand. I took care that
the stock and barrels should be evenly balanced, and
that the former should be bent exactly like my old
one; and, last not least, I was very particular not to
have the locks too stiff. In fact, I took care that I
should have something I could shoot with. Most
men order a gun as they would a watch or a bracelet,
and leave it to the maker to turn out an article,
pretty enough, 'tis true, but quite unsuited to the
owner's length of arm, neck, and style of shooting.
I always say to a man who is going to give fifty or
sixty guineas for a gun, ' *Caveat emptor*.' By-the-
bye, that reminds me of a story of my old school-

master, Mr. Byers, whose hard fate it was to have a very bad article, in the shape of a scolding shrew of a wife. One day he gave his first form ' *Caveat emptor*' as the theme for certain hexameter verses. Next morning the worthy pedagogue found amongst other copies the following lines :—

" ' CAVEAT EMPTOR.

" ' Buyers purchase a horse for better or worse,
As Byers has taken his wife;
A horse may be sold before he grows old,
But Byers must keep her for life.' "

" There she goes," said Villars, as a hare sprang from her form in the thick grass, and sped across the bog, throwing up a shower of spray on each side of her. The lurcher strained in its slips, and nearly pulled the Frenchman into a peat hole. "Let him go, let us have a hunt," said Michelet, who dearly loved a course. But this Dayrell would not allow; he had no idea of mixing the opposite pursuits of stalking deer and coursing. They skirted the forest for about two miles, threading their way through brakes of tangled brushwood, where they saw nothing but an occasional buzzard, either looking for game, or hovering over some unfortunate rabbit. At one of these Villars was going to shoot, but was prevented by his companions, who feared lest an unlucky shot should disturb some nobler prey. Michelet at last came to a sudden halt, he looked on the ground, swung his arms round like a windmill, then pointing to a print in a soil, asked, " *Qu'est que c'est ça?* " They gathered round, solemnly inspected it, drew a long breath and said, " Fresh slot of deer." " They are here, and we will find them," remarked Dayrell, as they trudged on after Michelet. The latter presently turned to the right, and leaving the wood, breasted a hill, from the top of which a good view could be obtained of the best glen. The rain and fog, as Michelet prophesied they would, had cleared off, and Dayrell, on arriving at the summit of the ridge, unslung his glass, and narrowly scanned every corrie in the vicinity.

In front lay a valley, between the precipitous sides of which a burn, swollen by the late rains, foamed and tumbled over the rocks that obstructed its course. At the upper end was a wide expanse of broken ground, intersected with ravines, and covered with fern and heather. On the right, but not visible from Dayrell's post of observation, were the two farms spoken of by Michelet, and the much-loved turnips that induced the deer at times to stray from the depths of the forest.

" A most likely place," said Dayrell, shutting up his glass, " and, with the wind in the right quarter, favourable for a successful stalk; but it is no use looking for deer on such a day as this. Now, however, we know the ground, and may have the chance of finding them here in more favourable weather."

Michelet was anxious to point out another glen, where he had found an out-lying stag more than once. His suggestion was not received with favour, it being thought better not to disturb the ground until a change in the weather took place. They therefore retraced their steps to the inn, the best course to pursue under the present circumstances. After dinner that evening, they arranged their plans for the next day's campaign. If the weather should be still unsettled, Michelet was to take them to another part of the forest to look for woodcocks, and where there would be no chance of disturbing the deer; for, independently of the sport, they thought a woodcock " served on toast " no despicable addition to the hard fare of an *auberge*. The morrow looked certainly more propitious than its predecessor, but as showers continued to fall, they followed out their plan of having a day's cock-shooting, for which purpose they impressed into their service two natives as beaters, shouldered their double-barrels, and went to Michelet's preserve. They had a good day's sport, killing eight woodcocks, and nine couple of snipe; but what most pleased them was, that they found the latter lay well—a happy augury of fine weather on the morrow.

On this, the third day, patience had its reward; a bright sun and a north-easter proclaimed it a deer-stalking morning. Dayrell and Villars trod the heather with quite a different step to that of the preceding days; they seemed to have that kind of foreboding, so often the real cause of success. They made the best of their way to the glen, so narrowly scanned by them on the first day, and, before ascending the hill, made their arrangements. The man with the dog was to remain in the valley, and not to stir till the signal was given, when he was to follow the stalkers at a respectful distance. Michelet was to accompany Dayrell to the top of the ridge, and received strict injunctions to make himself as small as he conveniently could. Villars was to stay where he was, an injunction which that young gentleman had no idea of obeying. On reaching the summit, Dayrell crept up to a small mound, and peered through his glass at the corries on the opposite side. After ten minutes' inspection, he directed his Dollond towards some broken ground on the right, where the fern and heather were more luxurious, and, drawing a deep breath, said to Michelet, "It is them, I believe. Just take the glass and look."

"Where?" asked Villars, poking up his head.

" You here?" replied Dayrell, hastily. " Do lie down, or you'll frighten every deer in the country."

The keeper balanced the glass in his hand, then turned it in the direction pointed out to him. The moment was one of intense excitement and suspense to the pair. Dayrell anxiously watched the keeper's face, but Villars had a fit of the buck ague, fidgeted with his rifle, and felt the point of his hunting knife.

" I can see them, now," said Michelet, slowly.

" How many?"

" I make out three hinds and a stag. But, Monsieur Dayrell, you can never approach them."

" Wait a minute," said Dayrell, taking a long survey through the glass. " It is to be done, and I will show you how. The wind at present blows up the valley, that is in our favour. We must stalk them from the upper end, though, even so, we cannot get near enough for a shot. You, Michelet, must remain where you are, until, by the aid of the glass, you see us under cover of yonder pile of rocks. When I hold up my hand, you may get up, and quietly descend the hill. The stag, when disturbed, is almost sure to make for the forest, and must pass near enough to give us a shot."

" And the hinds?" enquired the blood-thirsty Michelet.

"We don't want them to-day," answered Dayrell, laughing.

He and Villars then descended the hill, and having told the man to follow with the hound, proceeded to make their long *détour*. It is one thing to stalk a stag oneself, and in a fresh country; another to be in the hands of some canny Highlander, who knows every inch of the ground, and brings you at length within sixty yards' range. But Dayrell had a good landmark in the shape of a hill higher than the rest, which he kept in view, until he came in sight of two clusters of rocks. "Which are the rocks we marked," thought Dayrell to himself, then turning to Villars, asked him, if he had seen more than one from the other side.

"Not I, *mon cher*," gasped the excited youth. "Go to whichever you like, only not further than you can help. I am so blown."

"Then *en avant*. Let us hope we are right."

Ten minutes of alternate walking and running brought them within five hundred yards of the rocks. A short pause to gather breath, and steady the pulse, enabled Dayrell to whisper, "If you have a chance, mind you aim at his shoulder, and if he is galloping towards the forest, shoot well forward. By-the-bye, Villars, your cap; you really must put that red abomination in your pocket. Its colour is enough

to frighten every living creature into the next department."

Villars pocketed the offending head-piece, and,
with hair blowing about in the wind, followed his
leader up the steep and stony ravine. Dayrell made
for the right and Villars for the left of the rocks.
The former proceeded with the caution of an expe-
rienced hunter, until he caught a glimpse of two
hinds that were feeding out of gunshot, flapping
their ears, and snuffing for any taint that might
portend danger to their lord and master. There
was no possibility of a nearer approach; so having
seen Villars coiled up in the heather and in position,
he crept back, and gave the signal to Michelet. The
keeper saw it, left his hiding-place, and descended
the hill. The deer, when they perceived him, collected
together in a state of apparent indecision; then
having made up their minds, moved on slowly,
crossed a small burn, and passed within easy shooting
distance of the two. Villars' rifle was discharged in
a moment. None but the merest tyro could have
missed; but Villars' ball was not within twenty yards
of the deer, who turned and dashed up the hill-side.
Dayrell had a difficult shot, but he took time, and
that he hit him he was sure. The thud of the
bullet, and the quiet turn of the stag told him that.

"Let go the hound," he cried; and in a second

the animal was bounding across the heather, and in a minute more was out of sight behind the hill.

Hatless Villars follows in pursuit, while Dayrell remains behind to re-load his rifle. The boy is almost mad. He runs down the hill-side as though it was a level, well-kept lawn, and turns a somersault before he has gone a quarter of a mile. He is up again, following the course of the burn at a reduced pace. Now he stands on the edge of a pit, hollowed by the torrent, his hair blowing in the wind, and uncertain what to do next. The stag is at bay beneath him. Shall he attack him with the butt of his rifle or with his knife? when crack! goes a rifle behind him. The stag lowers his head, then falls on his side against a projecting rock.

"Take care, Villars," cries Dayrell, who had fired the shot. "Put your knife up, and don't go near him yet, there may still be some life in him."

But this last shot had killed him. He never moved after he fell, and in a few minutes Dayrell and Villars had slipped down the bank, and stood by his side.

"It is a stag, and that's all," said the former, in rather a disappointed tone. His horns are perfect, but small, and his weight will be nothing to talk of. Never mind, I dare say it is as much as Michelet and his assistants will care to carry to the inn."

Then the deer are larger in Scotland?" enquired
Villars. "Never mind if they are. Wait and hear
what my uncle and the others at the chateau will say.
They will call it a grand stag, and *we* shall be voted
the first chasseurs in the world. How I wish I had
hit him. I think, Dayrell, I must have touched him.
Don't you fancy he went a little lame up the hill
just before you fired? But here comes Michelet,"
and Villars ran to meet the keeper, clapped him on
the back, and plied him with so much brandy that,
had not the latter buried his head in the burn, and
drunk enough of the purer element to float a man-
of-war, he would inevitably have slept with the stag
on the open moor.

Villars was right in saying that their reception at
the chateau would be triumphant. The Frenchmen
could not understand how a man by his own unaided
genius had killed a deer. A successful shot in a
drive they could comprehend, but the manœuvres
and skill of a stalk were beyond them, and the result
hardly to be credited. Nor would they have believed it without the deer and its antlers as evidence
to the fact, for the testimony of Michelet was value-
less; an unlimited number of *gouttes* of brandy had
fired his fancy. Every time he told the story he
added a few more kilometres to the distance, and a
few more minutes to the time, until none but the

ignorant peasants who flocked to the chateau to see the deer believed a word he said. By the time that Michelet had lapsed into a state bordering on delirium tremens, and the peasantry had reverted to their old habits of tobacco smoking and habitual lethargy, the Frenchmen had found *magnifique, é tonnant,* and the like expletives sufficiently strong to describe their opinion of the deed; and, when looking on the antlers hanging in the hall with "Dayrell, 185—" written underneath, shrugged their shoulders, more than ever convinced that the talents *ces diables Anglais* exhibited in hunting and shooting could only be attributed to a very dark agency.

CHAPTER XII.

It was market day in Villeneuve—*the* event of every
fortnight in the lives of the peasantry living near
that salubrious but dull little town.   On every road
converging on the Place the natives are trooping, and
chattering in their patois, and dragging themselves
on as fast as unwieldy high-heeled sabots will allow.
Some are carrying merchandise, and some are carrying calves just three weeks old to sell to the butchers,
who are ready to murder such innocents.   Some, by
the aid of furze bushes, are driving gaunt, long-
legged pigs, keeping them straight by means of rope
harness wound round their bodies.   Even the harness may be bartered at the fair, as the wag Latour
told Dayrell on their return that evening, when pigs,
loose and unfettered, declined to go whither their
owners wished.   " Funny fellows these natives of the
Garonne.   If they cannot get rid of their pig, they
will make their expenses by selling his harness for a
few sous !"   Some are carrying hares and some are
carrying partridges, and some are not ashamed to

bring a bunch of yellow-hammers or thrushes for
Villeneuve to turn into soup, or serve upon toast. In
the town, although lawyers are busy and granting
audiences; although the tradesmen are employed
behind their counters, instead of smoking, as on
other days, in the Place; although the tax-collector
sticks to his desk; and although many have care,
thought, and calculation imprinted on their foreheads,
there are plenty of idlers who find time to loiter
about the Justice Hall, and canvass the merits of
the case of " Cordon-noir v. De Vismes."

It is ten o'clock by the village clock. The doors
of the Hall are opened, and De Vismes, his party,
and the crowd, rush upstairs into the Court, if that
could be called a Court which was only a white-
washed apartment, with the upper end railed off to
prevent the intrusion of strangers. On a dais within
this sanctum sat the judge, looking in his black robes
and round cap like the grim inquisitors in Spain. On
the left sat the *greffier*—the most nonchalant of secre-
taries, who noted the words of his superior in a book
at one moment, and at another combed his hair and
stared out of the window as if disgusted with his
thankless office. The only other persons allowed to
remain in the privileged enclosure were two representatives of the French bar, and an officer of the Court.
Outside were congregated plaintiff, defendant, wit-

ness, and spectators in one confused mass.   Happy
he who found a window-sill or wall for support, and
was not, like Dayrell, wedged between a young lady
who trod on his toe, and a brawny blacksmith, whose
elbow performed a gamut of pokes on all his ribs in
succession.

The case of "Cordon-noir v. De Vismes," stood
first on the list, but the opening was of the most uninteresting character.   The gens-d'armes' depositions
as to facts, names, and dates, in connection with the
assault on Cordon-noir at the ball, were read by the
judge, and when his dull prosy reading was finished,
the public were as wise as at the commencement.
For the men had spent that hour in whispering to
their neighbours, or making signals to comrades at
the other end of the hall; and the women, pulling
their knitting needles out of their hair, had set to
work at their new worsted stockings with their accustomed zeal.

"Monsieur Cordon-noir," shouted the officer of
the Court, at the termination of the judge's exor-
dium—a call which was followed by a shuffling of
feet, a squeezing through the living mass, and the
breathless plaintiff's appearance at the bar.   But
what a change from the dapper steward of the ball.
No black coat; no hair parted down the middle; no
studs emulating the real diamond in brightness; but

seedy clothes and unshaved face, while misery lurked in a blood-shot eye. A murmur of pity broke from some of the knitters, who sent their needles home into their hair, and breathlessly expected his evidence.

Cordon-noir's lip quivered—his arm trembled, as he raised it with well-feigned difficulty on repeating the customary oath, "Je jure—"

"*C'est un pauvre*—" cried some one in the crowd, using in addition an inadmissible expletive.

"Remove that man," said the judge to the gens-d'armes.

In two minutes the offender was seized, and taken down stairs, amidst the suppressed laughter of his friends.

This little episode over, Cordon-noir commenced his tale. He and his fellow stewards—the young unmarried men of Villeneuve—had given a ball on the fête of St. Cecilia. To show hospitality and to amuse their friends was their object, as well as to keep up a custom as old as Villeneuve. His task it had been—while his fellow stewards performed in the band, or kept the circle open for dancing—to see that all were happy, or, as he beautifully expressed it, "*bien comfortables.*" De Vismes had waltzed with energy supernatural—no one admired it more than himself. De Vismes' dancing was distasteful to

T

the ladies sitting on the benches. He and his partner were too violent. So he, Cordon-noir, had ap-
pealed to monsieur, asking him to moderate his
transports—monsieur had refused—he applied to
monsieur a second time; then the cruel barbarous
assault was committed. He was knocked down; he
was kicked; he was bruised about the arms, legs,
and head; he had had a doctor to attend him next
morning; he could not work; and he thought he
was entitled to 150 francs damages.

The judge read this evidence, and the *greffier* put
it down in his notes.

Monsieur Le Bas, a quiet barrister, and De Vismes'
barrister, rose to cross-examine.

"Bootmaker you are to all Villeneuve, Monsieur
Cordon-noir—happy man! Making 5,000 francs a
year, I dare say, eh? (Monsieur C. opened his eyes.)
Not so much—well, now-a-days, alas, bootmakers
must rough it on 3,000. You don't even get that?
Nor 1,000, nor 500, but only 300? You must
be joking, when you ask for 150 francs damages
for being prevented working, as you allege, for three
days. A very modest request. I hope, Monsieur le
Juge, you will bear it in mind. Then you were so
ill you could not go to the café? Oh, you did go to
the café; and played billiards and écarté the whole
of an afternoon and part of an evening?—a friend

asked you to do so?—no need of any explanation, Monsieur Cordon-noir, the judge will understand about the health of a poor man who could play billiards and cards for eight hours at a stretch. But I have not done with you."

"Do you know a young lady in Villeneuve, a Mademoiselle Bien-gentil?"

"I know her—yes—I know her; but she has nothing to do with this case."

"Thank you, Monsieur Cordon-noir, I am the best judge of that. Now answer me on your oath. Did she refuse to dance with you?"

"*Moi*," replied the Frenchman, gnashing his teeth, the *spretæ injuria formæ* rankling in his bosom. "*Moi!* she refuse me! The prettiest girls in Villeneuve are proud to accept me!" and forgetting the presence of the judge, Cordon-noir finished with a *par exemple* and a blank expletive.

"Monsieur Cordon-noir will recollect where he is, or he will be committed to prison," said the judge, solemnly.

"He says he never asked Mademoiselle to dance, and ——" continued Le Bas.

"I beg my brother's pardon, my client admitted no such thing," struck in Cordon-noir's counsel.

"Did you ask her to dance, and did she refuse?" enquired the judge.

Cordon-noir hesitated a moment, and answered, " No."

" He may go down, Monsieur le Juge," continued the advocate, " I have nothing more to say to him at present," he added significantly.

Two of Cordon-noir's fellow-stewards were called as witnesses of the assault, the one a hair-dresser, the other a tailor. The former described the attack upon his friend as " *barbare*" and unprovoked; said, that when on the ground his friend had been kicked, and that his life would have been in danger had the defendant not been a coward and run away.

" Pray, where were you when it happened?" asked Le Bas, in cross-examination. " At the top of the staircase, you say. Well, it was quite dark in the passage at the bottom of the staircase, the indictment says, yet you saw the assault committed. Oh, you did not see it, but you heard the noise. Pray, how do know that De Vismes did it? Oh! Monsieur Cordon-noir told you so afterwards. Monsieur le Juge will please to make a note of that."

The doctor deposed to attending Cordon-noir at his request. Did not think him much hurt—more frightened than hurt, perhaps. Did not believe there was any necessity for his being called in. Would be glad to receive a fee for a hundred such cases, they took up so little time. Had received his fee of five francs on writing a prescription for his patient.

Cordon-noir fairly boiled over on hearing this evidence. " *Cu-ill-on,*" muttered he to the doctor, handing him at the same time a five-franc-piece (for witnesses in France must be paid after they have given their evidence, and before they have left the box). " *Cu-ill-on,*" he reiterated; to which the medico replied with a shrug of his shoulders, and a promise that he would send the " poor infant" a ptisan as a cooling draught that evening.

Here rose the counsel for the plaintiff—a burly, bullying barrister, who coughed oracularly, and addressed the Court with all the declamatory vehemence and gesticulation peculiar to the French bar.

" Monsieur Le Juge,* I rise with mingled feelings of surprise and pain—surprise that the facts of this case should have been so wilfully perverted, and pain that any Frenchman should be found to defend such a cause. The facts of the case are these :—On the *fête* of St. Cecilia, the young men of Villeneuve always give a ball and send invitations to residents in the town and neighbourhood. This year they extended their hospitality to the gentlemen staying

* The author wishes it to be understood that this trial and speech is only a summary of what actually occurred in a French Court of Justice, and of which he took notes.

at present with the Comte d'Artois. Amongst the
visitors is an Englishman—I don't know his name,
but the people tell me that it means courage and
love of fighting—'Dare-all,' Monsieur le Juge, I
understand it is, and that this Monsieur Dare-all
came also to the ball. In England, I need hardly
tell you, it is the fashion for every one 'to box.'
The higher classes have exhibitions of 'the box,'
and go to them as often as we do to the opera; the
middle classes, if they do get a holiday, take a
special train and see 'a box,' in which one of the
two combatants is often killed; and the poorer
classes, if they have no quarrel on hand, make one,
so that they may finish with 'a box.' The upper
classes, again, of which Monsieur Dare-all is one,
will go to a place of entertainment, not for the purpose of being quiet spectators of what the manager
has provided, but for the sole purpose of 'making a
box.' They are rude to some people, use insulting
language to others, and even push and hit; in a
word, do anything to provoke a disturbance. When
these gentlemen from the chateau came to the ball
at Villeneuve, they—I blush to say it of Frenchmen,
my compatriots—had been tutored by this Englishman, and were prepared to make a scene. But,
mark me, they found our young men too well-
behaved, too orderly. Those Parisian gentlemen

found country people quite different to what they expected—much more polished than those they had been in the habit of consorting with. What did they do then? Listen to this. They sent to the nearest café for intoxicating drinks, invited all to partake, and turned the heads of these well-disposed youths. The defendant then set off to dance with an indecency of which Mabille would be ashamed, and with a vehemence highly disproved by the ladies of Villeneuve. My client was a steward. He, as in duty bound, stepped forward, and in the politest terms requested him to desist. Monsieur De Vismes refused, and danced more indecorously than before. My client again remonstrated. The result—a box— a *veritable box Anglais*. My client was knocked down and kicked; then the defendant and his dastardly friends ran, yes, ran away. This is the real case, Monsieur le Juge, and I say that every law that governs society has been broken. I say that, when the youth of this town, holding out the hand of good fellowship to yonder aristocrats; when my client, remembering the *entente cordiale* between England and France, cemented by mutual sufferings in the Crimea, invited an Englishman to the *fête*, and when all this was repaid by a barbarous outrage on my client, that you, Monsieur Le Juge, must redress his wrongs. Suppose the doctor did speak slightingly of

the bodily injury my client has received. What of
that? Can the prescriber of medicines and the
wielder of the knife estimate the poignant sufferings
of that client's honour? I would put you, Monsieur
le Juge, in Monsieur Cordon-noir's place. Could
you hold up your head amongst your fellow-citizens,
who so well know and appreciate your impartiality,
discrimination, and good sense, had you been as-
saulted as he was on the night of the ball? No; I
am sure you could not; therefore, I say, this is a
case for heavy damages. Show that the strong
cannot attack the weak with impunity. Put down
at once the bullying spirit imported here by a foreign
intruder. Trample under foot the spark before it
bursts into a flame. Let the defendant feel the
whole force of the law; in other words, I say, *Fiat
Justitia !*"

In answer to this inflated harangue, De Vismes'
counsel gave a correct account of the affair from the
commencement; pointed out how lamentably the
plaintiff's case had failed; and dwelt upon the testimony of the doctor as conclusive that little or no injury had been inflicted on Cordon-noir. But to show
how little dependence could be placed on what the
plaintiff said, he would call one witness.

"Call Mademoiselle Bien-gentil."

The

"Causa mali tanti, coujux iterum," &c.,

in all the plenitude of crinoline, and cap of the country, after a serious struggle, pushed through the crowd, and appeared at the bar, blushing and smiling.

"Was nineteen years of age. Had been at the ball. Did not care much for country balls; liked those at Bordeaux better. Spent three months with her aunt at the latter place. Liked them because the men danced much better, talked more, and were more *comme il faut*. Monsieur De Vismes danced like the monsieurs at Bordeaux; that was the reason she danced with him five or six times. Refused to dance with Cordon-noir because she was engaged, not because she wished to make him jealous, or because De Vismes told her. Why should he be jealous, when she was going to be married to some-one else—never mind who—in six months? Heard Monsieur Cordon-noir speak angrily to De Vismes; saw no fight, and heard no disturbance."

"Are there any more witnesses?" asked the judge, drearily, as mademoiselle retired.

"No," replied both the barristers.

"Then this Court is adjourned to Thursday, when the verdict will be given," said the judge, who straight-way retired to his ill-furnished apartment, where a supper was prepared for him, the chief component parts of which were *vin-ordinaire* and nuts; and that evening he strained his eyes over voluminous returns

from the farmers of his commune, about the amount
and quality of the cereals grown on their acres, a
careful summary of which the government requests
him every year to send.   On the morrow he went to
an "audience," in a village fifteen miles distant, and
returned wet through and dispirited, to find a messenger waiting to take him to the bedside of a dying person to witness his last will and testament.   The next
day there was an "audience" elsewhere; besides interviews with gens-d'armes and the mayor, leaving
scarcely a moment to look over the notes he had
taken at Cordon-noir's trial.   Nevertheless, this
justice of the peace, who did his duty for fifty pounds
a-year, came into Court on Thursday jaded and
haggard, and delivered this sentence.

"De Vismes is condemned to pay seventy-five
francs damages, the costs of the action, and to be
imprisoned one week."

The cordwainer and his friends rushed exulting
into the street, leaving Dayrell and De Vismes in
Court, astonished at the verdict and appealing to one
another if what they heard was true.   Still the judge
took no notice of them, but called on the next case.
The gens-d'armes, however, did not step forth and
take De Vismes by the collar, and lead him to prison
—French law on this point is kind and accommodating—De Vismes might spend his week in durance

vile just when he liked; so he waited till the end of
the shooting and hunting season, and when Lent had
commenced he went quietly and comfortably to
prison; but having bribed his gaolers, he was allowed
to break the rules, and spent the week in playing
écarté and giving dinners to his friends.

CHAPTER XIII.

THE best friends, we all know, must part, and pleasant as life at the chateau was, the party broke up after the trial, and dispersed, by no means rejoicing, in different directions. Dayrell's route lay southward, to the far-famed town of Pau, whose climate has induced more than one worthy doctor to dip his pen in ink, and give the world a notion how wrong it was not to go there. He retraced his steps to Bordeaux—beyond all comparison the most delightful of cities devoted to money-making and commerce. Let us take a turn round it on a fine morning in early autumn. Let us pay our two sous and step on to the bridge that spans the Garonne, whence we shall have a bird's-eye view of the handsomest town in Europe. Beneath us sweeps a noble river, and happily unpolluted like our whilom silver Thames. Its surface is dotted with comers and goers to and from all parts of the world; its banks, formed into quays, some three miles long, teem with countless shipping. And yet here, in the midst of commerce, we miss the noise and confusion of a Liverpool dock scene, and even the glare of a southern sun fails to discover the dirt that clings to business places in our metropolis. The Gascons do not rush hither and thither, like Bristol porters or London dock men, but treating their business as a pastime, lazily roll the bran-new casks to their stations on the quay. We think we feel the most excited of the two when we try to guess whether these same casks contain the unrivalled Lafitte, or *the* pure and unadulterated (?) Jullien, offered by Messrs. Logwood and Bark at 20*s.* a dozen to the British public. Abutting, but not encroaching, upon the causeway, are edifices of the Italian order of architecture,—palaces, a fervid imagination might fancy them, but simply warehouses for magnums of rosy wine. In the background shoot up Gothic towers and antique spires, quite as handsome as those we go so far to see in Southern Italy.

We leave the bridge, and walk up the principal street. That magnificent building is the theatre, and the two gorgeous establishments by its side, we need not add, are cafés. The knots of happy Frenchmen sitting outside, and sipping their favourite beverage, are sufficient evidence of a thriving business. In the thoroughfare there is life—*beaucoup de move-ment,* our French cicerone calls it; broughams glide

swiftly by, with fair faces within, but not Gascon, he
further tells us, but Béarnaises. If so, it must be
worth while travelling a hundred miles further south,
and seeing more of those dark flashing eyes and nut-
brown complexions. Great men, too, strut about
that street—lords of the Medoc and Haut Sauterne
vineyards—magnates in their own estimation, and
the Emperor's also, who selected them out of all
France to hear the famous speech that concluded
with the words, "*L'empire, c'est la paix.*" Stop,
traveller, for a day or two at the Hotel de France;
take our word for it, you will see, in your wanderings,
few cities to compare with this metropolis of the
South.

Dayrell, however, did not tarry long, but took
train to Dax on the morning after his arrival.
"What a change comes o'er the spirit of our dream"
after twenty minutes on that railway! The sensation of passing from a hot to a cold bath is as nothing
compared to the exchange of the princely town and
its environs, for the uncultivated department of the
Landes, and its demi-civilized inhabitants. Pine
trees, heather, sand—sand, heather, pine trees; the
latter, with deep scores in their sides, presenting a
woe-begone appearance, as though bewailing the
cupidity of man in thus extracting the resin from
their wounds. Anon we see an inhabitant mounted

on stilts, and gazing vacantly on his ragged flock. Scanty is his clothing, with the exception of his sheepskin-coat, his sole protection against rain by day and heavy dews by night. On through the same unvarying landscape, save when we halt at a station, to which no village or houses are attached, and, when our engine-driver, pitying the forlorn state of the ticket-collector, tarries beyond his time to detail small scraps of news. Still, onward, where no life is seen, save where a few ducks or teal, affrighted by the whistle, arise from the stream; still, onward, through monotonous heather-land, until we can lift our eyes and welcome the snowy peaks of the distant Pyrenees. We arrive at Dax in six hours, and more than one diligence is waiting to convey passengers to Pau. No sluggards are the latter upon the road; competition forces the pace. We trot up the inclines, and descend at a gallop, unmindful of occasional dismemberment of rope-harness, or the distressed condition of the steeds. *"Allez,"* cries the postilion, as we rattle through Orthes of the narrow streets; and it is some time after we have passed the actual scene of the combat, that we remember the battle Wellington won. *" Allez, Allez,"* over the flat, and galloping through Artix and other scattered hamlets, occupants of *coupé, intérieur,* and *banquette* are equally glad to see

the gas-lit Place at Pau.   Having landed Mr. Dayrell
at the hostelry of France, let us pause, and recover
the breath which the speed of Monsieur Bienvite's
malle-poste has nearly taken away.

Thus has it been written of the capital of Béarn,
"Pau is a delightful winter residence for such
invalids as would escape the cold and fogs of
England, and renovate a constitution impaired by
variable weather and nipping frosts.   It enjoys a
high character for its peculiar dryness of atmosphere,
and an absence of wind which renders it ——" but
really we are not Dr. Quinine; so we must stop this,
or we shall be infringing some valuable copyright.
We will begin afresh.   Although a free and enlightened public can never be expected to be unanimous
in their opinions on any point whatever, yet the vast
majority eagerly proclaim the fact that, as a winter
residence, Pau is without a rival on the Continent.
Here the fast, the slow, the clever, the stupid, may
each, according to his own taste, tranquilly float
down stream.   For some good genius, it would
appear, has awarded unto this city a fund of amusement suited to every taste.   Ask the hunter (biped,
not quadruped) if he is not content, when his coat-
tails are flying in the wind as he flits across the
landes at the tail of Mr. P.'s hounds.   Ask the
cricketer, the archer (male and female), the golf-

player, their opinion, when, on Bilhéres' broad plain
in the month of *February* (tell it not in frost-ridden
England), the first sends the middle stump flying
with a well-pitched "bailer," the second hits the
gold with Ford-like accuracy, and the third spins his
ball across the grass with such a speed as the eye can
scarcely follow. Make enquiries of the old fogies,
Messrs. Growler and Buttercup, if their declining
years are not soothed by whist at the English and
French clubs. Question Lightfoot on the subject of
dancing at Carnival-time, and that fast young gentleman will tell you it is "stunning." Even Snapshot
and Marchbrown, if not overloaded with game and
fish, return refreshed from their healthy sporting
trips. But supposing that these congenial spirits,
one and all, tire of the continuous round of pleasure;
supposing that the fragrant Léoville and the full-
flavoured Mouton have slightly disagreed with their
interior economy: still it is open to them to flit to
the pretty town of Bagnères, to see (perhaps) an
Empress at Biarritz, or witness the *Montagnards*
executing wild dances at Eaux Bonnes. Let them
change the scene for a few days, and I warrant they
return to Alma Mater (Pau) with what the dear old
Latin Grammar called

"Mens sana, in corpore sano."

But, Mr. Traveller observes, where so many

English collect, there must, of necessity, be divers clans, sets, and some struggles for precedence. In reply to you, Mr. T., let us quote the worthy man of the Rue des Tailleurs, who said, " Society at Pau, Sir, forms a republic *pure et simple*. No king or queen has ever been allowed to reign. True, like the brave old Romans, we have our consul who becomes dictator when any difficulty arises; but, having set things to rights, like his worthy proto-types, he lays aside the insignia of his office, and next day is jollily sailing with us over Sauvagnon hill in a run, or subsiding into a ditch (as the best of us must sometimes) on the flats round Morlaas. No, joking apart, what our republic has to fear is the self-constituted queen of a ' watering-place,' whose special duty in life it appears to be, to draw a line between presentable and unpresentable people—her own caprice, her own likings and dislikings, being her only guide to this undesirable end. A titled dame, ere now, has dropped down amongst us, and, in imitation of her English compatriots in the Eternal City, has invested herself with the tiara, and consti-tuted herself arbiter of society. For a time she has held her solemn receptions, and given her tea-parties, at which a few elderly ' sticks in waiting' and mild young tuft-hunters presented themselves. For a time, her attempt at forming a court interrupted the harmony that had hitherto prevailed; but the lasting element was wanting. The *salons* of the pretender were slow, those of society in general were the contrary. The 'Wednesdays and Saturdays' of the former were voted a bore, and the attendance of guests became more select; and, ere the season waned, our new Queen was compelled to lay aside the bauble she had grasped in an unlucky moment, and confess that our republic was not to be trifled with. No; Sir, the English system of exclusiveness never has and never will take root in Pau."

But Captain Finicking, of the Heavies, has a charge to prefer, and would include all foreign towns in his sweeping condemnation. He says that they are hotbeds of English sharpers, and tells stories of his brother officers, who have left Baden, Dieppe, and Florence with lightened purses. Let him try our model republic. He will not fall a victim to such adventurers as prey upon their kind. The latter thrive not at Pau. They may come, and they may stay for a few days, but, soon finding themselves in the position of "isolated birds," they take their places in the mail, and retire at the befitting hour of night to find another spot better suited to the development of their peculiar talents.

If, *mon ami lecteur*, you would wish to know more of the *dolce far niente* life of the denizen of Pau, place

yourself by the side of our hero as he smokes his
matutinal cigar on the Place. Can you conceive
anything more beautiful than the scenery? For a
back-ground to Nature's picture, there is the long
Pyrenæan range; its hundred snow-capped peaks
glistening in the sun. At their feet are hills and
dales, clothed with trees and vines, and dotted with
picturesque chateaux. Below, the tumbling roaring
Gave makes its way over a shingly bed, as yet un-
stained by the meltings of the winter snow. On
the promenade are groups of idlers, invalids, and
sight-seers, under cover of blue and red umbrellas,
which oftener do good service as a screen against the
sun than as a defence against the pitiless pelting of
the rain. In parties of twos and threes, the French
brunettes trip along the tree-lined alley—young
ladies who, by undeniable toilettes and sprightliness
of demeanour, bid defiance to the critics who would
find fault with irregularity of feature and sorry complexion. But, far out-stripping all competitors, you
see the "sunny," cheerful faces of our English girls,
who, disdaining extraneous adornment, trust to their
natural beauty and innocent ways to steal away the
hearts of us too susceptible individuals. Are you
still unsatisfied? Then step with us to the Park—
why called so we know not, seeing that it is a woody
ridge, admirably laid out, with paths, sequestered

seats, and an occasional peep cut through the foliage. Mrs. Mainchance says that these benches have witnessed many of those " promising" flirtations, and that those old cynics, the bachelors, dub them " seats of sacrifice,"—wrongfully we say, considering that it is at no ignoble altar that the victims have prostrated themselves; and we are sure that nobody can be surprised if, under (generally) cloudless skies, and amid beautiful scenery, the whole nature of man for once forgets its selfishness and inclines to languor and love.

But to our tale. There was a mighty congress at Pau in what we will call " Wild Dayrell's year." It may have been love of change, pleasure, or scenery; it is to be hoped it was not in every case incipient weakness of lungs that caused so unprecedented a gathering. There were English and Scotch, Russians and Americans, and last, not least, representatives of the Emerald Isle—not Mulligans, nor hirsute descendants of Brian-Boru, but pretty Irish girls, with good figures and just a smack of the brogue, reminding us of those we steered over Loch Corrib in days gone by, when we rowed past the wooded demesne of Clydagh, and skirted the banks of the Lake to gain a nearer view of the red-petticoated peasant girls, who, with pitchers on their heads, stopped to gaze in wonderment at us adventurous mariners; for

the rocks were dangerous, even when we steered into
the middle to see to better advantage the Connemara
mountains, and the small silvery clouds chasing each
other along their rugged sides; reminding us of the
pleasant, lively girls we took into dinner afterwards
at the hospitable mansion, who warbled Moore's
melodies when we returned to the drawing-room, and
danced to the voluptuous Olga and dashing Priscilla
airs into the smallest of the small hours; reminding
us of our companions at Killarney, whom we pic-
nicked with at the Punch Bowl and escorted to
Mucross, whom we ferried across the far-famed Lakes,
and walked with—but then it was *the* selected one—
in the fir plantations and by the mountain ravines.
And those we met in Ireland and those we met at Pau
made us such true believers in the beauty, kindness
of heart, and talents of the daughters of Erin, that
we were compelled to answer rudely their simpering
English sister when she said, " So you admire the
Irish.   Now, do tell me, don't they always let you
kiss them when you ask the favour."

One of these, Kate Berners, was a true Irish girl,
inheriting the characteristic beauty and wit of her fair
compatriots.   Do not imagine for a moment that we
are going to paint a terrestrial angel, or a seraphim in
petticoats.   We are only speaking of a blue-eyed lively
young lady of nineteen, with a good figure, and an

unaffected simple manner, that took immensely with the most critical audience. She and her mother and sister lived at some distance from the tittle-tattle of Pau, in a château on one of the hills between the Pyrenees and the town. The mother was the opposite of her daughter; a strong-minded woman, she looked to the main chance, that of marrying her daughters well, as the be-all and end-all of existence. No one knew better than she the relative value of pawns, knights, and bishops, on the matrimonial chess-board. Had the daughter but seconded her plans, the two might have given away a knight and a pawn, and fairly checkmated the cleverest of her opponents.

Dayrell first met the *famille* Berners at a dance, in the house of one of those philanthropic ladies who, having no daughters of their own, love to see others happy, or rather in fair progress to what they consider the *summum bonum* of human happiness—the tying of the conjugal knot. Now, since the sad event at Ems, Dayrell had quite altered in his behaviour to the fair sex. He never gave any preference to blonde or brunette, but, treating all alike, caused more than one Flora or Angelina to misinterpret (though they sturdily denied it) the *empressement* which he threw into his conversation. As a matter of course, a pretty girl like Kate Berners had, before

our hero's arrival, a string of admirers, all in different stages of the love-fever. A careful observer
might have ticketed them, beginning with number
one down to little Bouncer, who could get no higher
on the list than number ten. Kate's, or rather her
mother's, favourite was one Francis Townley, whose
property—his great recommendation in the maternal
eye—was a Yorkshire reality—at least so said Mr.
Burke, amongst other useful revelations. He had an
uncle too, not one of the "golden balls," but a *bond
fide* capitalist, who was supposed to have executed a
last will and testament in favour of his nephew.
When you had ascribed unto Townley the attributes
of a gentleman, you had said all you could in his
favour. Every other quality he possessed might best
be described by a negative. He was not amusing,
nor good looking, nor original (a dozen ancient
witticisms and wise saws being alone at his disposal),
nor was he a good dancer, or fond of field sports.
Let us add, that he was a "muff,"—a good natured
one, 'tis true; but it is not everybody who thinks the
latter epithet a compliment.

Dayrell was introduced to Kate early in the evening; and his fund of conversation and good waltzing
certainly made a favourable impression. He danced
three times with her, enjoyed "liberal sittings out"
over tea and negus in the other cool and refreshing

apartment, and congratulated himself on having thus early in his apprenticeship at Pau found a clever and amusing companion. Promotion in the good graces of our womankind resembles, in some respects, the much abused system in vogue in her majesty's army. To gain a step in the latter you must purchase. The highest bidder steps over the head of other competitors. Poor Couterbound's name is first on the list of lieutenants, but unto him is denied the entrance into the "glorious army" of captains. So the acre-less and fund-less individual lingers long on the bars of the matrimonial ladder, and often sadly sees the rich noodle promoted to the vacant post. But here the similarity ends, that is to say, as long our royal commander-in-chief considers promotion by selection *invidious,* for our young ladies will at times neglect the old system of purchase, and promote to the post of first favourite the most deserving, albeit, perhaps, the most penniless of their admirers. Dayrell reaped that evening all the benefits accruing from this weak point in the ladies' catechism, and jumped over the heads of many deserving candidates for Miss Kate's good opinion.

In the meantime, the maternal eye quickly mastered the situation. As we have hinted, that judicious matron had settled upon Townley as her future son-in-law, and oft as she turned restlessly in

the family four-poster, had pondered over the best
plan to make "that man" propose. In her eyes the
advent of Dayrell was a special interposition of Pro-
vidence—a kind of useful machine for awakening the
pangs of jealousy in the torpid soul of Townley; and
in her fluttering bosom she matured her scheme,—
yes, chuckled over her new idea, as we may suppose
the first Napoleon did, when he formed the "cutting
out" plan that won the battle of Austerlitz. Mothers,
as we all know, contribute more to the settlement of
the day sacred to bridesmaids and orange-flowers, than
even the strong influences that the "fair selected"
can bring to bear upon her swain. The former can
wield a potent weapon—it is called flattery. Let
them but use it with discretion, and speedily will the
booby man commit himself to that "for better or
worse" state, to the chances of which the matrimonial service candidly admits we must all be sub-
servient. In Townley's absence that evening, she
matured her plan. When returning Kate to the
shelter of the maternal wing, Mrs. Berners spoke to
Dayrell in terms the most flattering and motherly;
flattering to himself, and gushing over with affection
for her daughter. Then she hoped he would visit
them at their country retreat. "It is some little
distance," she said in excuse, "but then you have no

flowers or gardens at Pau, and no view to be compared with ours." And having fixed her arrow dexterously she sailed out of the room with Kate, leaving Dayrell in a pleasant state of flutter and surprise.

" Strange thing for me to meet such nice people the first night I go out at Pau; and Miss Kate, charming girl; no money, I suppose. Young ladies residing in foreign towns seldom have. All the more likely to find a husband who will marry her for her own merits. I should like to see a little more of them, and this ' retreat' of theirs," thought Dayrell. So three days after the ball, he was doing what the irreverent Bouncer called " the grind " in the direction of the Berners' house. It was three miles from the town, on a ridge of hills exactly opposite Pau. The *détour* that had to be made to cross the Gave took him through Jurançon, near the " Trafalgar" of Pau, where Madame Cuisine serves a dinner at a guinea a-head, and is accustomed to the sight of " flushed faces in a setting sun," and the songs that follow that disorderly symposium. Then through a well-cultivated plain to the ridge, where work for the back sinews began, and a self-imposed treadmill up a steep incline. Half-way up the ascent Dayrell stopped to take breath, and saw the trellis-work, where in summer—

" The vines (not nailed to walls) from tree to tree
Festooned, much like the back scenes of a play,
Or melodrama, which the people flock to see,
When the first act is ended by a dance
In vineyards copied from the South of France."

"Very pretty, is it not?" interrupted Crotchet, ex-captain in Her Majesty's 6—th regiment, who was paying a visit to the *famille* Berners with his friend Townley, and smoking his afternoon cigar on the terrace outside their house. "You have just arrived in time for the animated discussion going on in that drawing-room, as to how they are to put one hundred and fifty people into a room calculated to hold not more than fifty at the most, and how they can have an archery meeting in that field, surrounded, as you see, on the three sides by the public road, without seriously endangering the lives of the passers-by. I left Townley with the mother and daughters. He was then in great perplexity, stroking his moustaches, and suggesting that the bed-rooms should be turned into supper-rooms, an idea the ladies hardly relished. Do go in and help him. I will join you when I have finished my cigar."

"Can you help us to settle the point?" asked Mrs. Berners, after welcoming Dayrell to their chateau, and explaining their difficulty.

"The point settles me," he replied; "for archery I never practised. Yes, I beg pardon; I did once, speaking literally, not metaphorically, draw the long bow. It was in a new mown hay-field belonging to a clergyman *en retraite*, who devoted his time to improving the breed of cows and fowls, instead of attending to the 'cure of souls.' It may have been a judgment on him for his dereliction of duty; but my second arrow, winging an erratic flight, lodged itself in the haunch of one of his veteran grass-fed Alderney herd."

"What did he say, Mr. Dayrell?"

"Much the same as the Oxford crews did, when, on three occasions, they ran into and consequently upset my skiff on the Isis—' Now, stupid, why don't you take lessons at home before you come and practise here?'"

"I am quite surprised," said Mrs. Berners; "your county, Sussex, is famed for archers. You have Mr. Ford, at Brighton, and the Miss Mackays, at St. Leonard's, and other great performers to instruct you in the art. Besides, did you never try to win a prize at Coneyborough Park?"

"I forgot that celebrated occasion, when I won a real trophy. Small glory, however, for me, seeing that I was the only competitor for the visitor's prize. As a reward for putting one arrow into 'outer white,' the stewards offered me the choice between a curiously wrought-iron card-case and a silver arrow. I

selected the latter, intending to wear it as a breast-
pin, and was horribly disgusted at finding that, after
a few days, it lost its effulgency and displayed the
skill of the fabricator in transmuting tin, for the
time being, into the expensive metal silver. This,
perhaps, damped my ardour, and made me prefer
Lilywhite's bowling and the *ars cricketica* to the
science of archery. Sussex, in fact, only taught me
three things:—To play cricket, to ride down the
steepest hill-side fearlessly, and with a loose rein,
and to eat its far-famed pudding without fear of
indigestion. Still, it is fair to state, that I left it at
an early age, and have been a wanderer ever since."

" You would not have left Yorkshire so soon,"
said Townley. " It is the finest county in England,
has the prettiest scenery, and the most hospitable
inhabitants."

" I thought very little of it, when I stayed near
Malton on my return from the Highlands. I saw
nothing but flat moorlands, a cold soil, and had
indifferent shooting."

"Everything in this world is comparative" (a
stereotyped Townleian phrase). " If you had come
from any other part of the world but Scotland, you
would have told a very different tale."

" Mr. Townley is always comparative," said Kate.
" The other day he said our house, gardens, and

view, would appear quite tame to any person coming from Berne or Tivoli."

"Mr. Dayrell has not seen the garden," Mamma put in. "Take him out, Kate, and show him the view that all our visitors admire so much."

Exeunt Miss Kate and Dayrell through the open window into the garden, cut into those fantastic shapes — triangles, octagons, and crescents — that English horticulturists love, with grass walks between the beds and turfed slopes at the four sides, with knotted roots of trees for seats, and fanciful arbours, where roses and blackthorns grew most luxuriantly, the handiwork, for the most part, of Kate, *vice* the old Benedictine Abbot resigned. Pretty little heretic, as she appears in her garden-hat and long strings; verily, the old superior Benedictinus would turn round in his coffin yonder, and forgive the usurpation, could he but see her tripping along the walk in this whilom home of the faithful. Even the old carp in the pond—cotemporaries, they say, of many an abbot, and of any age from 50 to 500—must love the change of dynasty, and the fair hands that throw them crumbs of bread. See, how they testify their confidence by lazy rises to the surface, and still lazier descents to their sub-lily retreats; and our Kate's merry laugh rings through the summer-house that overhangs the perpendicular hill-side—happy change from the old abbot's solemn voice—not always so solemn either, if what they say be true, that ofttimes that holy man, with his brother *convivæ*, here passed the hours of eve, sipping the best of Bordeaux wine.

" So those, Miss Berners, are the remains of a real abbey, and you did not build an artificial ruin by way of adding to the natural beauty of the scene. I suppose the old lay brethren, like Sheridan's monks, used to waddle down to this summer-house with corkscrews hanging from their waists, and bottles in each hand to set before their Sanctissimus Pater."

" I am afraid, Mr. Dayrell, you are a very poor historian," answered Kate. " The art of making bottles was not invented in those days" (she had read that in the " Welcome Guest ; " Dayrell saw it open on the table at the very place, as he came in), " they used leathern jugs."

" You are quite right, Miss Berners, similar to those they had at Winchester College and the Hospital of St. Cross. We boys used to tell old Governor Swipes, as we irreverently nicknamed the porter of the latter place, to fill the ' flowing ' jug with my Lord of Guildford's mild ale. He did so. On one occasion, when his back was turned, we emptied a handkerchief of gravel and dust into the same receptacle of beer. He was not friendly after that, not at all; he literally drove us from his door when we petitioned for a refreshing draught."

" How very mischievous," observed Kate; " and yet I ought not to say much, for my cousins behaved quite as shamefully to their papa and his friends, when one 20th of August they abstracted the whiskey from the flask, and the beer from the case-jar, and refilling each with water, dispatched them with luncheons to the moors."

And so they talked, and left the summer-house for a peep, cut through the foliage, and which commanded one of the finest views of the Pyrenees. They saw in front the grand line of the snow-clad mountains, the pine forests clinging to their sides, and the green flax fields at their base, relieving the eye when dazzled by the whiteness of the snow, or wearied by the more sombre colour of the trees. To the north they had a severe contrast to the former, in the apparently interminable plain, in which the works of man—the white houses, the chateaux of Pau and Bizanos—were but as mere specks in the indefinite sweep of the landes and forests.

"Magnificent," observed Dayrell. "I must confess that this view is far more splendid and comprehensive than that which my friend the baron commands from his chateau near Rouen, and so proudly said of it —' Voila, monsieur, la vue de l'Univers.' I can see

x

the Pic du Midi and the Mount Perdue, but not the Maladetta."

"That is not visible from here," said Kate; "all our visitors ask for it, because it is the highest peak of the Pyrenees. Then they declare their intention of scaling it next summer, but in October are sure to find some excuse for their failure. Captain Crotchet came back and said that there was too much snow—far more than ever had been known before. Poor little Mr. Bouncer confesses to having mounted half-way to the summit, when the Spanish guides objected to ascending higher without an extra douceur, and 'you know,' he innocently admits, 'I wasn't big enough to threaten them with summary chastisement if they would not adhere to their original agreement.'"

Prattle on, pretty Kate, and enter fully into the spirit of the three-volumed novel that Dayrell says he will write, taking the legends of the Pyrenees for a subject, and your "eyrie" as the habitation of the haughty baron who wooed y⁰ fair maiden of humble origin, and who in consequence of the said baron's advances, thought proper to drown herself. For further particulars respecting which, apply to the author of that original work entitled "La Bidosse." Talk on, we say, while Townley is fidgeting in yonder drawing-room, and is sorely perplexed by the ques-

tions of your indefatigable mamma. That able
tactician knows how a little judicious rivalry fans the
flame of love; and has she not done well, in the
words of the sporting writers, to put in Dayrell to
make the running for the favourite Townley. Let
us—carrying out the same metaphor—hope that she
will not, like some clever trainers, make any mistake
in the capabilities of the respective competitors for
the Berners stakes. Even when at length she per-
mits Townley to go into the garden, she keeps him
by her side like a Blenheim spaniel with a string,
anxious, as she says, to have the opinion of an author
upon horticulture (Townley had once written a letter
to the *Field*, deprecating the use of manure water for
roses, and had been severely handled by Hawthorn,
Mignionette, and other correspondents in consequence), as it was her intention to make some new
flower beds in the spring.

"You cannot do better," drawled out Townley, in
answer to a volley of questions, and quoting a part
of his celebrated epistle to the paper. "Continue to
prick off the tender plants, and forward them as
much as possible."

"That is Kate's business," said mamma, innocently
adding, "I wonder where she has taken Mr. Dayrell.
Let us look in the arbour; every one goes there to
see our view of the mountains."

Totally unconscious of the maternal scheme, or of being the cause of inquietude to Townley, Dayrell sauntered back into the garden with Kate, and met Mrs. Berners and her victim.

"A splendid view you have," said he, addressing the latter, "and a delightful country, though hardly one that we fox-hunters should admire. Yet I cannot agree with my Leicestershire friend, who says he hates a country he cannot cross on horseback."

"That reminds me," said Mamma, "that Kate wants to see your hounds. Do you think it safe for her to go? If a party could be made for Wednesday, and you could join, Mr. Dayrell, I would place implicit confidence in your keeping her out of mischief and danger. Mr. Townley says that he rides but little, and would sooner drive to the meet."

Dayrell was far too good a judge to refuse such "crumbs of comfort" as chance threw in his way. So he remarked, glancing first at Kate, and then looking full at Townley, "We shall be highly honoured with the duties imposed upon us." An assumption that called forth at the moment no reply from Mr. T. Dayrell then took his leave, having refused an invitation to dinner, which Townley and Crotchet accepted, wisely preferring this hospitable table to the wretched *cuisine* of the Hotel de la Poste.

"Splendid girl, is she not, Crotchet? Did you hear her sing that, what's its name, from *Don Giovanni—Dolla sua pace?* No affectation about her, I tell you, like Fanny Tibbets, or Clara Fane, but her whole soul was in the music. Crotchet, old fellow, I will tell you a secret, but you must promise not to repeat it. A lady is the cause of my visit to the South of France. You ought to have seen the pretty girl in Yorkshire, with whom I fell desperately in love, to the horror of my mother and sisters, who were afraid of my marrying her. They disapproving the match, implored me, literally on their knees, to travel for a year, and so, if possible, forget her. Almost the first person I meet is the counterpart of my . . . . . The same hair, the same complexion, the same figure; upon my word, Crotchet, I hardly believe my eyes, but she is as like as ——"

But the simile was not completed by the speaker, who will at once be recognized as Townley, when, on returning to Pau, after the Berners dinner, he relieved his breast of his overwhelming secret.

The net has been skilfully laid, thought Crotchet; the lark is gradually coming down from that high flight it took some three weeks ago, when it warbled so melodiously about the absurdity of marriage, and a man tying himself up for life. Pretending igno-

rance, however, of his friend's design, he simply
remarked,—

"I suppose, Townley, you will ask her to sit
for her portrait, which you can hang in your room,
and keep as a constant reminder of your Yorkshire
original."

"Nonsense, Crotchet; you know what I mean,—
I ought to marry at once, and as —— in Yorkshire
is out of the question, why not Kate Berners? If I
only knew how to begin, I would soon find an opportunity of proposing. What did you say to Miss
Blades, Crotchet?"

"Said very little, as far as I can remember. A
squeeze of the hand (it was at supper after a ball),
a look into her eyes, and a whisper about 'mine for
ever,' finished the most important part. In two
minutes all was over but the task of persuading her
guardian to look at my governor's unpunctually-paid
subsidies in the light of a valuable property, in
which, as you know, I was unsuccessful. Popping
the question, my dear fellow, is the easiest thing in
the world, especially for acred and funded esquires
like yourself. Shake off all timidity; be natural for
once; go at the fence in earnest, and I warrant you
will land safe on the other side."

"Easy it may be perhaps; but I have an idea she
will refuse me point blank. Did you see how she

walked with that Dayrell this afternoon? You heard,
I suppose, the remark she made, when I told her
that I thought of applying for the post of attaché to
the embassy at Vienna—that she read in some book,
that a man only became a diplomatist, because he
was good for nothing else."

"Suppose she does politely 'remand' you, there
will be no great harm done. You must wear the
willow like a man, or wait a little, and then try
again. It is wonderful how young ladies, when
they have thought the matter over, and become,
as it were, accustomed to it, will change their
minds. Stay; I have it. Why not propose to the
mother?"

"Propose to the mother!"

"I mean for Kate. Make a long speech to
the maternal parent. Dwell pathetically on the
unalterable state of your feelings. Delicately hint
that you can make a respectable settlement, and
wind up by asking for her intercession with the
daughter."

"A capital idea," said Townley, as he stood on
Pau bridge, and looked down on the Gave, as it
sparkled in the moonlight. "Propose to the mother,
that will simplify the proceedings."

And the two worthies bid each other good night.
Crotchet wended his way to the French club to see

if Monsieur Diabole was following up his nightly
vein of luck at *écarté*, and Townley to his pillow,
where he conned over a masterly and effective speech,
every word of which he had forgotten by the time
he awoke next morning.

CHAPTER XIV.

ARCHERY is a pretty and lady-like amusement. On the plain of Bilhéres, below the park at Pau, it is conducted on much the same principle, and with about the same average of good and bad shooting, as elsewhere. But we have our doubts, whether it is a judicious field for the aspirant to matrimonial honours to practice her *role*. True, that at the meeting of the fair competitors, beauty's bow is strung by the hand of her admirer. By him are her "snakes" disembowelled from the tenacious sward, and her arrows picked up and restored at the end of each round. But when these opportunities for carrying on the game of flirtation have been enumerated, all has been said that can be put down to the credit-side of archery. There is too much attention required; too much absence of mind on the part of the fair performer; too much moving backwards and forwards between the butts; and too large a concourse of the fair sex, to render it a profitable occasion for "improving" an acquaintance. Besides, no girl, when in the presence of her fair rivals, likes to give too much encouragement to a suitor,—a fact that may, or may not, account for the indifference with which Townley was received by Kate at the next meeting of the Toxopholites.

Bravo, little Ellen Callister, you have hit the gold, and Fanny Tibbets, of the commanding stature and strong muscular development of arm, steps forward and congratulates the little girl in all the conscious-ness of her own superior talent. Townley calls it a *coup doré*, and is rebuked by Fanny, who remarks, that if, instead of making French jokes, he would abstain from treading on her arrows, he would render her a great service. Yes, Miss Tibbets, of the Basses Plantes, has the command of ἐπεα πτεροεντα. No one we should like better to have on our side in a tough discussion. So we will make a memorandum to dance the first and fourth quadrilles with her at Mrs. Mainchance's ball to-night. That attention may be returned with interest, ere many days have elapsed. Other good shots are made, and more applause is given; then the numbers are counted, and victory is awarded to the *blondes*, who, with becoming modesty, attribute their success to luck. An impro-vised luncheon in a tent follows, and Townley seizes the opportunity of letting off some bad jokes about long bows, Beau Brummel, &c., that would have brought tears into the eyes of that jocose individual, Joe Miller himself. Kate said nothing; but Townley was too conceited to put a right construction on her silence.

In comparison, however, with this scene, how differently every body turned out to meet the hounds on the appointed Wednesday. The sport of kings, as Mr. Jorrocks termed it, is quite the opposite to the tame *passer le temps* amusement of archery. Look at Kate with her feathers flying, and the colour mantling on her cheek, as by the lightest of touches she let her horse know that she has a whip, and could use it if she chose; and look at the steed itself, who, if it has not the points of an Eclipse, seems made to carry so light and lovely a burden. "Jolly companions every one," in pink and sable coats respectively, are jogging along the Bordeaux road, all of them determined to be in at the death of the wily animal, provided they are not spread-eagled first in some bog in the landes. There are carriages *en route,* with ladies inside, who for the nonce will talk sporting, and ask anxiously when the hounds will "throw off," and what covers are to be "drawn." Townley is not on wheels, as intended, but rides one of Boiteux's hacks, which that worthy tells him *ne tombe jamais.* "The *mechant* bit that piece out of his knee," continues Boiteux, seeing his customer glance suspiciously below, "*mais il ne tombe jamais, jamais.*" And Townley bestrides the animal that never falls, after the manner of a French priest who visits the distant parts of his cure once a month on horseback. He sits well forward on his saddle, his toes are turned out, the tips of his feet only being in the stirrup irons, and his bridle is nearer his chin than the pommel of his saddle. Yellow cords, glossy hat, patent leather boots, and white kid gloves, complete Townley's preparations for the chase. But master huntsman and hounds are at the meet, picturesquely grouped in the fern and heather of the race course, some minutes before the most punctual members of the hunt arrive.

"Remember, Miss Berners, you are under my guidance to-day," said Dayrell, riding up in full hunting costume. "Your mother made me commander-in-chief, so if we find a fox, you must allow me to pilot you through the lanes."

"Oh! never mind me, Mr. Dayrell, I shall be safe enough with"—this was said *sotto voce*—"Fanny Tibbets as a chaperone; Mr. Boiteux's horse," she added archly, "*may* run away, and then I cannot help seeing some of the fun. But look," continued she, pointing with her whip to an object in pink disappearing behind a bank; "that man will certainly kill himself. That is the second time he has alighted on his horse's neck. So unnecessary too. Why does he not stay in the road?"

"He officiates as amateur whipper-in," replied Dayrell. "He is a munificent subscriber to the hunt, and is allowed to show off in that questionable manner. You see his efforts have not done any good; for that hungry hound Bountiful, having pounced upon a rabbit, scented mischief from afar, and has retired into the brake with the remains of bunny in his mouth."

The hounds drew at least half-a-dozen coverts blank, and, when a fox was found, behaved scurvily, disappointing the ladies who came to view a pretty sight. We cannot record a fact like this; "that an old dog-fox broke cover, and, waving his brush in defiance, faced the open with all the gallant bearing of his species." On this occasion the wily one slipped away, and the field had to take it upon faith that they were pursuing a *bonâ fide* fox. They spent an uninteresting quarter of an hour in cantering along rides in single file, in threading their way through sylvan alleys, and, more than once, swishing through the overgrown brushwood. It even looked at one moment, by the sudden turn the hounds made, that Reynard's fate was prematurely sealed; in which case Kate would have received a brush, and certain timid people been delighted by the premature conclusion of the run. Happily, however, it was ordained otherwise; for the fox suddenly made up his mind that the woods were no longer tenable, and set his head northward for the stronghold of Sauvagnon.

That the first flight went well we are in a position to affirm, from having had many opportunities of witnessing their performances. But as, for the nonce, what befell the ladies, or rather lady and Dayrell, is of more importance, we must content ourselves with reporting the deeds of those who played the humble part of follow my leader. Boiteux's nag, with a light weight and a willing rider on its back, had not the slightest objection to the "obstacles," but took them in such legitimate on-and-off style, as to deceive Kate into the idea that hunting was all "plain-sailing." Her confidence, as well as her excitement, increased each minute; so much so that her handkerchief, which she accidentally dropped, was sacrificed to the goodness of the pace, and is, perhaps to this day, fluttering in some retentive furze bush. "How very unlady-like." Perhaps it is; but forgive her, madam, if you please, excitement may have once carried you beyond the strictest rules of decorum.

"Well done, Miss Berners, none but the brave deserve the brush," cried Dayrell, as he and Kate emerged into a lane. "Follow me, and, as long as the hounds run in this direction, we can, by riding parallel, keep them in view."

His orders were strictly followed by Kate, much to the detriment of her habit, so far as copious splashing and mud can injure that unsightly garment.

"Steady," said our pilot, checking his fair companion. "The hounds have turned to the right. *Can* you face the Landes a second time?"

The appeal was answered by Kate—or rather her horse—scrambling over a bank, and the pair were again within reasonable distance of the flying pack. We must be allowed in this hunting narrative to change the proverb, "Pride comes before a fall," into "A fall follows a display of pride." Look at young Skittles, how he plumes himself on the way he charged that Aylesbury double, and proudly alludes to his performance, as he gallops by the side of the steady, earnest Master of the Pack, who thinks jumping quite secondary to what the hounds are doing. The next yawning ditch provides a berth for poor Skittles, and the M. F. H., with a look of pity, mutters to himself, "Better for him if he had been thinking about what he had to do—a fall follows a display of pride." So—and we are very sorry to have to record it—our pretty Kate, in the exhilara-

tion of the moment, called Dayrell's attention to a
small brook over which she had triumphantly jumped.
This momentary diversion from the attention she had
hitherto paid to her horse, caused the animal to
blunder at a bank, and land its fair rider on the
green turf of a lane.   Dayrell was at her side, and
assisting her in a moment.   To his question, " Are
you hurt ?" he received a reassuring reply in the
negative.   Some valuable moments, however, were
lost in shaking out disordered plumes and re-adjust-
ment in the saddle.   But no sooner placed there than
she expressed her wish to go on, and strained her
eyes to catch a glance of the flying pack.   Alas !
pretty Kate, the loss of a few minutes in a run are
irrecoverable.   You may look where you will, but
you will neither see nor hear anything in those fields
where, but just now, men, hounds, and horses passed
in their joyous career.   Like Robinson Crusoe, you
may light upon the imprints of their feet, and so
hunt the trail; you may see the broken bank where
the tail scrambled over, and the open gates where
Messrs. Shirk and Crane passed through and avoided
a dangerous fence.   But no living thing will meet
your eye, unless it may be an old rook, who,
perched on a bough aloft, salutes you with its mocking
caw.

   " It is no use persevering, Miss Berners, we are

not likely to fall in with the hounds again; and, besides, I think your horse is lame. It would be better for us to look for some farm house, where the mud might be removed from your habit, and then ride slowly home. If you don't wipe out those ugly stains, the authorities at your house will never let you hunt again, and might, on your arrival, hand you over to the doctor's tender mercies."

Kate cast one wistful look in the direction the hounds had taken, one rueful glance at the line of hills topped by the forest of Sauvagnon, and said with a sigh, "We were going so well, when my horse made that stupid mistake. I had set my heart on winning the brush to-day. But I suppose, Mr. Dayrell, we must go home."

Dayrell was not one of those who subscribe to the idea, that every man admires the lily but loves the rose. Courage, better expressed by the word pluck, in his eyes, was of far more worth than the gentler attributes of the fair sex. Possibly a maid of Saragossa, a Joan of Arc (provided they were pretty), or a Beatrice de Cenci, would have won his heart in the presence of the powerful rivalry of drooping eyelashes and impassive beauty, yes, even of Andalusia. In a new light had Kate Berners suddenly appeared to him,—to him who for two years and a-half had been almost insensible to woman's presence, or at

Y

the most had treated such as he met to the barren
honours of common-place talk. No man falls so
surely or so precipitately as he who puts implicit
faith in his powers of resisting woman's fascination.
Like the water of a mill-dam that has been pent up
for years, and only niggardly poured its silver stream
on the wheel, when some chance causes it to burst,
its rush and flood are fearful. So Dayrell's feelings
seemed to break loose within him, and the old nature,
which never can be shaken off entirely, resumed its
sway, all the more strongly from the artificial barrier
that had so long enthralled it.

Dayrell could talk fluently and to the point on
most subjects. But now, when he breathed the
passion he felt into his conversation, his words fell
with an irresistible force. Kate listened, more astonished than convinced, to what he said. That the
immaculate Dayrell should descend from his pedestal,
was, after what she had heard of his character, an
unexpected result. Is he in earnest? thought Kate,
or is it only the infatuation of a moment? And she
might, there and then, have lent herself to the former
notion; she *might* have been led into the belief of a
good time coming; or, who can tell, *might* have
heard the all-important question asked, Will you or
will you not? Such things are at times done very
suddenly. But the solution of the mystery was not

to be. Certain goodly sail-of-the-line appeared in
the horizon, to wit, Fanny Tibbets with her convoy,
who, in all the gushing innocence of the unmarried
state, poured forth their endearing expressions, " So
glad you are not lost," &c., accompanied by signi-
ficant glances that were not lost upon Kate. Unlucky meeting! that consigned our Kate to the
cross-examining Fanny Tibbets, and Dayrell to Ellen
Callister, whom he endeavoured to amuse with such
stray ideas as came uppermost in his mind on their
road back to Pau.

Thus Dayrell, through Diana's agency, scored the
odd trick; but he was by no means sure of the game,
much less of the rubber. Townley still held cards
in his hand, such as a skilful player might easily turn
to advantage. He might finesse his queen of trumps,
or, if that manœuvre failed, he still had a rich hand
to fall back upon. That the latter lost to-day was
by no means his fault. As he said, on his return to
Pau, his horse was a puller, and carried him unwilling through briar and brake in the wood where they
found, the results of which were manifested in a
crushed hat, a barked nose, a scratched face, and an
unfortunate rent in the yellow cords. Altogether,
the consequences of his day's hunting much resembled
those of our tennis-playing tyro, who told us in
lugubrious accents how he had spent his last half-

hour. "I went to the court," he said; "I became very hot; I missed the ball; I tumbled down; I cut my knees; I scratched my hands; I broke my racket; and then the marker called out, 'Worse than nothing!'"

CHAPTER XV.

THREE years have elapsed since we had occasion to visit the legal sanctum. Tales still occupies his well-worn arm-chair, a thought more grey, perhaps, but plodding and persevering, as in days of yore. Dayrell's affairs have lately occupied much of his attention, and, more than once, has he grimly smiled, when thinking how his management has succeeded, and his prophecies have been fulfilled. Freeholds, leaseholds, and ground rents have not been hurried into the market, but sold gradually, and at the right moment. Debts have been paid with the funds thus realized; and, on his arrival at Pau, Dayrell received a welcome letter that informed him of the result. "There was but one thing wanting," Tales wrote; "your signature to certain deeds; and, if you cannot come here, my junior partner will bring the papers to you." A pleasant arrangement for our hero, who, for many reasons, did not wish, at present, to leave the South of France.

But a circumstance of far greater importance to

Dayrell had occurred in the interim—the sudden
decease of a maiden aunt. This excellent lady,
when the news of her nephew's pecuniary downfall
was communicated to her, in the sorry-to-tell-you
accent, that relatives love to affect, did not, as
some aunts would have done, wipe out the dis-
honoured name from her last will and testament,
but appointed two trusty guardians of the 20,000*l.*
she had intended to leave him, without whose sanc-
tion the capital could not be touched. When, after
the manner of flesh in general, she retired to that
bourne, where countless distributions of flannel and
coals to the sick and needy are no doubt rewarded,
Dayrell found himself in the possession of comparative riches, and the necessity for living in a garret,
which, by-the-bye, he had never recognized, entirely
superseded. In his present position, he felt like a
passenger coming by steamer from the opposite side
of the channel, who, at first starting, without being
in actual danger, has been rarely tossed about, and
rejoiceth when, under the lee of the land, he finds
himself in still water, and rapidly approaching the
port.

At this juncture arrived Tales' partner, the bearer
of parchments, with the red wafer in the corner,
which the law required Dayrell to touch and
solemnly declare, "This is my act and deed." We

never could understand the mystic rite, but suppose it is somehow connected with the dark ages, maybe with the practice of Crusaders and others, when they laid their hands upon altars, and bound themselves to undertake some unpleasant adventure. But, however important the touching of the wafer may be, we hope the personal character of the witness does not affect the binding nature of the ceremony. We presume it does not, on the ground that unworthy priests and judges may perform their respective duties, without detracting one iota from the benefits, which, by virtue of their office, they confer. Were it otherwise, Hamber, Tales' agent, would not have been a proper bearer of the legal documents.

Hamber was the son of a rich man, who, having made his money by industry, had no idea of allowing his hopeful to pursue an aimless life of indolence. " Sir," said paterfamilias one day to his son after dinner, " you must work, or you will never have a penny of my money." So, bowing to stern necessity, Hamber, junior, followed the paternal advice, and sacrificed himself on the altar of writs and parchments. In course of time, Tales, for pecuniary consideration, was induced to receive him as a partner, and straightway endeavoured to make the most of his new recruit. It would be doing Hamber much injustice to suppose that he was deficient in ability,

or shrewdness.   As a Bersagliero, or Guerilla, of the
legal profession, his talents were invaluable.   Were
you to offer him fifty or a hundred pounds to do
something out of the routine,—for instance, trace a
bill, for which no consideration had been given, or
arrange with Levi, or Solomon, for the return of
Spendthrift's acceptance—no one would be more
competent to hunt out the former, or badger the
latter.   It was to the drudgery of business that his
soul refused to stoop, and made Tales regret that he
had received such a partner.

Hamber's arrival at Pau was, of course, celebrated
by a dinner at the Hotel de France.   Garderes, by
express appointment, brought from the inner crypt
the cobweb-covered bottles of Lafitte, in which his
heart delighted ; at least, we may conclude so from
the price charged in the bill.   The first magnum
was rapidly waning and approaching the condition
known to the *cognoscenti*, as a "marine."   Jean, the
waiter, inwardly anathematizing the habits of those
English, had in vain warned them of the late hour
by frequent flourishes of his napkin, when it struck
Dayrell that his new professional adviser would be an
excellent confidant for certain love-passages between
Kate Berners and himself.   On hearing the name,
Hamber pricked up his ears.

"Berners—Berners—not the plaintiff in the chancery suit, is it? I thought I had quite done with that name. A few months ago, I had every reason to dislike its repetition, so often did it occur in a voluminous brief that I had to copy for the firm to which I was articled."

"The same, I should imagine," answered Dayrell. "I understand they claim some estate in Lancashire, and that the second hearing of the case has been anxiously expected for the last two months."

A low whistle escaped from Hamber. "Extraordinary circumstance," he began; "the most extraordinary I ever recollect. Independent of what I know from the papers I had to copy, I happen to be acquainted with a fact that might—I say *might*—go a long way to secure a verdict for your friends. The case, I believe, is this. The plaintiffs rest their claim on being direct descendants of a Mons. La Touche, who died more than a hundred years ago. He left a son and a daughter. Your friends have to prove that the former died intestate, and without legitimate children. Here is the hitch; no records can be found. The firm I belonged to issued advertisements asking for information. The only reply they received was an anonymous letter, in which the writer stipulated, first, that no questions were to be asked as to how the knowledge was obtained; and secondly, that a large reward should be paid before the trial

came on. This proposition did not at all suit our
chief. Still, not liking to throw away a chance, he
gave me a kind of roving commission to find out the
man, and bring him, if possible, to reasonable terms.
I went four times, at least, to the coffee-house in the
city, from which the letters were addressed, before I
met the writer. He was a tall, dark-complexioned
man, of perhaps fifty years of age, more like an
Italian courier than an Englishman, and with a
slightly foreign accent 'You know my terms, Mr.
Hamber,' he said, after I had introduced myself, and
stated the object of my visit. 'If you are prepared
to accede to them, we can do business immediately.'
'Your secret, Mr. Thompson,' I said, 'is worth
nothing to other people. You may as well tell us;
depend upon it, we shall be prepared to give a very
liberal reward if, through your agency, we get a
verdict.' 'Ahem!' remarked Thompson, looking
slily at me. 'You ought to know, Mr. Hamber, the
uncertainty of the law; for ready money down the
secret is yours, and not otherwise.' 'But consider,'
said I, 'my chief's position. Supposing he pays the
money you ask, and your information is useless, what
a scrape he will be in with his client.' 'I cannot
help that, Mr. Hamber, I can make no alteration.
Mind, I tell you I am the only person who can put
you in possession of such papers as you require.

You must come to me, sooner or later, if you wish to obtain them.' In short, I could do nothing with him, and as Mrs. Berners objected to paying so large a sum, Mr. Thompson's acquaintance was dropped. He gave me one hint, however, before I left the coffee-room, to show perhaps that his agency could not be dispensed with. 'The certificates,' he said, 'are not in England; you may search for them, Mr. Hamber, but you never *can* find them.' Thus the matter stood when I left the firm four months ago. Whether the *soi-disant* Mr. Thompson has become more communicative in the interim I have no means of knowing."

"Hamber," said Dayrell, "this must be worth an enquiry. If I could raise the money, and I can too, it would be the very thing for me to obtain this information of Thompson's. Help yourself. Why are you looking so grave?"

"It is all moonshine, my dear Sir; no good can come out of it. Mark my words, it is only throwing good money into the dirt."

"I 'll try it, Hamber, I will indeed, and you must go to town and find that Thompson. You know I am in funds again; and, if we succeed, I will make you a handsome present."

Hamber smiled at Dayrell's excitement, but, feeling that any attempt to dissuade him this evening would be useless, he trusted to a night's reflection modifying his client's scheme.

"No liqueur, you say, Hamber; suppose we adjourn the meeting. I will introduce you to one of the phases of life in these parts—a French club, not political, but where the cry instead of ' *Vive l'Empereur*,' is ' *Vive l'Imperiale.*' "

Representatives of various nationalities haunted the French *cercle* in those days. English, French, Irish, Germans, Spaniards, Americans, Moldavians, and Russians joined the nightly *réunions*, and watched with unwearying anxiety the cards dealt for écarté or Imperiale. Oh! for the graphic pencil of a Hogarth, to sketch the faces that flitted round that green table. Oh! for a Thackerœan pen to trace their characters and antecedents. Mons. Diabole, owner of the noisy voice, and distributor of apropos remarks, first demands our attention. His signal good luck, as much as his cast of feature, causing his name to be Anglicised, and dwelt upon with much emphasis. Report coupled his name with slave-trade transactions at Sierra Leone. People who visit him, say that he still retains a " bit of ebony" at his house in the Basses Plantes, as a sort of

Memoria temporis acti.

That stout and burly barrister yonder is Monsieur

Hautvoix. He gives good and well-meant advice to young England. "Don't play," he says, "with that *canaille*,"—elegant name for his compatriots. "They will win five francs of you, take them to market to-morrow, and buy themselves a cabbage!" That tall Russian is a hero of Kars, whom the English good-naturally call "the old card," and in their innocence believe that not only is he one of Alexander's spies (what Russian traveller escapes the imputation?) but that he is ignorant of the Saxon tongue. So, when the Russian once approached a table where two British youths, not liking their bad play to be criticized, were finishing a game of écarté, he heard one remark to his companion, that it was only "the old card." Fancy the astonishment of the speaker, when the colonel, looking him full in the face, said, "It is lucky, Sir, you have a *trump card* to deal with!" That pale man is the representative of the Court of Moldavia, whose good humour no amount of bad luck can upset; and opposite is the "insensate" Russian, who, no matter how the game goes, never moves a muscle of his face. The player is the French banker; see how affectionately he handles, and gloats over, his cards, if at all favourable. Last, not least, look at our countrymen, led, but not like lambs, to the slaughter, for with energy do they back the losing side, and "cover" countless

Napoleons, confidently exclaiming *"Je fais le jeu."*

Townley seldom played; but this evening was an exception to the rule. Fortune had honoured the side nearest the door with most of her favours. The wise men of Pau have been hanging back, or, like beasts of prey, awaited the moment when something should be thrown in their way. Townley now takes possession of the unlucky seat, smiles complacently on his opponent, the oily banker—deals the cards slowly, we may say primitively, and, with a *" Je vous salue, Monsieur*," bows to the red face opposite. England's representative would have fared ill if left to his own devices, but a white-visaged mentor sits by his side, and, in reality, plays the game for him. France pulls the strings, and England obeys the impulse. *Malheureusement*, grumbles the disconcerted banker at the end of an unsuccessful game, and yields his place to another, who is likewise discomfited by Townley, and retires more quickly than his prede-cessor. Backers flit to Townley's side. The vultures flock to the slaughter, and pile dollars where but just now the wheedling supplications of Diabole could not bring the paltry stake of twenty francs. Again luck follows old England. Dayrell winks to Hamber, and whispers the old proverb about bad luck in love being followed by good at play.

"The pass," of the evening collects stragglers from all parts of the room. Townley's politeness and "salutations" are pushed to a point verging on imbecility. Every time he dealt he bowed and repeated the complimentary words. Still further he pursued his winning way. An obdurate quartette alone faced the tide of luck. Even they retired disgusted, when Townley passed for the eighth time. There was a pause. Who would take up the gauntlet? France does not think it a good thing, and Russia hangs back. Then Dayrell stepped into the breach, and Moldavia brought up its supports, and the gallant pair challenged Townley plus the world.

"Put on as much money as you like, we will cover all," said the former to his opponents; an order they obeyed with such alacrity as to upset the calculations of Townley's mentor, quick and clever though he was at figures.

The money is counted, and piled on Townley's left hand.

"*C'est ça*," cried Dayrell; "*le jeu est fait*. Cut Townley, if *you* please. I have the queen—you the ace—it is my deal."

"*Combat à l'Anglais*," suggests the burly barrister.

"De race for de Derby," squeaks Diabole, imitating a common phrase amongst the English.

The sun continues to shine upon Yorkshire

Townley scores four points to his adversary's one. It is the former's deal, and he turns a King. Twenty hands drop suddenly on the money—grasping, pushing, seizing—emblematic of French politeness, so much talked of, and so seldom practised, when Dayrell discovers that his adversary has mis-dealt, and given him six instead of five cards. Such a restitution of dollars and such a hubbub ensues. We warrant there is not a Frenchman on the opposite side that does not connect the mistake with a robbery of the most barefaced description. The game is renewed. Four, scores Dayrell after the next deal, and so the point of " quatre a" is attained. Tremble, ye French backers of Townley, and reckon not on a dinner to-morrow. Your champion asks for fresh cards and is refused. He plays his miserable " nines" and " tens" only to be covered in succession by his adversary's three fatal trumps. *" Adieu*, Townley, *au revoir*," says Dayrell; and Hamber remarks to the latter, " What do you think now of the proverb you quoted a few minutes ago ?"

But this was only mild skirmishing. It was the grand final charge of lansquenet that was to invest the victor with something more substantial than a laurel crown. Diabole, Hautvoix, the pale mentor, and others, decline, under cover of urgent affairs at home. They are too clever to trust their barks to

the uncertain currents of lansquenet. A select—
very select—party retire behind the thick Lyons
curtains to a smaller salon of the club. Very quiet
is the commencement of the game, as the players,
unable to make a stand, pass the packs from one to
another. It appears to be a kind of trifling—just
like the first over of a cricket-match, or first half
dozen strokes at billiards—an attempt to get the
hand in for more effective business. By degrees the
dealers warm to their work. The fatal word " banco"
is repeated with more or less telling effect : but still
no great damage is done, no wonderful *coup* made,
till Dayrell took the cards for the fourth time. He
won gradually, till his doubled stakes became too
high for the habitual players to cover. "Banco,"
calls Townley from the lower end of the table ;
and two queens light airily upon the green cloth,
mulcting the caller of some 800 francs. "Banco
the whole," cried our friend from Yorkshire, and
many a card is turned before one in Dayrell's favour
dropped from the pack. " You had better stop," said
Dayrell good-naturedly ; "I have a run of luck."
To which Townley only answered, "Banco for the
whole again," and, amid much excitement, a third
adverse card turned up, and the whole stake passed
over to Dayrell.

The lamps were far from brilliant on the Place as

Hamber and Dayrell left the *cercle*—daylight already peeped from behind the eastern mountains. There was the red glow of dawn on the edge of the broken clouds, and a peaceful serenity in the air that ill harmonised with the thoughts of the two spectators. " You will take a fair instalment of the money with you, Hamber, for prosecuting the enquiry we talked about at dinner. Rather extraordinary that Townley should pay. Still, should he ever know it, he cannot regret the destination of his bank-notes."

" *Bon-soir, Mademoiselle,*" said the unabashed Dayrell on meeting Miss Gardéres, who was tripping down the hotel staircase with her basket of keys, and her natty little cap on the back of her head.

" *Bon mâtin,*" said the damsel, with emphasis, as she glided into some obscure retreat, unwilling to be seen talking to such a couple of reprobates.

Ere the day was far advanced, more than one mother of a family had heard the news from the *cercle,* and, in true gossiping spirit, had retailed the same to her neighbours ; ere the sun had set, Mrs. Berners was in possession of full particulars ; and, ere the night mail had carried off Hamber, armed with papers signed, and with instructions for his new campaign, Kate had been treated to a homily, that made the poor girl very depressed and sad. But here we must take the liberty of putting the clock back, and refer to a conversation that took place between Mrs. Berners and her daughter some few days before, when the tearful opposition of the latter defeated, for the nonce, the mother's designs.

Townley had followed Crotchet's advice, and, when paying a morning visit, had waylaid Mamma Berners, as, in garden-hat and gloves, she was sallying forth to the planting of carnations, or budding of roses, and poured his eloquence into her ear. "An hour on the gravel" sufficed to unfold his plans and prospects, and to persuade Mrs. Berners to undertake the office of ambassador extraordinary to our pretty Kate. So, scarcely had the sound of Townley's departing wheels died away, than Mamma, like a true woman, hurried to impart the secret to her daughter, who, guessing by intuition the object of the visit, was in her chamber, and heard with trepidation her mother's approach.

But thither we mount with reluctance. 'Tis no edifying sight to witness the opposition of mother and daughter. 'Tis not pleasant to hear a sad low voice reiterate, "Mamma, I cannot marry that man." We would prefer not to see the unnatural pallor that overspreads the brow, when, without answering, she listens to her mother's severe rebukes, when not a muscle moves in the beautifully chiselled face, when one tear glistening on the cheek and another hanging upon the eyelash, are the only evidences of the storm within. Under such circumstances it would be better to turn aside. Our presence is uncalled for. Still, who that has ever been the unwilling witness of such a scene, can forget the struggle, as marked in a lovely face—the struggle between the duty owed to the parent, and the determination never to yield to dictation in such a matter as the disposal of heart and hand.

" I will never marry Mr. Townley," was a bitter pill for Mrs. Berners to swallow, when, leaving poor Kate to find consolation in a passionate burst of tears, she reviewed the case in all its bearings.

" Silly, foolish girl," she soliloquized ; " she does not know her own mind. It is not every day that such a chance occurs. I am quite astonished at her conduct ; there can be no reason for her acting thus, unless ——" and this worldly mother dropped into a train of thought, and pictured to herself a kindly, manly face, yes, one that oft-appeared to her in her dreams, and her solitude, whose hard lot it had been to meet and love the matchless Kate La Touche of twenty-five years ago, to be rejected for the stale old reason, that it was a bad money-match, and to be killed, as she had read, when fighting his way to Lucknow under the undaunted Havelock. It was but a passing twinge. It was but for a moment that her old nature triumphed over the money-grubbing, Dives-toadying-ways of the world. The current of her thought relapsed to its former channel, and she endeavoured to make out the man who had thwarted her plans. " Could it be Mr. Dayrell?" she asked herself, and turned it over in her mind. By degrees the mist cleared away, and she fancied she saw her error and mistake.

Then Mamma Berners sought a second interview with Townley. It was an easy matter for her to pour into his unsuspicious ear a story about Kate's youth, and her difficulty in making up her mind before she took such a serious step. She recommended him to visit at their house, and promised that all should shortly be settled. Townley was not a wise man,—albeit, many a wiser than he has, ere now, been hoodwinked by the other sex,—and agreed to the proposition with unreflecting haste. " Depend upon it," he remarked to Crotchet, " Kate is prudent as well as clever. The difficulty of winning such a girl makes the prize all the more worthy of the trouble."

So, when the news of the lansquenet catastrophe was hinted about Pau, with just a slight amount of exaggeration—the multiplication, as well as the addition table, being freely applied to the sum lost by Townley —it is needless to say that Mrs. Berners' temper

was sorely ruffled. This lady's suspicions of Dayrell
being the cause of her daughter's obstinacy had
hardened in the last few days, and she was all the
more angry, because she had only her own tactics
to blame for the result. When the Honourable
Mrs. Hooker selected our old friend Couterbound
to escort herself and daughters to the Botanical
gardens, Swan and Edgar's, and the palace at Syden-
ham, and Mr. C., enraptured by a pretty face, carried
off the heart of the flower of the flock—intended,
by-the-bye, to grace the breakfast-table of some
country capitalist—did not that honourable lady
consider she had a right to be offended? " He had
been taken up," she said, " because he was useful,"
and, if neglecting his duty as a machine, he
exercised his undoubted right to volition, did he not
deserve the heaviest visitations her wrath could
devise? If Yellowplush, the footman, were to step
from behind his mistress's chair at a dinner party,
and tell her what to eat, drink, and avoid, he would
not, in her opinion, commit a greater solecism than
had the unfortunate Couterbound.

So argued Mrs. Berners with regard to Dayrell.
What right had he to appear as a free agent and make
use of opportunities that she had given him, simply
for the furtherance of her own ends. Leading Mr.
Townley, too, into gambling habits; it was quite

dreadful. Yes, pretty Kate listened to a dreary, dismal tale that evening; but she would have been no real true-hearted woman, if every thing she heard did not more than ever confirm her opposition to her mother's plans.

CHAPTER XVI.

DAYRELL's position at Pau was, at this moment, peculiar. Although no open rupture had taken place with the head of the Berner family, his reception at the chateau was now none of the warmest, a hint to him of the propriety of discontinuing his morning visits. Besides, the step he had taken with regard to the law-suit, no prudent man could approve. You have only to lend money to a friend, they say, and you make him your enemy for life. Dayrell had done something similar, with this difference, that his loan was *sub-rosâ*, and unknown to the borrower, and should his meddling in other people's affairs be discovered, he might be visited with rebukes more severe than kind.

A series of "cutting-out" manœuvres managed to procure him occasional interviews with Kate. It is happily ordained that our womankind must succumb to the temptations of shopping, and as Mrs. Berners could not turn a deaf ear to the invitations of French milliners, to inspect new Paris patterns, or curious assortments of silks, her visits to Pau, with her daughter, were, as little Bouncer termed them, "Angel's visits," no doubt, but unlike them in one respect, not few and far between. Dayrell watched his opportunities, and often, when Mamma was haggling with Pecune, the French banker, respecting the cash she was to receive for her letters of credit, or when complaining to Madame Gant of the infamous quality of her yellow kid gloves, did Dayrell promiscuously drop in, and, under the pretext of purchasing scent-bags and nicknacks, have a hurried interview with Kate.

Carnival-time, too, is prolific in soirées, and was this year celebrated at Pau with *éclat* extraordinary. When those noble-hearted bachelors, regardless of expense, gave their magnificent ball, which reminded the editor of the " Bayonne Vindicateur" (who had an invitation) of fairy-land, and the proprietor of the " Béarnais Regenerateur" (who had not been asked), of all that bad taste could devise, to gain which information, he was popularly supposed to have seen through a blind, shutter, and a double-fold of drapery,—when, we say, that event long thought of, and carefully managed in every detail by its promoters, was to bring together all the *élite* of beauty, such as the foreign as well as the home market could produce, it would have been hard if

Mrs. Berners had prevented Kate from being present. Not but that her fate hung some time in the balance, for Townley was laid up with an attack of bronchitis, and Mamma feared the presence at the ball of one whom she chose to consider an interloping rival. But reports came in thickly, describing the gorgeous preparations for the coming fête. Female curiosity and love of display could no longer hold out. It was ultimately decided that they would order new dresses, and go to the ball.

It is half-past nine in the evening. The Mairie in the middle of the town is no longer a large, desolate building, *sans* light, *sans* life, *sans* everything—*Messieurs les jeunes gens Anglais ont changé tout cela.* Flowers bloom, where flowers never bloomed before, on cold stones, in sequestered crypts, in empty niches, and wide arcades; ugly flights of steps have been turned into handsome staircases by means of carpets, festoons of laurel, and variegated lamps. The hall, sacred to deputations to the mayor, and sittings of the grand jury, hung with pink and white fluted satin, and ornamented with flowers and flags, made a magnificent ball-room. The band revelled in a green *parterre,* and over the heads of the performers the Tri-colour and Union Jack united in true fraternity. The "Queen of the Harvest" waltz is being played as the last arrivals press into the room. Well-matched couples float gracefully round to the inspiring strains, and bad performers execute evolutions, never contemplated by the inventor of the *deux temps*. Be-ribboned and be-turbaned mothers, unable to find seats, swell the circle that forms round the dancers. But amongst them is not Mrs. Berners. She is in good hands to-night, and reposeth her ample frame on a red sofa, thanks to the careful agency of a new friend of hers, one Captain Prattle, of Her Majesty's navy, the most amusing man in Pau, and a firm ally of Dayrell's. He it is that will lull that matron this evening, not to sleep, but to oblivion of the passing scene, by means of stories, which, any one hearing would have great difficulty in deciding where the fabulous ended, and the true began. Being in Dayrell's confidence, he has heard the story about Townley, and, like a trump, exerts his talents in the cause of injured humanity.

"Engaged to Dayrell for the third waltz—the supper-dance, I'll be bound. A capital engagement for Miss Kate, and I'll take care Mrs. Berners does not interrupt the *tête-a-tête* afterwards," thought Prattle, as he overheard Kate's answer to Dayrell of "Very happy;" and presently finding that matron on a bench in the ball-room without a soul, not even a dowager, to converse with, he took a seat by her side, as welcome as a shower to a meadow after a month of drought.

"Sir Arthur is the richest man in Pau. You said you'd take some perigord-pie," observed Prattle to Mrs. Berners, as that lady deposited her ample frame in an arm-chair and resigned herself to supper and indigestion. "Just arrived here. Yes, I ought to know something about him, considering my cousin was on the point of marrying his sister. An unfortunate display of temper on her part interfered with the nuptials. Just my own case, I assure you, when that beautiful widow, Mrs. Barbara Goldsmith, consented to become Mrs. Prattle. I basked in her smiles; I was happy. The wedding-day was actually fixed, when one morning she found out that I had been to Ascot, and told me that if I preferred the society of blacklegs and gamblers to the hallowed precincts of Exeter Hall, I might look for some one else. But Sir Arthur is quite the thing for your eldest daughter," insinuated Prattle to Mrs. Berners, who pricked up her ears. "Your youngest, they say, is happily placed on the roll of the engaged."

"Perhaps, she is," retorted the dame. "Rich, you say; he certainly is good looking. A little wine and water, if you please. Captain Prattle, you must introduce him presently, and ——" but here the conversation was interrupted by an explosion of crackers, which youth persuaded its partner to pull, albeit, with closed eyes and well-feigned terror.

Sir Arthur passed at the moment, and the Captain took the opportunity of introducing that simpering good-natured young man to Mrs. Berners. She straightway fastened on the Baronet, and plied him with questions about the health of Lady This, and asked where the Honourable Mrs. That was passing the winter,—a laudable proceeding on her part had those notables ever honoured her with more than a distant bow. Then suddenly recollecting her forlorn condition, she requested him to escort her to the ball-room, much to the discomposure of the Baronet, whose eye wandered in search of little Ellen Callister, the centre at that moment of the pyrotechnic display at the end of the supper-table.

In the meantime, the corridor leading out of the ball-room was not without its tenants. What, though the variegated lamps artfully placed amid festoons of laurel, cast but a subdued light. Glittering chandeliers are not absolutely necessary, when, like Kate and Dayrell, we would steal a quarter of an hour's conversation in a gallery removed from the public gaze. The couple paced up and down engaged in low and subdued conversation, and scared away more than one owner of a white dress, who, with her exhausted partner, would have sought the

cooler regions of the outer gallery, but, intuitively
aware of what was going on, forbore to interrupt
the *tête-a-tête*. We can guess what they are saying,
and our mind reverts to certain events—oasis in our
career—that we never, never can forget. Do we
not remember the ball-room, not a hundred miles
from Irun, and the verandah, where the black eyes
of the Spanish beauty met ours, and she whispered
in French, *Monsieur* (Oh, that horrible cold word,
Monsieur), *cela ne peut pas etre*. Would we not, at
that moment, have exchanged all we had in England
for a Castilian vineyard, and that Senora for a
blushing bride? Do we not remember the ball, "in
the halls of dazzling light," in Ireland, when, on the
lawn, Isabel, of the golden hair, walked by our side,
and asked with all the innocence of youth, "But,
what would the Connaught girl do in London?"
When, again, we earnestly wished for 3,000 acres,
even of bogland, and a life interest in the beauty of
the far west. Do we not recollect the *belle Anglaise*,
at Amiens, and Angeline, at Heidelberg? We hope
these fond illusions we still cherish will not be spoilt,
as was the case in London the other day, when one
of those beauties, so altered for the worse in face
and figure, introduced us to a be-wigged gentleman
—*her* husband, who straightway asked us to visit his
" 'ot-'ouses in 'Ertfordsher, and 'oped we would

come soon." Those side scenes of a ball-room have much to answer for. Still, all honour, say we, to the kind-hearted ball giver, who lights up her conservatories and galleries, and supplies the exigencies of many a timid, but loving couple.

The corridor, however, in the Mairie, with its subdued light, and tempting sofas, did but little to further Dayrell's plans. It was his fate to see Kate's eyes cast down upon the floor, and to hear her utter the *cela ne peut pas etre* of Irun's black-eyed maiden. "Mr. Dayrell, it is impossible; my mother never will give her consent." A bold man might have suggested the conventional chaise and four posters, or a timid one have urged dissimulation, as the best method of defeating the "powers that were." But our hero knew that Kate would not entertain such ideas, that she was far too well brought up to ignore the duty children owe to their parents. He was on the point of playing his last card, of trying what effect the disclosure of the "Hamber mission" might have, when the ungainly Crotchet appeared in the passage.

"Are you engaged for this quadrille?" asked he, sidling up to Kate, and holding out his arm with the characteristic awkwardness of a man who toils through duty-dances at the very few balls he patronises; and Kate, much to Dayrell's disgust, is led to a conspicuous place opposite the orchestra, where, to her unheeding, Crotchet blurts out such miserable *on dits* of the club, as his cloudy memory can summon.

" Done with you. Fifty francs, you bet, that I do not reach the top of the Maladetta before the end of October. You've lost your money, Greyling; you may as well pay me at once. I'll take thirty francs down, and scratch the bet ;" and Bouncer, whose potations of Champagne had rendered that youth more than ordinarily precocious, endeavours to inscribe the wager on his " card of the dances and engagements."

" You are a rich man, Dayrell; I will do the same with you," added Bouncer, as our hero approached the coterie, who, careless about dancing, paid their respects to the supper-table and the rosy god. " Stay. Fifty francs I scale the mountain before you marry Miss What's-her-name—Kate Berners." And the youth laughed as though he had made a most witty remark.

Bouncer, you are hard upon Dayrell, and, we may say, impertinent. You might have been treated with something worse than a sharp rebuke, had not your temporary secession from the strict path of sobriety been observed, and made some excuse for your misbehaviour.

Dayrell, however, swallowed his wrath and a glass of champagne, and returned to that much-frequented post of observation, the doorway of the ball-room. Most of the "wall-flowers," who, to the shame of the male sex be it told, had not stood up for aught but duty-quadrilles, had retired, as well as such discreet mothers as fear the effects of late hours on the blooming complexions of their charges. Couples take advantage of increased space, and sweep round the room at a pace detrimental alike to ten-franc bouquets and floral wreaths. Fanny Tibbets has secured for a partner—for this time only, let us hope—the solemn but imposing Laurie, and threatens annihilation to any adventurous pair who may cross her path. Sir Arthur and Ellen Callister pull up breathless beneath the orchestra, and that artless girl wields her weapons to such advantage as to render that simpering baronet—as all Pau remarked—singularly *distrait* and absent for just four days afterwards. There is a dead-lock at the bottom of the room, occasioned by the inexperienced Crochet, under the influence of champagne, attempting the reverse turn, and coming in contact with others who revelled in the goodness of the pace. Kate's pretty face looms over the shoulder of one well known in trenches of Sebastopol, yet unharmed by bullet, though, from the landing at Eupatoria to the taking of that stronghold, he never missed a day's duty.

And this contemplated, with anything but gladness of heart, poor Dayrell—one of the twenty stewards whose purse and energy had called the scene and ball into existence.   But mind, it is not the dross expended or the time wasted, that disquiets him. 'Tis the old, old story: the desire for something unattainable; the jealousy of what he interprets as another's success; the sense of desolation in a crowd that causes that gnawing sensation at the heart.   Are bye-gones to be ever bye-gones, and never to be a lesson to the love-lorn?   Is he to forget the termination of the affair in Sussex, or to reap no benefit from the lesson he received after the University boat-race?   *Par exemple!*   No.   His feelings are those that every one has at different periods of life, yes, every one, from those elderly gouty-toed bits of humanity we see in drawing-rooms, down to the beardless guardsmen just commencing the fashionable "rounds" in town.   Previous disappointments make not him or us wiser.   We endow the last novelty with all the attributes that we found her predecessors never enjoyed.   The last is the peerless beauty without fault—when straightway we congratulate ourselves, and say, "εὑρήκαμεν."   Happy that it is so for most people, otherwise their life would be a blank.

" May I have the next dance ?" said Dayrell rather dolorously to Kate, as she and her partner stopped close where he was standing.

" Mamma said this was positively to be my last waltz," she replied. " I shall be very happy if you can persuade her to let me stay for just one more galop," she added, on observing that eminent conductor of the orchestra, Signor Basso, rap twice with his fiddle-stick as a notice to his coadjutors to finish.

He gave her his arm, and walked to where Mamma, vehemently fanning herself, awaited them.

" No, Kate," said the elderly lady; " it is past three, and we must go home at once. Thank you, Mr. Dayrell," she said to our hero ; " Captain Prattle can find our carriage. Don't let us take you from the ball-room."

But Dayrell, aware that possession was nine points of the law, did not allow Kate to disengage her arm, but conducted her to the cloak-room, where, if he failed to put her opera-cloak straight over her shoulders, she neither blamed him nor even observed it, so intent was she on something he was telling her in a whisper. And a cloak-room, Mrs. Mainchance says, is not a bad place for such a whisper. Did not she receive at different times of her girlish career two proposals after a ball, the proposers in both instances being extremely well off? So now the confusion arising from false starts for carriages which did not as yet stop the way; the search for cloaks which bewildered maid-servants could not resurrectionize from the heaps of the unowned; and Prattle's kindness in relieving him from the duty of shouting for Mr. Berners' vehicle, were all in Dayrell's favour, and gave him an excellent opportunity of pressing Kate to say Yes or No.

"Only revoke the word ' impossible,'" said Dayrell, as they slowly descended the staircase. "In seven days I shall have good news for you," he added mysteriously.

Kate looked at him hopefully for a moment; then shook her head. "*Allez, allez,*" called the gens-d'arme on duty; and the carriage drove under the archway of the Mairie, leaving Dayrell on the steps wistfully gazing where last he had seen Kate's sad, desponding face.

*   *   *   *   *   *

"A lettare," said the Anglo-Béarnais servant of the hotel, coming into Dayrell's bed-room on the afternoon after the ball. "Three times since I call you," he added, as our hero lazily stretched out his hand to take the missive.

When things come to the worst, difficult though it is to decide when that period has arrived, they must mend. Thus, when things looked gloomy, Hamber's letter, written cheerfully, and to the point, arrived. "Our friend Thompson," he wrote, "I met yesterday, by appointment, in the City. He confessed all. While confidential servant to the Sous-Prefet of Bayonne, he used frequently to amuse himself by reading his master's letters, and, if time hung more than ordinarily heavy on his hands, he used to dip into the archives preserved in the Prefectorial bureau. In these were registered births, deaths, marriages, names of landholders, past and present, minutely and particularly, as only French officials can record them. He found some English names in the register of the departed, and amongst others that of M. La Touche, who died at St. Jean de Luz without making a will, and childless. The date given by Thompson shows this is the person we want. We now require a form drawn by a lawyer, attested by witnesses, and countersigned by both Justice of the Peace and Sous-Prefet. This you ought to see to yourself. Take a lawyer with you, and go to Bayonne at once, and send me the papers as soon as you can."

Dayrell was not long dressing that afternoon, or in calling upon that eminent counsellor, Hautvoix. He would have started that evening in the malle-poste for Bayonne, had not the latter refused, on the ground of his being engaged to defend a maid-servant, who was charged with the murder of her mistress, and the appropriation of about twenty pounds' worth of jewellery. So, adding his mite to the indignation every lady in Pau felt against the offending Swiss girl, he reluctantly waited till the following evening.

A man is not served the quicker in France, because he happens to be in a hurry. Not a bit more expeditious will an *employé* be in writing a receipt, copying a register, or brushing off the sand, that to this day serves for blotting paper in civilized France, because Monsieur says he has no time to lose. Simple as Dayrell's business appeared, its settlement was by no means so. He had to pay three visits to the Sous-Prefet before that functionary could be seen. True; when he and Hautvoix were admitted, they were received with the utmost politeness, with scrapings of feet, removal of hat, and enquiries about Pau society; all of far more consequence than a business discussion. Then, when the Sous-Prefet had mastered the case, his clerks had their turn. Innumerable cigarettes they smoked before they searched the registers, and finished the formalities such an occasion required, and when the "Justice of the Peace" was wanted, he was either at an audience in some distant village, or pursuing the

red partridge on the Uplands of Bidart, or enjoy-
ing his coffee and dominoes in a neighbouring café,
whither his Basque maid-servant was forbidden to
come in search of him—an order she strictly obeyed,
unmoved by Dayrell's compliments and persuasive
eloquence. " It is a piece of forty sous, she wants,"
whispered Hautvoix. At the sight of money the
demeanour of this "descendant of a thousand kings"
changed. Without cap or bonnet, she scuttled off
and would fetch her master in what she termed a
petit quart d'heure. But love will carry a man,—

> "Trans Gargara, transque sonantem
> Ascanium."

Not even the listlessness of the Sous-Prefet, or the
Justice's love for shooting, prevented Dayrell accom-
plishing his object. In four days he obtained his
papers, and in honour of the event, he and Hautvoix gave the clerks a " Punch," and several " con-
summations" at the café, when the barrister, under
the influence of eau-de-vie and cigarettes, held forth
copiously about the delights of Pau society, and the
gaiety, and the scandal, thus making those poor
employés (for Bayonne in the winter time is as dull
as ditch-water) as jealous and discontented as only
a Frenchman with 40*l*. a-year can be, and compelling
them at last to rush out of that caravansery, and

refresh themselves with the sight of some poor fellows worse off than themselves—the recruits on the Place, who, with straw round their right and hay round their left legs, were marching to the monotonous accompaniment " Paille, Foin—Paille, Foin."

CHAPTER XVII.

Spring is a cheery time in the Basses Pyrenees.
Then are ball-rooms voted hot and out of date by
the *beau monde*. Mercurial spirits are about paying
a flying visit to the Eaux Bonnes and Cauterets
before their return to England. Mothers are mindful
of the annual Exodus, and determine to give their
unmarried charmers one more chance of bringing
dis-ingenuous youth to book before the commencement of the summer migration. Hence they patronize
that valuable institution, the pic-nic. Who can tell?
Perhaps, *sub tegmine fagi,* on some bonny hill-side may
be spoken the word which the notes of the Traviata or
Queen of the Harvest Waltzes have failed to elicit.

Is not Gardére celebrated for his Mayonaises?
Who knows better how to mix the crisp white-
stalked lettuce with the yellow sauce peculiar to
that appetizing dish? Cannot Barton and Guestier
make up hampers of champagne and claret? Compare them with what Fortnum and Mason sends out
each Epsom Carnival, and the English firm would

be left far in the rear—if not at the post itself. So a day is fixed—no written invitations given—but time and place are appointed by simple word of mouth. Mrs. Mainchance is on the *qui vive*—looks up her oldest linen, her used-up knives and forks, and goes in person to market to select the fowls and tongues. Crohairée, having but two carriages at home, is bewildered at the orders he receives, and Boiteux bruises his shins amidst *debris* of old harness, to find materials for Sir Arthur Scapegrace's contemplated four-in-hand. Crotchet proposes two fiddlers and a cornopean, but his motion is negatived by the quiet element of the party, who have decided objections to an open-air dance. "You don't know what it may lead to," says one old lady, who remembers at Bagnére —— but scandal, we will not reproduce. "It is out of place, however," she says, "at a pic-nic, and will make it so late before they return home." So the fiddlers are to be left behind. Prattle, the life and soul of a party, furbishes up his best stories. In a word, all busy themselves in the good cause, and anxiously expect the appointed day.

No fear of rain in the South of France, when the sun shines high and bright above the Pyrenees, and when the clouds do not press heavily on the shoulders of the *Pic-du-midi*. The Place is the great starting-point of the expedition. Thither are collected French

idlers of the better sort, who, much perplexed, talk
of this *jour de campagne,* just as we should of a dip
in the sea in the height of winter. But the mass of
the populace are congregated about the Hotel de
France to inspect the four-in-hand. To see this,
even Mademoiselle Gardére comes out of her shell,
to wit, a bivouack on the first floor with two Lillipu-
tian chairs, a book shelf, and the tiniest of bedsteads
for furniture, and brings her little sisters, who have
been spinning cock-chafers all the morning, to salute
Monsieur Dayrell and the others, with *Bon jour,
Messieurs.* Mademoiselle is all admiration, and that
peculiar winning purr of her's is heard oft-repeat-
ing, " *Comme c'est beau.*" The road passes through
Jurançon, where the shuttle-turning females look up
and stare, and the old beggar-man, so astonished is
he, forgets to ask for sous. They trot up the valley,
past the flocks guarded by a sabotted boy and throaty
Pyrenean dog, or meet a long train of muzzled but
gaily caprisoned mules, under the tutelage of a dirty
but handsome-featured Castilian. They pass the
heavy roulage carts, with their tinkling bells, and
are a cause of wonderment to bagmen in the Oloron
diligence, as that vehicle tears past them in a cloud
of dust. They rattle through Gan, where the hill
begins; the horses are brought to the collar, and,
to ease them, the drivers dismount. The boys of

the country, true to their money-making instincts, seize the opportunity, and press forward, cap-in-hand, while one old veteran on crutches, with a St. Helena medal on his breast, asks boldly for a trifle to buy tobacco or some wine. He has a right to demand it. "Did not a cannon take off my leg at Toulouse? Yes, Sir, an English cannon-ball." In forty and four years we wonder how much our travelling myriads have paid for that one disastrous shot? But Bouncer and others are looking wistfully at the hampers, and would like a bottle of champagne uncorked. Alas, early hours and stern matronly presence forbid.

"How beautiful," exclaimed Mrs. Mainbrace to a bevy of elders, who, having shaken off their dust and pressed their crinolines into shape, stood and looked at the view from the summit of the hill. All echo the sentiment, while the young ladies are forming confidential clusters, and giggling at Townley's undignified efforts to carry a hamper, his white kid gloves grasping one end, and the post-boy's horny hand the other, presenting a marked and pleasing contrast. Prattle, Crotchet, and others help, and, by the time the carriages are emptied, have formed a barricade strong enough to stop that corps of brilliant uniforms, if not distinguished valour—the Bounders of the Pyrenees. There is much yet to be done. Champagne has to be carried to the icy-cold spring. Townley's idea of wrapping the bottles in wet flannel and exposing them to the sun, is treated with the scorn it deserved. Young ladies are on their knees, and busily unpacking. What are they lamenting now? Only that the salad bowl is broken, and that a soup plate will not hold an eighth part of the lettuce. Why that burst of laughter? Only, because the Mayonaise sauce has run out of the bottle and mingled freely with Gardére's apricot tart. Chaos, however, subsides into something like order, as fowls, tongue, and pies in their respective dishes, sink deep in the spotless cloth. Carriage cushions make excellent seats, and those who had the forethought to bring rugs, dispose them daintily for the convenience of their own particular vanity in crinoline. But the fate of Tantalus awaits the hungry and thirsty. Although the salad may be mixed, and the sherry —such sherry as it is in the South of France—may be uncorked, the sight-seeing mania must be indulged before the banquet is touched. "It is too soon," lisps a female, past the happy medium of life, "to sit down to dinner. Captain Prattle says there is a ruin we ought to see, and that he can get the key." "Let us go," echo the ladies, and, in batches of four and five, they follow Prattle, while discontented youth, who go to pic-nics only for the champagne and the dinner, abuse the gallant Captain, and lazily bring up the rear.

The keys turned gratingly in the lock, the doors are opened, and the company enter. A native, old in years, and smelling intensely of garlic, wished to officiate as showman. But Prattle waved him aside, and took the office upon himself. "This, ladies and gentleman, as you perhaps don't know," he began, "is a castle built in the fourteenth century to resist the attacks of the warlike and rapacious mountaineers. That room on the left was the banqueting-hall; this on the right the chapel. In the former, the Baron was compelled, by a vow made in his youth, to dine twice a month, and, in the presence of his vassals, drink a quart of Gan wine out of a human skull, which the prettiest girl of the neighbourhood presented on her bended knee. This font you see in the chapel is the identical one in which Henri IV. was christened. You perceive the crack in the middle. That was made when they brought it from Pau at the time of the Revolution on two sumpter-mules." Intense interest depicted on the countenance of the ladies, who minutely examine the relic. Prattle continues, " You have likewise read how, when the great Henri was born, his mother, according to Béarnais custom, rubbed his mouth with an onion. You see that iron safe in the wall. In it is preserved the identical herb, which is only exhibited on great fête-days, and on it the marks of that blessed baby's teeth may yet be seen." "That won't do," mutters Bouncer, " who ever heard of a baby born with teeth?" But nobody ever succeeded in silencing Prattle. He had a way of looking through his glasses as he answered, that precluded further controversy. "If I did say teeth instead of gums," he asked, "what then?" and his tongue wagged on about an apocryphal score of pictures, which he minutely described, mimicking the language of an English housekeeper exhibiting her master's gallery, and whose loss at the revolution he regretted. The party turned into an *allée* overgrown with weeds, which he opined was a place of recreation for the knights on wet days.

" Played at skittles in their armour," interrupted Crochet.

" Gentleman who will make bad jokes," he replied, " might have said in their *night*-shirts."

But in his banter Prattle had his object. " You shall have the opportunity you want," he had promised Dayrell one morning, when the latter confided his secret and asked his advice. " Wait till the picnic, where Miss Berners is going; you shall have half an hour to talk with her. You can tell her of Hamber's mission, and nobody shall interrupt you."

His lecture over, Prattle was arguing with the
native, who, angry at being relieved from his office of
cicerone, wanted a double fee, when he saw Dayrell,
who had joined the party unobserved just before its
conclusion.

"You returned soon—no success, eh?" remarked
Prattle.

"None whatever. Townley would walk with us,
and talk in that lackadaisical manner of his; so I
stopped their promiscuous wanderings by bringing
Miss Berners back to the party before our absence
was remarked."

"Never mind, you shall have a better opportunity
after dinner," said Prattle, and at the same time gave
him a few useful hints.

What young lady ever is fastidious at a pic-nic?
We never knew one, beginning with that arch
enemy of ours, the grim Miss Towler, down to laughing, bright-eyed Bella Sparkle, who did not love to
escape the restraint society's laws impose, to sit cross-
legged on the mossy turf, instead of a high-backed
chair, and last, not least, to have an amateur
"Jeames" in the place of orthodox Yellowplush.
The ladies must have their holidays as well as the
gentlemen. If they were never to taste a bit of
nature, is there not a chance of their becoming dull?
The party sitting round that cloth of snowy white-

ness were quite content to rough it, to sit closely packed, and in fear and trembling to balance plates upon their knees. What matter if the amateur waiters were awkward?—if one unfortunate wight upset the salt, was he not laughingly told to throw some over his left shoulder?—and if another poured a glass of champagne into beauty's lap (an accident which of course often happened), did he not hear, "that it was *only* a muslin," expressed in a manner so *naïve* that his heart was that instant led into captivity. The change of air and scene seemed to agree with all. Radiant with smiles was Ellen Callister—her attention divided between raised pie and what the simpering baronet was saying. Clara Fane, whose appetite was in general unequal to the conventional "little jelly" of an evening party, asked unblushingly for more Mayonaise; and Louisa Plantagenet, who on other occasions would have scorned the action, sipped champagne out of a tumbler in the absence of the tapering glass. The ladies having finished, the gentlemen waiters began to work on their own account. Dipping deeply into raised pies, or carrying off remnants of chicken, they, one by one, subsided into corners, or propped themselves against trees, taking care to keep an open bottle at convenient distance.

There was one, however, who did not condescend

to act as waiter. This was Prattle. He never
flurried himself or spoilt his digestion by serving
others. His business was to amuse, to be the pleasant
raconteur when the feast was done. So he ate calmly,
while the rest hurried hither and thither with salt and
salad, only occasionally lifting out of his plate his
full-moon face, and murmuring to the nearest gentleman, "Bread, please." Yet no one played him any
tricks. They either respected his age or his faculty
of telling stories, in which it was next to impossible
to separate the true from the false, and they laughed
heartily at their Munchausen, who had travelled all
over the world, and had thus a background for every
picture, and a fertile imagination to fill it in.

"What have you lost?" asked Fanny Tibbets of
the Captain.

"A ring—a mourning ring—I would not have lost
for worlds. I had it just now."

"Mourning, Captain Prattle, how can you say so?
I am sure it is as wicked looking as any I ever saw."

"Then you have found it."

"I never said so; but, poor man, as you are so
unhappy I will relieve your anxiety, on condition
that you tell us the story attached to it."

"Thank you, Miss Tibbets," he answered, heaving
a melodramatic sigh; "since you compel me, prepare
to hear a short but moving tale. I was but twenty-

six years of age, and had just been made lieutenant
in the navy. Unfortunately, I had not been gazetted
to a ship, so I was staying in Dublin, simply because
I had no ready money, and the tradesmen of that
town alone would give me credit. But even these
long-suffering men were at last in a state of disaffec-
tion. My tailor received me coldly, and my bootmaker not only threatened, but actually took steps
to deprive me of my liberty. In fact, I was miserable. In one of my desponding moods I was walking
up Sackville Street, when I met my elder brother,
the owner of thousands, but the stingiest man living.
'No sooner in town, Phil,' he said, 'than I meet the
happy middy, having his run upon shore, with more
money in his pocket, I warrant, than brains in his
head.' 'Lieutenant, if you please,' I answered;
'just passed his examination through having more
brains than money.' 'You have!' he said, looking
at me fixedly, and deliberating for a moment. 'Phil,'
he continued; 'I know the very thing for you, and
can do you a good turn.' 'Never wanted one so
much as at this particular crisis. What is it?'
'What would you say, Phil, to an heiress, with 800*l.*
a-year in her own right? Good tempered, if not
pretty; interesting, if not young. Shall I name
her? It is my wife's cousin, Miss Scorer. I will
introduce you, and you shall marry her!' 'Maid of

my soul,' I answered; 'with eighteen,—no, eight—
that will do—with eight hundred a-year of her own.
I am ready, and if she says yes, you may adjust the
halter about my neck as soon as you like.' I
wondered what kind of person Miss Scorer might
be. The word 'interesting' set me thinking. Does
it mean romantic? Has the germ of early love
been nipped in her gushing bosom, and has she
pined in solitude ever since? Am I to be the man
to restore her to life, to re-kindle the fire that has
burnt out? Or does it mean long eye-lashes, and
half-closed eyes; hair falling in neglected clusters
on a swan-like bosom; a figure pensively gazing into
the fire, and building castles in the coals, save when
it moves to the piano and warbles one of Mr. Moore's
melodies with the plaintive accent of the nightingale.
You see, Miss Tibbets, I was romantic enough once.
I was not kept long in suspense. I went with my
brother to the house. I ascended the staircase with
all the anxiety and trepidation of a lover. The
servant announced us, and I was face to face with
my enchantress; one glance, and all my castles
melted into thin air. I saw a lady, you understand
me when I say of a certain age, just discarding her
Berlin-wool work, and pocketing a pair of spectacles
with marvellous celerity. Of her personal charms
let me be silent, lest I overrate them. To her con-

versation my brother's epithet, 'interesting,' could
not apply. Her only redeeming point was her good
nature, and that, in regard to a thing I could have
dispensed with, was unbounded. 'What do you
think of her?' asked my brother, after dinner. 'Isn't
she a prize, and fond of you already? Why Phil, it
was a case of love at first sight.' 'On whose side?'
I asked mechanically. 'On both,—her's especially.'
'Bob,' I said solemnly, 'this is past a joke, or rather
I have had enough of it. I never could marry that
woman, so do not mention the subject again!'
'Zounds! man, and why not? Where are you going
to find another woman with 800*l.* a-year to throw
herself into your arms? Not marry her? you don't
know your own mind. Depend upon it, you will
like her well enough when you are better acquainted.
Another glass of wine, and we will go upstairs.' I
have a dreamy recollection of what followed; how
my brother played cribbage with the sister at one
table; how he joked with her in whispers, and, like
Mephistopheles, looked at me over his shoulder to
see how I was getting on—I, the unhappy Faust,
who played chess with Miss Scorer, and was of
course checkmated. To be checkmated in the real
game of life was my destiny. But what could I do?
In order to pay my debts I must marry well, and
here was the opportunity. I proposed when under

the influence, I believe, of a bottle of old East India sherry. It struck me afterwards that it was put on the table at luncheon for that special purpose. I was accepted, and the wedding-day fixed. From that moment I ceased to be a free agent; I was on foot day and night. By day I was shown, like an ex-wild beast now tamed, to congratulating friends; by night we played chess and backgammon, or did our moon-lit sentimental rounds in Merrion Square. One pleasure alone remained, I could walk Sackville Street in peace, for Bootlace, cordwainer, Cuttings, tailor, and others of the tribe, servilely bit the dust. I forgot, Miss Tibbets, to tell you, that Miss Scorer was what Mr. Anderson would call a healthy feeder. Supper was her favourite meal; for it especial luxuries were retained. I have even seen a lobster salad form the *pièce de resistance* of that social repast. Heaven bless her! I often thought there never can be a doctor's bill in our house. A week before the wedding,—it was a Tuesday, I think, but am not sure,—I left the house after the usual routine —chess, supper, and mutual good nights. Can you, Miss Tibbets, doubt my sorrow in parting? Can you think I omitted to walk round Merrion Square, and watch the light in an upper window till it was extinguished? I even abjured my evening cigar, so that there should be nothing between me and my——"

Here Prattle seemed overcome by his feelings; he remained silent a moment.

"And what happened?" asked Mrs. Berners.

"What happened?" echoed all.

"Madam," replied Prattle, "I am grieved to state that that excellent lady, from the effects, as the doctors said, of that heavy supper, came to a premature end, at—let me see—8.30 in the morning."

"Oh, fie, Captain Prattle," burst from more than one unbeliever. But the good man looked at the dissentients through his spectacles, and said, "I was with her the last thing at night, and I saw her in the morning; in fact, was sent for; so, I suppose, I ought to know."

"You are not worthy then of this ring," observed Fanny Tibbets. "I had a good mind to put it up to auction, and give a ball with the proceeds."

"Noble-hearted creature," he replied; "pray, do so. But be sure first that the stones in it are genuine."

While Prattle was thus entertaining a select circle; while Mrs. Berners, listening to his story, forgot Kate; while Mrs. Mainchance's eye slumbered, and her brain ceased to form new schemes, the young ladies who voted him a bore—a "stupid old man" Ellen Callister called him—had jumped from the grass, and, their bright eyes flashing in the setting sun, had slipped away, with arms locked together in sisterly embrace, and with the professed object of seeing the luminary disappear from a better point of view. These Sir Arthur and Dayrell intercepted. We don't suppose **Kate** was disappointed, nor Ellen, though she did act the hesitating maiden for a moment, was sorry at the intrusion. All we know is, that in a few minutes, two couples, one in the direction of the icy-cold spring, and the other of the ruin, might, in the language of Mr. James, have been seen to wander.

" How kind of you, Mr. Dayrell, to go to Bayonne on our account," said Kate, after hearing his elaborate story. " You must let me tell the news to mamma. I may, may I not? How she will thank you, and become quite friendly to you again."

" Friendly ! Miss Berners," said Dayrell in a tone of deep disappointment ; " I expected more than that, at least from you. Do you know what I really did expect? That I should have a grateful, sunshiny face turned up to mine, breathing, not only its thanks, but, may I say it, a return for my love, and one cheerful look to assure me of my happy destiny. But your answer has placed me within the cold and icy pale of friendship,—of friendship only, and the smile of love is reserved, perhaps, for another."

"How can you talk so, Mr. Dayrell? You don't know how much I have suffered, or you would not put such an interpretation on my words."

"I am so sorry to have offended you, Kate. (May I call you, Kate?) I did think you would have listened so cheerfully to me, when I told you how I had removed the last objection your mother could have against the match. For this is the only one, is it not, Kate? that I am not so rich as—as somebody I could name."

No answer.

"You know, Kate," he continued, "the evidence I have obtained must gain you the verdict; and by it you will obtain a great increase of income. I will go to London myself, and see that the lawyers are not dilatory. But, stay, a thought flashes across me. Your mother may think this fresh acquisition of fortune another reason against the match. She will fancy that her daughter ought to marry some one ——"

"I'll listen to this no longer, Mr. Dayrell," broke in Kate. "You have no right to ascribe such ideas to mamma, which are reflected again on me. Do you think I am to be biassed by such worldly considerations? No one shall ever force me to act so."

"Then I am not quite indifferent to you, Kate. May I hope some day ——" and Dayrell was on the

point of kissing her hand, when she drew it hastily
away.

"Mr. Dayrell," she answered, "you received my
reply once before—in the ball-room at Pau,—I have
none other for you to-day. I will never marry
without my mother's consent. You had better let
me tell mamma your secret, and if you will call to-
morrow at our house, you will doubtless be ——"

"The lost babes in the wood," exclaimed a person
just behind them. "Here they are, 'found at last.'
They thought, Miss Berners, you had met with an
accident—tumbled down a precipice, leaving only
this parasol for the coroner's jury to hold an inquest
on. I came to tell you they were packing the
hampers, and were nearly ready to start."

"I wonder you did not remain," said Miss Berners,
"and lend them your valuable assistance. On our
arrival you exerted yourself more than any one."

"Fair play is a jewel, Miss Berners. I worked
first. It is now their turn. Besides, I stand up for
the rights of labour. By rights, I mean rewards;
and those I have not received. I carried the hampers,
unpacked them, acted as waiter, and when, at last, I
sat down to my own dinner, I found they had drunk
all the champagne; and what Bouncer had given
me in a silver-necked bottle was only the common
wine of the country; and while I was searching

in the carriages to see if I could find something better, all of you went for a walk."

"Poor Townley. Hard, indeed, is your fate," remarked Dayrell. "Why is everything in this world comparative? Accustomed as you are to champagne every day, *vin de grave* must have been as vinegar. This is one of the sad effects of being a swell. Upon my word, I am glad I cannot afford to drink the wine of Epernay always; and so, when I cannot have it, don't feel the loss."

Townley stroked his moustaches, and only half-understanding Dayrell's meaning, took what he said as a compliment.

"But you are not going back so soon?" he asked of Miss Berners.

"Indeed, I am; mamma will be expecting me. Besides, we must not follow the bad example of some people, who will not help their friends."

Townley continued to walk with them, but in anything but a good humour. He pulled his moustaches, threw his legs about, and, plunged in deep thought, made no attempt to renew the conversation. It was nearly dark when they joined the rest of the party. By that time the table-cloth, the dishes, and the *debris* of the feast, had well nigh vanished. Some remnants the young ladies were distributing among the native population, others were munched by coachmen and post-boys, to whom Prattle also distributed measures of Gan wine. The more careful of the old ladies were foraging for odd spoons, forks, and napkins, and collecting the same in baskets, filled ordinarily with Berlin worsted, but enlisted to-day for this special purpose. "We ought to be leaving," observed one of the most prudent mothers. "It is becoming quite dark, and I am afraid Captain Prattle will give those men too much wine." So a move was made towards the carriages, into which they crowded indiscriminately. We don't know whether it was by chance, or design, but Dayrell and Kate found themselves on a front seat, with a horse-rug over their knees, very snug and comfortable, and opposite another youthful couple, the lady having taken advantage of the *mêlée* and darkness to leave her mother's wing. But though each couple were so near, one heard nothing of what the other said; and while their coachman raced with one or other of his brethren, and with his "Hoop—Hoop-o-la," passed his rivals, they talked, oblivious of their shouting charioteer, oblivious of even Mrs. Mainchance's maternal eye, which peered through the twilight, understood the situation, and murmured to herself, "I always said so. It is a case; after all there is nothing like a pic-nic."

Then Townley, in high dudgeon, found himself

perched on a box by the side of Crotchet, when the
latter poured his experiences and explanations into
the Yorkshireman's ears. "You don't know the sex
as well as I," he remarked. "They treat worst
those whom they love best; such as are indifferent
to their charms, they encourage to the utmost of
their power. Perhaps it is because in their pride
they would conceal from the sisterhood the attachment they really feel; perhaps they recoil from the
imputation that the love is all on their side; or
perhaps they fear lest you should feel secure in your
position, and wax lukewarm. Hence they teaze you,
and aggravate you in trifling matters until married,
when, perchance, they make pretty confessions in
the ears of their husbands, who, starting up in
amazement,—yes, awaking, as it were, from a dream
—wonder that they could have been blinded by so
transparent an artifice.

There is a picture of the Emperor Napoleon
nervously—we don't use the adverb in a pusil-
lanimous sense—nervously pacing a room with his
hands in favourite attitude behind his back, with
brow contracted into the deepest thought, before
signing his abdication at Fontainebleau. Thus, her
crotchet-work being tossed aside on the breakfast
table, Mrs. Berners walked, and pensively pondered
over her daughter's revelations on the morning after

the pic-nic. "Yes, mamma, he proposed to me, and,
in the kindest manner, without taking credit to himself, he told me what he had done about our law-suit.
I could not be unkind to him, mamma, dear, and I
would not, if it were ever so,"—and the girl, remarking her mother's contracted brow, had burst
into tears. But Mrs. Berners was not only obstinate, but had very little feeling. She utterly despised a person who owned to feeling love for another, that is, such as would prompt its possessor to
injure herself for the sake of the loved person. Self-
interest and her own pleasure were her leading
principles. It was her boast, that when she married
her husband in India, and he, poor man, wanted to
spend a quiet honey-moon with his bride, she replied,
"I'm not going to be immured to please any body; I
shall go to parties and balls as before." Thus she was
not likely to appreciate Dayrell's good-nature *per se.*
"What right had he to do anything of the kind, to
put me under pecuniary obligations to him? I
would sooner lose the law-suit than submit to that.
He is a meddler, and I will tell him so to his face."
During thirty turns up and down the rooms this was
the tenour of her thoughts. Then followed the reaction. He might, after all, not be so bad a match.
He had some money, expectations, and was of good
family. But then, what was to be done with

Townley? She had promised to intercede for him—almost told him that he should marry her daughter, and if after this she threw him over, what would he say? Talk of it everywhere—and the words of a silly man are more to be feared than those of the wise—and make Pau a most uncomfortable residence for her. In her disgust at the failure of her schemes a feather might have turned the balance. Still, whether Townley or Dayrell became her son-in-law, her difficulties appeared great.

" Mr. Townley," announced the servant; and that worthy, sucking his cane and attempting to appear at his ease, stumbled into the room. His dress was worthy of the occasion: unsullied boots, blue frock-coat, blue tie—not to mention his spotless white kids, four pairs of which he spoilt ere he found one without rent or stain. Then his hair fell in a graceful curl over his right temple, and his cheek was so rosy that he must have practised the young ladies' plan of having a good rub before going into a ball-room; in fact, to use a somewhat hackneyed expression he looked as if fresh from a band-box, and as though a touch would spoil all. He would have made Mrs. Berners believe that his visit was unpremeditated—a mere morning call; but that lady was not to be deceived. At a glance she read him through and through.

" Pray take a chair, Mr. Townley," she said. The pic-nic, I see, has done *you* no harm. Poor Kate has a headache, but will be down to luncheon. Of course you'll stay till then ?"

" I wish it was heartache," thought Townley. Perhaps it was, but not exactly for the person he wished. He muttered something about being sorry, sucked his cane, and fixed his eyes on the fireplace.

Mrs. Berners attempted to divert his thoughts into some cheerful channel. She talked of the picnic, the latest ball, of Ellen Callister's score of 520 at the last archery meeting, wondered whether the Tibbets were going to England this summer, and whether the Fanes would be at Biarritz. " For Mrs. Fane," she said, " has not forgotten the notice the Empress took of their family last season. I dare say, this time she expects permission to bathe in the enclosure retained for the imperial party, or at least to dine *en famille* with them twice a-week !"

Townley listened, and replied in monosyllables, till luncheon was announced. They found Kate in the dining-room. She was pale, but very composed. Her somewhat cold reception did not set Townley more at ease. The conversation flagged, till Mrs. Berners casually remarked,

" Mr. Dayrell said he should call to-day, did he

not, Kate?" (Oh, fie, Madam; what a mild stretch of imagination.)

"Not to me, mamma," replied Kate.

"What was he coming for?" asked Townley with interest.

"Merely to bring his race glasses. We wanted a better view of the mountains than our old one gives. Perhaps you have a better pair, Mr. Townley, and will kindly lend them to us. In the meantime I must write a letter for this post, if you will excuse me for half an hour; I dare say Kate and you will not quarrel," and Mrs. Berners left the room.

At Winchester we used a phrase, which (and no other so well) describes Townley's condition when Mrs. Berners retired. He was "hard up for action." His hand wandered to his hair, clung to his moustache, stroked an incipient beard, made a semicircle round his shirt collar,—although that article wanted no manner of setting up,—played about his waistcoat, and finally plunged into his trowser pockets, where, meeting with a key, a pencil, and half-a-franc, it expended its restlessness in gathering up those articles and letting them fall in a series of avalanches. Then his eye moved from the glass to his boots, from his boots to his waistcoat, from his waistcoat to the table. Then he made imaginary figures on the rug with the toe of his boot. Yet even these manœuvres failed to give him confidence. Kate, though in no laughing humour, was amused in spite of herself. "If I was in his place," she thought, "I would not be such a Zany. I fancy I should have courage to speak." She did not, however, tell him so; but, guessing the object of his visit, and wishing it over, she mentioned the gardens. "The rhododendrons are in flower now," she said; "and this is the best time to see them." So she took him into the garden, where she showed him the flowers, and the tame carp. Thence it was but a step to the harbour, the original monk's nest.

Kate is leaning over the rail, and looking down the precipice in the direction of the mountains. Townley, more embarrassed than ever, is trying to catch some inspiration from the contemplation of her pretty profile. At length he opens the trenches with, "You know, Miss Berners, why I am here to-day. Your mamma has doubtless told you."

"No," said Kate, inwardly despising a man who could make love by proxy.

A poser for Townley. He approached nearer, touched her arm—she still turning her eyes in the same direction. Then, growing desperate, like Punch's officers of the 13th Light Pokers, he broke the ice and disappeared.

"I have come to-day, Miss Berners, to ask you—

·to ask you—to marry me. I would have done so
before, at Mrs. Mainchance's ball, at the pic-nic
yesterday, but I had no opportunity. I should be
the happiest man in the world if I could hear you
say yes." No answer from Kate. "You don't know
what a capital county Yorkshire is," he continued;
"all the year round there is shooting and hunting,—
I mean, there are archery meetings, balls, and dinner
parties. 'Gad, there is the hunt ball at York, the
best in the world, and held every year. Then the
society is so good, a little stiff perhaps, but you
would be well received, Miss Berners. Then we
might come to town sometimes, or go abroad, if *you*
wish. I am sure I would be the kindest husband"
—and Townley commenced the recapitulation of his
own cardinal virtues; how he was a man of note in
the county, and how his mother and sisters doted
upon him. Then he described the glories of his
ancestral domain, how the acreage was so and so,
and how the arable and grass were equally distributed.
He even touched upon the new sort of draining tile
he was about to introduce, ("Oh, nonsense," says
a young lady to this. We beg your pardon, miss;
it may be nonsense, but it is nevertheless true,) and
wound up with saying that all—even to the last tile,
we may suppose—should be hers, if she would
say "Yes!"

c c 2

" You ask me to marry you ? "

" Yes."

" Then I must decline," replied Kate.

" What? Really? Think again. You cannot refuse me."

" I mean what I say; I cannot marry you."

" Why not? You don't like me well enough ? "

" No, I don't like you enough."

" Miss Berners," said Townley, as excited, and regardless of the damage to coat, hair, and trowsers, he fell on his knees in approved fashion, " once more, I ask you to retract."

" No," she said quite firmly.

" You love another better ? "

" Mr. Townley," she said, " you have no right to ask me."

" Is it Mr. Dayrell ? "

" I shall not answer any questions. Let us go back to the house, please," said Kate, moving from the arbour.

Townley caught her hand, as if to prevent her going ; another minute and his lips touched it. We believe, had he asked permission, she in pity would have allowed him to do so. But he took her un-awares, and Kate fired up.

" Mr. Townley," she said, " if you cannot behave properly, if you must take such liberties, you may look for another person, for I will not allow it. Let me go; here is mamma coming. Never! no, never!" she replied to his last appeal.

"You must go back to Pau immediately?" said Mrs. Berners, in a tone of intense disappointment that no interview in her cosy boudoir was demanded by Townley. "I hoped you were going to stay to dinner."

"So I would," he answered, "only I have business at Pau. My carriage, you see, is waiting—could not stop on any account—shall see you perhaps to-morrow—Adieu!" and in two minutes the noise of his departing chariot wheels was no longer audible to Mrs. Berners, as she stood astonished and perplexed on the steps of her house.

CHAPTER XVIII.

To use the language of the gentlemen of the turf, it was the week after the Two Thousand. That race—for nominally two thousand guineas, but, in fact, much more—is forgotten. No one cares now to ask why the favourite's coat broke out in blotches shortly before the event, or who gave the order that its legs should be beaten with a flogger every morning before sunrise. That question is one of interest to the gentlemen of the long robe only. It is a thing of the past, and the whole world, sporting and otherwise, are looking forward to the future—the result of the Derby. In order to solve the problem of which is to be the best three year old, all London is attacked by a kind of equine fever. Now the Two Thousand is supposed to be the key to the Derby. Horses beaten in the former race should have no chance for the latter. On paper it would appear so; but, somehow, the reverse invariably happens. Either the horses at Newmarket did not try, or were pulled, or were not in good form, or would prefer a longer course. For their own interest, people find excuses for the losers; the old names are introduced into the betting, by which the bookmakers profit, and the poor public bleeds. The uncertainty, however, yields plenty of excitement. At every club, smoking-room, and dinner-table, the chances of the favourites are discussed; any one supposed to be in a stable secret is besieged with enquiries; and all this intellectual energy is expended upon a few animals, who are about to run over the Epsom sward at best pace for about three minutes. Patter has heard from a ring man, who, by judicious betting, wins on every horse, and, therefore, can afford, so Patter says, to give an impartial opinion to a friend, that if he did back anything, it would be the renowned quadruped, " Old Gooseberry." Clatter has just seen two men round the corner, who declare " it is a duke to a chimney-sweep on two;" while Batter, Hatter, and others, have heard from some one, who saw somebody else, who had drunk a glass of brandy and water with Alfred Day, and learnt from him the secret, that Necromancer could not lose. All which conflicting opinions the neophyte takes in, and going to his chambers, vainly endeavours to digest, or, perchance, invests on each, and finds on the morning of the 27th of May, that he loses 20*l.* by his best horse and 380*l.* by his worst.

The discussion of turf topics is the pastime of the hour on the steps of the Polyolbion Club at 3.30 P.M. Dayrell has just joined the knot of triflers. It is his first appearance in public since his return from the South of France. Straightway he recognizes some of the old faces. "How are *you* ?" asks Cherub, with a slight emphasis on the pronoun, and holding out a little finger for Dayrell to shake. "Been abroad, eh! Hot out there, I suppose;" and Cherub, who for years lived on the sixty per cent. bounty of the children of Israel, but who now has inherited the fortune of a relation, and drives a four-in-hand, turns with an assumed languid air to an individual, whose cut of trowsers and hat proclaimed him, "All over Newmarket," and listens to some advice, to the meaning of which, the words, "saw him at exercise," and "goes like a stag," give a clue. Bantling, the hero in other days of many a *hazard*ous enterprise, and dictionary to every pretty face this side of Temple Bar, stops an instant to moralize with Dayrell. But a Hansom passes before he has finished his tale of London dulness compared with what it used to be. Into it sneaks Bantling, remarking, "We married fellows, you know, must be punctual," and drives to his nuptial bower in ——— Square, where his wife—as a kind of retributive justice for former sins—chides him for being so late,

and declares he shall not go to that odious club
again. Passes in his brougham, Boreas, who, from
the wilds of " Mesopotamia," in other days plodded
it on foot to the City. He kisses his white-gloved
hand to Dayrell, and with an air of patronage asks,
" What are you doing?" Waits for no answer, but
shouts imperiously to the coachman, " Spelter's,"
and still kissing his hand to various passers-by, is
driven to that colossal bill-loving establishment.
And Tipster, the most unlucky of turf prophets,
rushes through the folding doors of the club with
half a dozen unread letters in his hand, and turns
to Dayrell, " whose absence of four years he has
forgotten," with the query, " Who's to win?" Then
he goes on to lament how he did not see our hero
at Newmarket, or he might have put him on such
a real good thing, and that at Epsom —— But,
you do not bet, and you are not going there. Is it
possible?" Tipster says, and is staggered. Then on
Dayrell he casts a half-pitying, half-reproachful look,
—just such as a stage coachman might on seeing his
oldest passenger depart by the train ; and marking a
youthful speculator of more promising mould, is at
his side in an instant, detailing a most important
(if not mythical) trial Old Gooseberry has had with
Boanerges. There are as good fish in the sea for
Tipster as ever came out of it.

"Their ways are no longer mine," thought Dayrell. "Everything and everybody seem changed. It was so different five years ago, when I used to meet a good fellow, and it was, 'Where will you dine? and what will you do this evening?' when we straightway linked arms, and saw each other through a long, if not a very innocent, round of fun. But now the connecting link of kindred pursuit is severed. They only nod to me, and pass me with a simple, "How are you?' And why? Is it because I can tell them nothing new about what is to them the breath of life; because I know nothing of the women, the new racing moves; because I have not cast my lot with any party? Worse than all, I have not the heart, not the inclination to begin again. I should feel weary ere I had ascended the first steps of the ladder. I feel myself out of the race. Left behind by my rivals, I must finish it alone—yes, alone." And while the irreproachable cutlet of the Polyolbion was being prepared, and Oldbore flourishing a copy of the *Times*, repeated, as he does every day of the year to each fresh comer, "No news in the paper at all," Dayrell reviewed, with much bitterness of spirit, the course of events since the memorable pic-nic.

We also will put back the clock and review the same.

The morning succeeding that on which Towpley's advances had been repulsed by Kate, a scented, pink note lay on Dayrell's breakfast-table. "An invitation to dinner or an archery meeting," said our hero, breaking the seal. "Hallo! what's this? Bagnères de Luchon, Montpellier, and the beautiful Mediterranean! Why the old lady must be mad or is hoaxing me." Again he applied himself to its contents, and read—

"My daughter has acquainted me of the kind interest you have taken in the matter of our lawsuit. I had no idea you were so engaged, or had advanced money on our account. I have written to my lawyers to put us out of your debt. At the same time pray accept our best thanks, which I only regret I cannot render personally, but circumstances render it necessary for us to leave Pau immediately. We intend paying a short visit to Bagnères de Luchon, Montpellier, and other beautiful places on the Mediterranean. We start to-morrow morning, and with our united thanks for your disinterested conduct,

"I remain,

"Yours very truly,

"C. Berners.

"P.S.—We may be in London next June, and stay at my sister's house. I hope you will call there, as I am sure she will be glad to ask you to one of her little parties, and Kate would be pleased to meet you and talk over old times in the South of France."

"This is too much," said Dayrell. "Can such utter heartlessness dwell in woman's heart? That I who have braved the garlic of Bayonne, who threw my bank-notes into the scale, who have twice offered myself and all I have to her daughter, should be dismissed with 'the hopes' of my 'company to one of her sister's little parties.' Is it possible that the reward of love, that devotion's *médaille d'honneur*, should be a prospective invite to a 'muffin-worry?'" He tossed the scented note into the fire, but, before it was alight, withdrew its blackened corpse, thrust it and his hand into his pockets, and had a bitter tussle with the evil spirit that raged within him. The *spretæ injuria formæ* was the primary cause of this outburst. Alas! when is self, in the shape of wounded vanity, not uppermost in man's thoughts? "So I am to be tossed aside," he thought, "treated civilly, politely, and have a bit of sop thrown to me sometimes in the shape of an invitation to dinner, and a seat next Kate, till she with her handsome dowry becomes the prize of the first titled reprobate that offers himself. I shall be asked to see the wedding presents, invited to the breakfast, introduced to the son-in-law, and Kate, after the ceremony, will talk to me for five minutes, and do a bit of humbug by calling me her dear Edward. But she cannot be as bad as that. No; it is impossible. It cannot be Kate's fault: it is her mother's. I will send for one of Crohairée's carriages, go to their house, and wait in the grounds till I see Kate, and hear my fate from her lips."

So he sent for a carriage, but neither at Crohairée's, Boiteux's, or the other depôts, was one to be had. It was fine weather, and people had gone to pay their flying visits to the Pyrenees. Three hours must have been cut to waste before the porter brought one to the hotel. He was on his way to the Berners' house, and meditating what he should say; whether he should take the high injured line, or appeal to Kate's feelings and excite her pity. The latter seemed the best, for he knew how few women could resist a tale of sorrow of which themselves were the cause. His carriage was taking the last turn out of Jurançon, when he met another coming from the opposite direction, with the blinds lowered on account of the sun and dust. The people inside he could not see, but he recognised the man and maid-servant in the rumble: in fact, he could not be mistaken in their identity, for the former removed his hat and saluted him in French fashion. "It is them, and I am too late !" he ejaculated. " Shall I follow ?" But one glance at his wooden-legged, jaded old horse con- vinced him that pursuit was hopeless. Besides, what had he to gain by an interview? A few hypocritical words from Mrs. Berners, and scarcely a syllable from Kate worth listening to when her mother was present. So he stopped the coachman, left his car- riage, and returned to Pau on foot, for fear some of the lynx-eyed gossips should know of his failure, and have a good laugh at his expense.

The Berners secession was a terrible blow. Now that she was gone—gone without a word of explana- tion—gone with but a slender chance of his ever meeting her again,—he felt, for the first time, how much he had loved. To think that every hour put so many more kilometres between him and her, that their post-horses were even then bowling down the inclines on the road to Toulouse, while the riders, in their Napoleon boots and short-tailed jackets, shouted, " Hoop-Hoop-o-la " more lustily when they thought the *belle Anglaise* was watching their efforts. He would gladly have changed places, or seats, with one of the latter even for one short stage. Pau now was utterly distasteful to him. Every walk, shop, and turn in the streets reminded him of Kate. Here was the cir- cuitous path, and there the seat in the Park, where she told him that town-life could have no charms for

her, when in the country she could find such scenery
and beauty as that before her. If he went near the
Mairie it reminded him of the bachelors' ball; if he
took a walk near the chateau he thought of the
archery meeting on the plain of Bilhéres, and how
Kate, in ascending the hill with him alone, was tired,
and having with one hand gathered up the folds of
her dress, looked around to see if any gossiping
people were near, and, not seeing any, placed her
other lightly on Dayrell's arm. It was but little
consolation for him to hear that Townley's offer had
been refused, or that the tongue of scandal said that
Mrs. Berners was furious because Mr. Townley had
proposed to her daughter instead of her, and that
that was the cause of their sudden departure. But
although he took some pains to refute such reports,
Townley cared for none of those words. In fact, no
one wore the willow more contentedly—we may say,
more proudly—than he did. It brought him into
notice : he strutted on the Place more consequentially
than before, and his vanity was tickled by the atten-
tions of more than one young lady, who had no
objection to link her fortunes with those of the rejected swain.

So refusing Mrs. Mainchance's pressing invitation
to one more—the very last—pic-nic, or to join a party
of rash speculators who had lost at the Club at Pau,

and were going to Bordeaux for the race week under
Diabole's guidance to win back all their losses—a
trip that might be reasonably expected to end in
disaster for the English, and keep Diabole in drink,
food, and lodging for the next eighteen months—
Dayrell returned to England with but two ideas: first,
to consult Hamber, and next to see Mrs. Berners'
lawyers.

Early in the day on which we just now found
Dayrell melancholy and moralizing upon the steps of
the Polyolbion Club, he had been to Hamber's offices
in Lincoln's Inn. He had driven to the square—
the deserted, yes! even by cabmen, who are not
sufficiently credulous to expect a back-fare from
thence—that square of dingy-window frames, through
which no one ever seems to look on the grass, for fear
Nature should prove antagonistic to parchment—
that square of arches and nooks, which remind one
of the places we used in childhood to see placarded
with " Beware of the big dog," and inspiring us with
equally uncomfortable feelings as we crossed the
threshold—and, after some trouble, he found his
friend's chambers.

" Here they are, and in a new building," he said
to himself, as he read the name on the side panel.
" Bravo, Hamber, you march with the times; you
have nothing to do with the rickety staircase and the

cobweb-hung office, but patronize plate-glass windows and the very latest novelty in architecture,—the only modern house, I see, in the square. I shouldn't wonder if Hamber has introduced the glass of sherry and sandwich system; baits his trap with the driest Montilia and the crispest Abernethy biscuit. Here is the door; let us open and see." Hope, alas! told a flattering tale. The boy-clerk, on being questioned, replied in one breath, "Mr. Hamber's out—not be back to-day—leave your name." If Hamber marches with the times, he likewise marches every Saturday to ——; he supports the early closing movement, and is also a volunteer. Dayrell in disgust descended the staircase, and betook himself to the Polyolbion for consolation, with what results we showed in the opening of this chapter.

But even the idle Apollo does not always bend his bow; nor is Hamber always smoking the normal pipe of the volunteer and shouldering a long Enfield. There is a Monday in every week, and in more than a moiety of the Mondays in the year our lawyer returns to his desk with a headache, and a nervous feverish state of body.

"Who did you say called on Saturday? Mr. Quod —Sir Arthur Scapegrace—Mr. —— who? Sir— Daniel, did you say? Now remember, you are on your oath, and fancy yourself in the august presence of judge and jury, repeat that name. Daniel, you answer? And pray who is Mr. Daniel, and what was he like?" were Hamber's interrogatories to his boy-clerk.

"Please, Sir, he was tall and thin ; said he would call again, and hoped he should catch you."

"Much obliged to you for nothing, Mr. Daniel. But tell me, boy, how was he dressed? Was he a gentleman or a Hebrew? Had he a straight or a hooked nose?"

" Please, Sir, I did not observe."

" You young villain," exclaimed Hamber, flourishing a ruler about the boy's head. " Do you think I keep you to spoil sheets of foolscap paper with your scribbling, and to stain the desks with ink? Now, Sir, brush up your wits, and recollect something about the gentleman. What sort of a nose had he?"

"Please, Sir, I don't know."

"Was it hooked?"

"I am not quite sure."

"Will you swear, Sir, it was not hooked?"

"No, I will not."

"Well cross-examined,—keeping your voice in practice," interrupted Dayrell, as he came into the room.

"That's him! that's Mr. Daniel," said the urchin, to the amusement of Dayrell and the discomposure

of Hamber, and slipping off at the same time to his high stool out of reach of his master's ruler.

But his master took no notice of him, but turning to Dayrell, said, "You overheard our conversation; I beg your pardon, it was about you. That little villain said a Mr. Daniel called here on Saturday. That name is not on my list of clients; and I began to think I had had a visit from a sheriff's officer on pressing business. Sit down, Mr. Dayrell, I hope I have to congratulate you."

"On my return to England? Yes. On success in a certain quarter? No. But I see 'Private' on the door yonder; I suppose we can have a quarter of an hour's quiet talk."

"Certainly," said Hamber, leading the way into an ill-furnished room, littered with every description of docketed papers.

"So the old lady was unkind to you," Hamber answered, when Dayrell had concluded his story respecting his misfortunes at Pau. "Sad to think that so much time and trouble were wasted. But, Lord bless you, the ladies are quite as bad as the male sex. They will coax you, and make much of you so long as you can be useful. Their object gained, they will throw you aside as coolly as possible, and without remorse."

"You are wrong, Hamber, Mrs. Berners has not

thrown me over. You forget I volunteered the search for the certificate; of my own free will and choice I went to Bayonne. I never consulted a soul but you. She shows her gratitude in her own way; she asks me to a tea-party in London. Perhaps she thinks that the height of bliss; I must not quarrel with her because we differ in opinion. Besides, I am not beaten yet; I shall have been the means of their gaining a fortune. Perhaps, when they come to town, they will have something better than tea-parties to offer to the 'author of their well-being.'"

"Well done, you will not give in. Now I'll tell you what I have been doing since my return to town. I have seen Mrs. Berners' lawyers more than once. They hope to get a verdict; but you know, we lawyers are an incredulous suspicious race. We make certain of nothing; at least, so we tell those who consult us. We congratulate no one till the verdict is given, the last appeal set aside, and every paper signed, and hidden in our strong boxes. We only hope for a good result; we keep our clients in a state of doubt and uncertainty. Mrs. Berners' lawyers have sent for her to come to town. First they will require a guarantee for the expenses of the trial; then they will weary that good lady with a beautiful combination of hopes and fears, which will make her the most humble, and at the same time,

the most disgusted of mortals. That is your moment
to step in—a month from this, when she is fairly
embarked in the legal sea of trouble. Not a scion
of the Berners' family can tell their benefactor to
step out. In a few days you may be in-and-out of
that house like a tame dog. You can be always
calling on the excuse of business. I will keep you
well supplied with legal phrases and information. In
a word, make yourself the connecting link between us
and the ladies. If you will follow my advice, I
wager, that before the judge puts on his spectacles,
and sums up the case, you are engaged to Miss
Berners. Stay; I'll bet no money, but only a dinner
at the Star and Garter, that what I say comes true."

"I like to listen to you," said Dayrell; "it puts
one in good spirits. By your own showing, you are
no lawyer, or, rather, don't follow the legal receipts
of success. You not only predict, but stake a dinner
on the event. Being, therefore, of no use as a professional adviser, suppose you put on your hat, and
introduce me to Mrs. Berners' lawyers. She told me,
you know, to call on them. Now, will you come?"

"And leave my poor *clientelle* to thirst for information, and unable to invest their superfluous six and
eight-pennies; leave them to walk disconsolate round
my rooms, stare at the maps, and badger my clerk—
that villainous boy, I mean—with questions, until, in

his confusion, he will 'execute and assign' that draft in a way by no means contemplated by its original drawer. Still, in the cause of friendship, and, with ulterior views to a glass of soda and brandy, I am yours to command. Boy, give me my hat. Say to all who come that I am with the Attorney-General, and shall be back in half an hour."

"That's the room where you would have been obliged to wait an hour, if I had not accompanied you," said Hamber, showing Dayrell a cabin, 16 feet by 12, with maps on the wall, and with a London Directory and advertisement sheet of *The Times* on the table. "They put a poor client in there sometimes, who is so utterly disgusted at the time they keep him, that he rushes out, and declares to the clerk that he will take his case out of their hands. 'I'll let my principal know,' says the clerk, coldly. Two minutes, and a ruddy, pleasant fellow, of two and twenty, and heir to large estates, calls, and is sent up to the sanctum without a moment's delay. We know which side our bread is buttered," added Hamber, with a wink. " First come are not the first served."

"Good morning, Mr. Hamber," said the legal owner of the cabin, and professional adviser—magnificent term—to Mrs. Berners. "This is Mr. Dayrell, you say. I will attend to his business at once."

The lawyer whistled down a pipe. A clerk obeyed the summons, and brought some papers. The former extracted from the mass one, which was a minute of Mrs. Berners' last letter. He consulted it for a moment, then fumbled with his cheque-book, and handed Dayrell a piece of pink-tinted paper.

"You will find that the right amount, I think," he said. "You will excuse me, gentlemen, for dismissing you at once, but I am very much engaged at present. Mr. Hamber knows what a busy time this is for us poor lawyers."

"You can tell me, perhaps, when Mrs. Berners is coming to town?" asked Dayrell.

"No, I cannot," shortly answered the lawyer.

"But she is coming; at least, I have heard so," persisted Dayrell.

"Have you?"

"But you don't know who I am," continued Dayrell. "It was I who found the evidence you required at Bayonne, and for that purpose spent three or four days there."

"Pretty place, they tell me—pretty place," answered the lawyer; "but you must not waste any more of my time. Robert, show Mr. Broadacres in. Good morning, gentlemen."

And Dayrell and Hamber left the office.

"By the powers, he tried to cross-examine a

lawyer," said Hamber to himself. "Poor fellow; does he expect to draw water out of a stone? Did he think anything short of the rack would have elicited the smallest particle of information? Poor creature—poor creature!!"

CHAPTER XIX.

"I found the court small, hot, and crowded. Why crowded, I could not for the life of me divine. Nothing could be more uninteresting than the subject, nothing more ungraceful than the Vice-Chancellor's delivery. When the little man's nose was not in close proximity to his notes, it was in the air, sniffing inspiration for the coming sentence; and after every full stop his body moved backwards and forwards like a crooked pendulum. Of the bar, some members slept, some read the newspaper, scarcely any one listened to his lordship, save a junior with ferret eyes, who seemed to drink in the words of wisdom, wholly unconscious of the slip of paper labelled, 'Brother to Cicero, scratched at ten P.M.,' which a facetious brother had slipped into his wig. It was a will case, and the summing up will not be finished to-day. There is no chance of your trial beginning before the middle of next week. So, if you will take my advice, you will leave town for a few days. These visits to your lawyers have made you nervous and uncomfortable. A change will do you good. What do you say to Windsor for a week? Wednesday is the fourth of June, the Eton boys' holiday. Shall we go?"

Thus spoke Dayrell to Mrs. Berners in the quite-at-home tone of a confidential adviser. That lady, but lately arrived from Montpellier, in consequence of a peremptory letter from her lawyer, was now in London, and staying with her sister. She had already paid several visits to Lincoln's Inn, and was weary of legal personages and papers. Her brain comprehended not the explanations, to her more enigmatical than a sphynxian riddle. She yearned for some one to take her part; or at least to explain bit by bit what it was necessary she should know. At that moment Dayrell called, primed with forensic lore and verbiage, partly found him by Hamber, partly invented by himself. Not that his language was strictly *en régle*. As the would-be yachtsman, who has never been on the sea, talks to the un-initiated about " luffing the taffrail," and " boxing the fo'castle," so Dayrell selected the longest and most imposing phrases, without the slightest regard to sense. At one moment he would fit in a " contingent remainder " to an odd corner of his discourse, and at another would earn a reputation for the pro-foundest knowledge of the law by talking of a " *nolle prosequi.*" Mrs. Berners seized the crutch that was offered her; leant on it, and in a few days could not walk without it. Kate at first did not like this monopoly of the crutch by her mother; she pouted and worked at her crotchet in moody silence; but by and bye she began to believe in Dayrell's forensic wisdom, and to listen attentively while he expounded the law.

Now people who have lived much abroad dislike the orthodox restraint of an English household. Mrs. Berners, weary of the punctuality and fussiness of her sister's establishment; weary of hearing the chimes of the clocks, and that one in particular on the staircase, which played the Old Hundredth at nine o'clock so regularly every morning; weary of that philanthropic sister, who spoke in such gleeful terms of how she had sent flannel to the South Sea Islanders, and *English* Testaments to the hearse-drivers of Madagascar, quite ignoring the wants of the unenlightened populace living within stone's-throw of her house, was quite delighted with Dayrell's proposition. Kate, too, pined for the country and her flowers. Report spoke well of Windsor Park and its ferns. It was country, and not like that horrid London, where she could not go out without a body-guard. Besides, she had a little pride of her own. She didn't like to be seen in her aunt's dingy

brougham, whose horse was rough in coat, and
whose old coachman looked on his box like a chim-
panzee with the cramp. If she could not ride in a
barouche, attended by a Jeames with legs un-
matched in the great calf-market, wherever that may
be, she would sooner stay at home. Even Kate's
maid, accustomed to the flower of foreign *cafés*,
pricked up her ears when she heard of the *cravates
blanches* of the Eton boys. The greatest conquest
she ever made was a Bordeaux barrister, who under
his grey Napoleon-cut beard wore a white tie, since
which epoch she had always a lingering penchant
for the colour and the blend.

But although the " Fourth of June" was the osten-
sible cause of their visit to Windsor, none of them
had the slightest idea of what they were going to see
on that festive occasion. They had a sort of vague
notion that there would be a gathering of boys in
freemasons' aprons round a banner, planted on a
place called Salt Hill, to be followed by an exciting
race on the river between a ten and eight-oar.
Afraid of parading their ignorance, they asked no
questions, but went to Windsor in a delicious flutter
of expectation. Thus it came to pass that the programme disappointed them. True, they occupied
conspicuous seats while the speeches were made, and
thus exhibited Madame Devy's last triumph in the

floricultural bonnet-line; but they thought it too bad that there should be no boat-race, no planting a banner with time-honoured rites. A procession of boats and the fireworks were set for the evening; but these did not fulfil their foreign notions of what a fête should be. Besides, a cold prevented Kate attending the festivities of the evening. But Mrs. Berners had made up her mind to do the river, to see all that was to be seen; and Dayrell, much against his will, was obliged to leave Kate, and accompany her. On such a night, when the river was studded with craft of every size, when punts laden with sight-seers shot out every moment from the shore, when Bills and Sams, of the chaffy, beer-drinking, waterside stamp, steered their boats with a reckless disregard of what they bumped or whose timbers they shivered, it was venturous for an amateur to attempt to wield a pole. Dayrell's experience of the vagaries of a punt was confined to a cruise or two on the Cherwell, when some towing power up stream, and the current down stream respectively did the work. So, on the evening of the Fourth of June, when he essayed to wield the punt-pole, like Mr. Robinson riding the camel, he did it in a sort of way—a sort of way unsatisfactory alike to his freight, whom he splashed with water, and other mariners whose barks he fouled without remorse.

" Now then, where was you brought up ?   Is that
the way you use your tooth-pick ?   For a tanner I'll
steer you better with my little finger ;" were among
the remarks elicited by Dayrell's mild efforts on the
water, and, by the time that good luck and the
current had drifted their punt to a station—the worst
possible for seeing the boats and fireworks—Mrs.
Berners had made up her mind that it was all very
dangerous, and congratulated herself at having
escaped the fate of all those who go down unto the
sea in ships.

" No, don't do so," said Dayrell, as he fixed his
pole firmly in the mud.   " We were in Chancery,
but now——" and he looked towards the people in
the boats near his, as though he deserved some κυδος
for being where he was.   " It was a severe trial.   I
have not punted these eight years—certainly not
since I left Oxford.   Out of practice, you know,
Mrs. Berners.   How Kate would have laughed had
she seen my efforts to keep her head straight."

" Whose head, Mr. Dayrell ?   I am sure you are
not very complimentary."

" This ship's, Mrs. Berners.   Vessels, you know,
are feminine, because the sailor loves his old crafty so
well.   He might like, but he could not love anything
masculine or neuter ; so he must talk of *her* head.
But sometimes, Mrs. Berners, the vessel does not

return the love. She is faithless, she throws him overboard, or she leaves him behind at some foreign out-port, or takes on with others more to her liking. Then she is the same to him as though she had struck on a rock or sunk in mid-ocean, for, as it appears, he is separated for ever from her whom he loves best."

" What a melancholy idea, Mr. Dayrell."

" But sometimes the sailor meets her again in a home-port, forgives his old crafty, and stands happily and proudly on that deck as before. Has he not returned to his first and only love? Yes, Mrs. Berners, you cannot believe it," he continued, emboldened by that good lady's silence; " but I have been in the position of the sailor who loved his vessel. I have served for a time, and have found no favour with her captain. I have been separated from my first love for a short space, and have found her again in port. If she is to start on another voyage, I hope to be on that good ship's books. Do you understand my meaning, Mrs. Berners? Then I must come to the point at once. You remember how intimate we were in the South of France, and how you left suddenly, without giving me or any of your friends notice. I was prepared at that moment—at least, on that very day—to ask your consent to my marriage with your daughter. I was separated from her for a time, but have, by good luck, met her again. I take this opportunity of telling you that all I have done —small as that is—was for her sake—all done to gain your consent to our marriage. Whether you win or lose the trial, it is the same to me. I still offer my-self, and am prepared to assist you in any way as regards that matter. You know, as your accepted son-in-law, I can offer to do more than a mere stranger. You cannot, I am sure, refuse me. If you have any conditions, name them, and I will cheerfully accept them."

" Hooroosh ! Hullabaloo ! That chap's in the water. Here he is up again, with the shilling in his mouth. Brayvo, brayvo !" shouted the mob on the bridge, while at the same time a crowd of boats put off to render help if necessary.

" I tell you, it is five pounds I have won. Here, give it me," exclaimed a well-known voice. "I will have it before I change my wet clothes."

" Will you ?" replied a laughing subaltern. "Done for once, Limmer. True, I bet you five pounds. You thought I meant pounds sterling; it was the lbs. weight of anything, mud, rags, or something in that line."

" Hurrah ! here's a sell," shouted the mob, as it followed the disputants over the bridge. " I'll bet you a pound, Captain, you don't do it again," "and I," " and I," " and I," reiterated different members of the unwashed fraternity.

" It is only a man I was with at Oxford," replied Dayrell, to Mrs. Berners' interrogatory. " He is always betting with somebody. He is very sharp, and he seems to have met his match to-day. But you have not answered my question, Mrs. Berners."

" Really, Mr. Dayrell, your proposals have taken me by surprise. Suppose we talk it over to-morrow morning. Look, here are the boats. Could not you move us into a better position to see the fireworks? That is the signal rocket," she exclaimed, as a fiery messenger soared on high with a fizz, a rushing sound, and ended in an explosion that called forth, " Oh, oh, ohs," of real or pretended admiration from the spectators.

Then Dayrell put off once more from the shore, and flourished his pole more recklessly than ever. The Sams and Bills may execrate him now as much as they please. He scarcely hears them; he certainly don't care for them.

There was great joy in the little house at Windsor that evening. Kate's cold vanished, like the morning mist, on hearing the news, which Dayrell communicated to her, while Mrs. Berners underwent an hour of self-imposed banishment in an upper chamber; and this good mother passed a night of meditation. No doubt, she turned restlessly in the maternal four-poster, and picked her fingers to pieces before she

came to the conclusion that it would not be such a
bad match after all. When she met Dayrell next
morning in the study—there was a study even in
that house, gloomy, bare of furniture, and in which
the imprisoned air struck coldly to the bone—she
offered no obstacles, did not even propose the forma-
tion of a "Limited Liability Company," being content with Dayrell's simple word, and an assurance
from Tales that all arrangements could soon be
made.

Strange to tell, the trial never came off. When
the solicitors on each side had worked every engine,
and discharged every shot, for which the law per-
mitted them to demand remuneration ; when folios
of foolscap had been covered with costs, resembling
in detail the account rendered by a fashionable
upholsterer, where every nail, screw, cord, pulley,
polishing, and repairing is set down with painful
accuracy ; the other side proposed a compromise.
" A compromise !" Mrs. Berners exclaimed, when she
heard of it. " I won't listen to it. Their case is
weak, and they know it. I will go on." But the
terms proposed were very advantageous, the uncertainty of the law very great,—a fact Mrs. Berners
was prevailed upon to recognize after a mighty ex-
penditure of words and quoting of examples. With
this happy termination of the great Berners' lawsuit

Dayrell had much to do; and as the last paper was signed by Mrs. Berners, and witnessed by himself, he turned to his pretty Kate, and said, " It is now, dearest, our turn. To make my prophecy come true, that you should become an heiress and my wife at the same time, you must fix as early a day as possible,—a day on which the sceptre of bachelordom is to pass from me, and on which I am to lay down my title of 'Wild,' declaring solemnly that that soubriquet shall know me no more."

* * * * * *

Dr. Moberly, Grand Master of St. Mary's College, Winchester, entered the school-room one day, the boys, "up to books," greeting him with a rise *en masse.*

" Stand up, Cheekey, the elder," said the Master, selecting a copy of verses out of those in his hand, "and tell me why you have begun yours with an ' Et.'"

Cheekey, the elder, well-known for his pilferings from the *Gradus ad Parnassum,* and his laborious attempts to make the " barest" of hexameters scan, rose from his seat, stammered out, "Please, Sir," and took breath.

" Well, Cheekey, the elder," asked the Grand again, " what explanation have you to give ?"

" Please, Sir," a stop. " Please, Sir, you gave us

that theme six weeks ago. You said my copy of
verses then were very spirited, and that I was to
take two places. All my ideas could not be exhausted in that effort. The same carried out with,
I hope, more spirit, you will find in the copy you
have in your hand, and connected with the former
by the word 'Et.'"

Thus, instead of drawing the threads of our story
together, and dismissing the *dramatis personæ* with
a few words, we may, like Cheekey, the elder, introduce their names into a second volume, more
especially, if the earlier incidents of their career
meet with public approval. There is only one
character that demands a word, or rather, a kindly
dismissal. It is little Ellen Callister, whose pleasant
ringing laugh, and whose happy sun-shiny face is
still bound up with our memories of the past. We
left her, the night of the pic-nic, walking with Sir
Arthur—a walk that ended in an engagement, and
congratulations from the whole English body trans-
pontine. Sir Arthur went to England that April.
They were to be married as soon as the usual lawyer's
business had been completed. But that wedding
was never solemnized. Either Sir Arthur met some
one he liked better, or he repented of his hasty engagement. That match was broken off, and Ellen
never saw him again. If Ellen had had a mother to

give her advice, and to have "managed" Sir Arthur, this might not have happened. It was hard that her inexperience should have been so cruelly punished. She was, after this, the life of many a circle in Italy and France; she laughed and prattled as of yore, and the world voted her the same light-hearted girl. But we remarked the change when we met her at a *bal masqué* in a box, with half-a-dozen hangers on clustering round her. She was flirting first with one and then another, even with poor Meekling, who meant more than he could speak, and who was prepared to go, not only to the altar (as he told us over a cigar at 1.30 A.M.), but to the end of the world for her, and though she was glad to see an old friend, and had a playful remark ready for us, there was a want of cordiality, arising, perhaps, from a fear that her motives were understood, which made us turn on our heels, and leaving her, feel apprehensive for the future fate of Ellen Callister.

But destiny decreed otherwise. Her fate was different to what we expected. We took up a sheet of the *Times* some weeks ago; our eye glanced down the list of those summoned to a better world, we read, " On the — inst., Ellen, the beloved daughter of Colonel Callister, of fever, at Hyères, South of France."

FINIS.

LONDON:

Printed by Truscott, Son, & Simmons,
Suffolk Lane, City.

www.ingramcontent.com/pod-product-compliance
Lightning Source LLC
Chambersburg PA
CBHW050901130726
47900CB00015B/1358